# THE WAY TO A WOMAN'S HEART

# THE WAY TO
# A WOMAN'S
# HEART

Christina Jones

**WINDSOR**
**PARAGON**

First published 2011
by Piatkus
This Large Print edition published 2011
by AudioGO Ltd
by arrangement with
Little, Brown Book Group

Hardcover  ISBN: 978 1 445 85838 8
Softcover    ISBN: 978 1 445 85839 5

British Library Cataloguing in Publication Data available

Printed and bound in Great Britain by
MPG Books Group Limited

# *Acknowledgments*

With deepest gratitude to all at Piatkus, my publishers, especially Emma Beswetherick and Donna Condon.

And with loads of love and thanks to Broo Doherty, my agent, for being brilliant.

And special posthumous thanks to my grandmothers who left me the recipes.

# THE WAY TO A WOMAN'S HEART

# Chapter One

'Please, please, please . . .' Ella Maloney implored the straw-chewing gods of all-things-rural as she squinted at the signpost. 'Please, let this be the right one. P-l-e-a-s-e don't let this one be another dead end.'

Having slowed the car to a halt and pushed her sunglasses into her newly done salon-smooth cinnamon-and-honey hair in order to read the faint lettering, Ella actually wasn't holding out a lot of hope.

Almost as soon as she'd left London and its sprawling suburbs behind, she'd discovered that one overgrown country crossroads looked much like any other overgrown country crossroads. And also, sadly, that one weathered rustic signpost looked exactly like every other weathered rustic signpost.

After already experiencing several false starts and a few serious dead ends—once teetering on the edge of a duckpond and twice sailing straight into someone's garden—there was absolutely nothing to indicate that this particular crossroads and signpost combination would be any more help than any of the others.

So there was no point in getting over-optimistic, Ella thought, blinking through the blinding dazzle of a perfect May morning, because this one wasn't going to be the right one either, was it?

But . . . Hallelujah—yes! It was!

And there they were . . .

Fiddlesticks . . . Lovers Knot . . . Hazy Hassocks

. . . Bagley-cum-Russet . . .

The faded names that would, hopefully, change her life.

'Yes, yes, yeeeesss!' Drumming triumphantly on the steering wheel and doing a little happy dance with her feet beneath the pedals, Ella held her own small in-car celebration-for-one. 'At last!'

The drowsy names sounded like enchanted fairy-tale places. Ella could already feel the tension and tiredness simply seeping away.

'Yay!' Ella blew an extravagant double-handed kiss at the lopsided signpost whose delightful destinations were almost completely obscured by burgeoning shepherd's purse and convolvulus. 'I've really, really made it!'

She'd been playing a solo version of 'are we nearly there yet?' for the last thirty miles. Having ignored the sat nav because both her route and her pre-programmed target seemed to be causing it some confusion, Ella now embraced the appearance of the ancient signpost with as much enthusiasm as a weary lone explorer suddenly stumbling across friendly human civilisation.

Not, she thought, that her journey from North London to Berkshire could be remotely compared with a Ranulph Fiennes trek, but for a committed townie like her, it had been a pretty testing couple of hours.

There had been more than a few times while driving through the green and golden countryside on this gloriously bosky May morning, when she'd begun to wonder if her destination even existed.

Hideaway Farm, she'd been told in one of Poll Andrews' letters—real letters, not texts or emails—was halfway between the exquisitely named Lovers Knot and Fiddlesticks. Not actually in either village though, and if she reached Hazy Hassocks she'd have gone far too far.

The farm was, Poll had said, signposted at the end of Cattle Drovers Passage—if the sign hadn't fallen down as it was apparently wont to do—and then she just had to drive along Hideaway Lane, round its various twists and turns, until she found the farmhouse at the end.

If in doubt, Ella should ask anyone she met for directions. Everyone local, Poll's letters had assured her, knew the way to Hideaway Farm.

Hideaway Farm . . . Ella had giggled delightedly to herself. How magical was that? The name alone conjured up memories of childhood storybooks and tales of wild, free madcap adventures in a rustic paradise.

Hideaway Farm—yes, she could just see it—all haystacks, and lazily droning tractors, and grazing, er, sheep? Or maybe cows? And pigs? Ella was a bit hazy on the sort of animals that might inhabit Hideaway Farm. But she was sure there'd be smiling apple-cheeked women and beaming suntanned men and happy bare-footed children scampering through dappled buttercup and daisy meadows.

It was all going to be absolutely perfect.

Earlier, when she hadn't seen a human being for at least fifteen minutes, and for ages had been scarily surrounded by nothing but fields and trees and a big, big sky, Ella had become a little concerned, but not now. This was the countryside for heaven's sake, what else could she expect?

And then there had been a bit of a problem with everything being so *green*. Well, apart from the

3

huge expanse of sky, of course. And that was the most unbelievable blue. Far bluer than the sky she'd left behind in London. And there was so much more of it somehow. To be honest, the size of the sky and the mass of greenery had all become a little bit overwhelming.

But now, Ella beamed again at the signpost, it was going to be all right.

How fantastically relaxing it must be, living in villages with these sleepy, bucolic names, and having neighbours who probably still danced round maypoles, and had probably never even seen a spreadsheet, or heard of an iPod nano, and who thought Gok Wan was a small Indonesian island.

No doubt about it now. Abandoning her going-nowhere life, chucking up her city job before she became burned out at twenty-seven, and answering Poll Andrews' advert for help in one of those posh magazines that were always filled with things like 'Lady Hermione Pugsley-Grossbody seeks live-in companion. Must be able to drive, speak fluent Mandarin and emote with llamas' *had* been the right choice—whatever Mark had said to the contrary.

Mark . . . Ella shook her head. No, she wouldn't think about Mark. Not yet. After all, she wouldn't be doing this at all if it hadn't been for Mark, would she? And if she thought too much about Mark now, she might just give up and turn around and scoot back to London which would solve absolutely nothing . . . No, she was going to stick to her guns . . .

Determinedly, Ella replaced her sunglasses, started the car, and headed in the direction of

4

Fiddlesticks and Lovers Knot. Anyway, after all the upsets and arguments of the last few weeks, Hideaway Farm was going to be heaven on earth. She just knew it.

## Chapter Two

Ten minutes later and hopelessly lost in yet another maze of tangled lancs and deserted sleepy cottages and single-track roads leading to nowhere, the euphoria was a thing of the past and Ella began to wish she'd never heard of Hideaway Farm.

Somewhere between the turning for Fiddlesticks and the fork to Lovers Knot she'd lost her bearings. Again. Ask someone for directions, Poll Andrews had said. Hah! Like who for instance? Chance would be a fine thing . . .

This was totally, totally ridiculous.

Hot, tired and extremely irritable, Ella drove even more slowly and peered through the further haze of unremitting green-and-gold countryside for a safe place to stop and phone Poll. There was nowhere . . . nowhere on these insanely narrow lanes where she could park without blocking the road, and where were all those earlier handy gateways when she really, really needed one . . . ?

Her phone started to ring from the depths of her handbag on the passenger seat. OK, Ella thought as she glanced across at it, just let me find somewhere to stop—and if you're Poll Andrews with foolproof directions, I'll definitely kiss you.

The phone stopped. Ah well . . .

5

Turning yet another overgrown cloned countryside corner, Ella suddenly brightened. Just visible ahead was a baked hummock of scrubby grass surrounded by gravel—oh, and deep joy!—to one side there was a small stone-walled, slate-roofed building, and—even more and ever deeper joy—the small building had a wooden seat outside—and yes! The seat had two people on it! People who no doubt could and would point her in exactly the right direction.

Spirits restored, Ella parked carefully alongside the grassy hummock behind a van, three bicycles and a minibus. Maybe, she thought, this building was a village hall—although there had been no visible evidence of a village in the vicinity—or maybe even the local doctor's surgery? A small rustic medical centre covering all the tiny hamlets and remote farms?

Whatever it was, it indicated civilisation and it definitely had human life outside it and surely someone must be able to tell her the way to Hideaway Farm, mustn't they?

However, it was possibly best to check the phone call first in case it was Poll . . .

Scrabbling in her bag, she scrolled down for the missed-call number and groaned.

Mark.

Ella could picture him, with his spiky gelled hair and his designer shirt, sitting in the office across the corridor from hers—well, what had been hers before all this started—probably with his designer-shod feet on the desk, and with the daily stack of empty coffee cups and sandwich wrappers already mounting up. He'd be flicking through his computer screen and iPhone with one hand and

6

answering the desk phone with the other, doing some work, but also laughing with the other men in the office and talking about football and F1. And thinking about her?

She hoped so. After the previous night's rather frigid farewell, when he'd clearly been expecting her to have an eleventh-hour change of heart, they'd both said things they probably shouldn't. Ella sighed and pushed the phone back in her bag. There was no way she was going to return his call now. It was less than twenty-four hours since they'd parted company, and they'd agreed she'd ring him when she arrived at Hideaway Farm. She laughed ruefully to herself. Typical Mark . . . How on earth were they ever going to work this out if he couldn't even stick to the basic rules?

Scrambling from the car, reeling slightly in the heat and stretching her cramped legs, Ella scrunched across the gravel. Beneath the sun's glare it reminded her of childhood seaside holidays and she had a fleeting—very fleeting— moment of violent homesickness for her family left behind, like Mark, in London.

Hopeless . . .

Pulling herself together and fixing her best 'I'm a stranger and completely lost and I wonder if you could help me, please?' smile, she approached the elderly couple on the bench.

As she got closer she realised she'd been very wrong about both them and the building.

She'd assumed the couple were both men, dressed as they were in battered tweed jackets and thick corduroy trousers despite the heat, but as one of them was wearing a slash of orange lipstick beneath its stubble, she now fervently hoped they

7

weren't. And the building wasn't a village hall or a doctor's surgery either.

With its stacked boxes of fruit and vegetables outside and racks of postcards and newspapers and plastic kitchen utensils dangling from festoons of string round the doorway, it was clearly a small general stores.

WEBB'S MIRACLE MART the sign over the door proclaimed proudly. WE SELL EVERYTHING.

Trades Description Act looming, Ella thought darkly, also reckoning the only miracle about it was that anyone could ever find it.

'Excuse me.'

The couple on the bench blinked rheumily up at her without smiling and said nothing.

'Er, hello, I just wondered if you could tell me the way to Hideaway Farm, please?'

They pursed wrinkled lips and screwed up the watery eyes and sucked in a joint wheezy breath.

'Ah,' the lipsticked one nodded. 'Reckon we can.'

Her companion gave a sudden toothless grin. 'You going to see that mad Poll Andrews?'

Ella nodded. She really, really didn't like the sound of 'mad'.

'Good luck, then—' the lipsticked-one also grinned gummily '—you'll bloomin' need it.'

Great, Ella thought. 'Um, right, but if you could just tell me how to get there, I'd be really grateful.'

'Ah . . . Well, all you need to do is turn back away from Angel Meadows.'

Ella frowned. 'Where's Angel Meadows?'

They gave joint cackles of laughter. 'This here is! We're in it, duck. Don't you know nothing? Anyway, once you've turned round, you go back to the Fiddlesticks road—up that-a-way where you've

8

just come from—OK?'

Ella nodded.

'Right, then just keep going straight on, past the turning for Lovers Knot, past all the turnings until you come to what looks like a dead end. That's what throws people—it don't look like it leads nowhere but it's Cattle Drovers Passage. Hideaway Lane is at the end of that, right?'

Ella nodded again, smiling her thanks.

The lipsticked-one looked pleased that their information had been so well received. 'Poll Andrews' place is the only house up there, duck. Go right to the end of the lane and you can't miss it.'

Ella smiled even more. 'Fantastic. Thanks so much for the directions. It sounds easy enough. I'm sure I'll be able to find Hideaway Farm now.'

The couple nodded in tandem. 'Course you will—though whether you'll want to stay there is another matter. Good luck, duck.'

## Chapter Three

Within fifteen minutes, having followed the couple's directions and ignored all the turnings and negotiated both Cattle Drovers Passage and Hideaway Lane with no further mishaps, Ella triumphantly pulled the car to a halt outside the pillared and worn-stepped front door of an exquisite mellow-brick-and-slate picture-book farmhouse.

She grinned happily to herself. Made it! At last!

Hideaway Farm: all sun-kissed with softly

9

billowing trees, and birdsong, and the rich fragrance of freshly cut grass. And silence. Absolute silence.

It was, as she'd known it would be, a perfect haven of rustic tranquillity.

With an ear-splitting groan the front door was suddenly yanked open and a tall, slim woman tripped over the hem of a flowing Indian print dress, lost a sequinned flip-flop, and stumbled clumsily down the steps.

'Oooh—sod it! Sorry, that wasn't directed at you—are you here already? Goodness me, that was quick! I'm simply thrilled to see you. I thought you'd be ages—not that I've any sense of time at all, but . . .'

Ella, easing herself from the car, stopped and blinked at the dishevelled hippie vision. 'Er, hello. Are you Poll Andrews?'

'I think so.' The woman beamed, bending down to retrieve the flip-flop, hoik up the bottom of her dress and disentangle several rows of brightly coloured glass beads which threatened to strangle her, at the same time. She straightened up, still beaming. 'Although on days like these I'm not really sure.'

Ella laughed. It certainly wasn't the new-job welcome she was expecting. And Poll was certainly nothing at all like the *Archers* matriarch she'd imagined.

The elderly couple's 'mad' immediately sprang to mind . . .

Mad or not, Poll had wonderful cheekbones, and smiling dark eyes, and with that sun-kissed complexion would never need facials and chemical peels and other salon enhancers—although, Ella

10

reckoned, possibly some decent moisturiser wouldn't go amiss. And her hair needed the dry frizzy ends tidied up a bit but otherwise it was simply naturally lovely.

And how effortlessly cool Poll looked in the flowing ethnic frock that owed nothing to the latest fashion fads and everything to comfort and individuality.

With those vivid beads and her wild hair and un-made-up face, Ella thought with a pang of envy, Poll was absolutely everything she aspired to be now she'd escaped the corporate rat race.

Ella held out her hand. 'Hello, then. I'm Ella. Ella Maloney.'

'Yes, of course.' Still beaming broadly, Poll drifted across, and clutched both Ella's hands in welcome. 'Please excuse my appalling manners. How wonderful to meet you at last after all our letters. And how young and pretty you are! I'm just a little confused because you'll never believe what's happened this morning and—oh, please mind the—ah, too late . . .'

A power-burst of dogs, cats, two hens and one small boy clutching a muddy bucket exploded from the open door behind Poll and poured down the steps.

'Oh—' Ella smiled in delight at the gorgeous blond boy '—and is this George?'

'Ooops—so sorry about the mud. Yes, this is George, my son. George, meet Ella.'

George, who Ella knew from Poll's letters was a few months shy of his third birthday, smiled hugely and politely held out a tiny muddy hand.

Completely overwhelmed by maternal longings, Ella beamed back at George, the reason for her

11

being at Hideaway, and shook his hand. Then, misty-eyed, she blinked over his head at Poll. 'Oh, he's an absolute poppet.'

George grinned some more, and gabbled something completely unintelligible.

Poll smiled. 'He's got his own language, I'm afraid. I understand him of course, but—'

'And I'm sure, once we get to know each other, that I will too. Won't I, George?'

George nodded, gabbled some more and hugged Ella. Oooh, bless him. Suddenly awash with love, she absolutely longed to pick him up and cuddle him.

Poll sighed happily. 'Well, this seems to be a mutual admiration society, thank heavens. Oh, Lord, sorry about the animals.'

Ella found herself being sniffed and investigated from every conceivable angle. She patted and stroked in return, and hugged George again and didn't care at all that he'd smeared the muddy bucket across her jeans and pale-green T-shirt.

This was all she'd ever wanted. Well, almost . . .

'Oh dear . . . I'm so sorry.' Poll looked distracted again. 'This chaos really isn't what I'd planned for your arrival. I got my dates muddled, you see, which means—well, you don't want to know what it means, honestly.'

Ella continued patting and stroking. 'We did say today, though, didn't we? I haven't got it wrong?'

'Nooo.' Poll ran an agitated hand through her frizzy hair. It stood on end. 'It's not you, it's me. Oh, I'll tell you all about it when you've settled in. I'm so sorry about the welcome. I'd planned it all so differently . . .'

'It's OK—honestly. I'm just delighted to be

here.'

'Are you? Really? Oh, I'm so pleased.' Poll looked very relieved. 'I do hope your journey wasn't too awful.'

Ella smiled manfully as the hens eyed her sandalled toes with beady speculation. 'The journey was fine once I'd left London and got the hang of the countryside, and your directions were great—although I did get lost at the end and had to ask directions at the Miracle Mart.'

'Did you?' Poll looked askance. 'How awful! And did Mrs Webb—she runs the Mart—tell you where we are? I'm surprised if she did. She always thinks people are undercover reporters or the Home Office. Watches far too much television, poor dear.'

'No, I didn't see Mrs Webb—a couple of the villagers told me.' Ella felt it was possibly best not to elaborate on the conversation.

'Good.' Poll looked relieved. 'We always go into Hazy Hassocks for our shopping. We don't go to the Miracle Mart if we can help it. We only use it in dire emergencies. Angel Meadows is a bit odd.'

'Mmm, it was a bit strange. I didn't even see a village.'

'No, it's more a hamlet, even smaller than Lovers Knot. Anyway, you'll have plenty of time to explore the area once you're settled in, won't you?'

'Hopefully, yes—oh, and this house is just beautiful.'

'Thank you. Oh, let me rescue you.' Poll hurried towards her, shooed at the cats and hens and attempted to remove the dogs and George. 'We don't get many visitors. They're just a bit overexcited. We've been so looking forward to

13

meeting you. I'm really sorry.'

'Please don't apologise any more, it's all wonderful. I'll just get my bags out of the boot, shall I?'

'Yes, of course. My manners have completely deserted me along with the last of my brain cells. Oh, and yes, you can leave your car there, it'll be quite safe. It's a dead end—just barns and things. Let me give you a hand with your luggage, then I can show you your room and we can do the guided tour—or would you like a drink first? It's very warm for May and you've had such a long journey and . . .'

'Whatever is easiest for you.' Ella was still valiantly admiring the rapidly drying mud in the bottom of George's bucket as she flipped open the boot of the car and hauled out the first designer-tagged holdall. 'A drink would be lovely, though. Maybe it would be better to get my stuff inside first? There isn't very much.'

'So I see. Just two bags,' Poll sighed. 'Aren't you clever? I never seem to manage to travel light. Here, let me help you . . . Lovely. Now, in through the front door, along the passage and the stairs are straight ahead . . .'

They made their way, each hauling a holdall and hampered by several cats and dogs, and with George clinging to Ella's hand and chattering non-stop in what sounded like a childish version of Esperanto, into the farmhouse's gorgeous cool flagstoned darkness.

Poll pointed out the rooms as they passed.

'This is my sitting room which we'll be sharing from now on, and this one was originally a morning room I think, it doubles up as George's

14

playroom now, oh, and that's the formal dining room—we haven't made much use of it really although hopefully we will now—and those two rooms are sort of extra living rooms which will come in handy, and that's a kind of study-cum-office that is rarely used because I tend to just pile stuff up on the hall table and . . .'

By the time they'd manoeuvred the twisting staircases to the third floor, with Ella making appreciative noises about each of the rooms, the huge wild flower arrangements, and Hideaway's nubbly walls and ancient tiles and original wooden balusters, Poll seemed to have regained some sort of composure.

'I know I'm sounding like an estate agent. I always babble when I'm nervous—and I am. Nervous. Very. If only Ash Lawrence hadn't thrown me into a complete tizz this morning by phoning and telling me that I'd got my dates wrong.'

Ash Lawrence? Who was Ash Lawrence? Ella frowned. Had she already been told about Ash Lawrence in Poll's avalanche of chatter? No, she didn't think so. The 'mad' word was rearing its head again. It was probably best not to say anything.

Poll pushed open an oak-panelled door. 'Here we are. This is your room. And George and I are just along the corridor. This floor was originally one huge attic but had already been converted into three double bedrooms when we moved in, so I just added the en suite in here, and a Jack and Jill bathroom between mine and George's rooms. I do hope you'll like it.'

'Oh, wow!' Momentarily forgetting all about

15

wrong dates and Ash Lawrence and Poll's general confusion, Ella dropped her holdall just inside the door of a vast and lovely pale blue and cream room. 'It's beautiful! Thank you so much—you've gone to so much trouble. I really appreciate it.'

Poll smiled. 'I want you to feel at home. I want you to be happy. I want us to be able to live together without any problems at all. This venture is very important to me.'

Venture? Ella frowned again. She didn't remember any mention of a venture in the advert or the subsequent letters. 'Er, and to me.'

'Oh good. I'm so glad. Come down as soon as you're ready and we'll be able to have a proper chat over lunch about, er, everything.'

Ella nodded. 'Thanks. I'd really like that. And sorry, but the house is so vast . . . Will I be able to find you?'

Poll corralled the dogs and cats and George in an untidy group. 'I'll be in the kitchen. Bottom of the stairs, straight across the passage, then third door on the right. Take your time—we don't run to any sort of organised timetable at Hideaway, as you'll soon discover.'

Ella grinned. 'That sounds totally blissful. I've been so looking forward to not being stressed and always having to be somewhere or doing something at a set time. I don't suppose you do a lot of clock-watching in the country?'

'Er, no, not really.' Poll paused in the doorway. 'Although we might have to be a little less spontaneous from now on when—no. No, let's leave that part of it for now.'

Ella, still slightly overwhelmed by the gorgeous room, the ditzy Poll, and the wonderful non-stop

16

chattering George, smiled happily. 'Oh, I know I'm not here on holiday. I know I'm here to work and I guess I'll be pretty busy with nannying, oh, and hopefully some cooking . . .'

'Cooking?' Poll raised her eyebrows. 'You enjoy cooking?'

'I love it. Especially making puddings. Cooking's my favourite thing in the whole world,' Ella said, then cast a longing look at George. 'Well, nearly . . .'

'I love cooking too, especially big main courses, but the kitchen is at your disposal any time you want it,' Poll chuckled. 'It's huge so we won't get in each other's way. Mind you, you might hate working in it. It's very old-fashioned—I don't have any modern gadgets at all.'

'That's not a problem for me. Most of my best puds are from my gran's handed-down recipes, and I learned to cook them in her 1950s and definitely non-technical kitchen while she watched me like a hawk. It was like taking part in my absolutely favourite cookery programme only without the fear factor.'

'Cookery programme? Fear factor?' Poll frowned. '*Masterchef*? *Hell's Kitchen*? *Come Dine With Me*?'

'*Dewberrys' Dinners*.'

'No way!' Poll beamed. 'That's my favourite too! Oh, brilliant—we can watch it together.'

'And laugh at the culinary disasters concocted by the contestants and squirm at the full-on carping between Gabby and Tom.'

'For a married couple who are both Michelin-starred chefs, they're truly awful to each other, aren't they?' Poll grinned. 'I'm never sure if they're

17

going to manage to stay married until the end of each show. They seem to hate each other, don't they? Do you think it's all for the television audience's benefits—or are they really that bitchy to one another?'

Ella shook her head. 'No idea. Gabby really is an appalling woman, isn't she? So harsh to the contestants and even more so to poor Tom. Reality telly with teeth and claws. Gabby and Tom make Simon Cowell look like Mother Teresa.'

'Mmm. But what does that say about us, then? Tuning in in our gazillions to watch some poor saps fail miserably and a marriage disintegrate?'

'Christians and lions for the twenty-first century,' Ella agreed. 'But very clever casting and a brilliant idea. I just think the contestants are really brave— inviting the whole crew and those two self-obsessed Michelin-starrers into their own homes, and then having to cook all those courses *live* with just their own things, no help at all—and then have to put up with all that criticism.'

'It must be hell.' Poll nodded. 'But worth it in the end. Most of the previous winners have gone on to open their own restaurants, haven't they? And they get all that prize money.'

'Surely no amount of money would ever be enough to make up for the public humiliation of having your very best dishes trashed by those two ego maniacs?' Ella shuddered. *'Dewberrys' Dinners* is great to watch, but I'd never take part. Never in a million years. Nah, I'll stick with experimenting with my gran's recipes, and making my mistakes in private.'

Poll nodded fervently in agreement. 'But we'll still watch it, won't we?'

'Definitely. Wouldn't miss it for the world.' Ella laughed. 'Which makes us pretty two-faced, doesn't it?'

'I suppose it does. Or maybe simply human? Whatever, I'm just thrilled to bits that you're another fan. Now, I must sort out George's lunch and let you finish your unpacking. Oh and—' Poll scuffed at the floor with a sequinned flip-flopped toe '—there's something else I need to talk to you about. My plans for Hideaway Farm. Oh dear, I knew I'd fluff this bit. It's so tricky to explain, but you see, I'm afraid I wasn't strictly honest in my advertisement . . .'

## *Chapter Four*

Ella, her heart rapidly sinking, stopped smiling and stared at Poll. 'Really? Um, how not strictly honest? Which bit of the advertisement wasn't strictly true?'

'Only a little bit,' Poll said cheerfully. 'And as long as Ash Lawrence doesn't arrive too soon, I'll explain it properly over lunch. We can have a lovely long chat then, and get to know all about one another. It's nothing to worry about, I promise you.'

Hmmm, Ella thought darkly. In her experience, that phrase usually meant there was an awful lot to worry about indeed.

Was this brief rural dream all going to be way too good to be true? However much vetting the posh magazine had done, had Poll Andrews slipped through the net? And what exactly had Poll's advert said?

*Happy-go-lucky, honest, non-judgemental person
who wants to change their life into the slow lane,
required to help out with child-care in idyllic
rural farmhouse in return for small
remuneration. Car driver preferred. Must like
animals. Own room and full board provided.*

Fairly non-committal really, Ella thought now.
And of course it had been the *child-care* followed
by *slow lane* and *idyllic rural farmhouse* that had
leaped out at her on that most stressful of city
days. But what about the *non-judgemental*? What
was that all about?

At the time she'd assumed that it meant
someone liberal-thinking without any radical views
to either left or right who wasn't going to get
involved in crusades of any sort—and this had
more or less been confirmed by Poll in her letters.

More or less . . .

Ella frowned, her imagination whizzing into
overdrive.

So, what if Poll Andrews and Hideaway Farm
were just a cosy front for something far more
sleazy? Hadn't the Great Train Robbers holed up
with their stash in some rural farm umpteen zillion
years ago? What if Poll was part of a gang? Or a
gangster's moll? Or an internet fraudster? Or a
drug baron? Or a money launderer?

What if . . . ?

Poll interrupted this manic runaway train of
thoughts. 'Oh, please don't look so worried; it's
nothing awful, honestly. Look, let me get George
downstairs and fed and watered while you unpack,

20

then we'll have lunch and talk things over and—'

George had galloped across to the window and was waving frantically.

'Ooh, no!' Poll groaned.

Ella frowned. 'What's the matter? Who's George waving at?'

'It's a car turning off Cattle Drovers Passage,' Poll said shortly. 'George loves cars and lorries and buses. He waves at all of them. I hope it's the plumber from Hazy Hassocks come to fix the kitchen tap at last, but I bet it'll be Ash and Roy—oh, Lordy. Two more for lunch, and no time for us to discuss things . . .'

Bugger, Ella thought. She frowned again. She seemed to be doing a lot of frowning. 'Who exactly is this Ash Lawrence? He seems to be causing you quite a lot of trouble.'

'Oh, bless him. It's not his fault. It's all mine—I always seem to get things muddled. Ash is lovely. Really lovely. You'll adore him. It's just—I thought he was arriving on the fifteenth . . .'

'Today's the fifteenth.'

'I know that now,' Poll said testily, hurrying across the room and removing the still waving George from the clutches of the sash window. 'Ash told me that this morning on the phone when he said he was on his way. I was looking at the wrong month on the calendar. I'd kept it on the view of Derwentwater because it was so pretty.'

Ella nodded. From what she'd gathered about Poll so far, it sounded horribly plausible.

'And,' Poll continued, now giggling with a struggling George, 'I thought Ash and Roy were moving in next week.'

'Moving in? Here? Two of them? So he's—

21

they're—going to be your lodgers, are they? Is Hideaway a B. & B.? Is that what you didn't say and why you need to employ me to look after George?'

'Sort of,' Poll said evasively as George and his coterie of animals scampered off downstairs. 'It's very sad. Ash and Roy lost their previous home, poor things. Oh, but you won't believe how divine Ash is. Late twenties, absolutely gorgeous looking, and he's a chef. Or he was—although he's looking for another post now of course. His accommodation went with his job, but the restaurant owner didn't take to Roy, Ash's companion—clearly a nasty case of homophobia—and Ash was given notice to quit.'

'Oh dear,' Ella said. 'That sounds very unfair. But there must have been some really good reason or else this Ash could have sued for wrongful dismissal, couldn't he? You can't just sack people because of their sexual preferences, can you? So, is he a friend of yours? Is that why you've offered him a home?'

'No, not really. It's a bit more complicated than that.'

Ella, already in brain-meltdown and deciding that Poll's explanation about just how complicated would definitely make things even more convoluted, didn't ask. 'And what about, er, the unsuitable boyfriend? Roy? Is he a chef too? What's he like?'

'No idea,' Poll said cheerfully. 'But he's not a chef. I've got the idea he's an older man and I think Ash said he does something with pylons.'

'Pylons? You mean like in the "Wichita Lineman"?'

22

'I guess so. The job probably means he's away a lot and possibly explains why he didn't come to any of the meetings I've had with Ash. Or he was probably too embarrassed after being the cause of them being thrown out of their previous home.'

And he's probably also a twenty-stone biker with tattoos who plays loud thrash-slash-clash-rock with a penchant for devil worship and biting the heads off bats, Ella thought darkly. 'But surely, with George to consider, you must have checked this Roy out too, if he's going to be lodging here?'

'Oh, yes. Um, actually, no. I've, um, made bad business decisions in the past so I left my solicitor to do all the investigations and stuff this time. He assures me he found absolutely nothing doubtful at all. So we can safely assume Roy is as pure as the driven snow.'

Hmm, Ella thought, still far from convinced. Roy had probably simply changed his name to duck under the investigative radar.

Oh, God—not only was she no longer entirely sure why she was at Hideaway Farm, but she was now going to be sharing it with a homeless chef and the gay Berkshire equivalent of an early Ozzy Osbourne.

Fantastic.

Poll fiddled with her beads. 'Look, there's so much I need to tell you, but I'll just go down and say hello to Ash again and introduce myself to Roy and get them settled in, if that is them in the car, of course, and make George's lunch, then hopefully we'll be able to sort things out . . . OK?'

'OK.' Ella nodded, trying to fix on a cheerful I-can-cope-with-anything smile. 'That sounds lovely.'

23

Ella waited until the door had closed behind Poll, then exhaled in confusion. Well, whatever was going on, she'd agreed on three months' trial and she was just going to have to make the best of it.

And at least Hideaway Farm was exactly what Poll had said it was in her letters. Digging out her mobile from her handbag, Ella quickly texted her parents, her sister, her ex-flatmates, three ex-work colleagues, and her two best friends to let them all know she'd arrived safely, the decision had been the right one, the countryside, house and especially her room was fabulous, all was absolutely hunky-dory, and that she'd be wearing a daisy-chain tiara and cherry earrings and saying 'me duck' before they knew it.

She hesitated slightly before texting Mark. She wanted to speak to him, to hear his voice, but knew it would probably end in tears, so she quickly sent a non-committal and brief 'arrived safely. beautiful house. lovely people. all ok so far. speak soon. Love E x'.

Then bobbing beneath the low, sloping ceiling, she ran across the polished floorboards and stared out of one of the large open sash windows at the back of Hideaway Farm.

Below her was a dusty yard enclosed by a tall wall, a faded blur of grey slates and old-gold sandstone, glittering in the sun like encrusted gemstones, and dotted with lichen and moss—and yes, there were lots of hens scratching happily about in the borders that glowed with tumbled flowers.

And beyond the yard she could see snaking glimpses of Hideaway Lane, just visible over the wall and through the lilac bushes, and the end of

24

the quaintly named Cattle Drovers Passage—and then, there was nothing.

No houses, no people, no traffic. Just trees, and blossom, and fields, and so much sky—as far as the eyes could see—all wrapped up in a warm, drowsy silence.

It was, as she'd known it would be, absolutely perfect.

Well, apart from the little niggle about Poll, of course. She already knew that Poll was in her forties and divorced—Poll had been very open about her circumstances in her letters—and now she also knew, by her own admission, that Poll was not completely honest.

Ah well, Ella thought as she sorted her pared-down clothes into neat piles on the gloriously downy bed, she'd discover more over lunch, wouldn't she? Unless lunch was totally dominated by the homeless gay couple, of course.

Hey-ho . . .

Finding homes for her things in the lavender-fragranced drawers and wardrobe, Ella hugged herself in delight at the sheer gorgeousness of her room. It was exactly like a suite in a country-house hotel—simply too lovely for words. Poll had provided everything she could ever need. Cool on the scorching day, voile curtains floated sensuously at the windows, there were jugs of flowers everywhere, and a small television set and stereo sat on top of a bookcase, which in turn was crammed with a mixture of old cloth-bound editions and sparkly new paperbacks.

How long was it since she'd even opened a book? Although, maybe now she was a country girl she'd be able to catch up on her reading which would be great . . .

And—ohmigod! Look at that!

There was even a tiny fridge and courtesy tray and a Teasmade beside the bed!

How fantastic!

Ella laughed in delight. Her grandparents had a Teasmade. She thought they'd died out in the 1970s.

Oh, this place was bliss . . .

'Ella!' Poll's voice echoed distantly up the stairs. 'I'm so sorry, but it looks as though we're going to have to delay our little chat for a while. Please come down for lunch whenever you're ready. George is in the garden having his, but Ash Lawrence has just arrived.'

## *Chapter Five*

As she reached Hideaway's front door, Poll sighed. Typical. The day which had started so well had now disintegrated into chaotic confusion. Again. This definitely wasn't how she'd planned things. Her last hope that she and Ella would have more time alone to discuss her plans for Hideaway without interruptions had definitely bitten the dust.

The tall, slender, deliciously dark man in jeans and T-shirt uncurling himself from the driving seat of the loaded estate car had seen to that. Not, of course, that it was his fault. That—as usual—was all hers.

Poll took a deep breath, carefully lifted her long skirts, safely negotiated the steps, and held out her

26

hand to Ash Lawrence.

'Ash, hello. How lovely to see you again. You've made good time. And I'm so sorry about the mix-up in the dates.'

Ash Lawrence stopped stretching, smiled and shook her hand firmly. 'I just hope we haven't caused you too much trouble by arriving unexpectedly.'

'None at all,' Poll lied cheerfully. 'It was my mistake.'

'If you're still not quite ready for us I could go away and come back tomorrow. I've been sleeping in the car for a while now—one more night won't make any difference.'

'No!' Poll was horrified. 'You can't do that—no. We're all ready, honestly, and—oh, yes, please bring your stuff indoors and I'll show you to your room and—ah—and this must be Roy.'

She turned her welcoming smile to the tall, thin, gawky Art Garfunkel lookalike who was emerging from the estate car's passenger seat.

'Er, no.' Ash shook his head. 'Actually, Roy's been staying with someone else on a very temporary basis since we had to leave the restaurant, but there wasn't room for me as well. This is Joe. A mate of mine. He's going to help me move my heavy stuff in. Roy'll be along later.'

'Oh, right. Hello, then, Joe.' Poll turned back to Ash. 'I'll look forward to meeting Roy when he arrives. Look, shall I just show you to your room? Then you and Joe can get your bits and pieces in without too much interruption.'

'Lovely, thanks.' Ash flashed the devastating smile again. 'You've no idea how grateful I—we—are. Right, Joe, if you start unloading, I'll find out

27

where we're going.'

*     *     *

Coming downstairs and after several false starts, Ella eventually found her way to Hideaway's kitchen. As there was no sign of Poll on the stairs or in the house, she assumed the Ash-arrival was still taking place outside.

Wow, though—she looked around in delight—whatever else Poll had not been truthful about, she certainly hadn't lied about the kitchen. It was exactly how she imagined a farmhouse kitchen would be: quarry-tiled floors and nubbly plastered walls, with a huge refectory table surrounded by ancient Windsor chairs, and several gorgeous floor-to-ceiling dressers loaded with china, and pots and pans hanging from a clothes airer contraption—oh yes, and herbs drying there too! Ella inhaled the wonderful scent of thyme and basil and parsley. Cooking in here was going to be absolute bliss.

And wow again! Walking from the cool kitchen into the searing heat of the garden, Ella was met by a tidal wave of warm, honey-sweet air and a deluge of butterflies.

In the lee of the farmhouse, the yard was exquisitely country cottagey, with a little patch of lush lawn and flower-packed beds to one side, shaded from the sun by fronding trees, and set out with a canopied swing seat and parasoled wooden table and chairs. It was idyllically pretty, like something from a child's picture book.

On closer inspection, the floor of the high-walled dusty yard was actually mellowed bricks, with a sort of hollowed out bit in one corner which was clearly George's dirt pit. Ella smiled delightedly, watching him now as he industriously chugged his vividly coloured lorries in and out of the miniature quarry, helped by the sturdiest dog, while the remaining dogs, cats and hens had all found respite from the heat beneath the overhanging branches of the heavily blossomed lilac trees.

The remains of George's lunch were on the table, and Ella flicked the buzz of inquisitive wasps and bees away with her hand.

George looked up and waved at her, yelling some unintelligible and lengthy greeting. Ella waved back.

She sank on to the canopied swing seat and rocked gently back and forth, watching George playing, swamped with pleasure. Why, oh why couldn't Mark be here to see this? Surely, seeing this place, meeting George, he'd understand that this really was her dream come true. She'd always adored children, and had always wanted to be a nanny for as long as she could remember, but had been persuaded to do business studies and find a 'proper job' by her teachers and parents. So, reluctantly, she'd gone along with it until the urge became just too much to bear. And now, she thought, gazing up at the cloudless sky, and listening to the sound of country silence and George's cheerful prattle, she'd made a stand and taken a life-changing decision.

Why did everyone seem to think it so wrong for her to have these incredibly strong maternal feelings? Why should she be made to feel as though she'd somehow let down the sisterhood by not striving for a career but simply wanting to spend her life with children: initially other people's, and then eventually her own? Why was it considered so dreadfully old-fashioned to actually aspire to being a contented homemaker and mother?

It was not only her family who thought she was throwing away her life on looking after children. Mark thought so too . . .

Ella pushed the thoughts of their last angry row out of her head. She was here now, and Mark was in London, and they had agreed on three months apart to resolve their differences.

She definitely wasn't going to think about Mark. Well, not right now anyway.

George looked across at her again and waved a plastic shovel in the air. Ella smiled at him. He was just so cute . . .

Chattering happily, he beckoned her over to the dirt pit.

'Sorry? Ah, right . . . you'd like me to help you with the digging?'

George nodded enthusiastically and picked up a second shovel.

'Great.' Grinning in delight, tucking her hair behind her ears, Ella eased herself up from the swing seat and hurried to join him.

## Chapter Six

Poll ushered Ash upstairs to the second floor room he'd be sharing with Roy, and to her relief and delight he was as volubly pleased with his accommodation as Ella had been with hers. Poll

30

wanted to kiss him.

She beamed. 'Oh, I'm so pleased you like your room—and I hope Roy approves too, of course. I know it'll all be a bit strange to start with—but please just make it your home. If there's anything at all you need, just ask. Oh, here you are—two front door keys—and if you forget them I always leave a spare one hanging in the back porch. I'll leave you to settle in now, go and sort out lunch, and pop back in a minute. OK?'

'Perfect, thank you.'

And relieved that so far Ash's arrival had gone without any problems, Poll hitched up her skirts and practically skipped downstairs.

Finding no sign of Ella or George anywhere in the house, she hurried through the kitchen, peered into the garden, and chuckled to herself. They were kneeling side by side in the dirt pit, industriously chugging lorries back and forth, lost in their own world.

Maybe for once she'd made the right decision, Poll thought happily, watching them together. There had been plenty of better qualified applicants for the job of mother's help, but Ella's openness and honesty about her lack of formal experience had been endearing, and her overwhelming love of children had outweighed any last doubts. And to be honest, Poll admitted to herself, she'd have been terrified of most of the Career Nannies who'd applied. No, it was far better this way—to have someone who not only loved George but was also, hopefully, going to become a friend.

'Enjoying yourselves?'

'This is the best fun I've had for years.' Ella, now

fairly grubby, looked up, shading her eyes from the sun. 'George and I are building a new motorway. It's going to have a special lane just for lorries, and one for buses and another for cars, and lots of sweet shops and a funfair, oh, and a swimming pool.'

Poll laughed. 'Sounds perfect. You'll have to submit the idea to the Ministry of Transport. And does this mean you and George are already starting to talk the same language?'

'Absolutely.' Ella sat back on her heels. 'I've not managed to get all of it yet, but give me time. As it is, we're communicating OK with the basics.'

'Amazing—and oh, Ella, I'm so sorry for all this confusion and delay because you must be starving.'

'Hungry, yes,' Ella admitted, 'but you're busy and I can wait. Have Ash and Roy moved in now?'

'Ash has. Well, he's in the process. With a friend called Joe helping him.'

'Not the mysterious Roy?'

Poll shook her head. 'No, not yet. Roy's been staying somewhere else and will be along later. I said we'd give Ash and Joe a few minutes to get the stuff upstairs and then I'll introduce you.'

Ella nodded. 'Fine—but I still wonder why isn't Roy here helping with the move.'

'I've no idea. Maybe you'd like to ask?'

'And maybe I'll just do that,' Ella laughed. 'Are you suggesting that I'm nosey?'

'As I don't know you well enough yet, I wouldn't dream of it.'

Ella chuckled. 'I'll save you the bother, then. I am. Very.'

'Me too.'

They smiled at one another.

Grabbing his favourite lorry, George suddenly clambered from the dirt pit and scampered happily towards the kitchen door.

'I think he wants to go and see what's happening and do the introductions now, too.' Ella grinned. 'So clearly we're not the only nosey ones.'

Poll stood up. 'Come on then, I expect they're still unpacking, but I promise you, you will adore Ash.'

As they reached the front door, there was no sign of Joe outside, but Ash was dragging a final heap of bags from the estate car and George and the dogs rushed to issue their customary greetings.

Ash, as Ella had done, was reacting very nicely to the onslaught, Poll noticed with pleasure. He certainly was very charming.

Ash paused in the introductions and patting and stroking and smiled again. He really did have the most devastating smile. 'I'm almost done here. We've got most of the stuff in. It's a fabulous room—absolutely perfect. Thanks so much.'

'You're very welcome.' Poll winced slightly at the warmth of the reception George and the dogs were giving Ash. 'I hope you'll both be very happy here and—'

'Oooh.' Ella's eyes widened as Ash strolled past Poll. 'Wow. He's really fit—and absolutely gorgeous.'

'Mmm,' Poll chuckled. 'And maybe I've got this wrong, but didn't you say in your letters that you'd got a boyfriend in London?'

'Yes, well, yes, but it's a long story.'

Poll raised her eyebrows. 'Which, as I'm incurably nosey, you'll tell me all about sometime soon?'

Ella laughed. 'Maybe I will, and maybe I won't.'

'Of course you will.' Poll smiled. 'I'm a good listener. It goes with the nosiness. Anyway, even if you didn't have a boyfriend at home, *he* is definitely not your type.'

'Actually, he is,' Ella said happily. 'In a totally hypothetical way, of course, given that I'm no longer young, free and single. But he's drop dead gorgeous. I love dark hair and blue eyes, and look at those cheekbones and the length of those eyelashes . . .'

'Yes, gorgeous he may be, but he's definitely not your type.'

'Oh, believe me he is—a girl can look and appreciate these things, can't she? What did you say his name was again? Joe?'

'No . . . No, Ella, listen. He's *not* Joe. Joe's the friend who's sorting stuff out upstairs. *He's* Ash. Ash Lawrence.' Poll stretched her eyes and lips in exaggerated agitation. '*Ash Lawrence* . . . Get it? Gay chef, boyfriend called Roy . . .'

'Ah—damn.' Ella nodded slowly. 'That's Ash Lawrence, is it? Now I see why he's very not my type. What a shame, because he's too stunning for words. Blimey then, I wonder what Roy's like?'

'Beautiful,' Ash Lawrence said smoothly, appearing between them and hauling various bags and suitcases up the steps, 'and the love of my life.'

Poll was amused to notice that Ella was blushing. 'Ash, this is Ella. She's just arrived too and—'

'Another waif and stray?' Ash beamed at Ella. 'I can see I'm in good company. Ash Lawrence.'

'Ella Maloney. Great to meet you. And not a waif and stray, a mother's help and a willing convert to the rural life.'

Once George had insisted on shaking hands solemnly again, and Ash had been introduced to the dogs, the cats and three of the hens by name, and they'd all helped in hauling the remainder of his luggage from the estate car into the hall, Poll suggested to Ella that it might be kinder to Ash if she removed George and the animals to the relative calm of the garden again.

'OK.' Ella nodded, grabbing George's hand. 'Is there anything you'd like me to do for lunch?'

'Good heavens, no, you've only just arrived yourself. I'm being a completely useless hostess.' Poll shook her head. 'Actually, lunch is all ready, thanks. And as soon as Ash is unloaded we'll be able to eat and drink all afternoon and have a lovely chat together.'

'Great.' Ella grinned. 'Come on then, George, we've got a motorway to construct.'

Once they were alone again, Poll looked at Ash. 'As soon as you and Joe have finished, please come and have some lunch with us.'

'Thanks, but I did promise I'd drop Joe off at work and then go and pick Roy up as soon as I'd unpacked. It's not far so we shouldn't be long. We don't like being apart.'

Poll smiled happily at such devotion. 'Of course you don't. Maybe you and Roy could join us, then? I've done loads of food and we can all get to know one another. Come straight through the house and into the garden when you get back. Oh, I'm so pleased you're here. It's going to be such fun.'

Ash nodded. 'I think it is, too. Thanks so much for this, Poll. I'm really grateful.'

Poll waved her hands. 'Don't mention it. And we're all going to get on brilliantly. Ella is a lovely

35

girl and—'

'Very pretty.'

'Very,' Poll agreed. 'And she's left her boyfriend behind in London to come and work here. I do hope she won't miss him too much. Still, at least you and Roy will soon be reunited, won't you?'

Ash smiled. 'We will. I can't wait to get him settled in. He's really going to love it here.'

*    *    *

Poll was lovely if ever-so-slightly mad, Ella decided as, with the sun beating relentlessly on her back, she and George industriously tunnelled through the dirt pit. And Ash Lawrence was, she thought with only a momentary flicker of guilt about Mark, without doubt the most beautiful man she'd ever seen. She'd be sharing her life—her perfect new, albeit crazy, rustic life—living in the same house as the Most Stunning Man in the Entire World.

Oooh, damn it. The Most Stunning Very Gay Loved Up Man in the Entire World. And all her friends had told her she should make this break permanent, and that she was bound to find a far more suitable man and forget about Mark, and Ella had robustly denied it, scoffing at the very thought that she should be so shallow.

And then, with no warning, there he was—Ash Lawrence—her ideal man. Except, of course, he wasn't, because one, she didn't know him at all and two, he was gay, and three—great big three—she was in love with Mark. She sighed and concentrated on channelling away at another dirt tunnel.

Poll drifted out of the kitchen door and collapsed on to a wooden seat. 'Whoo, it's sooo hot. We've had so many wash-outs recently I'd forgotten what hot summers were like. Is George OK?'

'Fine,' Ella said, blowing strands of dusty hair away from her face. 'Says he likes Ash a lot and wants to meet Roy now. And I hope you don't mind but I found some juice in the fridge so we've both had a drink, oh, and I found a sunhat for him in the kitchen.'

'Bless you, I can see you're clearly going to be a godsend. I didn't mean for you to start work straight away—you must be so tired after your journey—I do appreciate it.'

'No problem,' Ella said cheerfully, as George issued a string of construction instructions. 'And if this is work then I'm more than happy.'

'Well, I'm still mortified. I'd planned to serve up jugs of iced fruit juice and lashings of food and welcome you properly. My life never seems to run to plan—but you're obviously brilliantly resourceful. I just knew you would be. So? What do you think?'

'About what? Oh, Ash Lawrence? After my embarrassing little girlie fan gush, you know very well what I think.'

Poll laughed.

Ella pulled a face. 'Not funny. I only hope he didn't hear. So, I gather the devastating Ash is happy up there? And where's Roy hiding?'

'Ash is very happy with the room, yes, and is just about to go and collect Roy from the place where he's been staying. Ash has been sleeping in the car

37

because there wasn't room for him. Isn't that sad?'

'Very. And it's also very sad, given that he's possibly the sexiest bloke on the planet, that he's gay. But I still don't understand why Roy doesn't have his own car. Why can't he drive here himself here? If he's working on pylons as the Berkshire equivalent of the Wichita Lineman he must have transport. Has he lost his licence do you reckon?'

'I don't know.' Poll shook her head. 'But you'll be able to ask him all those questions yourself pretty soon—that sounds like Ash driving off along the lane now to fetch him. He shouldn't be too long.'

\*   \*   \*

He wasn't. Less than half an hour later, heralded by George's screams of excitement from his dirt-pit quarrying, Ash Lawrence appeared in the kitchen doorway.

'Hi!' He looked around with appreciation. 'Oh, this is gorgeous out here, isn't it? I've collected Roy. I'll just get his stuff upstairs, and is it OK if I put his food in the freezer?'

'Of course,' Poll said. 'Does he have a special diet? You should have said. I'd have got some things in for him specially.'

Ash smiled the melting smile again. 'I wouldn't dream of it. Roy's well stocked up. Look, I'll just do the food thing—he's still in the car. Why don't you go and say hello?'

Poll and Ella nodded and, with George and the lorries following, made their way through the house.

'I don't want to be non-pc here,' Ella whispered

38

as they reached the front door, 'but do you think Roy's, well, OK? I mean, it all seems a bit odd. Him being the one staying somewhere while Ash slept rough, and not helping with the move, the special diet, and now not getting out of the car—you don't think he's, um, sort of well, disabled in some way, do you?'

Poll shook her head. 'Lord knows. I hope not because I haven't fitted ramps or anything and I would have if I'd known. But Ash didn't say anything about it at our previous meetings, and my solicitor certainly didn't mention anything in his searches.'

Ella peered at Poll. 'These legal searches and reports—how closely did you read them?'

Poll shrugged. 'Well, I didn't read *every* word, naturally—I mean, once the solicitor had assured me that the criminal records checks were all clear, and I'd skimmed through the basics . . .'

'You gave up?'

'Well, yes. There were dozens of pages of the stuff. But Roy was OK. The solicitor said so, in fact, he laughed when he said it, so I knew I'd got nothing to worry about. And Roy *works* shinning up and down those massive pylons, doesn't he? He can't be, um, disabled or ill in any way, can he? Maybe he's just shy?'

'And maybe he's just slightly ashamed of being a hell's angel or something equally antisocial?' Ella said as they clattered down the steps towards Ash's estate car. 'And maybe the solicitor has a warped sense of humour. And maybe the special diet is bats and fresh blood and—Jesus Christ!'

'What?' Poll stopped walking. 'What's the matter?'

39

Ella jabbed a finger at the car. 'Works on pylons my eye! Dear God, Poll—I'm not surprised the solicitor laughed. Why the hell didn't you read those legal reports?'

Poll frowned. 'Why? What's wrong with him? Oh, poor Roy. Is he badly incapacitated? Awfully disfigured? Doesn't he work on pylons, then?'

'No, Poll. Roy definitely doesn't work on pylons. In fact, Roy doesn't work anywhere at all. Roy's a bloody *python*.'

## *Chapter Seven*

Recoiling mesmerised, neither of them spoke. Oblivious to their stunned silence, George was standing on tiptoe, excitedly peering into the car, making cooing noises.

'Poll?' Ella whispered. 'Breathe. Say something.'

Poll, still staring at Roy, grabbed a protesting George to safety and cleared her throat. 'Right—yes, OK—what? Such as?'

Ella swallowed. 'Anything. Anything at all that might be reassuring. Anything that won't make me more shivery than I already am.'

'Are you frightened?'

'Frightened? Of . . . him . . . it . . . Roy? Yep, I think I am. Aren't you?'

'A little disturbed, yes. He's come as quite a shock. OK, er, so, let's be practical . . . I'm a vegetarian, so what do pythons eat?'

'Cats, dogs, chickens and small boys?' Ella hazarded, her eyes transfixed on the mass of softly undulating coils crammed in the small tank on the back seat of Ash's car. 'Lord knows, but you can bet your life it won't be Quorn or tofu.'

'Oh, God.' Poll swallowed, anchoring George firmly to her side. 'And whatever it is, Ash has just put it in the freezer.'

'Look on the bright side, then, at least it must be dead.'

'Thanks.'

'Are you a snake-o-phobe?'

'Ophidiophobic?' Poll said faintly. 'No idea. Are you?'

'I didn't think I was, but I think I might be now.'

Ella, feeling involuntary shivers prickle her skin despite the searing heat, stared at the python. The python slowly raised its head and stared back. Then, clearly bored, it gave a sort of shrug and subsided into its coils.

'It's . . . he's . . . Roy's actually quite pretty,' Ella said, rubbing her arms and wishing the goosebumps would subside. 'He's got lovely markings—like a big tabby cat—and he's got very, um, kind eyes.'

Poll cleared her throat again. 'Yes, I suppose he has. And I know he has to be marked like that for camouflage, but don't you think he'd be slightly less intimidating if he were turquoise or pale pink? With sequins?'

Ella frowned. 'Er, no.'

Poll shrugged. 'Oh, is it just me, then? Am I the only one who always visualises spiders in pastel shades to be able to cope with them? If you think of them as lilac and lemon and rose and sky-blue stars scuttling around it makes them a lot less scary.'

'Yeah, OK, I'll take your word for that.' Ella

41

stared doubtfully at Poll. 'But Roy isn't a spider, pastel or otherwise, neither is he turquoise with sequins. He's a huge brownish python—and we've got to live with it, er, him.'

'I know. Oh dear, will it be safe to be sharing the house with him?'

'I really don't see what else you can do, having invited Ash and . . . him . . . Roy—weird name for a snake—to make their homes here. Obviously Roy being a reptile was the reason for them being chucked out of their last place and, as you've rescued them from that, you can't do the same thing, can you?'

'No,' Poll sighed. 'I can't.'

'And anyway, he'll be living in a sort of python secure unit, won't he? It's not like he'll be slithering up and downstairs for breakfast, or wanting to share the sofa to watch telly or anything, is it?'

'Don't!' Poll groaned. 'I told you I always got things wrong. I could have sworn he said *pylon*. I really should have listened more carefully and, yes, OK, read the solicitor's reports. How big is it, do you think?'

'About three miles,' Ella said with a shudder.

'Slightly under six feet, actually.' Ash Lawrence leaped nimbly down the stone steps. 'He's just a baby. And he's a ball python, not a Burmese or a Royal, so he won't get much bigger. Isn't he fabulous?'

Poll and Ella nodded doubtfully. George clapped his hands.

'Would you like to stroke him?' Ash opened the car's door.

Poll and Ella squeaked, shook their heads in

42

synchrony and retreated. George clapped his hands even more and rushed forwards. Poll grabbed at him again.

'It's fine,' Ash said soothingly. 'Roy doesn't bite—he's not venomous. He's a constrictor.'

'Thank goodness for that,' Ella said faintly. 'That means we only have to worry about being squeezed to death.'

Ash chuckled. 'Roy's very well behaved and only squeezes when he's hungry or frightened. And he's currently neither of those. He's been well fed this morning. He won't need another meal for a week or so.'

'Um, good,' Poll croaked. 'And actually, I've just said to Ella that I'm a vegetarian, so, about the feeding . . . ?'

'Small rodents.'

'No!'

'Sorry, yes, but pre-packed and pre-frozen. Nothing cute and furry and scampering.'

Ella frowned. 'Not now, maybe, but once upon a time . . .'

Ash sighed. 'I know, but I can't change nature, can I? Much as I'd love to throw him a handful of pine nuts and a small spinach quiche, it isn't going to happen. Poor Roy—he's had such a bad time.'

'Has he?' Poll's eyes immediately softened. 'Oh, dear.'

'He'd been abandoned by someone who thought having a python was cool, then discovered it wasn't. Then he had a short stint as a nightclub dancer's accessory, which was awful for him. So, I took him on and nursed him back to health—but my employer had a no pets rule, and I got found out, and, well, you know the rest. Then you were

43

so wonderfully kind and unprejudiced about reptiles, and amazingly generous with your offer of a new home, and here we are.'

'And you're very welcome,' Poll said stoutly. 'Both of you.'

Ella chuckled to herself.

'But,' Poll said quickly, 'I really must be sure that he . . . Roy . . . won't escape or want to eat George or the cats or dogs or the chickens. You hear such awful things, don't you?'

'I solemnly promise you,' Ash said, straight-faced, 'that no one, or nothing, is at risk. Believe me, I wouldn't have imposed on your generosity if I knew differently. Roy has a securely locked vivarium, and is more than happy with his, um, frozen ready meals. Even if he escaped—which he won't—he'd only be looking for company and somewhere warm to sleep, not foraging for food.'

'OK.' Poll heaved a sigh of relief. 'That's absolutely fine then—I think.'

Ash leaned into the car and opened the travelling tank. 'Come and stroke him.'

Ella dragged her eyes away from the tight T-shirt and jeans stretched over a fabulous body.

'Stop drooling,' Poll hissed. 'You're attached and, remember, he's gay.'

'Actually,' Ella hissed back, 'he might not be, because you only thought he was gay because you thought Roy was the Berkshire Wichita Lineman. Now we know Roy is—well—reptilian, it might mean that Ash is superbly heterosexual, mightn't it?'

'Well,' Poll said doubtfully, 'since you put it like that, he *might* be, I suppose.'

Ella beamed. Every cloud and all that. Not that

44

she was going to think about Ash in *that* way, of course—she had more than enough on her plate with Mark—but it was nice to *know*.

Ash now had most of Roy looped over his arms. 'Come and say hi. He's really friendly—lazy and laid-back. And I must get him upstairs into his permanent home fairly quickly. This little box is only for transport and whatever happens he mustn't get cold—even today's heat would feel Siberian to Roy. Oh, Joe and I have already set up his tank in my room—' he glanced over his shoulder at Poll as George reached forwards eagerly '—and I know I'll have to sort out extra payments for the electricity. There!' He grinned down at George. 'He's smiling. He likes you.'

George stroked Roy's blunt-nosed head gently and cooed happily. Despite Ash's earlier assurances, Poll and Ella still stared anxiously.

'Come on.' Ash held the armful of python towards Ella. 'Snakes get a rotten press. They aren't cold and slimy. Roy's warm and smooth and totally adorable.'

Pretty much like his owner then, Ella thought, stretching out a tentative and slightly trembling hand and touching Roy's perfectly patterned velvety skin.

She stopped, surprised. 'Oh . . . he's nothing like I thought he'd be, and I can feel him breathing. Oh, bless him. He's lovely.'

Ella and Ash shared a proud-parent eye-meet moment. Ella, suddenly feeling very warm, looked away first.

Poll, clearly not wanting to be outdone, also ran a reluctant hand briefly over Roy's beautifully marked skin, then smiled at her own bravery. 'Oh, yes, he's cute. Not cold or scary at all. There. Now we're all friends. So, would you like to pop him upstairs into his new quarters? And come and join us for some late lunch in the garden?'

'That sounds wonderful,' Ash said, hoisting Roy round his neck and looking at Ella. 'Would you mind just taking his tail end so that it doesn't knock against anything as we go upstairs? Snakes bruise very easily. Look, just hold out your hands and take the weight—he's quite relaxed. Thanks, that's great.'

Ella, carefully carrying several feet of surprisingly heavy python, felt ridiculously proud of herself. And with Poll opening doors and George dodging between them stroking whichever bits of Roy came to hand, they made their way up to Hideaway Farm's second floor.

Ella couldn't help thinking as she climbed the stairs that life had taken a pretty crazy turn. Somewhere around that overgrown signpost her old normal life had ended and this new bizarre existence had started. This morning she'd been in London, and it could have been decades ago.

Now, merely hours later, she was in a remote Berkshire farmhouse with ditzy Poll, a very cute small boy who'd already stolen her heart, an even cuter homeless maybe-gay ex-chef, and carrying the tail end of a python.

Ah well, she'd told Mark she'd wanted a complete life change, hadn't she?

They'd just reached Ash's room when the phone rang noisily in the hall below.

'Sorry.' Poll pulled a face. 'I'll have to go and answer it. It might be important. It might be the plumber—or maybe even Billy or Trixie letting me know when they're arriving.'

'Billy and Trixie?' Ella asked.

Poll shrugged. 'Er, yes. I'll tell you about them later. Sorry, I've got to get the phone.'

Ash hoisted Roy up gently. 'Won't they ring on your mobile if you don't answer the landline?'

'I don't have a mobile.'

Ella and Ash looked at her in amazement.

'Never got the hang of having to charge them, and even when they were charged I always pressed the wrong buttons and cut people off, so I've stuck to the landline,' Poll said happily as she hurried towards the stairs. 'Come along George—yes, you can come and see Roy again later.'

Ash shook his head as they disappeared. 'No mobile? How on earth does she manage?'

'Goodness knows,' Ella said, out of breath. 'I couldn't imagine life without a mobile—although I'll admit to leaving my laptop with my parents.'

'Sadly, I refuse to be parted from either. And my MP3 would be hard to live without, too.'

Ella laughed. 'I reckon Poll would think MP3 was a division of the police. And I don't think she has a computer because all her letters to me were, well, letters. Oof—can we put Roy down, please? He weighs a ton.'

'Sssh.' Ash grinned. 'You'll hurt his feelings. He's very sensitive about his weight—but, OK. You let your end of him go gently—that's great—and now if you could just make sure the lid is fully opened while I pop him in and let him get acclimatised.'

'Blimey.' Ella gazed at the massive tank running along one wall. 'That's one huge snake pit.'

'Vivarium. State of the art. It comes in sections that all bolt together and the heat and light unit

47

just plugs in. But that's why I needed Joe's help in getting it up here. Right, are you ready to introduce him to his new home?'

Between them, with a considerable amount of huffing and puffing, they eventually managed to slide a still very relaxed Roy into the large vivarium.

Ella smiled at the way Roy seemed to sigh happily as he moved slowly across the shaved bark, investigated the mounds of sphagnum moss, the rocks, the little caves, the watering hole—all illuminated by carefully shaded spotlights—then, clearly confident that he'd come home, curled himself up and stared at them with his unblinking eyes.

Ash snapped the locks securely into place. 'He's nocturnal so he'll just want to go to sleep. Thanks so much—you were great.'

'My pleasure,' Ella said loftily, proud of her snake-charming prowess and really relieved that Ash hadn't witnessed her earlier terror. 'So, are you coming down for lunch now?'

'When I've unpacked, yes. That'd be great.'

'Poll loves cooking, so we should be well fed—although as that's your area of professional expertise maybe I shouldn't say that.'

Ash shook his head. 'I'm no culinary diva. It's always a pleasure to have food cooked for me. Although while I'm out of work maybe I should offer to take a turn in that wonderful farmhouse kitchen. It'll give me an opportunity to try out my soups. I'll cook anything, but I love inventing new soup recipes from really fresh local produce.'

'Oh, yes, Poll's kitchen is brilliant.' Ella beamed. 'And as you do soups, Poll specialises in mains and

48

I love concocting puddings—although of course I'm very much an amateur—between us we'll be able to provide a proper dinner.'

'A *Dewberrys' Dinner*?' Ash laughed. 'My favourite programme.'

'No way! Really? Poll and I have already discovered that we're both fans, too.' Ella sighed happily, already visualising snuggling up close and personal to Ash on Poll's vast cushiony peaches and cream sofa while Tom and Gabby Dewberry ripped some other poor wannabe chefs to shreds on the small screen. 'We've both said we never miss it.'

'Me neither. I always record it to watch after a shift,' Ash said. 'Or at least I did until I became one of the unemployment statistics.'

'Mmm, Poll explained about—everything.'

'Hopefully I'll find another restaurant before long. I can't afford to live on fresh air.' Ash smiled. 'But Poll's amazing, isn't she? Thank God for people like Poll. You have no idea how difficult it is finding somewhere to live that'll take a python. Although, I must admit the set-up here is a bit curious. I mean, you said you weren't another lodger, so why are you here?'

'Mother's help, as I said,' Ella said quickly, deciding to leave out all the other more painful details. 'New job. I was frazzled by working in sales, worn out by impossible targets and bad-tempered customers, needed a change of lifestyle and wanted to escape from city living for a while. And I only arrived here this morning, although it seems as if I've been here for several lifetimes already. Of course, I wasn't expecting—' She stopped.

49

'Expecting what?'

'Expecting you to be moving in—or Roy to be a python,' Ella said, deciding that honesty was the best policy.

'Really? Didn't Poll tell you anything about us?'

'Not a word until I arrived a couple of hours ago.'

'She's a bit dizzy, isn't she? Lovely, though. And so what did you think Roy was, then?'

Ella grinned. 'Oh, I thought you and Roy were a gay couple. And Roy worked on pylons and looked like Ozzy Osbourne.'

Ash laughed.

Ella decided it was possibly not the best time to tell him that none of this was a joke, so she simply smiled instead. Ash smiled back.

Oooh, but he had such a fabulous smile. Ella suddenly wanted to open the tank again and kiss Roy. Brought together to live under the same roof with the sexiest man in the universe—even if he *might* be gay—by a ball python. How cool was that?

Not cool at all, her inner voice reminded her. Remember, you've got Mark and more complications than any girl needs . . .

'Ella!' Poll's voice echoed up the stairs. 'That was Billy Booker on the phone. Because I got the dates muddled, he's arriving the day after tomorrow instead of next week, and I've managed to ring Trixie too, just to check what dates she had, and she's coming the day after tomorrow too. Isn't that wonderfully convenient?'

As she had no idea who Billy and Trixie were, Ella made a murmur of assent. 'Er, yes. That sounds, um, perfect.'

'So,' Poll continued cheerfully, 'we'll have one day to get to know each other better, and then another day of complete mayhem to look forward to.'

'Oh, yes—lovely.'

'And if Roy is happily installed,' Poll's voice echoed up the stairs, 'is Ash ready for lunch yet? Everything's wilting, including me.'

'I think so,' Ella called back. 'I'll just ask him.'

Ash surveyed the mountains of luggage strewn around his room and nodded. 'Actually, I'm starving so I'll leave this lot until later. I'll just ring Onyx and let her know Roy and I have arrived safely, then I'll come down and find you.'

'Onyx?'

Ash nodded, flicking through numbers on his mobile. 'She used to work with Roy—I think I mentioned it earlier? He shared in her stage act and she really loved him, but she wasn't happy about it from a welfare point of view so she gave him to me.'

Ella nodded, walking—she hoped—casually towards the door. 'Oh, of course, that famous double act: Morecambe and Wise, Cannon and Ball, Ant and Dec, Onyx and Roy—they just trip off the tongue.'

Ash laughed as he lifted his mobile. 'You're really funny. I do love a girl with a—Oh, hi . . .'

Ella, really, really not wanting to hear Ash cooing seductively at Onyx-the-stripper, who she hoped against hope was really called Olive and looked like a welder, stomped downstairs.

'Blimey.' Poll frowned in the hall. 'What's up with you? Oh—Roy hasn't escaped or bitten anyone has he?'

51

'No, Roy's nicely at home in his secure snake pit.'

'Thank goodness for that, but I thought you and the superb Mr Lawrence were getting on just fine?'

'We were . . . are . . . were.' Ella swung crossly round the newel post. 'And, on the plus side, he makes divine soups and wants to cook for us in your kitchen, and he's another *Dewberrys' Dinners* fan. And still on the plus side, he thinks I'm funny. Oh, and on the plus side again, he definitely isn't gay.'

'Really?' Poll chuckled. 'There's a mercy. London boyfriend in the picture or not, you'd clearly be hell to live with if he was. And all those pluses sound pretty good to me. So, do I sense a minus coming up?'

'Oh, yes, a big, big, b-i-g minus. About a nanosecond after finding out he wasn't gay I discover he has a girlfriend.'

'And you've got a boyfriend,' Poll pointed out reasonably.

'Yes, but it's not the same thing at all. Mark's just a normal bloke with a normal job. *He's* involved with an exotic dancer called—can you believe it?—Onyx.'

'Pretty name. Did he tell you she was his girlfriend?'

'I didn't ask—anyway, there was no need. He went all soppy on the phone. A girl knows these things. And I bet she can do the splits and cartwheels and everything. And,' Ella said quickly, 'if you laugh, I'll resign now before I've even got started and be back in London before you can say "glittery G-string".'

52

'I wouldn't dream of laughing.' Poll laughed. 'Ooh, sorry, but it is quite funny.'

'Is it?'

'Yes, well, Ash goes from gay to heterosexual in the blink of an eye and Roy is replaced by Onyx— and you're still frowning. Sorry, I'm not laughing at you, honestly. And as you're romantically attached too, I don't see the problem. Now, do you think you could just stop scowling long enough to eat some lunch?'

Ella wrinkled her nose. 'Oh, tough one . . . Go on then. I might just try and force something down.'

## Chapter Eight

'At long, long last,' Poll sighed as she put the final lunch dish on the wooden table in the garden and poured tall ice-clinking glasses of juice for Ella and Ash. 'I do apologise for all the delays. It's so hot and you must both be starving, dehydrated and completely bewildered. Please help yourselves.'

As Poll felt that making sure everyone was well fed was the most important thing in the world, she'd produced a sort of extended ploughman's lunch which would probably feed at least thirty people, but she didn't want Ella and Ash to think she *skimped*.

'It all looks wonderful,' Ash said, helping himself liberally to something of everything.

Ella, her mouth already full of bread and cheese, nodded her agreement.

Poll, piling her own plate, was delighted that Ella seemed to have recovered her equanimity, and also that she clearly didn't intend to follow any sort of lo-cal diet to keep that stunning figure. She allowed herself another covetous glance at Ella's long, long, jet-back eyelashes and her perfect peachy youthful complexion. Not a line or wrinkle or open pore in sight. Like porcelain.

Ella, Poll thought, was exactly what she'd longed to be in her youth—and had never been able to be, and never would be now. Damn it.

'George is having his nap,' Poll said, 'so it seems like an ideal opportunity to explain a few things to you both. Oh, do have some more bread, and all the cheeses are home-made from the milk of Hideaway-grazed cows and goats.'

Ella groaned greedily. 'I won't be able to move an inch after this. It's all absolutely fantastic—and I'm sorry—I know zilch about farming. I didn't see any cows or goats. Are they, er, in stables or something?'

Poll laughed, dropping a dollop of pickle in amongst her cascade of beads. 'Oops . . . No, we don't keep animals on the farm. In fact I don't farm it all. I rent out the land to neighbours for growing stuff, and for grazing when it's needed, but then only for dairy purposes. The hens are mine and they're part of the family and wander around and lay eggs in some odd places, and we do eat those of course. The eggs, that is, not the hens. But Hideaway Farm is totally arable.'

'Arable?' Ella frowned. 'Crops and things?'

'Wheat. Barley. Potatoes. Greens. Even oil-seed rape. I'd have never come here if I thought anything was going to be slaughtered. Actually I hope the vegetarian thing is OK with you?'

Ella helped herself to more cheese and a large

54

spoonful of tomato chutney. 'Of course. It's fine. Actually, I've never thought about being a non-meat eater, but I'm willing to give anything a try.'

'Me too,' Ash agreed. 'And all this is amazing if it's totally veggie—I mean, you've even got pâté—surely . . . ?'

'Mushroom and cheese and herb,' Poll said proudly. 'Tasty as anything concocted from something that breathed—well, at least in my opinion. But I'm afraid food without a face is all that I cook here at Hideaway.'

'Not a problem for me,' Ella said, spreading pâté on a chunk of bread.

Ash nodded. 'Not for me, either.'

And thank goodness for that, Poll exhaled. So far so very good. In a minute she'd be able to tell Ella—and now Ash as well—exactly what her plans were. But not just yet, not while things were going so well. Best stay on safe ground for the time being. Food. She'd stick with food.

Poll smiled at Ella. 'So, what sort of puddings do you like to cook?'

'Rich, old-fashioned ones. Huge gooey ones. With oodles of cream and sugar and real custard. I used to drive my size-zero housemates crazy! Eve's pudding, Midsummer pie, real Victorian trifle, Manchester tart—that sort of thing.'

'Fantastic.' Ash raised his eyebrows at Ella. 'All this retro stuff is very fashionable at the moment, and they're definitely some of my favourite puds. I can see we'll all have to join Weight Watchers before long. Are you self-taught?'

'Yep. My gran taught me how to cook all those, and more, when I was a kid. I just watched her, then helped, then went solo.'

'The best way to learn anything.' Poll slowly buttered another chunk of bread. The butter spread itself amongst her beads as she leaned forwards. Ella was certainly full of surprises. 'They sound wonderful and, as Ash and I are more savoury cooks, we're going to make a great cooking combination. And I love old-fashioned recipes. You'll have to teach me some of your favourites.'

Ella nodded happily. 'Of course, but will I have time? With everything you want me to do . . . ? Which is obviously looking after George—but what else exactly? What exactly haven't you told me about?'

Poll laughed. 'Ah, yes. I really can't put it off any longer can I? And maybe it's as well that Ash is here too as he doesn't actually know any of this either.'

Reaching under the table, she produced a battered box file.

'Don't look so worried, Ella. I only lied by omission. I honestly do want someone to help with George, but not because I intend to be a lady of leisure who lunches while you skivvy—far from it. I know that's what the ad sounded like, but what I really want is for you to share in my dream.'

'Dream? What dream? I don't remember anything about a dream in the advert.'

'Sorry. I told you I went about everything the wrong way round. Right, well, my inherited money—another long story which I'll tell you one day—like everyone else's, has taken a bit of a knock in the credit crunch years, so I know that I'll need to make sure there's plenty left for George. Which means earning some to make up the deficit.

56

As I'm totally unemployable I thought I could do something to earn money while also helping other people. So I decided to marry the two together.'

Ella and Ash exchanged confused frowns.

Poll handed the file to Ella. 'Maybe if you just look at these first.'

Still completely bemused, Ella flicked through the papers. There were masses of newspaper cuttings, copious notes and dozens of letters. It would take weeks to study them in any depth.

She looked up at Poll. 'Could you give me a clue about what I'm supposed to be looking for? At a quick glance these all seem to be stories about people who've been in the news for various misdemeanours.'

'Not necessarily,' Poll said, leaning across the table and lifting out the top sheaf of papers. 'Some have, of course, and I discarded those. I spent ages collecting this information from news programmes and the press, and even longer sifting out the wrong'uns. And in the end I made my decision, so please read these.'

As the sun spiralled overhead and one of the cats wove its sinuous way round her feet in the table's shade, Ella skimmed through the papers. Eventually she looked up.

'OK, so as far as I can see these people have got absolutely nothing in common, except they've been in the news this year for, well, for being antisocial . . . I'm sorry, but I still don't understand . . .'

Poll sighed. 'They do have one thing in common—as have all the poor people in those reports—they've lost their lives and their homes. Oh, Ella, you've no idea how much heartache there is out there. It was so hard to choose . . .'

57

'Choose?'

'Mmm.' Poll nodded. 'I had so many sleepless nights trying to pick the ones who really, really needed my help. I could only pick three to start with, of course, but hopefully one day, with more income, I'll be able to expand. Then there was George to consider. I couldn't expose him to anything or anyone who might cause, well, problems.'

'No, of course you couldn't. So, are you going to sponsor them or something? Make a donation to Shelter on their behalf or what? I still don't understand where I come in.'

'You will. Don't you see? These people have lost everything. Through no fault of their own. Which is why I've invited them to live here.'

'*What*?' Ella nearly fell off her chair. '*Live*? *Here*? At Hideaway Farm?'

Poll nodded, smiling hugely. 'Yes. It's the one thing I can do. I can make a difference. I've got everything I'd ever dreamed of now, but most of my early life was pretty rubbishy and I never thought I'd find this sort of happiness. These people deserve a second chance too. I've got all this room here—so now I can give it to them.'

'Unbelievable,' Ash breathed.

Ella wasn't so easily impressed. 'By taking them in? To live at Hideaway Farm? Are you mad? They're all weird, and dangerous . . .'

'They're not. I promise you. I've met them—so has George and my solicitor.'

Ash looked interested. 'So am I in there too?'

'You are.' Poll nodded. 'Yours was the first case I found. You were the first person I contacted.'

'And thank goodness you did. I was at rock

58

bottom. I'll never stop being grateful to you.'

Ella shook her head. 'OK, I understand about why Ash lost his home, but who are the others? And why . . . ?'

'Just two more to start with, and they're both lovely.'

'Two more?' Ella queried. 'Ah, right, the mysterious Billy and Trixie?'

Poll beamed. 'Ten out of ten. And of course I've had them properly checked out and vetted—police checks, criminal records and everything. They're misunderstood and currently unhappy and a bit confused by the bad hand life has dealt them, but not dangerous or weird.'

'Really? Everyone in this file sounds pretty scarily weird to me.' Ella glanced quickly at Ash. 'Present company excepted, of course.'

'Of course,' Ash chuckled, filling their glasses with more iced juice.

Ella smiled. 'Thanks. OK. So, you're going to turn Hideaway Farm into a refuge, and you want me to . . . ?'

'Do exactly what I advertised for. To look after George so that I can make sure I give everyone the best start possible at Hideaway. I don't want this to disrupt George in any way at all. So, you're here as a mother's help—it was only the *reason* I left out of the ad.'

'Amazing,' Ash said before Ella could answer. 'Poll, that's just wonderful.'

Ella frowned. 'Well, yes, it is—or at least in theory—but how will it work?'

Poll took a long drink. 'Easily, I hope. Ash knows this bit. I'm going to let them make Hideaway Farm their new home. I'll be their landlady and

59

they'll pay me whatever rent they can afford according to their current circumstances, which will give me the regular income I need, and they can get on with working or whatever, and rebuilding their lives.'

Ella was still in a state of shock. 'So, let me get this straight—are they moving in with all their stuff? Furniture and things? Lock, stock and barrel?'

'I've fully furnished their rooms because none of them had many possessions, but of course they'll be bringing whatever bits and pieces they have to make them feel at home. We've already discussed what they'd need, and worked all that out.'

'And is Hideaway going to be their permanent home?'

'It'll be whatever they want it to be. My solicitor has dealt with all the tenancy agreements and health and safety and boring legalese stuff. We've settled on a six-month period to start with. They may want to stay longer, they may well have found their feet and a new home by that time. Anyone who moves out will be replaced by another poor soul needing my help.'

'Wow. Like Ash said, you're amazing . . . mad, but amazing. Most people would run a mile from doing something like this.'

'I'm not most people, as you've probably gathered,' Poll chuckled. 'And I'm a pretty awful housekeeper so with all these extra people living here I knew I'd have to have some help with George so that his life stayed stable, and I wanted someone who would understand. Someone, like you, who wanted to change their lifestyle too.'

'Well, I'm relieved that's all it is. I'd imagined all

sorts of things, but certainly not this . . .' Ella looked across the table at Poll. 'So, as well as Ash, you've invited Billy, er, Booker—a failed small businessman with kleptomaniac tendencies?'

'Wrongly accused,' Poll said stoutly, her eyes growing misty. 'Poor Billy, such a lovely man. He's a widower and he had his own small bakery business which went bust in the recession. He was living in social housing. Awful rabbit hutch flats. Stuff went missing from the other residents, and turned up in Billy's flat. Food mostly. Billy's an absolute sweetheart so someone obviously planted the things on him. But he was evicted after being branded antisocial—and with no family and no income except his tiny pension and nowhere else to go, he was inches away from living on the streets and simply *needed* me.'

'Poor bloke.' Ash looked shocked.

'Or,' Ella said, 'he might really be light-fingered, a liar, greedy and unpleasant to boot.'

'Ella . . .' Poll shook her head. 'You don't mean that. You wait until you meet him. You'll adore him.'

'OK, I'll suspend judgement.' Ella smiled at Poll. 'I just hope you're not being taken for a ride. So, that's Billy. What about Trixie?' She looked down at the next sheaf of papers. 'Oh, yes—Trixie Pepper, a middle-aged woman who's—*What*? No way! An *arsonist* . . . ?'

Ash laughed.

Ella looked at him. 'It's not funny. That's what it says here.'

'Alleged—nothing proved—and you'll really like her,' Poll interrupted quickly. 'Poor Trixie. She lived in a grace and favour cottage in the grounds

61

of some big house—she was the cook/ housekeeper—and sadly let one of her concoctions catch on one night while she was—and this'll make you laugh—glued to watching *Dewberrys' Dinners.*'

Ash frowned. '*Catch on?*'

'Oh, yes—poor Trixie—she was absolutely entranced by the latest goings-on between Gabby and Tom Dewberry and took her eye off the ball so to speak. She was lucky to get out alive. The cottage was razed to the ground. Apparently it wasn't the first time she'd set fire to things by lacking concentration, so they terminated her employment just like that.'

'Not surprising,' Ella said sharply. 'Pyromania is probably not one of the top qualities anyone would be looking for in a cook/housekeeper.'

Poll giggled. 'I know—maybe we'll have to keep a discreet eye on her when she's here if she's a tad forgetful in the kitchen.'

'Or be burned alive in our beds.'

'That won't happen. I've got George to think about. The whole thing was overexaggerated anyway,' Poll said firmly. 'Goodness me, haven't we all done the same thing when we've been distracted while cooking?'

'Not destroyed an entire house, no,' Ash said doubtfully.

Ella sucked in her breath. 'Dear God!'

'What?' Poll frowned.

Ella's finger jabbed at the page. 'This Trixie, not only is she an arsonist—OK, *alleged* arsonist—but it says here in the newspaper cuttings that she blamed the *fairies* for the fire . . . . She must be completely mad.'

'No, she isn't. Don't take things so literally. Just

62

some nasty chit-chat around the village she lived in. Trixie was well known for believing in the little folk . . . and where's the harm in that? Plenty of people do. Apparently everyone said she brewed herbal tinctures and experimented with a few fairy-led incantations when she was cooking. When we met, she said that the wicked fairies had given her the wrong measurements which meant her timings were all awry and that's why the pan caught fire—'

'Absolute crap!' Ella exploded.

Poll laughed. 'Nice to see you're keeping an open mind. Actually, Trixie also said that she thought a bad elf—'

'Oh, Poll,' Ash spluttered, 'come on. Bad elves and wicked fairies, please . . .'

'You and I may not believe in fairies—although I'm not entirely sure about me—but if Trixie does, and it makes her happy, then who are we to point fingers?'

'But she blamed the fairies for setting fire to her house!' Ella snorted. 'Which means she's totally barking and won't take any responsibility for anything because she can always blame it on the fairies. I think she sounds like one huge risk.'

'Which is exactly what everyone once said about Mitzi Blessing in Hazy Hassocks.'

'Mitzi Blessing?'

'Oh, you'll love Mitzi. Everyone does. She's become quite a good friend since I moved here. And, come to think of it, she's got a couple of lovely girls working with her who're roughly about your age. Amber Flanagan and Cleo Maguire. We'll have to get you together. You'll need some youngsters to pal up with locally. I'm sure you'll be itching to get out on the town before too long.'

Ash looked serious. 'Sounds like a good idea, Ella. I've heard there're some great whist drives and barn dances in these villages.'

'Oh, ha-ha.' Ella poked out her tongue.

'Children!' Poll frowned. 'Where was I? Ah, yes, Mitzi. Mitzi has a really successful herbal cookery outlet—Hubble Bubble—and several uninformed people have accused her of witchcraft over the years. You'll see—it'll be just the same with poor Trixie. Mocked for believing in things that other people don't understand. Anyway, Trixie couldn't possibly be mad. She wears twinsets.'

'Oh, that's OK then,' Ella giggled. 'An insane arsonist fairy-believer in a twinset. Super.'

'Don't prejudge either of them, Ella. You wait until you meet them. They're both sweethearts. Like Ash.'

Ash blushed.

'And I thought it might be nice if we cooked a special welcome dinner for them. Ash can do the soup, I'll do the main and you can do the pud. Does that sound OK with you two?'

'Great,' Ash said, leaning back in his chair. 'It'll be fantastic to work in your kitchen.'

'Lovely. Ella?'

'Yes, of course. You'll just have to remind me what kleptomaniacs and arsonists like to eat.'

'Now I know you're teasing,' Poll laughed. 'But, seriously, now you know what I want to do and why I need you here, it hasn't put you off, has it?'

'I'd agreed to a three month trial—so I'm not going to renege on that. But I'm still honestly really not sure about it . . . them.'

'You will be.' Poll leaned across the table dangling beads in the cheese and pickles again and

64

hugged her. 'Thank you so much. You're a real star. And you'll love them as much as I do—and once you've met them, you'll never want to leave here, I promise you.'

## *Chapter Nine*

'Sleep well?' Poll looked up from the cooker as Ella, in cut-off jeans and a pale-blue T-shirt, pattered into the sun-filled kitchen the following morning.

'Zonked,' Ella said happily. 'I haven't slept like that in years. The bed just sort of snuggled round me and just as I was thinking I'd never get used to the darkness or the silence or being away from home, it was morning again. I didn't even hear my alarm clock. Sorry if I've overslept. I know I should be working and getting George up and seeing to his breakfast and everything.'

'Not today.' Poll handed her a glass of orange juice and a mug of coffee. 'Today we can all take things easy and get settled in properly before Billy and Trixie arrive tomorrow.'

'But George—?'

'Has been up since five and helped me collect the eggs for breakfast and is out in the garden adding more embellishments to your motorway.' Poll grinned. 'Actually, I thought maybe you and Ash could get to know a bit about the surrounding area—although Ash has lived fairly locally anyway—but even I still get lost on some of the back lanes. And I do need some shopping, so I thought maybe you could take George and drive into Hazy Hassocks.'

'With Ash as a tour guide?' Ella grinned. 'Sounds good to me. When do we start?'

'After breakfast,' Poll said firmly, heaping scrambled eggs on to chunky slices of toast. 'Grab that tray please. There's a love. It's so hot, I thought we'd have ours in the garden.'

'Bliss.' Ella scooped up mugs, glasses, the jug of juice, knives and forks and plates on to the tray. 'Oh, I'm so pleased I took this job.'

'Are you? Really? Even though you're not sure about why I'm doing it?'

'Really.' Ella nodded, following Poll out into the sweetly fragranced, sun-drenched garden with animals sprawled somnolently beneath the low-hanging lilac branches. 'And I think I know why you're doing it, Poll. And I think you're amazing— it's just . . .'

'You're not sure about Billy and Trixie?'

'Well, no.' Ella pulled out a chair and waved at an already dusty George. Oh, what a sweetheart George was, Ella thought as he waved a grubby fist cheerfully back at her, and what a lovely childhood he had. So safe and innocent and old-fashioned. 'Especially Trixie and the fairy stuff. But if you say they're OK, then I'm going to trust you.'

'You'll love them,' Poll assured her. 'They've had such a rotten time of it and I know all about rotten times, believe me. And I just thought if I had the chance to make a difference to other people's lives then I simply had to do it.'

Ella nodded round her scrambled eggs. 'Yes, I understand that part—but rotten times? You? With all this? Surely not?'

'It wasn't always like this.' Poll poured more

66

coffee and juice. 'In fact, it was all far from like this. Until Dennis—my husband—went, my life was pretty grim.'

'Really? And I know I said I was nosy, and I don't really want to pry, and you can tell me to mind my own business, but didn't Mr Andrews want to be involved in this . . . altruism? Is that why he, er, you . . . ?'

Looking amused, Poll sipped her coffee. 'Mr Andrews wouldn't have wanted anything to do with this, no, and anyway, he's dead.'

'Oh, God, is he?' Ella put her fork down quickly. 'I'm so sorry. I thought you said you were divorced?'

'I am.' Poll laughed cheerfully. 'Dennis wasn't Mr Andrews. Mr Andrews was my father. He's dead. Dennis is alive and well and living blissfully in Berne or Bulgaria or Brussels or somewhere with a Much More Suitable Woman.'

'Ah, right.'

'I kept my maiden name.' Poll beamed across the table. 'Because Dennis's surname was Perkins— and with me being Poll—well, I certainly wasn't going to be known as "Pretty Polly Perkins of Paddington Green".'

Ella frowned. Who the hell was Polly Perkins? And did Poll come from Paddington? 'But what's wrong with being Polly Perkins?' she queried. 'I'm not with you. And Paddington Green? Is that where you're from?'

'No! I'm Reading born and bred.' Poll laughed loudly. 'Bless you. I'd forgotten you're so young. "Polly Perkins" was clearly way before your time. It's a childhood rhyme, nursery rhyme, sing-along song, you know? I had enough problems with low self-esteem without adding that one to my repertoire. Dennis and I should never have got married—and not just because of the Polly Perkins thing . . . Still, once we were divorced, everything improved hugely.'

Ella frowned. Did this mean it was only after the divorce settlement that Poll could afford to renovate, furnish and decorate Hideaway Farm on a scale to rival Chatsworth? Hah! Right! Ella had always been scathing about women who bled their ex-partners dry. Poll's selfless benevolence suddenly took a massive dip in her estimations.

'Look,' Poll said, smiling, 'I wasn't going to go into any of this until much later, but since we've started . . .'

Ella listened in increasingly stunned silence to Poll's story of a venture into innocent middle-aged speed-dating and a rapid brief-lived marriage and the delight of George's arrival and the even more rapid divorce.

'. . . so you see, I made a huge mistake in marrying Dennis, the first man I'd ever been out with—the only man I've ever slept with—but it was worth every mismatched minute because it resulted in George.' Poll smiled happily. 'Married at forty, a mum at forty-two, divorced by the time I was forty-five. Not a great track record, but still, nothing's ever truly bad, is it?'

'Er, no, probably not. But, hadn't you had, um, *any* boyfriends before?'

Poll shook her head. 'Dennis was my first—and last—attempt at a relationship. Oh dear, it's probably better to start at the beginning. You see, my parents weren't particularly young when they met and had been married for well over twenty years when I was born. Unlike my own venture into unplanned mature motherhood, my arrival was, well, a complete disaster for them. They didn't want me.'

Ella winced.

Poll topped up their juice glasses. 'Oh, don't look so upset. It's a long time ago. I assume my mother thought she was menopausal. I don't know—we never talked about anything like that. They were old in mind and body when I was born. I grew up in a sort of strange, grim, restricted and unloving house. Then they both got ill. And I was their carer. From the age of sixteen when I left school, until they died twenty-three years later. I've never had a job—or a life.'

Ella swallowed. Poor, poor Poll. What an appallingly sad story. What a hatefully miserable life. No wonder she wanted to change it completely.

'Um,' Ella said, lowering her voice as George abandoned his convoy of small lorries and scrambled up at the table with a *Thomas the Tank Engine* colouring book and a fistful of crayons, 'that's truly awful. And I'm so sorry, but then, why after all that misery, did you get married to someone you hardly knew?'

'Because I wanted to be loved. I'd never been loved. I thought having a husband would guarantee it. It didn't.'

Ella sighed. This really was turning into a two-hankie saga. Poor Poll. 'But surely, you could have just, well, started going out, and meeting people and having dates?'

'I was thirty-nine. I'd had no teenage years to experience that sort of thing. No experimental

69

time. I had no idea how to go about *dating* or talking to men or anything. My one and only friend, Marie, suggested the speed-dating as a joky way to ease me into meeting blokes.' Poll laughed. 'Poor Marie. She was horrified when I told her Dennis—my first speed-dating experience—and I were getting married.'

'Blimey, yes, I can imagine. And I can understand why you—given the circumstances— might have dived in head first. But surely, Dennis—'

'Oh, Dennis went to speed-dating and married me because he simply hadn't had time to meet women socially. He was always too busy. Dennis had reached the stage in his life where he just wanted a nice compliant non-ambitious yes-woman to keep his out-of-work hours running smoothly.'

'And you sort of clicked?'

'Well, it certainly wasn't love.' Poll sighed. 'But we at least both thought we'd found what we were looking for. We were, of course, both bitterly disappointed.'

Oh, God . . . Ella scraped up the last of her scrambled eggs. How truly dreadful. 'Still, at least you got George and this lovely house from your marriage.'

'George, yes.' Poll nodded, pushing her wayward hair behind her ears and helping George with a tricky bit of colouring-in. 'And from George, I got the unconditional loving and being loved that I'd always craved. But the house, no. Hideaway Farm is all mine. I paid for it outright—Dennis had no claim on it at all. Dennis kept his corporate businessman's flat in town. He came down here at weekends or whenever he was in England after we got married, but he loathed it. It was never his home; Hideaway has always been mine.'

Oh, blimey . . . Ella pushed toast round her plate, how wrong had she got this?

'If you cry I'll join you, so don't.' Poll laughed. 'Please don't look so sad. It's all OK now. It's worked out so well. My parents might have been hard and austere, but they were also very astute with their money. No, OK—let's be honest here— they were as tight as a duck's thingamabob. They never spent a penny they didn't have to. I had no new clothes, very few toys, no treats, no holidays— and neither did they.'

'That still sounds like a pretty gruesome life to me. Far from OK.'

'Well, maybe, but it all worked out brilliantly. I was so lucky. You see, when they died, the mausoleum I grew up in sold for a small fortune, and as the only child of only children I inherited everything. I didn't, don't, and never will, need a penny from Dennis.'

'Oh, right.' Another assumption bit the dust.

'Living on a farm was the dream that kept me going throughout my growing-up years and beyond,' Poll said. 'All through my isolated childhood unhappiness, I read all the time, and simply adored Enid Blyton. I wanted to escape to the sort of life her fictional children had. I wanted to live on a farm. In the country. It was the most wonderful thing I could imagine—all that peace and quiet and happiness and lots of animals, and cosiness and blissful freedom, and being surrounded by kind people who actually liked me. All the things I'd never had.'

71

Ella, who had had all those things all her life without question, albeit without the idyllic rural setting, bit her lip. 'Yes, I can imagine—and I'm so sorry—but so pleased that things have worked out for you now.' She leaned across the table, picked up a random crayon and helped George colour the Fat Controller in lime green. 'And that's why you want to help others in a similar position?'

'Exactly.' Poll beamed. 'I know what it's like to be so far down that you can't see any way up and would give your eye teeth for a—'

'Fairy godmother? Like Trixie Pepper?' Ella giggled.

'Well, perhaps not quite a fairy godmother,' Poll chuckled, 'but yes, something like that . . . Anyway, that's my story. What about yours?'

'Mine? You know all about mine.'

Poll ran her hands through her wild hair. 'Phew—I'm baking already. This is going to be a real humdinger of a day, I reckon. And no, I don't. I know nothing at all about the, um, boyfriend. Of course you don't have to tell me . . .'

Mark . . . Ella sighed. What could she possibly say about Mark? She played for time by helping George, bored with colouring-in, scramble from the table and watched him as he trotted happily across to his dirt pit again.

'OK . . . Mark's funny and lively and sort of cute-looking. We've been going out for two years . . .' She stopped and stared up at the cloudless blue sky. 'And we've reached a sort of impasse in our relationship.'

'Oh dear.' Poll pulled a sympathetic face. 'Has he met someone else?'

'Nooo, nothing so simple.' Ella sighed. 'It was

72

just after two years we were going nowhere. He—Mark—was just happy to let things drift on in their usual routine—you know, some time spent together, other time spent apart—so he still had his football and nights out with his mates and I did girly stuff with my friends, but . . .'

'It wasn't going any further along the commitment route? And you wanted it to?'

'Yes . . . No—I honestly don't know, but it couldn't just stay like it was for ever and he'd never discuss it.'

'Do you love him?'

Ella stared at the sky again. 'Yes . . . well, yes, I love him. But I'm not sure if I'm in love with him any more . . . because . . . because of other stuff . . . and I think if I really, really loved him I wouldn't have chosen to be here now away from him for three months, would I?'

Poll spread her hands wide. 'I'm hardly a relationship expert, am I? But I'd say probably not, unless there was a really good reason.'

'Oh, yes, there's a really good reason.'

'Now I do feel guilty about probing.' Poll leaned across the table and patted Ella's hand. 'Please don't tell me anything else if you don't want to.'

Ella shrugged. 'It's OK. It's nothing sordid. It's just that Mark simply doesn't understand why I've always wanted to work with children. Doesn't understand why I want my own children. Couldn't understand why I'd want to give up a lucrative sales career for looking after other people's children.'

'Ah, right—tricky.' Poll nodded. 'And does he want children too, eventually?'

Ella shook her head. 'No. And that is the main

problem. Not just that he wasn't showing any signs of wanting to settle down and enjoys being one of the lads, but he said he hadn't given much thought to marriage and even less to having a family.' She stopped. 'Actually, he said he doesn't like children much. And, even if we did move in together or get married he wasn't keen on having a family . . .'

'Ah, tough one. But you didn't want to end the relationship?'

'No. Neither of us did. So we agreed on this break to be apart for a while and try to sort things out.'

'But wasn't it a bit drastic? Throwing up your job? Moving away? Couldn't you just have agreed to not see one another for three months?'

Ella shook her head. 'We work—worked—together. In adjoining offices. I had to get right away. And anyway, this way I also get to fulfil my dream of working with children.'

'Which,' Poll said, 'you seem to be born to do if the way you and George have clicked is anything to go by. But if you and Mark discover that you can't live without one another then you'll make some sort of compromise about the rest of it?'

'Something like that.' Ella smiled sadly. 'And the trouble is that my parents and my sister and most of my friends think he's right and I'm wrong. They simply couldn't understand why I was actually envious of the young girls congregating in the shopping precinct with their buggies and their gorgeous babies.'

'Oh, I can,' Poll said quietly. 'Not that my opinion stands for much, of course. But yes, I know only too well what it's like to yearn so much

74

for something you think you'll never have . . . Oh, Ella—not that I want you to go—but I hope your Mark will realise what he's going to lose and at the end of the three months you'll fall into one another's arms . . .'

'And live happily ever after?' Ella sighed. 'Yeah, well, maybe . . . maybe not . . . In the meantime, we'll stay in touch while I'm here and talk about anything and everything—except the whole career-change/settling-down/having babies thing, that's definitely a no-go zone.'

'We're a pretty pair, aren't we?' Poll smiled gently.

Ella shook her head. 'My problems are nothing compared to what you've been through. Anyway, I'd really appreciate it if you kept this between us. I mean, I'm happy to let everyone know that Mark's my boyfriend and we're having a break, but not the reasons behind it.'

'I won't say a word,' Poll promised. 'And you can always invite him down for a visit.'

'No way!' Ella was vehement. 'That would defeat the whole object. We have to stay apart and see what happens to us and how we feel and— Oh, hi.'

'Hi.' Ash, barefooted and looking devastatingly dishevelled in jeans and T-shirt, stood in the kitchen doorway, blinking. 'I seem to have slept in. What a fabulous morning!'

'Come and have coffee and juice—' Poll pushed her chair back '—and I'll go and scramble some more eggs.'

'Stay there, Poll, please. I can do it,' Ash protested.

Poll laughed. 'No way. Not today. And as Ella will tell you, you're going to earn your breakfast

75

because I'm turning you both loose on the joys of shopping in Hazy Hassocks.'

## *Chapter Ten*

Ella drove carefully away from Hideaway Farm. They'd decided to take her car as Ash's was apparently prone to breaking down without warning.

'As soon as I've got a job,' he said cheerfully from the passenger seat as they manoeuvred the twists and turns of Cattle Drovers Passage, 'I'll get it fixed. I prefer to drive—I'm not the greatest pass—oh, mind that bend. That was a bit close.'

'And you can get out and walk if you're going to criticise my driving,' Ella snorted, leaning down and racking up the air con. 'You're only here to act as tour guide and sat nav, OK?'

'Sorry—self-preservation. Hey, look at the road, and watch the hedge!'

George chuckled from his booster seat in the back.

'See?' Ash said cheerfully. 'Male solidarity. George agrees with me. Women drivers—huh!'

'Right.' Ella braked sharply and glared at him. 'Not funny. Now, are you going to shut up and give me sensible directions or am I going to kick you out?'

George chuckled some more.

Ash laughed. 'Sorry—no, really. OK—turn right down here, I think, towards Fiddlesticks . . . Aaargh! Too fast!'

Laughing, she thumped him.

As she steered the car slowly along the single-track lanes, head-high with shepherd's purse, moon daisies and dog roses, with the sun spiralling higher and hotter, and the delightful George singing happily behind her and Ash—OK, yes, also delightful—beside her, Ella smiled to herself. As sorting-out-emotional-life-crises went, so far, this one would take some beating.

'Poll said you were fairly local,' she said as Ash slumped beside her, hands over his eyes, peering exaggeratedly between his fingers, groaning and making George rock with laughter. 'So you should know the way well, shouldn't you?'

'Local as in Newbury,' Ash said. 'Miles from here. And I've lived in Reading too. OK, still Berkshire, but not much use for finding my way round these unmarked lanes. Although I do know my way to Winterbrook, which is the nearest large town to here.'

'Is it? So why aren't we going there for shopping? Why are we going to Hazy Hassocks?'

George chattered loudly from the back seat.

'Ah, right.' Ella nodded. 'That makes sense.'

'Does it?' Ash frowned. 'Do you and George speak the same language, then? Ah—slow down! No, seriously, slow down—next turning on the left. Left! LEFT!'

Ella skilfully manoeuvred the car round a sudden right-angled bend and took an immediate left with ease. 'There? See? Perfect. And yes, George and I understand each other very well. And he says Poll always shops at Hazy Hassocks because she likes Big Sava and they go to Patsy's Pantry for a milkshake and a sticky cake.'

Ash shook his head. 'He didn't say all that.'

'Nah, not all of it. Poll told me some of it before we left. Oh, we've reached a crossroads . . . Now where?'

Ash peered through the windscreen. 'Um, straight on?'

'You don't know, do you?'

'Nope. But straight on seems safer than veering ever deeper into the hinterland. Now, remember, take it steady.'

Ella wrinkled her nose, poked out her tongue and took it steady.

Miraculously, a mere fifteen minutes later they reached civilisation.

'Oh,' she said in surprise, looking around at the bustling village of Hazy Hassocks, 'it's lovely.'

Hazy Hassocks High Street curled and curved from the Faery Glen public house at one end to the dental surgery at the other, beneath a canopy of stately sycamores, passing the odd collection of shops—some crookedly ancient and half-timbered, others modern and plate-glass-fronted like Big Sava—along the way.

Ash nodded. 'And I bet you can get practically everything anyone could ever want here. No chains or big names, of course, and no designer outlets—which might be a bit of a drawback for you, you being a city girl and therefore a shopaholic, of course.'

'Blimey,' Ella sighed as they nipped niftily into a suddenly vacant space in Big Sava's car park—a move that made Ash yell and George laugh, 'do you have any other stereotypical remarks you'd like to offload?'

'Not at the moment, thank you.' He grinned at her.

She looked away quickly and concentrated on finding Poll's shopping list and a massive collection of bags-for-life.

Actually, Ash was right; the bucolic Hazy Hassocks shops would no doubt scandalise her London friends, but for country-living necessities and impulse buys alike, the bustling High Street probably had it all.

Ash scrambled from the passenger seat and released George from his confines. Ella tried really, really hard not to stare at his long, lean body.

She sighed as she locked the car. Ash was simply divine. Sexy, friendly, funny and intelligent. And beautifully un-gay. And living under the same roof.

What more could a girl ask for? Not a lot in her opinion. But no doubt he'd soon be spending his days job-seeking and his nights—huh!—well, Ella could only imagine his nights would be spent ogling the exotic and erotic Onyx as she undulated round a pole or bounced pneumatically on a lap or something.

It was an image she tried hard to ignore. And of course, there was Mark . . .

'OK,' Ash said, his hand holding George's. 'Shopping first? Or this milkshake and sticky bun thing?'

Ella's heart turned over as she looked at Ash and George. Beautiful man and beautiful child—they looked so perfect together. Clearly most of the hot and harassed women shoppers thought so, the way they cast longing second glances in Ash's direction. Treacherously she thought no one had ever ogled Mark like that, and even more treacherously she hoped people would think they were a family. How wonderful would that be?

She dragged herself back from her impossible-dream fantasy. 'Oh, er, we'll leave that to George, shall we?'

George chattered loudly and started to tug Ash away from Big Sava.

'OK.' Ella laughed, catching George's free hand, delighted as he swung backwards and forwards between them. 'Decision made. Milkshake first, obviously. Shopping for the feast to celebrate the arrival of Billy Booker and Trixie Pepper second.'

'I wonder what they'll really be like?' Ash said as they negotiated a knot of women in floral frocks and sturdy sandals, who also gave him covetous and appreciative glances. 'I wonder what difference they'll make?'

'None, according to Poll. I'm still reserving my judgement.'

'They won't be a problem,' Poll had said airily earlier that morning as Ella had got George cleaned up after the quarrying in preparation for the shopping expedition. 'We're already getting along really well, Ash has settled in nicely, so why should Billy and Trixie make any difference? Goodness—there's loads of room for all of us to live together. Trixie and Billy will fit in beautifully, you'll see. It'll only be like having the large family that Hideaway was designed for.'

And Ella had laughed. Because surely no family, whatever the size and however dysfunctional, had ever included so many disparate and desperate people?

Oh well, this break was only for three months, so if it was all unbearable when Trixie and Billy joined them, it wouldn't be for ever, would it?

80

She'd be leaving them behind by the end of August, wouldn't she?

But, she thought as they ran and swung and swooped their way round hot shoppers along the High Street, would she be able to easily walk away from the adorable George, and the animals, the ditzy but lovely Poll—and even the glorious Hideaway Farm—and return to London and Mark?

And what about Ash?

She glanced sideways at him as he laughed with George, swinging him ever higher.

Oh, she definitely didn't think she'd be able to walk away easily from Ash—with or without the addition of the exotic Onyx.

'Where's this café, George?' Ash puffed. 'Are we nearly there?'

George tugged at their hands as he stopped on the pavement and nodded enthusiastically towards a very pink frilly-curtained doorway.

'Is this it?' Ash frowned. 'Patsy's Pantry? Ella?'

'Er, sorry, I was miles away . . . Oh, yes—' she looked down at George who was still nodding excitedly '—I guess so. In we go.'

As they stepped inside, heads turned, conversations stopped, and they were immediately treated to curious stares from everyone else in the café.

The large woman enveloped in a pink coverall behind the counter, beamed. 'Morning, young George. And who's this, then?'

George gabbled happily, shook his hands free and galloped over to a vacant window table.

'Love him.' She smiled fondly. 'Can't make 'ead or tail of what he says but he's a proper little

81

cherub. I'm Patsy, and you must be Poll's mother's 'elp. Postman said you'd arrived yesterday. Emma, is it?'

'Ella,' Ella said, stunned that the jungle drums had already spread the information about her arrival.

'That's it.' Patsy nodded, then looked Ash up and down. 'My word, you're a handsome lad. I'm guessing you must be one of Poll's other lost causes?'

'Um, yes, I'm Ash.' Ash gave Patsy his most winning smile. 'And definitely a lost cause.'

'Ah, I'm never wrong. Bless 'er, Poll's heart's in the right place but her brain went AWOL years ago. Another scorcher, ain't it?' Patsy said cheerfully, ignoring any hint of irony. 'No, you both go and sit down with the little un—I'll bring your order over.'

'We haven't actually ordered yet,' Ash pointed out.

'Get away,' Patsy sniffed. 'I knows where young George always sits and what he always has—and I'm sure that with Ella being a mother's help she ain't going to change his routine, are you, duck?'

'Er, no . . .'

'Well, you go an' sit down, then. And mind—' she glared at Ash '—handsome is as handsome does. I don't know what you're at Hideaway for—if you're in trouble with the police or what—but I've counted me spoons, so don't you go nicking anything, right?'

Ash nodded seriously. 'I wouldn't dream of it. And I've never been in trouble with—'

'That's what they all say.' Patsy rearranged her vast bosoms beneath the pink coverall. 'Just don't think you can take liberties here. Poll's one thing, I'm quite another. Off you go and sit down. I'll be over toot-sweet.'

Biting their lips, they meekly followed George to his favourite window table where he was industriously building a sugar lump castle.

The Pantry's clientele, having resumed their inter-table chatting, continued to regard them with ill-disguised interest.

Sitting down, Ash immediately helped George with the ramparts and Ella giggled. 'She's probably counted the sugar lumps too, so don't go popping any in your pockets.'

'Damn.' Ash carefully helped George with the third cube in a small crystal tower. 'It's one of my weaknesses. How long do you think we're going to be branded as law-breakers?'

'You speak for yourself. I'm a bona-fide employee; you're clearly the one with the light-fingers. And until the twenty-second century at least, I'd say,' Ella chuckled. 'They seem to have played judge and jury on hearsay and found you guilty.'

'Which is what we've done to Billy and Trixie, isn't it?'

'No! Well, yes, OK a bit, but then we know things about them, and they might well be, um, doubtful.'

'We'll soon find out—Oh, bugger . . .'

George shrieked with laughter as the sugar cube castle collapsed across the table.

Ella, glancing over the top of her pink laminated menu card, was amazed at the way that everyone else in the café seemed to know one another. And as Patsy already seemed to know everything about her—and Poll—and what was happening at

83

Hideaway Farm, presumably that meant Patsy's customers did too.

The rural jungle drums were a revelation. In her London flat, Ella had barely spoken to her neighbours, and wouldn't have even recognised some of them if they passed in the street. But here, clearly, no one was a stranger for long, and there were no intimacies too delicate to be aired and shared with all and sundry. It was all very peculiar.

As if reading her mind, a very old woman, wrinkled like a tortoise, leaned over from a nearby table, flaking Danish pastry crumbs down her floral frock in the manoeuvre. 'Young Poll got the last of them odd 'uns turning up at Hideaway soon, 'as she? I'm Jean Turvey, by the way, but everyone calls me Topsy.'

Ash chuckled.

'Well, they're not really odd.'

'Ah.' Topsy Turvey nodded. 'I think you'll find they are. We knows all about Poll and her latest daft scheme. We told her it was a mistake bringing you in to look after young George while she fills that farm with miscreants.'

'They're hardly . . .'

'I'm Lavender Banding. *Miss* Lavender Banding. And this is my sister Lobelia,' a skeletally thin geriatric lady interrupted from another table. 'And you're wrong, you know. We know Poll's got a bank robber coming. And an axe murderer or a serial poisoner, isn't it? Ah, we know all about it. She's asking for trouble, is Poll. You'll all be a-massacred in your beds afore the month is out, you mark our words.'

Ash turned his laughter into a spate of coughing and demolished the second attempt at a castle much to George's amusement.

Ella looked at the elderly spinster sisters who were sharing one iced fancy and a very small pot of tea, and who were both wearing cycle helmets although surely they weren't strong enough to control bicycles, were they?

'Oh, I don't think so. I'm Essie Rivers, dear,' an elegantly dressed lady put in quickly from a third table before Ella could leap to Poll's defence. 'I don't think any of them are that bad, are they? Aren't they just homeless? Poll's very kind-hearted. I know what it's like to be homeless and unhappy, and then being lucky enough to meet someone generous and be given a second chance. Good luck to her I say.'

'Ah.' Essie's male companion grinned. 'Slo Motion, local undertaker, at your service, duck. Should be more like Poll if you asks me. Compassion is a rare commodity these days.'

A free-for-all discussion flared up then, with Slo and Essie on one side of the argument and several other tables, including Lavender and Lobelia Banding, on the other, and with a very oddly matched couple, who introduced themselves as Gwyneth Wilkins and Big Ida Tomms, chipping into the rare silences from their table in the corner.

'There,' Patsy placed three strawberry milkshakes and three Chelsea buns on the table. 'Don't you take no notice of them, Ella, duck. What will be will be as Doris Day always says. Poll's well known round here for making a dog's bollocks—excuse my French in front of the little 'un—job of most things. She always rushes into her harum-scarum ventures willy-nilly, and I doubt this one will be no different. Mind, personally myself I hopes she makes a go of this one.'

'So do I.' Ella nodded fervently. 'So do I.'

'Anyway—' Patsy folded her arms across her bosom-straining coverall '—we've got more exciting things to think about round here than Poll Andrews and 'er daft schemes, 'aven't we?'

'Have we?' Ash, still trying not to laugh, reached across the table to manoeuvre the recalcitrant milkshake straws into George's mouth. 'Er, like, um, what?'

'Lord above!' Patsy looked scandalised. 'I know Hideaway's well off the beaten track—but you must *know*?'

'We've only been there for a day,' Ash pointed out reasonably.

Ella, whose head was still reeling from the thought of sharing—within a matter of hours—life at Hideaway with a mad bad fairy arsonist and a petty thief, really hadn't had any time to notice much else either. 'Sorry, no . . .'

Patsy still looked shocked. 'You mean you 'aven't seen the posters? Or the bit on Meridian news? Or the splash in the *Winterbrook Advertiser*?'

Ella shook her head. 'None of those, no.'

'What have we missed?' Ash tore into his bun with perfectly even white teeth.

'We're going to be on the telly!'

George blew ecstatic bubbles into his milkshake.

'Really?' Ella said, quickly dissecting George's Chelsea bun into manageable pieces. 'Wow. How brilliant. So is it going to be a documentary about village life here? Or a local news item about you and featuring the Pantry?'

'No!' Patsy snorted. 'I don't mean Hazy Hassocks

86

or the Pantry—I mean, one of *us*. Someone from Hassocks or one of the other villages . . . Look, over there, duck, on the wall. The big poster. They're everywhere. Can't think how you've missed them round the town.'

Neither, once she'd looked at it, could Ella.

'Bloody hell!' Ash muttered. 'Sorry, George.'

In vibrant day-glo orange, and with the oh-so-familiar faces of Gabby and Tom Dewberry grinning out at them, the words *Dewberrys' Dinners* were printed in huge Comic Sans font.

'They're looking for volunteers for their next live show. Here. In this part of Berkshire,' Patsy said proudly, ignoring the small queue of customers at the counter. 'Mind, you'd have to be mad as a box of biscuits to want to take part—so it should suit young Poll down to the ground.'

Ella and Ash, exchanging glances, joined in the laughter. So did George—which resulted in a froth of milkshake spurting across the table. Ash and Ella both dived to wipe it up.

'Ah.' Topsy Turvey broke off her still-heated conversation and leaned towards them. 'She's right there, about being barmy to want to be on that darned show. But I can tell you there's plenty round here who've applied already.'

'Like who?' Gwyneth Wilkins paused mid-cuppa. 'Young Mitzi, I'll be bound.'

Ah, Ella thought: Mitzi . . . that must be Mitzi Blessing—the local witch.

Topsy Turvey nodded, looking more like a tortoise than ever. 'So I've 'eard. And that Geordie geezer what runs Giovanni's restaurant over at Willows Lacey. Not that 'e'll be allowed in as 'e's a pro so to speak. And Tarnia Snepps.'

'Blimey!' Big Ida Tomms snorted. 'Tarnia Snepps 'as never cooked a meal in her life! My money's on young Mitzi then.'

Slo Motion shook his head. 'Mitzi won't be allowed neither, duck. She'm a proper prerfessioneral cook like yon Giovanni's bloke, ain't she? *Dewberrys' Dinners* only 'as amachewers.'

'God help us if they picks on Tarnia Snepps.' Topsy Turvey shuddered pleasurably. 'Snooty cow she is. Her an' that Gabby is bound to come to blows.'

The Bandings tittered pleasurably at the thought.

'Nah.' Slo shook his head. 'It won't be no one like Tarnia. They'll go for a normal person.'

'Won't find many of them round here then,' Essie giggled.

Gwyneth nodded her agreement. 'Mind, I can't see anyone we knows really wanting to take part— unless they thinks it's worth the 'umiliation for the money at the end if they wins?'

Patsy reluctantly headed back towards the crowd round her counter. 'Ah, there's always them as is willing to take the devil's shilling. More fool them, I say.'

Ash sucked up the lovely ice-creamy sludge at the bottom of his milkshake, grinned at George who was doing the same, and leaned across the table. 'Pretty amazing . . . *Dewberrys' Dinners* filming round here.'

'Mmm, you're not kidding.'

Screwing up her eyes, Ella scanned the poster. Not that she was really interested, of course, but it was rather exciting—a top-rated television show taking place right on the doorstep . . .

She giggled to herself. She'd joined the country village mindset already. Getting excited about 'being on the telly'. But *Dewberrys' Dinners* was her—and Poll's and Ash's—absolutely favourite show and it was pretty cool that they'd be filming locally.

'We might even do the groupie thing and hang around the chosen venue and catch a glimpse of Gabby and Tom Dewberry—oh, Poll would love that, wouldn't she?'

Ash nodded. 'I reckon she'd love anything to do with *Dewberrys' Dinners*. Wouldn't we all? Look, I'll keep an eye on George—you go and see if there's anything in the small print to say they're looking for, um, victims in this area only. Then we can tell her when we go back, can't we?'

Ella pushed her chair back. Celeb-spotting the Dreadful Dewberrys would possibly make Poll very happy indeed. And didn't Poll deserve to be happy more than anyone Ella had ever known?

Ella edged her way across the crowded café, and took a closer look at the poster.

Gabby and Tom Dewberry, teeth twinkling and eyes sparkling, loomed large, looking for all the world like the happiest couple ever, um, coupled. They were very handsome, Ella had to admit. And smiley. She wondered again just how much of the on-screen carping and bitching was an act.

'*Love good food? Love home cooking? Live within a five mile radius of this poster? Then what are you waiting for? We want you to cook dinner for us and the whole country in your own home,*' Tom and Gabby oozed in unctuous unison from a star-spangled speech bubble. '*We can't wait to meet you and watch you create your best dishes, on live*

89

television, just for us. If you can wow us with your food, we can change your lives forever. Don't miss out on the foodie opportunity of a lifetime. See you very soon in your own kitchen.'

The closing date for applications was only two weeks away. There was a London phone number and a website address for further information.

Knowing that she wouldn't do any more about it, but also knowing that Poll would never forgive her if she didn't at least take down the contact details so that they could discover who the Dewberrys' unfortunate local victim was going to be, Ella quickly scribbled down the details.

'You surely ain't going to go in fer it, are you?' Patsy frowned from behind her counter. 'Not with what young Poll's already got on her plate? You wouldn't risk looking a prat on telly, surely? And God forbid that you'd let all them fillum people crawl all over Hideaway—there'd 'ave to be lights and electrics and cameras and what 'ave you. Surely, in God's name, you ain't going to risk any of that? Not when you'll already 'ave a houseful of villains and ne'er-do-wells.'

'Nooo.' Ella shook her head. 'Of course not. But Poll's a big fan and she'll be interested that the programme is being filmed locally. I'm not going to *apply* for heaven's sake—this is for information only.'

'You make sure it stays that way,' Topsy Turvey advised darkly. 'You don't know Poll as well as we do. That gel hasn't had it easy. Mind, she's her own worst enemy half the time with her dappy ideas. She's had enough trouble. She certainly don't need you to go encouraging her into no more daft schemes.'

90

'Wouldn't dream of it,' Ella said cheerfully, tucking the phone number into her back pocket and making her way back to a rather sticky Ash and George and a third demolished sugar-lump castle. 'Goodness, that'd be the last thing I'd do.'

## Chapter Eleven

The next morning, Poll sang happily to herself as she swept the kitchen floor. She had the house to herself having despatched Ella, Ash and George on a further tour of the local countryside.

Bless her, Poll thought dreamily, Ella was such a lovely girl. She'd already fitted in so well, and George clearly adored her. Sad about the boyfriend, Mark, not wanting children though. That was a hugely insurmountable problem. Still, hopefully, he'd miss Ella so much during her time here at Hideaway that he'd be prepared to change his mind.

Anyway, right now, there were more important things to think about, because today her new family would be complete.

Poll, wearing a baggy, saggy skirt, a well-past-its-best shirt, her blissfully comfortable but falling apart espadrilles, and with her newly washed hair covered up with a pair of George's pants clean from the laundry basket, beamed to herself.

Trixie would be here this afternoon, and before long, Billy Booker would be arriving . . .

Her heart gave a little skippety-skip of excitement.

Dust motes swirled and danced around her in

the shafts of sunlight on the increasingly hot May morning, and Poll stopped sweeping for a moment and leaned on her broom to gaze at their twirling prettiness. They looked like tiny sparkly fairies, twinkling and darting in the sun. A sprinkling of Trixie's fairy dust to bring magic into her life? No, she laughed to herself, that was far too fanciful—even for her—but she was so looking forward to seeing Billy Booker again.

Everything was, she thought, resuming her sweeping, going to be absolutely perfect for Billy's arrival. There was very little left to do. Billy's room was all ready, with fresh flowers, spare linen, tea, coffee and little packets of homemade biscuits, gung-ho books and blokey magazines—and everything else anyone could want. Poll was sure Billy, like all the disenfranchised newcomers, would be feeling very strange to start with, and wanted to make him completely at home.

And this time she'd be doing it without the welcoming committee as she'd rather cunningly, she thought, suggested that before today's marathon cook-in, Ella and Ash would like to investigate the neighbourhood further, and if that involved finding somewhere for George to paddle and indulge in ice cream on this scorching morning, so much the better.

'Fiddlesticks would be perfect,' Poll had said artlessly. 'It's not far and a lovely fat shallow stream runs right across the village green there. Crystal clear, a little bridge where you can sit and dangle your feet in the water, and perfect for paddling. And the Weasel and Bucket on the green do superb ice cream sundaes. All the local children gravitate there on days like this. I wish I could join you, but I must wait for Billy.'

Shortly, Poll thought now, as soon as this last-minute sweeping was done, she'd be able to shower off the sweat and grime and turn herself into a proper neat-and-tidy hostess. She'd wear her best Indian print frock and her amber beads and her favourite flip-flops, the purple ones with the sequins, and she'd be ready to welcome Billy Booker into his new home.

And later Trixie would be here too and then her new family would be complete. It was going to be a lovely fresh start for all of them.

Ah . . . but, nooo, surely not? Poll dragged herself from her reverie—surely that wasn't a car on Hideaway Lane, was it? Yes, it was, and it had stopped. Outside the farmhouse. Oh, Lordy, surely it couldn't be Billy arriving, could it? He'd said late morning but—was it? Already? Poll had lost all sense of time.

Propping the broom in a corner, wiping her grubby hands on her skirt and blowing the dust from under her nose, Poll, accompanied by two of the dogs, hurried through the cool, sweet-scented house to find out.

Billy Booker's car, standing rumbling outside Hideaway Farm's front door, was an ancient rusting Austin Allegro in an unfortunate shade of cowpat.

Billy, early fifties, shortish, with plentiful fair hair, a cherubic face and the gentlest of dark brown eyes, was fiddling with the handbrake.

Poll's heart gave a little leap of pure pleasure. Silly, she told herself sternly. Very, very silly indeed.

'Hello!' Billy struggled out from the driver's seat,

93

holding out both hands. 'Not too early, am I? It's wonderful to see you again, Poll. And what a fabulous place you've got here. I'm feeling at home already.'

'I hoped you would.' Poll grinned delightedly, taking Billy's hands in a sort of confused squeeze-cum-shake, then belatedly remembering the rag-bag housework clothes and the grime. Too late. Way, way too late. Damn it. 'Oh, please ignore the dogs.'

'I love dogs.' Billy continued to smile, releasing Poll's hands as he patted and stroked. 'All animals are better than most people in my opinion.'

'And mine,' Poll said with feeling. 'Anyway, we've got the place to ourselves at the moment, so you'll be able to get settled in without having to face a million other people.'

'A million?' Billy's pale-blue eyes twinkled. 'I knew you were a generous lass, but even so . . .'

They laughed together, and then in a slightly less chaotic rerun of Ella and Ash's arrivals, Poll helped Billy with his luggage—a hotchpotch collection of elderly suitcases, zip-up shopping bags, and black bin liners this time—through Hideaway Farm and into his room next door to Ash's.

'Blimey . . .' Billy looked around him in wonderment. 'This is like the Ritz. You have no idea how grateful I am, Poll, love.'

Poll blinked quickly. She always cried when people were nice to her. It hadn't happened very often.

'You're very, very welcome. Now, I'll leave you to get settled in and then I'll be downstairs. Would you like something to eat? A drink?'

94

'A nice cuppa would go down a treat,' Billy said. 'Although I can see you've given me all the stuff up here to make my own. I honestly don't know what to say—I didn't expect anything like this.'

Poll blinked quickly again. 'I'll go and make a pot of tea. We can have it in the garden. Come down when you're ready. Shall I put out some cake? Biscuits?'

'Not for me, thank you.' Billy was still staring round his room with something close to awe. 'I stopped off at the Little Chef on the way here and had one of them Olympic Breakfasts—filled me up a treat that did.'

Poll smiled. 'George loves going to Little Chef. He likes the pancakes.'

'Ah, me too. Specially the cherry ones with ice cream.'

'We'll have to get Ella to make us some. She's living here too, and you'll meet her later, because she loves making puds. And Ash and, er . . .' Poll hesitated for a minute, then decided the identity of Roy could wait until another time. 'Er, yes, Ash, he's next door to you just along the corridor, his speciality is soups—and yours is bread of course. Oh, there's an ancient bread oven in the kitchen; I'm sure it'd love to be put to good use again.'

Billy beamed. 'Sounds perfect to me. I've missed kneading the old dough. And what about you? Do you cook as well?'

'Every chance I get. Robust main courses are my thing—nothing fancy. I couldn't do nouvelle cuisine if you paid me—not that anyone would of course. I love dishing up big dinners. Hearty stuff.' Poll nodded eagerly. 'Pies are probably my best things, really. Dennis—my ex—rarely

95

complimented me but he did say that my pastry was the lightest he'd ever tasted.' She stopped. Did that sound like bragging? She hoped not. And could mentioning Dennis-the-ex sound like she was advertising herself as single? Oh, Lord . . . Blushing madly, she swallowed. 'Anyway, I'll leave you to settle in and you come down when you're ready.'

'I'll do that, thanks.'

Still blushing, Poll turned away and caught sight of herself in the triptych mirror on the dressing table.

Aaargh—noooo!

She was still wearing George's pants on her head.

'Bugger!' Rushing towards the staircase, Poll wrenched the underwear from her hair and shoved it up her sleeve. 'Oh, God, what must he think of me?'

Still smarting with embarrassment, Poll quickly showered and changed, scooped up George's discarded toys from their potential death-trap positions on the twisting stairs, made tea in her mother's fat china teapot—the one with the scattered roses and forget-me-nots—and set out the matching tea set on the wooden table in the garden.

And in what seemed next to no time, looking outwardly calm at least, Poll sat beside Billy on the canopied garden swing.

'This,' Billy said, looking around the sun-drenched garden, happily sipping milky tea with three sugars, 'is heaven on earth.'

'I want you to be happy. I know you've had a rough time.'

Billy nodded. 'Ah, it's been pretty hard lately.'

'Oh, yes. Losing your business must have been an awful blow.'

Billy nodded. 'But then, with all them superstores doing their own bread, and the high streets being like ghost towns, you can't really blame people for abandoning the little independent shops, can you?'

'I suppose not. Mind you, we're lucky round here. Hazy Hassocks still has a bustling high street, and all the smaller shops survive happily even though they've got Big Sava in their midst. It's a lovely village.'

Billy sipped the tea appreciatively. 'Everything around here seems lovely, Poll. I know I'm going to be very happy. And after what I've been through I could do with some happiness. After Mary died—'

'Yes, of course. You poor thing. You've been through so much. Losing your business and your wife.'

Billy set down his cup and saucer. 'Oh, me and Mary were never Romeo and Juliet. I missed having her around, course I did, because you get used to things being as they are, but truth be told she was a mean-spirited woman.'

'Really?' Poll pulled a face. 'Oh, I'm sorry.'

'Don't be.' Billy crinkled his gentle dark eyes. 'I was just glad we never had any kids. She'd have given them a hell of a life like she gave me. To be honest, the last two years without her have been a bit of a relief. She never stopped nagging and complaining. Not that she deserved to go before her time, poor lass, but there you are.'

'Oh, dear.' Poll hoped she wasn't going to cry.

97

'That's why the neighbours in the flats wanted me out, you see. That's why they planted stuff on me and then complained to the housing people that I was a thief—damn nonsense of course!—and started the rumours and that. See, everyone said I'd murdered her.'

'No!' Poll's teacup rattled in its saucer. Oh, God, Ella was going to love this! 'But, I mean, you didn't, did you? I mean, when I offered you a home here, and the solicitor did all the CRB checks, there was never any mention of a murder or an arrest or a court case or anything like that.'

Billy chuckled. 'Lordy, it never got that far. There wasn't nothing like that. There was no police involved. It was just malicious rumours. Mary didn't have many friends, she wasn't a friendly sort, but she had a couple of cousins living in them flats and they'd never liked me. It was just small town tittle-tattle. But it was enough to make my life hell.'

'But you didn't, did you?' Poll insisted. 'Murder her?'

'No—course not! Not that I hadn't thought about it on more than one occasion when her carping morning, noon and night drove me mad—the way you do. But I'd never have laid a finger on her. I never even raised my voice, let alone my hand. Bless you, I can't even kill a fly, love. I've not got a violent streak in my body.'

'So, how did she die? Oh, no, you don't have to tell me—but obviously she wasn't ill or anything.'

'Choked on a bloomer.'

Poll blinked.

'Fresh from the oven. Still warm. Still moist. Swelled right up. Mary was a bit of a pig for me fresh bread, not to mince words. Always gorged down her food. She'd never listen when I told her to let the loaves cool down a bit first, just snatched at them and shoved them in her mouth. Well, she'd been doing it all our married life and gave me hell when I tried to stop her and there'd never been any problems before, so I just let her get on with it.' Billy sighed. 'I did everything I could. Heimlich manoeuvres and artificial respiration and kiss of life and all that. But it was no good. Even the paramedics said I did all I could—they were there really quick, but they said they couldn't have done any different.'

'Oh God.' Poll was truly shocked by the horrific picture. 'Oh, how really awful for you—and for poor Mary.'

'Ah, it was. Terrible. One minute she was there large as life, mouth full of warm bloomer—the next minute, puffed up all puce, then, gone.'

They sat in silence. The birds sang happily in the sweet-scented lilac branches and the bees buzzed lazily in and out of the honeysuckle. It was a world away from sudden death and sadness.

'The biggest mistake I ever made,' Billy said softly, 'was marrying her in the first place. I thought I could make her happy and I couldn't. No one could.'

Without thinking, Poll reached across and squeezed his hand. 'But you tried and that's the main thing. You can't blame yourself if she wasn't happy. And I do know how you feel—I made the same sort of mistake. In fact I've spent my life making mistakes.' She quickly snatched her hand away again.

'I can't believe that. Not from what I know about

99

you.'

'But we don't know each other at all, do we?' Poll put her cup and saucer down. 'We've obviously got lots to find out about each other, haven't we?'

'Loads,' Billy said happily. 'But one thing you can tell me right now—do you have a handyman on tap?'

Poll shook her head. 'No, why? Is there something wrong with your room?'

'No!' Billy laughed. 'Of course not. The room's perfect. No, it's just that I used to do a bit of DIY, building work, that sort of thing in my spare time. I'd like to keep my hand in while I'm here. So, if you've got anything that needs a bit of renovating . . . ?'

'Practically the whole farm,' Poll said with feeling. 'I could keep you busy until the next millennium. But seriously, a couple of the barns have been half-repaired because I'd sort of planned to turn them into something and didn't, and they're desperately in need of some TLC.'

'Sounds right up my street,' Billy's eyes gleamed with enthusiasm. 'I've got all my tools with me and I'd certainly like to earn my keep or pay my way— and if I can take on the repair work, then that sounds like a bit of a plan, doesn't it?'

'A lot of a plan.' Poll beamed. 'Look, why don't I show you round the farm before the others get back and Trixie arrives? I know it's hot but we can keep in the shade, then we can chat at the same time?'

'I'd like that.' Billy smiled gently at her. 'Lead on, Macduff.'

So, with the dogs snuffling round their feet, Poll

and Billy wandered slowly along Hideaway's shingle pathways and across the flower-spangled fields and surveyed the half-repaired barns. And after Billy had practically capered on the spot with delight at so much pending DIY, haltingly Poll told him about her childhood and about marrying Dennis, the world-travelling businessman, about Hideaway Farm and her dreams.

Billy sighed sympathetically when she'd finished. 'Right pair, aren't we? Doing all the wrong things for all the right reasons.'

Poll laughed. 'It's lovely to have someone who understands. I just seem to have made such silly mistakes.'

'But not now,' Billy insisted. 'Now you're doing something amazing to help others—no one can say this is silly.'

'Dennis probably would.' Poll laughed. 'Mind you, I have done some really stupid things, just because I was trying too hard to please him. Do you know, when we first moved in here I painted the farmhouse's interior walls—and ceilings—deep purple.'

'Nice. I like purple.'

'Me too. I was sure that once I'd hung up some watercolour landscapes and added velvet curtains and dozens of softly glowing lamps, it would make the jumble of rooms and all those passages homely and far more cosy.'

'And?'

Poll giggled. 'It didn't. The all over purpleness made everything dingy, bleak and slightly menacing. And I tripped over things in the gloomy corners. And it took weeks—and cost a fortune— to have the rooms returned to their natural rustic

101

cream. By professionals. And Dennis—when he came home from Belgium—was furious. Again.'

'Lord,' Billy chuckled. 'I can see his face now. Bet it was a picture.'

'Hmm.' Poll nodded. 'But not quite as bad as when he was in the States for some time, and I wanted to prove that I was independent and self-sufficient and as business-savvy as he was.'

'What happened?'

Poll grinned. 'Oh, I rented out the farm's unused greenhouses to some really nice young men from Winterbrook who said they wanted to grow organic veg for their market stall. Dennis arrived back from Washington just in time to discover the drug squad confiscating all the flourishing plants and the cleverly intricate watering, lighting and heating systems, and sealing off the greenhouses with flutters of blue and white scene-of-crime tape.'

'No way!' Billy laughed. 'A cannabis factory? He must have gone barmy.'

'Oh, he did. He was incandescent. And even more so when the whole thing went to court. Luckily, I was cleared of any involvement in the wrongdoing, but it was the talk of Hazy Hassocks and all points north, south, east and west for weeks. Dennis never really got over it.'

'And he didn't support you? Try to understand?'

Poll shook her head. 'Dennis never understood me. It was my fault, I suppose. I'd lived alone for so long I wasn't much good at sharing my dreams. Mind you, after the drugs thing, I still wanted to show him that I wasn't as useless as he thought I was, so I opened up one of the smaller barns as a farm shop.'

102

'Sounds like a good idea.' Billy nodded. 'The townies love that sort of thing.'

'That's what I thought, but I soon discovered that Hideaway didn't actually produce enough of anything quickly enough to sustain a business, so I bought eggs and potatoes and pies from Big Sava in Hazy Hassocks, and sold them as farm fresh at a loss. Just until the stuff I'd planted started growing and the chickens started laying. Just to gain a regular customer base.'

'Right,' Billy said slowly, 'and—?'

Poll chuckled happily. 'And this resulted in a visit from an officious man from Trading Standards who said some very harsh things about fraud and closed me down overnight.'

Billy laughed. 'I'm beginning to see a pattern emerging, here. But having young George—that must have pleased your Dennis, surely?'

'Not really. Not at all, actually. Oh, I embraced motherhood wholeheartedly, and was, surprisingly, pretty good at it. I'd never expected to have children, and George was a total delight, and even if being a first-time older mum was pretty tiring, I absolutely loved every minute of it.'

'But not Dennis?'

'No. Poor Dennis simply wasn't cut out for fatherhood. He was disgusted by the mess and disruption a baby creates. He just accepted more and more far-flung posts and left me to it. And when he did come home he was horrified to find that my conversations ricocheted between plotlines from *In the Night Garden* and the Piplings of Nara, and if we went out and anyone asked me for my favourite piece of music, I always said it was "The Wheels on the Bus".'

Billy roared with laughter. 'Miserable bugger, your Dennis. Clearly couldn't appreciate a gel with a sense of fun. You're well shot of him, if you ask me. So, where is he now?'

'Somewhere beginning with B with a pert, polished, degree-laden EU solicitor called Melissa.'

'And you don't mind?'

'Not at all,' Poll said with feeling. 'I'm just glad he's happy.'

'So it's just been you and young George and the animals for a while?'

'Until now, yes. And before long George will be starting playgroup in Hazy Hassocks—I'm determined he won't have my problems, and will learn the social skills so often lacking in only children—then it'll be on to full-time schooling, so I knew I'd need something to fill my empty nest, so who better than people who needed a home?'

'You're a remarkable woman,' Billy said. 'Truly a one-off.'

Poll knew she was blushing so she looked away. 'Not really. Just a silly dreamer. And goodness, I hope I haven't bored you with all this. I never meant to say so much about myself. You're a good listener.'

'Bored? Never on your life. I've spent years listening to our Mary and never saying nothing back. This has been a rare treat for me. Having a proper give-and-take conversation. You've got no idea how happy I am now. With a new home, and new friends and a new start in life—all thanks to you. There aren't many who'd give people like me a second bite of the cherry so to speak.'

'But it's for my benefit too. I've always wanted a

huge family—and now I've got one. George and Ella and Ash and, er, um, Ash and you—and Trixie will be here this afternoon.'

'Can't wait to meet the rest of them. Ella and Ash are already here, you say? And what's this Trixie like? Another youngster?'

'No, more our age I think. I'm sure you'll get on really well. She was a cook/housekeeper—so we've all got something in common.'

'Apart from being lost souls adrift on life's lonely ocean?' Billy chuckled as they completed the Hideaway circuit and fetched up in the garden again. 'And all of us keen on cookery. That's going to be fun—although you know what they says about too many cooks spoiling the broth, don't you?'

Poll nodded. 'If we all want to cook at the same time it could be pretty chaotic. Still, with different areas of expertise—although I'm not exactly sure what Trixie's speciality is yet—hopefully, we shouldn't step on one another's toes too much.'

'Ah.' Billy grinned at her. 'It'd be like being on an episode of *Dewberrys' Dinners*, won't it? All shouting and bickering and having creative tantrums like them Dreadful Dewberrys. Blimey Poll, love, I honestly can't wait to get stuck in.'

# Chapter Twelve

'Right,' Ella said above the whirring of the electric fan as she leaned across Poll's massive kitchen table later that scorching afternoon, 'now what do we need next?'

George, kneeling on a chair beside her, stopped chattering about the earlier delights of Fiddlesticks, drew in a huge breath, and pointed excitedly at the heap of shiny, acid-green apples.

'No, not yet,' Ella laughed. 'And don't try eating them, sweetheart, they're very sour—they'll make your eyes water and your mouth go all screwy up— like this.' She pursed her lips exaggeratedly and crossed her eyes, making George scream with laughter.

'You OK?' Ash, dressed in his chef's whites, appeared in the kitchen doorway.

'What?' Ella quickly unpursed and uncrossed and felt very hot and excruciatingly juvenile. 'Yes, yes, we're fine, thanks. Oh, you look the business. Are you going to start on your soup? Do you need some space?'

'Please. Just enough room for a bit of chopping and mixing. So, what *do* you need next?'

'Sorry? Oh, right—yes . . .' Ella moved her paraphernalia to one end of the table and nodded at George. 'We need the stale bread next, don't we? The loaf that Mummy says is as hard as nails. So if you could get that for me, sweetheart— lovely, thanks, and you mix the spices and sugar in this little bowl while I grate it—no, I'll do it. The grater eats little boys. And we don't want this

106

pudding to have bits of George-finger in it, do we?'

George waggled his fingers and chuckled again.

Ash paused in assembling his ingredients and grinned along the table. 'What's it going to be, then? You've been secretive about it all day. Let me guess . . . Lovely smells. Apples and cinnamon? So . . . apple pie?'

Ella swiftly grated the stale loaf into a pile of breadcrumbs, watching carefully from the corner of one eye as George laboriously mixed ginger and cinnamon with a generous measure of demerara sugar. 'No, nothing so ordinary. It's a Brown Betty.'

Ella turned to look at Ash with what she hoped was a suitably superior expression. It was difficult. He looked extremely sexy. He'd looked extremely sexy earlier too, when he'd rolled up his jeans and, clearly blissfully happy, had waded through the stream at Fiddlesticks with George, catching minnows and sticklebacks, then released them, glinting like quicksilver rainbows as they darted away. Her heart, as then, was doing silly little bumpetty-bumps under her ribs.

But only because, she reminded herself firmly, he's here and Mark isn't and you're missing him. It has nothing—absolutely nothing—to do with the fact that Ash is gorgeous and lovely and friendly and funny and clearly adores kids. Nothing at all . . .

'Ah, right.' Ash nodded. 'Brown Betty. Lovely. A proper retro pudding.'

Ella quickly reached for the apple corer and briskly set to work peeling and removing the innards of the pile of Bramleys with possibly a touch too much unnecessary concentration. 'Well, let's just hope it works. Poll wants this first family meal to be a success. Assuming Trixie ever gets here, of course.'

Ash grinned as he started on the first butternut squash. 'After all our expectations, as long as she arrives in a cloud of sparkly dust with her wand on fire I'll be more than happy. Mind you, I reckon we've got it wrong, and we'll be disappointed. Billy hasn't lived up to his kleptomaniac press, the little bit I've seen of him. He seems like a really nice bloke.'

'For a wife-murdering kleptomaniac?'

'Well, yes, naturally.'

They smiled at one another.

'And,' Ash said as he started to chop garlic and onions, followed by bunches of coriander and dill, at the speed of light, 'Poll says he's going to start all sorts of renovations and DIY on the tumbledown barns and generally make himself indispensable about the place.' He measured red lentils into the old-fashioned weighing scales. 'Makes me feel guilty—he's in his fifties and I'm only a youngster in comparison—I should be doing that sort of thing for Poll.'

Ella cored another apple, keeping an eye on George's spice-mixing at the same time. 'But you can't be here all day—you have to be out job-hunting and eventually working—Billy doesn't. He's got his private pension to live on. He told me. Mind you, he managed to find time to knock up some herby rolls for tonight's dinner even though it's supposed to be in his honour.'

'Impressive.' Ash reached for the pepper grinder. 'I'm already feeling inadequate. Out of

108

work and generally pretty useless.'

'You'll find a job soon,' Ella said quickly, before she could say anything too embarrassing about Ash being the least inadequate man she'd ever met. 'How's it looking on the job front, anyway?'

'Well, let's say I'm not expecting a call from Gordon or Jamie anytime soon,' Ash sighed, easing past her to measure water into a massive saucepan, sprinkling in seasoning, and setting it on the hob. 'My last boss is unlikely to come up with a reference, and there are lots of out-of-work chefs at the moment. Hopefully today's interview might be just what I'm looking for.'

'An interview? Today?' Ella blinked. 'You didn't say anything about that when we were in Fiddlesticks.'

Ash shook his head, peering into the saucepan, clearly willing it to boil. 'I didn't know then. I only got the phone call about an hour ago. I'd left a message with them on the off-chance, and they want to see me at five. Anyway, we spent all our time in Fiddlesticks discussing *Dewberrys' Dinners* and catching fishes, didn't we?'

They had—and it had been lovely.

'Congratulations. Is it local?' Ella started to grate the apples. 'A restaurant in one of the villages?'

'I exhausted all those weeks ago. No, this one's called Maxi's and it's recently opened in the middle of Winterbrook. Not sure what it entails, but I'll take anything—I'm long past being picky. And at least this time I have an address, which might just help. It's been impossible to try to get a job while having no current references and being of no fixed abode. And shouldn't you be chopping

109

the apples?'

'I prefer to grate. It's quicker and they cook better.'

There was no way on earth she was going to admit that yes, of course she usually fine-chopped the apples for Brown Betty, but didn't want him watching with his professional eye and then laughing if they skittered all over the table or she sliced her fingers and cried.

'And why all the old-fashioned equipment? You could do it much quicker using a food processor.'

'I know—' she looked loftily at him '—but have you actually seen a food processor or anything dated after nineteen fifty-five in this kitchen?'

'Come to mention it, no.' Ash looked around the huge array of ancient cooking equipment. 'Which means I'll have to sieve my soup, not blend it. I haven't done that for years.'

She watched him as he moved from the table to the cooker and back again with professional ease. He'd measured nothing but the lentils, adding a pinch of something here and a dash of something there and tasting it all the time without even seeming to concentrate.

It was extremely impressive.

And pretty damn sexy, she thought, growing hot despite the fan, watching as his long fingers worked their magic on herbs and spices.

Oh, he was good . . .

Ash looked across at her. 'You're really very clever at this old-fashioned sweet stuff. If I ever manage to get my own restaurant I'd give you a job in my kitchen any time.'

'Thanks.'

Why did she feel so ridiculously delighted? It was

110

just a throwaway remark. And anyway, there was Mark . . . and Onyx. Way too many complications.

'Um . . . right . . . now, let's see how you're doing.' Ella leaned towards George who was still stirring the spices and sugar, his tongue protruding from the corner of his mouth. The mixture had taken on a rather unpleasant consistency. 'Oh, that's lovely. Yes, it is a pretty colour. Yes, just like dog poo.'

Ash chuckled then looked at his watch. 'Damn. I'll have to dash—can't be late, and parking in Winterbrook is a nightmare.'

'Is it?' Ella reached for the buttered pie dish.

'Chronic. It's a nice place, though. Good nightlife and plenty of shops—but crap parking. At this time of the afternoon I'll probably have to park at Onyx's place and walk.'

So, Ella thought irritably, as she wrested the sugar-and-spice mixture away from George, Onyx lived in Winterbrook, did she? And Winterbrook was relatively close, wasn't it? And Ash, if he got this job in Maxl's, was going to work there, wasn't he? Huh! He'd probably never come home to Hideaway Farm again.

The combination of facts depressed her more than she wanted to admit, so she compensated by beaming far too broadly at George. George recoiled, looking slightly scared. She stopped beaming.

'Right, sweetheart—now we start the really nice bit. I'll put in a layer of apples, then you dollop some of your sugar and spice in on top and we'll spread it out, then we'll add some of the breadcrumbs, then we do it over and over again until there's nothing left.'

111

Excitedly, George leaned further across the table and together they started layering breadcrumbs, spices and apples into the dish, scattering a final layer of crumbs and a dusting of demerara over the top.

'Superb.' Ash applauded. George joined in.

Ella straightened up. 'There, that's that done. We'll make some real custard later. Thanks George, you're the best sous chef in the world.'

George grinned proudly and immediately started spooning the leftover mixture into his mouth.

Ash and Ella laughed together.

'I always did that at my gran's,' Ella said. 'I couldn't wait to lick the bowls and the spoons.'

'The best bit,' Ash agreed, unbuttoning his chef's jacket to reveal a pale-grey shirt over darker grey trousers. Ella thought he looked sensational and that anyone who didn't give him a job had to be completely insane, references or no references. 'Although frowned on in the top restaurants. Sadly. And now I really will have to run. I'll finish the soup off later when I'm back. It'll only need sieving and warming through.'

'It smells fabulous.'

'Let's hope it tastes the same. Can you keep an eye on it—give it a stir, and let it simmer for another half an hour then just turn the heat off?'

'Sure—and good luck.'

'Thanks.'

'And don't be late for this dinner—Poll will have your guts for garters, as my gran always said.'

'Mine too.' He grinned, hurling his chef's whites over a chair. 'OK, I'm off. See you later.'

Despite the gloriously hot golden afternoon, the kitchen seemed grey and cold once he'd gone.

Stupid, Ella told herself, too, too stupid.

She was loading the dishwasher and George was driving his plastic lorry convoy through the Brown Betty residue on the table when Poll drifted into the kitchen.

'Oh, it smells absolutely gorgeous in here—is the pud all done?'

'Yep.' Ella straightened up. 'In the fridge ready to cook later. And Ash's soup is on the hob. He'll heat it through when he gets back. Did you know he'd got an interview?'

'He mentioned it just now. I gave him a kiss for luck.'

'I didn't,' Ella said shortly. 'Anyway, we should blow Trixie's socks off with this meal.'

'Possibly not the best phrase to use given Trixie's unfortunate circumstances,' Poll chuckled. 'But I get the drift. Actually, I wanted to ask you if this was important before I threw it away. I found it on the stairs. It must have fallen out of your pocket.'

'Really?' Ella squinted at the screwed-up piece of paper. 'What is it? Oh, yes! I'd forgotten all about it. I wrote it all down when we were in Patsy's Pantry, but what with going to Fiddlesticks and then getting back here and meeting Billy and starting cooking, it went right out of my mind. Here . . . take a look.'

Poll frowned at the paper. 'A London phone number and a website address . . . that's no use to me, I haven't got a computer. Sorry, is this supposed to mean something to me? Ah . . . the website . . . yes . . . oh—*really? Dewberrys' Dinners?* Here? Really?'

'Apparently so.' Ella nodded. 'They're looking for local volunteers for their next show. There's only a couple of weeks left to apply now I think. Not that I took the details for that reason, of course.'

'I should hope not.'

'But I thought, well, it might be funny to find out who they'd chosen and if it's very local, we could go along and star spot or something.'

Poll grinned delightedly. 'Oh, yes! I'd love to see Gabby and Tom in the flesh. I wonder who's put themselves up for it?'

'Oh, loads of people according the Pantry's regulars. They must be mad.'

'Totally,' Poll agreed. 'Who'd be daft enough to want a whole film crew in your kitchen, not to mention Tom and Gabby criticising you and each other, and the whole country watching while you cooked a three course meal *live*?'

'Hell on wheels.' Ella grabbed a handful of wet wipes and removed most of the stickiness from George's chin and fingers. 'Although of course, if you get through to the final and win the public vote, Tom and Gabby help you to set up your own restaurant and—'

'But we don't want our own restaurant.' Poll shook her head. 'Do we?'

No, they didn't, but Ash did . . . Quickly, Ella shook her head. 'No, of course not.'

'And it would never be worth all that hassle and embarrassment and public humiliation . . . would it?'

'No way.'

They stood in silence for a moment, watching as George slid from his chair and disappeared outside with his lorries and the dogs.

'Don't get too hot, darling,' Poll called. 'And put

114

your baseball cap on.'

George grinned, nodded, and waved.

Ella, waving back, said, 'But the *Dewberrys' Dinners* thing being filmed locally is still pretty great, isn't it?'

Poll nodded. 'Yes, from a theoretical point of view. I'd never want to take part, of course . . . especially now that we have the house full with Ash and Billy and Trixie. It would be far too much to contemplate . . . wouldn't it?'

'Oh, yes. Far too much.'

Ella and Poll looked at one another then looked away.

Poll smiled. 'Still, *Dewberrys' Dinners* . . . I agree it's very exciting. Whoever they choose, it'll certainly put this area on the map in a fifteen minutes of fame way, won't it?'

'Mmm.'

'Ella, you don't think . . . I mean, you don't want to, do you?'

'No, of course not! Why—do you?'

'Absolutely not. No way. No, it's the last very thing I'd want to do.'

## *Chapter Thirteen*

'Right,' Poll said. 'What do you think?'

'I think it looks wonderful.' Ella gazed at the kitchen table, set for six, with the old-fashioned mismatched china and cutlery gleaming in the last rays of the evening sun, and a pink jug filled with a rainbow mix of flowers as a centrepiece. 'You're great at this front-of-house stuff. I hope Trixie

115

appreciates it.'

'You don't think we should have used the dining room?'

'Nooo.' Ella shook her head. 'Far too formal. This is perfect, and everything smells fantastic. I wish Trixie would hurry up. I'm starving.'

'Me too.' Poll looked anxiously at the huge station clock on the kitchen wall. 'I wonder where she's got to?'

'Is she driving? She might have got lost on the way here. I did, didn't I? Loads of times.'

'Trixie doesn't drive apparently. I did offer to collect her but she says she's getting a taxi direct from Reading station. It seemed easier than trying to change trains and find her way from one of the smaller stops, but even so, she's very late.'

Not as late as Ash, though, Ella thought.

Ash still hadn't returned from Winterbrook. Either the interview at Maxi's had gone spectacularly well and he was celebrating, or spectacularly badly and he was drowning his sorrows, or—much, much worse—he'd got delayed by Onyx . . .

No, Ella shook her head, she really mustn't think about Ash and Onyx. Or maybe she should . . .

'I do hope the others turn up soon.' Poll looked distracted. 'Otherwise it'll just be you and me. Billy went upstairs once he'd made his rolls to get ready ages ago and has probably fallen asleep, there's no sign of Ash, and George has already had to have a cheese sandwich and some ice cream to stop his tummy rumbling, and now he's outside playing and will probably be too full up to eat or too tired to join us, and the dinner, if Trixie doesn't arrive soon, will be totally ruined.'

116

Ella stopped twiddling the napkins—real linen napkins, slightly discoloured and creased but real none the less in Billy and Trixie's honour—and smiled, she hoped, cheerfully. 'I'm sure it won't. It's all keepable, isn't it? Ash's lentil, squash and coriander soup will reheat nicely, and Billy's herby rolls are in the warming oven, and my Brown Betty is on a low heat and I can put the custard back on later . . . That just leaves your main course. What did you decide on eventually?'

Poll sighed. 'A ready-five-minutes-ago steak and kidney pie.'

'Really? Blimey—you've gone carnivorous in Billy and Trixie's honour, have you?'

'I have not,' Poll said indignantly. 'It's steak and kidney pie without the steak or the kidney.'

'Right.' Ella grinned. 'Two layers of pastry filled with veggie gravy then?'

Poll looked suitably haughty. 'Quorn instead of steak, and field mushrooms instead of kidney. Trixie—if she ever arrives—and Billy will never know the difference.'

Ella secretly thought they might.

'Ta-dah!' Billy, his fair hair slicked down damply, beamed shyly from the kitchen doorway. 'Will I do? It's my Sunday best.'

Poll and Ella nodded in approval at the outfit of badly ironed white shirt and slightly crumpled beige chinos.

'You look lovely,' Poll said softly. 'Thanks so much for making the effort.'

'Well, you two girls look just the ticket and even young George has been scrubbed up. Couldn't let the side down, could I? Where's everyone else got to?'

'Don't!' Ella and Poll groaned in unison.

But before they could utter anything else about the absentees, George—not quite so scrubbed up after half an hour in the garden—galloped into the kitchen, excitedly waving a small red lorry in one hand and a large yellow shovel in the other.

'A car?' Ella said hopefully. 'Really, George? Is it? A car? And it's stopped outside?'

George nodded excitedly.

'Thank God.' Poll cast a frantic look at the simmering pans. 'We might be OK.'

'You stay here with me, George,' Billy said, 'while your mum and Ella go to see who it is.'

'Thanks, Billy, and please let it be Trixie's taxi,' Poll said, hurrying towards the hall.

Please let it be Ash, Ella thought, hurrying after her.

Sod it, Ella frowned, emerging from the hall and spotting the taxi outside the front door.

Then she laughed.

The short, cuddly woman with the tightly permed greying hair and the too long crimplene floral frock, the double string of pearls, the sensible sandals and the capacious handbag over one arm, fussily removing her cases from the cab and arguing with the taxi driver, was as far removed from being an arsonist bad-fairy as it was possible to get.

Trixie Pepper looked exactly like everyone's idea of a storybook grandmother.

'Trixie!' Poll billowed forwards in her scarlet and purple print frock. 'Lovely to see you. And right on time, too.'

Ella sniggered at the blatant Pinocchio moment.

'The train was late,' Trixie said, finally agreeing

118

on the correct fare with the taxi driver who, clearly tipless, reversed crossly and roared away in the direction of Hideaway Lane. 'Then I couldn't find a porter, then someone said you had to get your own trolley for your luggage, and then there was all sorts of hullabaloo with getting through the turnstiles, and then the taxi rank was empty when I got there—still, I'm here now, and what a lovely house, dear.'

'Thanks.' Poll beamed. 'And I hope you're hungry because we've planned a welcoming dinner in your honour.'

'Lovely. I could eat a horse, dear.'

Poll looked slightly shocked at the carnivorous reference.

Ella chuckled to herself.

'And this,' Poll said, lifting one of the suitcases, 'is Ella Maloncy. Ella is my new best friend and my helpmate and is quite amazing and I really can't imagine what I'd do without her now. Ella, this is Trixie Pepper.'

After a slightly embarrassing hesitant moment of shall-we-shan't-we kiss cheeks, Ella stooped down and they shook hands.

'Lovely to meet you, dear.'

'And you.' Ella smiled. 'Oh, let me take that bag for you—oooh—damn me—I mean . . . Lordy, that's heavy. No wonder you wanted a porter at Reading.'

'Books,' Trixie said as they all trooped back into Hideaway Farm. 'I can't be doing with being parted from my books.'

Compendiums of magical spells? Ella wondered as they hefted the luggage up the twisting staircases to Trixie's room. Encyclopaedias of fairy enchantments? Twenty-three ways to hex your faithless lover? Nine fail-safe recipes to heal warts? Or ruin crops? Or turn your neighbour's wine into vinegar—or your neighbour into a toad? Or bring on a plague of locusts?

Or maybe they were do-it-yourself fire-starting manuals?

And were these new books, seeing as presumably all Trixie's old ones had been incinerated in her self-imposed arson attack? And how had she managed to accumulate so much luggage anyway after razing her cottage to the ground? Surely all her belongings would now be a pile of ash? Oooh, no, don't think about Ash . . . Presumably she'd managed to salvage something from the ruins? But, what if—

Poll broke into this thrilling train of thought. 'I'll just get Trixie settled in. We shouldn't be long. If you'd be an angel and pop back to the kitchen and make sure we're all ready to go?'

'Yes, sure,' Ella said, rapidly translating 'ready to go' as 'not burned to a cinder' which might be a touch insensitive in Trixie's hearing, and very relieved to dump the weighty suitcase on the landing. 'And maybe I should try ringing Ash again and remind him to get a move on?'

'Good idea.' Poll nodded. 'If you don't know it— which I'm sure you do—his number is on the kitchen wall. On the pinboard with everyone else's. And tell him to be here in the next ten minutes or we'll have to start without him otherwise. Now, Trixie, this is your room. Oh, please mind the step down.'

120

# Chapter Fourteen

Back in the kitchen, Ella discovered Billy was snoozing in the cushioned rocking chair, snoring gently. He looked lovely. Like a little contented elf. Trixie would probably love him. She couldn't wait to tell him about Trixie.

Tiptoeing quickly to the cooker, lifting lids and checking the ovens, making sure nothing had burned, Ella giggled to herself. Trixie . . . Not a sparkly wand or set of gauzy wings or glittering tiara in sight. Hah! So much for Ash wanting Trixie to arrive in full panto fairy godmother mode. He was going to be sooo disappointed. If he ever came home, of course.

She'd ring him. Now. It wasn't as if it was a social call or anything, was it? She had a really good reason—and Poll had asked her to— and, no, she didn't know his number—yet . . .

Making sure she didn't disturb Billy, Ella skirted the kitchen table and squinted at the massed jumble of scrappy paper, Post-its, business cards, photos, postcards and George's artwork on the pinboard. How the heck did Poll ever find anything she wanted on there?

Ah—Ella grinned. There was the piece of paper with the *Dewberrys' Dinners* details on it. So, Poll hadn't thrown it away . . . Ella glanced across at Billy. He was still sleeping. And George was playing outside. And Poll was still upstairs . . . And—oh, hell—why not?

She quickly copied the *Dewberrys' Dinners* contact number into her mobile.

Then, feeling slightly guilty, she rummaged through the rest of the assorted papers until she found Ash's number and quickly entered that into her mobile too. Not that she'd be using it on a regular basis, or the *Dewberrys' Dinners* one either, of course, but just in case . . .

She punched out Ash's number. It went straight to voicemail.

'Oh, damn,' Ella muttered, then deciding that a text would be better than leaving some garbled and probably unheard message, she sent: 'Poll wants you here asap. Trixie's arrived. Dinner's burned. Two not necessarily connected. VBG!'

Message delivered in a light-hearted way. Nice and non-committal.

'Ah!' Billy woke up with a start and blinked wildly. 'I wasn't asleep, Ella, love. I was—'

'Just resting your eyes, yes, I know. My gran used to have to rest her eyes a lot too. You carry on. You must be exhausted anyway, after all that driving, then the tour of the farm and cooking as well. Trixie's here at last and she seems lovely but I reckon she'll talk the hind leg off a donkey so you'll need all the rest you can get.'

Billy yawned, stretched and chuckled. 'And is she all in pink net with a little crown and a big wand?'

'Sadly, not. She's all floral and mumsy. Ash is going to be bitterly disappointed.'

'Not to mention you, eh, love? See, Poll told you Trixie was a normal person, didn't she?'

'Yes, but Poll's idea of normal—'

Ella stopped talking and Billy sat up briskly as the kitchen door flew open.

'Here we are!' Poll announced brightly, ushering Trixie into the kitchen, beckoning George in from

122

the garden and casting a frantic eye at the cooker. 'Welcome to the Hideaway family, Trixie. Ash will be here soon, Ella you've already met, and this is Billy Booker, and my son, George. I hope you'll be very happy here.'

'I'm sure I shall be, dear.' Trixie beamed happily at Billy and shook George's slightly grubby hand without wincing. 'This is wonderful. Simply wonderful. I'm so very grateful to you, dear. I don't know what I'd have done without you. You're so very kind.'

'Ah, she is,' Billy agreed, winking at Ella. 'She's a one-off is our Poll.'

'No sign of Ash yet?' Poll whispered as George was despatched to wash his hands, and Billy and Trixie sat down at the table. 'Did you ring him?'

'Texted,' Ella whispered back.

'That's clever. I've never texted anyone.'

'He hasn't replied.'

'Hasn't he? Oh, well, he probably has a really good reason for being late. Do you think we should dish up the soup even though he isn't here?'

Ella nodded. 'Definitely, otherwise it'll all spoil. If you do the soup, I'll grab the rolls from the bottom oven and start pouring the wine.'

'OK, but—' Poll looked slightly distressed '— don't you think this is all wrong?'

'What is? The wine? We've got water as well for anyone who doesn't want alcohol. Or do you mean the welcoming dinner in general? The fact that we've all played a part in the cooking which might lead to a case of too many cooks? Or the fact that Ash isn't here?'

Poll shook her head. 'None of them. I mean the

123

food itself. If it was the middle of winter, this would be fantastic, but it's a warm May evening. I feel like I'm in a sauna already, and we've concocted a really hearty meal. It should be salads and ice cream . . . Oh, why do I always do everything wrong?'

'You don't.' Ella grinned at her. 'OK, maybe it is a little, um, robust, but everyone's really hungry, the door's open, the fan's going, there's a nice breeze, and it all smells fantastic. They won't mind that it's a winter menu, they'll love it, Poll, honestly. Once they get started they'll be ecstatic about Ash's soup and it'll be all onwards and upwards from there, you'll see.'

And, much to Ella's relief, it was.

Within minutes, wine glasses filled, they were all oohing and aahing over the soup course.

'. . . oh, this is wonderful . . . delicious . . . so unusual . . .'

'. . . tastes like curry—mild, but spicy at the same time—like the best curry I've ever had . . .'

'. . . ah, that it does. Young George is on his seconds already, love him . . .'

'. . . yes, Ash is clearly a marvel with soups. A genius at blending flavours . . . such a shame he isn't here . . . more bread?'

Trixie dabbed delicately at her mouth. 'This is fantastic. Billy made it, did you say, dear? My compliments to the chef, then, Mr Booker. It's wonderful. You can taste the fresh herbs in the bread and the soup. Now, I love cooking with herbs. I could recommend some of the more unusual ones, dear.'

Ella smiled into her soup bowl. Bad-fairy herbs no doubt—hemlock and henbane and mandrake and aconite.

Oh, yummy—not.

'. . . you and Ash must get together, then. Concoct some recipes between you.'

'Ah, we should all have a little bash at that!'

'What a good idea. Oh, yes, this soup is the best I've ever tasted.'

'. . . more? Lovely, pass your bowl across, there's plenty.'

Oh, yes, Ash could certainly cook, Ella thought, spooning up the sublime lentil, butternut squash and coriander soup. It was quite, quite incredible.

Great cook—lousy time-keeper.

On cue, the kitchen door flew open again.

'Hi! Poll, I'm so sorry I'm late, but it all took much longer than I'd expected, and then there was a bit of a transport problem and . . .'

Ella looked up and registered two things at the same time. One, that Ash was wearing a funny little white hat which oddly didn't detract one iota from his gorgeousness. And two, that he was accompanied by the most beautiful girl she'd ever seen.


# Chapter Fifteen

The rest of the kitchen spotted Ash's headgear at the same time. George pointed at him and shrieked with happy laughter. Everyone else simply stared, then Trixie startled everyone by clapping her hands in delight.

'Oh! I love it! He looks like one of them old films—you know, the ones with Frank Sinatra.

125

where he's a sailor on leave and he dances in fountains and . . .'

'A sailor's hat!' Poll nodded. 'Of course it is!'

Ella looked at her with deep misgiving. Really Poll was so suggestible, so very easily led.

'Er . . .' Ella tried to force her tone in neutral, which was, she considered, pretty tricky when the sight of Ash's companion had sent her heart sinking into her stomach as rapidly as her herby croutons had disappeared into the bottom of her soup bowl. 'Seriously, Ash, what the heck are you wearing on your head?'

'Oh, this.' Ash tapped the hat and looked amused. 'Yeah, well, I had to try it on for size and then I sort of forgot to take it off and—'

Ella frowned. What sort of weird dressing-up games did he play with this stunning girl? Oooh no—it didn't bear thinking about.

Ash grinned. 'And sorry to disappoint you, but it's not a sailor's hat. It's part of my uniform.'

'Uniform?' Poll smiled, naturally the only person still seemingly unfazed by the hat. 'Oh, how wonderful—but if it's not a sailor's hat, a uniform must mean you've got a job?'

Ash nodded. 'At Maxi's.'

'Oh, congratulations,' Poll trilled excitedly. 'How lovely. Clever you. As a chef?'

'Er, not as a chef, exactly.'

Ella frowned again. She really shouldn't. She'd end up with a forehead like a ploughed field before she was thirty. 'Congrats on getting the job, but if you're not a chef, then what's the hat thing for?'

'I know! Of course! Everyone wears them at Maxi's!' Poll interrupted delightedly. 'Oh, George

126

loves Maxi's! It's only just opened and . . .'

Definitely not an odd dressing-up game then, Ella thought, her eyes now riveted on the stunning girl in the doorway. Silly mistake—any games involving any couple as beautiful as Ash and *her* would never involve silly hats, it was bound to be all sensuously fragranced oils and creams and . . .

'Maxi's,' Poll informed the rest of the table, 'is the latest must-go-to place for the children. They all have their birthday parties there. It's just like Tom and Jerry.'

'Cartoons?' Billy queried. 'Cats and mice killing each other? That doesn't seem too suitable for the little 'uns, if you ask me.'

'Nooo,' Poll chuckled. 'I don't mean Tom and Jerry, do I? Silly me—of course—it's Frankie and Benny's, isn't it?'

Ash laughed. 'Hardly in their league.'

Poll shook her head. 'Oh, dear, I was sure it was Frankie and Benny's. All those lovely sundaes and fab flavours.'

'Do you mean Ben and Jerry's?' Ella suggested, a touch tersely. 'Luxury ice creams? Does Maxi's do things like Ben and Jerry's?'

Ash nodded. 'It's an ice-cream parlour.'

'That's it!' Poll looked excited. 'Ben and Jerry's! Well, they make their own ice creams at Maxi's, they don't sell Ben and Jerry's obviously—but it's fab. Like one of those 1950s American soda pop places you see on the films. Clever girl, Ella! I knew we'd get there in the end!'

Ella peered at Ash. 'But you're a chef, not an ice-cream maker.'

Ash shrugged. 'Yes, I'm a chef, but an unemployed one. Or at least, I was.'

Poll stopped smiling. 'Lovely, Ash, I'm so pleased for you . . . Oh, but you said there was a transport problem, didn't you? Oh, don't say your car's broken down just when you've got a job? That would be too cruel.'

Ash shook his head. 'No, the car's fine, but I, um, get company transport which I had to drive home, which meant my car would still be in Winterbrook, so I asked—'

'A company car!' Poll crooned blissfully. 'How amazing, Ash. They must think very highly of you to give you a company car.'

Ash, eventually tugging off the funny hat and ruffling his hair in a way that made Ella's toes curl with lust, grinned at Poll. 'Actually, it isn't exactly a company car, it's an ice-cream van.'

*What*? Ella blinked. 'No way! An ice-cream van? You mean a tinkly-jingly stop-me-and-buy-one ice-cream van?'

'Exactly.'

Everyone clapped their hands again. Everyone except Ella who somehow felt that Ash selling ice creams from a van was wrong on so many levels.

'Don't tell me it's pink and white and pale green and has a big ice-cream sundae thing on the roof?'

'OK.' Ash grinned. 'I won't. But it is and it has. I've parked it at the back, by the biggest barn. It's well out of sight. And no, before you say anything, it isn't the job of my dreams, but any job is better than none and as I'm on a short-term summer contract they might not mind about my lack of references . . . Oh, and, Poll, I'm so sorry, in all the excitement my manners are sadly lacking. This is Onyx.'

All eyes immediately diverted from Ash to his

128

stunning companion. Everyone smiled and said hello. Onyx smiled warmly and said hello back. Ella really had to force herself to do both because she certainly hadn't needed to be told it was Onyx.

Onyx the exotic dancer. Huh, so much for Olive-with-the-welder-look . . .

Poll beamed even more. 'Lovely to meet you, Onyx. I've, um, we've heard so much about you from Ash.'

Ash beamed as well. Ella was getting a bit tired of the beaming.

'I hoped you wouldn't mind if Onyx joined us,' Ash said to Poll. 'I was pretty sure you wouldn't—because I had the ice-cream van, she had to drive my car back, you see and—'

'And I've already said,' Onyx, tall, black and traffic-stoppingly beautiful in tight jeans, skimpy vest and stilt-high glittery sandals, interrupted cheerfully, 'that I wouldn't dream of arriving unannounced and intruding on a special occasion. I just did the driving job to make sure the car got here. I'll be off now.'

Good, Ella thought, crumbling one of Billy's herby rolls.

'Goodness me,' Poll said, standing up. 'I won't hear of it. There's simply loads of food and the more the merrier. I'll just get some more cutlery. Ash, grab that chair—yes, that one—shake the cushion in case it's a bit hairy . . . lovely, now Onyx, you squeeze in here, next to Ella—oh—let me introduce you to everyone.'

Introductions were made—Ella noticed that Ash greeted fairy-Trixie with some disappointment—and then everyone started to talk at the same time.

'Soup OK?' Ash raised his eyebrows at Ella.

129

'Fine. I sieved it when you weren't back in time.'

'Thanks.' Ash pulled up the extra chair. 'You're a star.'

Ella tried very hard not to stare as Onyx slid her eighteen miles of incredibly slender legs under the table beside her.

'I still feel like the world's worst gatecrasher,' Onyx confided happily, leaning closer to Ella in a waft of gorgeous scent as Poll bustled between them to dish up more soup and rolls. 'I know how important this get-together is to Ash. He already adores Poll.'

'We all do,' Ella said, still trying to block out the image of the stunning Onyx entwined half-naked round a pole, or, even worse, round Ash.

'Yes, he said so—Oh, wow!' Onyx said, spooning up the soup. 'You can tell this is one of Ash's recipes, can't you? He's a genius in the kitchen.'

And no doubt in the bedroom, Ella thought, trying really, really hard not to be childish and failing miserably.

For the first time since she'd arrived at Hideaway she really regretted not having used her hair straighteners and her almost make-up-free fresh-faced look. Onyx's glossy short black hair was tousled and designer-layered, her make-up was flawless and her eyelashes—false, surely?—were like long ebony feathers.

Ella sighed.

As they moved on from Ash's soup and Billy's herby rolls to the non-steak-and-kidney pie and more wine, Poll seemed to have commandeered the conversation at the other end of the table. It seemed, Ella thought, to be revolving around the joys of being a vegetarian. Trixie, Billy and Ash—

carnivores to a man—were exclaiming happily over every mouthful. Ella sighed with relief. There really had been no need for Poll to worry.

'So—' Onyx leaned across to Ella again '—Ash tells me you're all foodies here. That must be so much fun. I'm a hopeless cook.'

Good, Ella thought. Nice to know you're not totally brilliant at *everything*. 'Well, no, we're not foodies, as such. Ash, of course, is a proper chef and Billy had his own bakery, but the rest of us are just happy amateurs.'

'Still—' Onyx swallowed a mouthful of non-steak-and-kidney with obvious enjoyment '—it means you all have something in common. Lovely for you all, living here, sort of communally. I know Ash was devastated when he lost his flat, and he says Poll has welcomed you all in with open arms.'

'Yes, she has—' Ella pushed her fork through her potatoes '—and she's amazing. Although I wasn't homeless—I came here to work for Poll.'

'Oh, yes. Ash told me that, too. He's told me all about all of you.'

Ella, not sure whether to be pleased that Ash had talked about her or not, decided to shift the conversation towards less personal matters. Poll would never forgive her if she started a cat-fight.

'Has he? Then you'll know we're a pretty mixed bunch and—'

Onyx laughed then lowered her voice. 'I know—actually I thought he was making it all up to start with, but—' she glanced round the table '—obviously not. Mind you, he's probably said plenty about me, too. Ash is a terrible gossip.'

'Is he?' Ella manfully attempted to do the grown-up supper-party thing and catch the conversational

131

ball. 'Well, yes, he's told us something about you.'

'I bet he has!' Onyx chuckled. 'He's a bad boy!'

The bad boy shot a scorching glance across the table. Ella gulped her water.

'Go on, then,' Onyx continued, 'what's he said?'

'Oh, nothing, um, personal, really. Just about you being, er, friends and you being a dancer.'

Onyx shrugged. 'Not much more to tell, really. I'm pretty boring.'

Yeah, right.

Ella concentrated on her meal for a moment. 'So, is Onyx, um, your professional dancing name?'

'Nah!' Onyx giggled. 'It's real. And I've got an older married sister called Pearl and a younger single sister called Ebony and a brother called Jet. All on the *black* stone theme, see? My parents are very proud of their roots, but they've also got a sense of humour. Sadly our surname doesn't follow the trend.'

'No?' Ella raised her eyebrows.

Onyx giggled again. 'No. It's Smith. How disappointing is that?'

Ella laughed. She couldn't help it. It was almost impossible not to like Onyx. Damn it. And she still itched to ask why Ash hadn't moved in with Onyx when he lost his flat. It seemed a little early in the supper-party conversation to throw in a casual-but-tasteless 'why isn't he shacked up with you, then?' line. But the itch wouldn't go away.

'So,' she tried to sound non-committal. 'You and Ash? How did you, er, get together? Did you meet at one of your, er, shows?'

Of course Ella was sure it had been; probably at some drunken stag do. In some sleazy club. Probably one that specialised in lap dancing. With

132

Onyx glistening and wearing tassels and a G-string and Ash, completely trollied, lusting disgustingly.

'Oh, no. We met ages ago, at uni.'

## Chapter Sixteen

Ella choked on a baby carrot. Onyx, the exotic dancer, had been to *uni*? Goodness, wasn't that almost exactly like Belle de Jour or something? Hadn't she been a high-class call girl by night and some massively well-qualified and respected scientist by day?

Was Onyx the world's leading expert on particle physics or nucleonics or marine biology or something equally mind-boggling?

'Uni?' Ella said weakly. 'I didn't know Ash had been to uni.'

Onyx nodded. 'Oh, yes. We were both at Reading, living in halls, and met when we were first year neighbours. Ash was doing Food Marketing and Business Economics with the intention of one day running his own restaurant. I was reading English—with the intention of doing who knows what, actually. Despite heavy partying, we both graduated with good degrees.'

Ella eventually swallowed the baby carrot. 'Really? Then why the, um, dancing?'

Onyx shrugged. 'Oh, natural greed I suppose. And a bit of laziness on both our parts. You see, we'd both been doing evening jobs while we studied to make ends meet—Ash was cooking in other people's restaurants, and I've always danced, so I found it easy to get club work—and once we

133

graduated we just slipped into making our part-time jobs full-time and carried on. A waste of our education, as my parents keep telling me.'

Ella exhaled and chased another carrot round her plate. Onyx, the pole dancer, was way, way better educated than she was . . . As was Ash . . .

Oooh!

'I've promised my mum and dad that I'll settle down and use my degree one day when I get too old for the bump and grind,' Onyx continued happily. 'And hopefully, Ash will get the recognition he deserves and open his first restaurant. But until then, me being a nightclub hoofer and Ash being a Maxi's mobile ice-cream vendor will pay our bills.'

'Er, yes, I suppose it will.' Ella didn't know what else to say.

Well, she had a trillion things just waiting to trip off her tongue but none of them would have been remotely suitable. She settled on something safely non-committal that wouldn't lead to hair-pulling and nail-gouging. 'And fancy you and Ash knowing each other for such a long time. Since you were eighteen.' Ella did the maths. A long-term relationship then. Far, far longer than she'd been with Mark. Oooh, Lordy . . . 'That's a lifetime.'

'Yeah, it does seem like forever.'

'And yet he was staying with his friend, Joe, and didn't move in with you when he lost his flat?'

Oooh, nooo. Ella cringed. Why had she said that? 'Sorry—' she shook her head '—none of my business. Forget it.'

Onyx chuckled. 'Oh, ask away. I don't mind. But as I still live at home with my parents, as do Jet and Ebony, because, one, we're all broke, and, two, we've been brought up to believe family is king, and because our house is a three-up two-down and Ebony and I share a bedroom and Jet's room is like a shoebox, even if I'd wanted to move him in, it would have been an impossibility.'

'Oh, right.' Ella did a little mental air-punch. Lots of questions answered there. Great.

'Oh, thanks so much.' Onyx smiled at Poll as she collected up the plates. 'That was amazing. The best pastry I've ever tasted. And as I'm a veggie, I ate every single scrap—as you can see.'

Poll looked at the empty plate with pleasure. 'I'm so pleased you enjoyed it. Are you and Ella getting to know one another?'

Onyx nodded happily. Ella simply nodded.

Poll raised her eyebrows and swished away. 'Good, good—now let's hope you all have room for Ella's fab pud.'

There was a mock groan round the table and a joint declaration that they couldn't possibly eat another thing. Except Onyx who smiled again at Ella.

'I can't wait for your pudding. I love food, and Ash says you specialise in retro puddings.' Onyx stretched like a well-fed cat. 'He says you're very, very good at them. He says you could turn pro.'

Ash seemed to have said an awful lot on a very short acquaintance, Ella thought, wondering again if this was a good thing or not. She supposed it was.

'Really? That's very kind of him. But yes, I do enjoy making old-fashioned puddings.'

'Which is exactly why you should go on *Dewberrys' Dinners*,' Onyx said as Poll dished up the Brown Betty. 'All of you. As soon as I saw the

135

posters in Winterbrook today I told Ash. They'd love you on there.'

'We've seen the posters too,' Ella said. 'But we've already discounted it. We all decided we couldn't put ourselves through it.'

'Really?' Onyx looked surprised. 'But if you won it, you get the opportunity to open a restaurant and the Dewberrys have mega-zillions to invest and—'

'Custard?' Poll passed the jug down the table. 'It's real. Not packet or powder. Ella made it from scratch with vanilla pods and what have you.'

Everyone helped themselves to custard.

'Yes, I know,' Ella continued after her first tentative mouthful of Brown Betty. It had worked perfectly. Thank goodness. 'But we don't want a restaurant and we don't want to look stupid on telly.'

'Oh, this is fabulous.' Onyx waved her spoon over the Brown Betty. 'Really fab. The whole meal is incredible. Which is exactly *why* you should apply to go on *Dewberrys' Dinners*. You'd kick the rest of them into next week. And you might not want a restaurant, but Ash does.'

'Are you talking about me?' Ash looked across the table.

'Yep,' Onyx said cheerfully. 'Don't listen. I'm just going to tell Ella all about your disgusting habits.'

Ash laughed.

Oh, Lordy, Ella thought, he was soooo gorgeous. And he was having to waste all his culinary talents by working on an ice-cream van when he sooo wanted a restaurant . . .

136

## Chapter Seventeen

Poll sat back in her chair and gazed happily round the table now strewn with empty bowls, crumpled napkins and discarded cutlery. She sighed with deep contentment. It had been OK. It had been very OK. The meat-eaters hadn't minded it being veggie, and no one had complained about it being a meal more suited to a freezing winter's night. There were no leftovers and everyone was relaxed and happy.

Who could ask for anything more?

Tonight was everything she'd ever dreamed of. The farmhouse was cosily filled with noise and people and the smells of delicious food. Her Hideaway family was complete—together, safe, and chatting in post-prandial bliss.

Nirvana.

She smiled fondly at Ella, Onyx and Ash talking and laughing together. It was wonderful that Ash had a job at last. And what a lovely one. Out and about in the fresh air throughout the summer, meeting people . . . Lucky Ash. Although, she thought, it probably was an awful waste of his considerable talents. If only she could magic up a restaurant for him as easily as she'd been able to provide him with a home.

And of course Onyx was devastatingly beautiful, and clearly she and Ash were very close, but Ella, obviously remembering Mark, was handling the situation in her usual sunny easy-going way. Bless her.

Such a shame Ash wasn't available, though. It

137

would have been wonderful if Onyx wasn't on the scene, and if the frankly blokeish-sounding and selfish Mark could just fade away and then there could have been a romance between Ash and Ella—maybe even a Hideaway wedding . . .

'Um, right, are we all done?' Poll managed to drag herself back from her daydream of a gauzy ceremony in Hazy Hassocks church, with Ash and Ella looking radiant, and umpteen tiny bridesmaids in floaty rainbow chiffon, and George as a pageboy, and Billy and Trixie beaming proudly from the front pew and herself in a layered frock in shades of gold and cream and possibly a big floppy hat with matching ribbon streamers. 'Everyone finished?'

'Ah, right full up.' Billy patted his stomach. 'That was a feast fit for a whole royal family. A great joint effort. Thanks, Poll, love.'

Poll smiled at him. He returned the smile and she gave a little shiver of delight. Billy had such a lovely smile. And he was obviously going to become indispensable round Hideaway, being able to turn his hand to anything that needed doing. He was such a lovely gentle man. The sort of man she should have met years and years ago. Although, she reminded herself sharply, if she had, and hadn't met Dennis, then there would be no George. And that was simply horrifying.

Still, she hoped Billy was happy and never wanted to leave Hideaway. Life without Billy, even if he was completely unaware of it—and Poll fervently hoped he was—would, for her, be unthinkable.

'Yes, a really lovely meal, dear.' Trixie interrupted the dreamy thoughts, her copious rows

138

of beads rattling with enthusiasm. 'Absolutely lovely. Couldn't have done better myself.'

Poll heaved a sigh of relief. 'I'm so glad you enjoyed it. Now I'm sure both you and Billy must be tired after your journeys, but as soon as I've got George off to bed, I'm going to make some coffee. I thought we'd have it outside because it's such a lovely evening. I know it's getting dark, but I've got lots of candles.'

'I make candles,' Trixie said, carefully wiping her mouth on her napkin. 'I ask the fairies to help me to pick fresh herbs—always with the dew still on them, of course—and add them to my candles when the wax is wet with a few spell words to ward off the evil spirits and make nice things happen. I do love a bit of a flickering flame.'

'Ah, so that's how you burned your house down, was it?' Billy said, chuckling. 'One too many flickering flames?'

Trixie bridled. 'Indeed it was not! That was a cooking accident, pure and simple. I just took my eye off the ball for a moment, so to speak, and whoosh! Terrible, it was. Terrible.'

Billy nodded. 'It must have been. Losing everything like that. I'm really sorry for you. Mind, we're all in the same boat here.'

'Hardly.' Trixie patted her plentiful curls. 'You weren't burned out, were you? I was left with nothing. My past was gone in a jiffy. Everything—photos, letters, me little trinkets and mementoes—all burned to a crisp.'

'Sorry,' Billy looked mollified. 'I didn't mean to demean your tragedy, love. I know that must have been really awful for you. Didn't you manage to save anything from your cottage?'

'I only managed to salvage a few books and whatever other nearby bits and bobs I could grab, and the clothes I was standing up in.' Trixie gave a shudder. 'It was terrifying. The flames and the smoke were something chronic. They rampaged everywhere—so quick, it was . . . so terrifyingly quick . . .'

'Ah,' Billy nodded, 'it must have been. So, if it wasn't your, er, fairy candles, was it a bit of, um, mystical cooking you was doing at the time of the inflagration? A clash of magic ingredients?'

'Mystical cooking?' Trixie stiffened. 'Magic ingredients? Let me tell you it was normal cooking, plain good home cooking—that's my forte. Yes, I may brew one or two little herbal tinctures—solely for my own consumption, in the privacy of my own home—but if you're alluding to my herbs and fairies and whatnot in a mockery way then I'll have to ask you for an apology.'

Billy chuckled softly. 'Wouldn't dream of mocking you, Trixie. Each to his own, that's what I always say.'

Trixie was still looking slightly miffed. 'When I've settled in proper like, I'll show you what the fairies can do—then you'll be laughing on the other side of your face.'

'Probably literally if the spell goes wrong.'

Trixie huffed and straightened her necklaces. 'Because I'm a lady and because we're all having such a lovely time here and I know my manners, I'll ignore that. But just to prove that you're wrong to mock, I'll let you into one of my little fairy secrets, shall I?'

Billy stifled a snigger.

Poll shot him a warning glance. 'Go on.' She

smiled encouragingly. 'Oh, and yes, George, go and find a lovely book for your bedtime story, sweetheart, I'll be up in a minute. No, go on Trixie, tell us about the fairies.'

'Well—' Trixie rearranged her beads and fussily smoothed the front of the floral frock '— fairies are good people. There are fairies for every occasion. Fairies who can be called on to help out when earthly methods simply don't work.'

'Really? And can we actually see them?' Poll looked expectantly at her.

'Oh, yes. But everyone sees them differently. Most people just say it's like a vivid swirl of fast-moving light, or a cascade of falling stars, or simply a sense of light and movement and colour.'

'Oh.' Poll was entranced. 'How very lovely! It sounds so beautiful.'

'It is. They are.' Trixie's curls nodded rigidly. 'And everyone has a special fairy. A fairy who is there, in the enchanted world, just for us. And our special fairy has a name for us that reflects our personality.'

Billy hooted with laughter.

Poll, sensing a scene threatening, felt soothing intervention was called for. 'Ah, yes, I've heard about something like that . . . I remember Mitzi Blessing's younger daughter found something on the inter-web-thingy—she stopped calling herself Lulu and wanted to be known as Moonwand Frostblizzard for ages. Really confusing it was. Mind you, Lulu Blessing is a confusing girl at the best of times.'

Trixie nodded. 'Oh, yes, the fairy generator name sites are lovely and a bit of fun, but that's not what I'm talking about. I'm talking about Real

141

Fairies. I'm talking about each one of us having our own fairy guide who knows us by our Given Enchanted Name.'

'Really?' Poll gave Billy another warning glance and hoped Ella wasn't listening. She'd never believe this. No, Ella was still chattering to Onyx and Ash. Thank goodness. 'Do you mean like a guardian angel?'

Trixie shook her head. 'No, that's something else again. But we really do each have a fairy who looks over us, takes care of us, and knows us not as Trixie Pepper or Poll Andrews but by our Enchanted Name, and whose mission is to make sure we do the right thing at the right time.'

'Yours had the night off when you burned your house down, did she?' Billy asked innocently. 'Or had you taken one too many of your herbal tinctures?'

'That,' Trixie hissed, 'as I've told Poll, was the work of a Bad Elf while I was cooking my supper and watching that edition of *Dewberrys' Dinners* from Cornwall where they were making pasties and got to the bit where they realised they'd left the veg out and were trying to get it into the cooked pastry without that ghastly Gabby Dewberry noticing and I got riveted and my pan caught on, and whoosh!'

Billy bit his lip and chuckled.

Trixie ignored him and looked plaintively at Poll. 'Oh, it's so difficult to explain about the fairies to non-believers—'

'I wouldn't bother then,' Billy said kindly. 'It'll like as not be nonsense.'

Poll tried not to laugh. 'Don't be such a nay-sayer, Billy. I'm fascinated, Trixie. Go on.'

Casting a further baleful look at Billy, Trixie took a deep breath. 'Well, my fairy name is Gossamer Snapdragon.'

Billy hooted with laughter.

'How lovely!' Poll exclaimed quickly. 'And does it have a special meaning? For you?'

Trixie nodded. 'All the given fairy names accurately reflect their owner's personality. Mine means I'm imbued with a lightness of spirit, in tune with the burgeoning of youthful spring, and can also be tough but fair when needed.'

'Poppycock!' Billy spluttered. 'I've never heard so much old baloney in my life!'

Poll flapped her hands. 'Take no notice of him— tell me what mine is then, Trixie. Can you do that?'

'I can't, but the fairies can if I ask them to.' She narrowed her eyes at Billy. 'Now, I don't know either of you properly, do I? I've only just met you today, have only been able to form a sketchy opinion of your characters from this dinner party, but the fairies will tell me your names which are linked to theirs and reflect your personality.'

'Party tricks.' Billy grinned. 'I love party tricks. Go on then, give us a bit of a laugh.'

Trixie leaned back in her chair and closed her eyes. Poll and Billy exchanged amused glances.

'Right.' Trixie opened her eyes again. 'Poll's fairy guide says her name is Thistledown Dreamer— soft, gentle, generous, easily distracted, kindly and loving. And you—' she stared at Billy '—your fairy guide says you're Pumpkin Scoffer. You're honest, robust, hard-working and loyal, but inclined to mock others, albeit in a non-hurtful manner.'

'Well!' Poll was impressed. 'That's amazing,

143

Trixie! Thistledown Dreamer . . . how pretty! And how very apt for me. And Billy's is very accurate, too. Pumpkin is so sweet.'

'Damn Pumpkin, my foot!' Billy snorted. 'She's making it up. She's just picking bloody silly, um, I mean, fairy names that go with what she's already sussed out about us.'

Trixie's cheeks turned very red. Poll really hoped she wasn't going to have a heart attack. She'd forgotten most of her elementary first aid unless it was fastening a splint. She could do splints. Splints, she felt, wouldn't be much use in a cardiac arrest.

'All right then, Mr Scoffer.' Trixie raised her eyebrows in a superior way. 'So, what about the rest of the party? The three young 'uns down t'other end of the table? I don't know anything about them at all, do I? I can't even begin to guess at their personalities, but I'll ask the fairies to tell me their names too, shall I?'

Billy chuckled. 'Ah, go on then. But I think you should leave out Onyx because none of us knows her so we wouldn't be able to say yay or nay, would we? You just do Ella and Ash, but I'm betting you won't get it right this time.'

'Actually,' Trixie said, 'Ella should be easy as the literal interpretation of her name is "fairy maiden".'

'Nooo! Is it?' Poll beamed. 'Really? I wonder if she knows. Sorry, Trixie, I know you want to concentrate . . .'

Trixie closed her eyes again.

'Nodded off,' Billy said softly to Poll, his brown eyes crinkling with mischief. 'Probably won't get another peep out of her until bedtime.'

'Ssssh, Pumpkin,' Poll said softly. 'Let the fairies

do their work.'

Trixie's eyes suddenly shot open.

'Blimey,' Billy said. 'That were a bit scary. Like summat off a ghost train ride.'

Poll giggled.

Trixie ignored him. 'Ella's fairy name is Sunshine Strangeflower. A happy-go-lucky girl with a warm heart and a willingness to tackle anything that life throws at her and always with a ready smile.'

Poll nodded. 'Well, as far as I know, that's Ella to a T. Come on, Billy, you've got to admit it.'

'And as I hardly know the girl, I'll have to trust you on that one. Come on, then. How about young Ash?'

Trixie did the eye-closing thing again. Poll held her breath. This was really quite fascinating. And how lovely it would be if there really were fairies. She wasn't sure if she believed in them or not. She'd always hoped they existed, always been fascinated by the idea—mainly after reading about the Cottingley Fairies. She'd never believe that was a hoax. Never. If the explanation had been good enough for Sir Arthur Conan Doyle then it was certainly good enough for her.

'Ash's Enchanted Name,' Trixie's eyes opened wide, 'is a bit odd. I hate to admit it, but I may have got this wrong.'

'Surely not,' Billy chuckled. 'You tell us what the fairies are telling you about young Ash, and Poll'll soon put you straight.'

'I'm sure you will, Mr Scoffer. Well, I'm being told he's known as Kalen, um, Aspeeday. Kalen indicates a warrior king—someone loyal and honest and hard-working, who slaves for what he wants to achieve but who will also fight to the

145

death to protect those he loves or the ideals he believes in.'

Billy nodded grudgingly. 'OK—young Ash strikes me as a lad who'd fight—not literally, of course—for the rights of anyone and everything he holds dear.'

'Yes, but,' Trixie said, 'where the Aspeeday bit comes in I've no idea. It's not the usual sort of Enchanted Name at all and, as far as I can see, has no meaning or any relevance.'

'That's absolutely amazing,' Poll exhaled. 'And it has loads of relevance, actually. You see, A-s-p-i-d-e means serpent or snake.'

Billy's dark-brown eyes widened in admiration. 'Fancy you knowing that, Poll, love. That's very clever.'

Poll blushed at the compliment. 'I had an old-fashioned education.'

'Really?' Trixie frowned. 'And is Aspeeday Latin, then, dear?'

'Old English,' Poll said. 'You don't want to know how boring it was, but things learned by rote seem to stick, don't they?'

'They do, dear,' Trixie agreed. 'I still know all my times tables. And the fairies use a lot of Old English language—not that I'm au fait with it all, of course . . . but even if you're right—and I'm sure you are, dear—I still don't understand why a snake should be relevant to Ash.'

Poll nodded enthusiastically. 'It is, believe me. Oh, I don't mean in a sort of creepy way or that Ash is a viper in the bosom or a wicked tempting serpent as in Adam and Eve, but, and of course you couldn't possibly know this, he has a much-beloved pet snake called Roy.'

146

'Bloody hell!' Billy snorted. 'In the bedroom next to mine?'

Poll nodded. 'Very securely locked in.'

'Oh, good.'

Trixie smiled broadly. 'Really, dear? Oh, I am pleased! Fancy that! I've never been let down by my fairies before but I must admit I thought they'd got it wrong. Ash must love this, um, Roy very much for the fairies to have linked it to him in his name.'

'Oh, he does,' Poll assured her. 'Roy's the love of Ash's life.'

Oh dear, and if only that were completely true. Poll glanced along the table. Onyx's chair was empty and Ash and Ella were laughing together. Of course Ash loved Roy, but it really seemed tonight, having seen them together for the first time, that he loved Onyx too. Poor Ella. Even if she and Mark called a halt to their relationship, Ash was clearly off limits. Life was so unfair sometimes.

Abandoning the age-old complexities of the eternal triangle, Poll stood up. 'Now I really I must go and see to George—it's way past his bedtime and he'll be wanting his story. Trixie, thanks for the fairy names thing—it was fascinating. You must tell us more about the fairies really soon. But now we know about the names, does it mean we'll have to call each other Gossamer and Pumpkin all the time in future?'

Trixie shook her head. 'Definitely not, dear. Those names are only used when the Magic Comes Upon Us. Fairies are very secretive folk, you know.'

Billy laughed. 'Thank the Lord for that. And

your secret's safe with me, Trixie. I swear I'll never tell another living soul that I've got my very own fairy. Now, while Poll's getting young Georgie tucked up in bed, what say that we start clearing this table and sort out some coffee?'

'Good idea. You do the dishwasher, Mr Scoffer, and I'll make the coffee if someone tells me where everything is.' Trixie cast an arch glance at Billy. 'And it'll be just coffee, no herbal tinctures or magical fairy brews. At least, not this time.'

Billy laughed.

Poll beamed at them both. They seemed to be friendly enough again now. Phew. She gathered her voluminous skirts up and squeezed along the table, pausing behind Ella's chair. 'I'm just getting George off to bed then we'll have coffee in the garden.'

'Lovely.' Ella smiled up at her. 'It all went brilliantly, Poll. Happy now?'

Poll nodded, then glanced at the empty chair beside Ella and lowered her voice to a whisper. 'Where's Onyx? I didn't see her go.'

'She's just popped to the loo.'

'Oh, right. So, how are you getting on? With her—Onyx?'

Ella sighed. 'Oh, she's lovely—I mean, not just beautiful, but a really fab person too . . . And she's *clever*—and I really like her—sod it.'

Poll pulled a sympathetic face. 'I know—even from the little I've seen of her, I do too.' She raised her voice to a normal level. 'So, maybe if you could just help Trixie find the coffee stuff while I do George's bedtime?'

'Of course.' Ella nodded. 'And Ash can help Billy clear the table and stack the dishwasher.'

Ash looked across the table. 'Love to. And I will if he can hang on for a while. As soon as Onyx comes back from the loo we're going to pop upstairs to my room so that she can say hi to Roy again—she hasn't seen him for ages. Oh, and don't count us in for coffee, sorry. I'm running Onyx back to Winterbrook because she's working later tonight, and I've no idea when I'll be home.'

## Chapter Eighteen

'. . . so you see, dear,' Trixie said earnestly to Ella several days later as they, accompanied by all the dogs and most of the cats, collected eggs in the depths of the hens' coop, 'the fairies can help us all.'

'Mmm, I'm sure they can.' Ella pushed her hair behind her ears, adding another still warm egg to her basket. 'And it's all fascinating—especially the name thing. I quite like being Sunshine Strangeflower. But, maybe you shouldn't go on about them, the fairies that is, too much . . . you know, away from here.'

'In case people think I'm doolally?' Trixie straightened up. 'I'm used to that, dear. But you wait—one day I'll be able to show you just what the fairies can do. One day, when you need their help, they'll be there, then you won't doubt their existence.'

'Oh, I don't,' Ella said quickly, shutting the hen-house door behind them. 'I wouldn't dream of it.'

'Now you're teasing me,' Trixie said, smiling, as they made their way back towards the kitchen. 'But you wait. One day you'll believe in them as much as I do.'

Ella strongly doubted it, but she liked Trixie and certainly didn't want to hurt her feelings.

'The fairies are very much linked to flowers and plants and all things natural,' Trixie said happily as they trudged across the sun-baked garden. 'See— here—there's speedwell and cowslips and scarlet pimpernel just in this patch of grass.'

Ella, who knew nothing at all about wild flowers, stared at the arid ground. 'Really?'

'Yes, and they each have their own fairies—all dressed in bright blue and yellow and scarlet—and each fairy has a special day and a special magical task. They'll appear exactly when you need them most. So pretty. And they each have their own little magical song, too.'

'They do?'

'Oh, yes.'

Trixie suddenly grabbed her floral dirndl skirt in her one free hand, swished it from side to side in a carefree girlish manner, then threw back her tightly permed head and sang in a frighteningly high-pitched warble, 'Pretty speedwell blue as the sky/Pimpernel red is nature's spy/While cowslip yellow/Makes folk mellow/Tra-la-la.'

Trixie stopped singing and dropped a small curtsey. 'There's lots more verses, dear, and they should be three separate songs. I sort of concertina'd those three in together to give you some idea—and of course I didn't want to awaken the fairy magic.'

'Oh, of course not.' Ella stared at Trixie, completely stunned. 'Er, yes, lovely . . . And, er, each fairy has a flower and a song? How, um,

150

lovely.'

'Oh, it is, dear.' Trixie trotted happily towards the kitchen door. 'Oh, and that reminds me, I really must get a complete set of Cicely Mary Barker for young George.'

'Who?'

'The Flower Fairies, dear.' Trixie looked shocked. 'Surely you know all about the Flower Fairies? Cecily Mary had it spot on.'

'Ah, yes, I do know the Flower Fairies books.' Ella, still completely bewildered, nodded. 'Lovely, but I'm not sure they'll replace Thomas the Tank Engine in George's affections.'

'Maybe not—' Trixie hefted her egg basket on to the kitchen table '—but everyone should keep an open mind, don't you think? And it's always better to teach children these things from a really early age before cynicism sets in. Right, now I'm going to sort out my smalls—I do like a tidy knicker drawer, don't you, dear? What have you got planned?'

Blinking slightly at the sudden switch to such a prosaic subject, Ella shook her head. 'Um, nothing very exciting. Poll's just taken a cool box down to Billy in the barn so she'll be gone for ages, and it must be ninety degrees already, so I'm going to take George out in the car—probably to Fiddlesticks so we can paddle and have ice cream.'

'I'll happily join you on the first, but please don't mention the second,' Ash said with a laugh as he opened the kitchen door. 'I've already had enough of ice cream to last me a lifetime.'

Ella raised mocking eyebrows. 'After what, you lightweight? Less than a week?'

'Less than a week of the hottest days anyone can

ever remember,' Ash pointed out. 'When every man, woman and child wants ice cream. And wants it *now*. This is the hardest job I've ever had in my life. Give me a sweltering kitchen, a full restaurant and a homicidal chef any time.'

'Excuse me, dear.' Trixie eased past him in the doorway. 'I've got a lingerie drawer to sort out and a little herbal tincture with my name on it waiting upstairs.'

Ash chuckled, watching Trixie head for the staircase. 'Lingerie? And these herbal tinctures?'

'G and t I reckon,' Ella said. 'And who knows what Trixie's underwear is like.'

'Not a subject I want to spend much time pondering on, thanks.'

'Ash, she just sang at me.'

'Who? Trixie?'

'Yep. A song about fairies and flowers. It was really scary.'

'I can imagine. Wish I'd been there.'

'No, seriously, she really does believe in all this fairy magic stuff. She isn't—well—certifiable, is she?'

'I doubt it. No more than the rest of us.' Ash opened the fridge-freezer. 'Sorry, frozen furry thing alert—avert your eyes. I've just fed Roy.'

'Oh, ugh. And why aren't you at work?'

'I'm on lates today, lucky me.' Ash straightened up. 'Which means I have the joy of parking outside the schools this afternoon and being roundly abused by pock-faced lads who wanna win *X Fac'or* and plump girls whose life ambition is to marry a foo'baller. None of whom have ever learned to say please or thank you.'

'My-my.' Ella grinned. 'You do have a high

opinion of your customers, don't you?'

'Some of them are really lovely,' Ash admitted, 'and I am very grateful to have a job—any job—at last, but there's nothing like being exposed to the Great British Public en masse when they're hot and tired and irritable, and when I'm the same, to bring out the worst in all concerned. Which is why I was serious about coming out with you and George for a paddle.'

'Oh . . .' Ella hastily suppressed the beam of pleasure. 'Oh, OK then. But no criticism of my driving.'

'Sod it.' Ash pulled a face. 'You always spoil my fun.'

*     *     *

'We're lost,' Ella said half an hour later as they drove along yet another high-hedge, flower-filled lane. 'Aren't we?'

'Possibly, probably,' Ash said, turning to the back seat. 'George?'

George chattered and waved a small red plastic lorry to illustrate his theory.

'He says it isn't Fiddlesticks,' Ella said, peering through the windscreen. 'Thanks, George, but we knew that. Ooh, how annoying—just when I thought I'd got all these little lanes sussed.'

Her phone rang.

'Your phone's ringing,' Ash said helpfully. 'You should answer it. It might be *Dewberrys' Dinners* urging you to apply for the show before it's too late, *or*—and this is more likely—it might be Trixie's favourite Fairy Sat Nav to tell you exactly where you are.'

Laughing, Ella pulled into the side of the lane praying some tractor or other massive vehicle wouldn't come thundering from the other direction.

'If it's private, shall I get out?'

'No.' She glanced at the phone and sighed. 'It's Mark—and please stay there. Hi. Yes, fine, thanks. You? Oh, really? Good. . . . Yes, scorching here too. . . . Are you . . . ? With who? Oh, right. Have a nice time, then. Look, I can't talk now, I'm in the car. I'll ring you later, when you're back, OK? Bye.'

Pushing the phone back into her bag, she started the car again.

'I could have got out,' Ash said. 'I didn't want to spoil your chat. Poll told me—well, she told me that you had a boyfriend in London and, well, you must miss him.'

'Mmm, yes it's a bit odd being alone,' Ella said non-committally, hoping that Poll had kept her word and not divulged any of the rest of the Mark information. 'Still, we both agreed on me taking this job and it's hardly on the other side of the world, is it? And it's not for ever. Anyway, now we have more important things to think about.'

And definitely not about Mark, she thought sadly. Mark, it appeared, was missing her, but not enough to prevent him embarking on a stag weekend to Prague with the lads. Not, she thought, that it would have stopped him going even if they'd still been together.

George suddenly chattered happily from his booster seat.

'Did he just mention *Dewberrys' Dinners*?' Ash queried.

'No—he said we were going the wrong way. You're the one who keeps mentioning *Dewberrys' Dinners.*'

'Having withdrawal symptoms. Can't wait for the next series—especially as it's local. I wonder if they've chosen anyone yet?'

'Doubtful—' Ella pulled up at yet another minuscule and overgrown crossroads '—seeing as they haven't even reached the closing date for applications yet. Why? Do you want to apply?'

'Do you?'

'No, of course not.'

'Me neither.'

'OK—now, can you see any traffic from your direction?'

'Nothing. Just a lot of hedge . . . Go straight on and we'll find someone to ask.'

After a further five minutes of what seemed like driving through the Hampton Court maze, they emerged into fairly clear countryside and Ella gave a little yelp of recognition. 'I know where we are!'

'Fiddlesticks?' Ash said hopefully.

'Angel Meadows! I came here on my first day—I was lost then, too—and got directions to Hideaway. It's a funny place but it does have a shop of sorts, so we should be able to find someone to ask.'

And with any luck, not the odd couple of her first visit, Ella thought, turning the corner towards the Miracle Mart.

'Good God!' Ash exclaimed. 'Are they having a public hanging?'

Ella blinked as she stopped the car. There was a crowd, several deep, clustered round the Miracle Mart—and, more worryingly, an ambulance.

155

George whooped with delighted excitement at the sight of an unfamiliar vehicle.

'Stay there, sweetheart,' Ella said, undoing her seat belt.

'OK.' Ash grinned.

Laughing, with the relentless sun baking on her head, she made her way towards the back of the throng. Whatever was going on she really didn't want to be involved, but with so many people, someone surely would be able to tell her how to get to Fiddlesticks, wouldn't they?

'Excuse me.'

'Not now, duck.' A plump woman turned and scowled at her. 'Can't hear what's going on in there.'

'Oh, right—sorry—but I just wondered . . .'

A mass 'shush' was hissed by the crowd.

Ella, ignoring the glares of those nearest to her, wriggled her way through the perspiring throng. At least all those tedious rush-hour tube journeys had taught her a thing or two about using her elbows to their best advantage, and despite the massed efforts of the crowd to hamper her progress, she rapidly reached the front.

Squeezing in between two children of indiscriminate gender dressed in Manchester United replica shirts and a woman wearing a quilted housecoat and a chiffon scarf tied over a startling array of vibrantly coloured rollers, Ella tried again.

'Excuse me.' She looked hopefully at the roller woman beside her. 'I wondered if you could tell me—'

'What's going on in there right now?' The rainbow rollers jiggled alarmingly. 'That's what

156

we'd all like to know. We haven't had an update for ages. I only popped out for me sliced white—the kiddies won't eat any of that wholemeal stuff, disgusting the way they leaves them gritty bits in—and found Mrs Webb standing outside like the bloomin' Gestapo saying we wasn't allowed in.'

'Mrs Webb?' Ella queried. 'Is she the owner?

*Is she the owner*?' The roller woman looked aghast. 'You a newcomer round here? Course Mrs Webb owns the Mart. Did you see another shop anywhere for miles? No, you did not. Bloomin' monopoly Mrs Webb's got.'

'I can see that she must have, but—'

'Lovers Knot don't have a shop at all any more, hasn't done for years now, and the other little place here shut down eighteen months since. So everyone has to come to the Mart, see?'

Ella, really not wanting to get enmeshed in a heated political or social discussion on the wholesale closure of rural businesses, nodded. 'Yes—but could you tell me . . . ?'

'If you wants to do a proper big shop there's Hazy Hassocks, they've got all sorts there.' The roller woman was in full swing now. 'And course, there's Coddle's Post Office stores over in Bagley-cum-Russet, which is fine if you've got a car, which I haven't. We're not a two-car family and anyway I can't drive and my Pete has the car for work. So Bagley's no use to me, is it?'

Ella made sympathetic noises.

The rollers waggled. 'Or then there's the village shop over at Fiddlesticks, which is nearer and not too bad for walking—'

'Ah, yes, Fiddlesticks.' Ella pounced joyfully on the name. 'Now, please can you tell me—'

157

Roller woman ignored the interruption. 'But Mona Jupp what runs the Fiddlesticks shop, she's gone all Fortnum and Mason recently.'

'Really?' Ella said, trying to control her mounting irritated impatience. 'That must be lovely.'

'*Lovely?*'

'Yes, well, not that I've ever been able to afford to shop at Fortnum and Mason myself, but if there's a call for those sort of delicacies round here then it must be a good thing and—'

'*Good thing?*' Roller woman looked confused. '*Delicacies?* Mona Jupp don't do delicacies. She does bog-standard like everyone else. No, like I said she's gone Fortnum and Mason. Self-service! Self-service, I ask you. Lost a lot of trade because of it, she has. People don't want to be fiddle-faddling about with little baskets in a proper shop, do they? Stands to reason. If you wants self-service then you goes to a supermarket, don't you?'

'Yes, I suppose you do, but I'm not sure Fortnum and Mason—'

'So, when you go into a proper little shop you wants to stand at the counter and have a chat about this and that and then ask for what you wants. What do they get paid for? Standing behind the counter chatting and serving you—that's what. And there's no serving if you're helping yourself and putting stuff in your own little basket, is there?'

'Well, no, but—'

'So most of Mona Jupp's regulars have come over to the Miracle Mart, but they won't be standing for all this nonsense. I just wish they'd get a move on with it in there.'

158

So did Ella. Whatever it was.

'Um, so could you just tell me how—'

'And don't get me started on pubs.' The rollers jiggled. 'All gone. There's no pub for miles round any more. My Pete, he has to go to the Weasel and Bucket in Fiddlesticks for his pint.'

'Fiddlesticks—yes. Can you give me—'

'And because you can't drink and drive he has to walk and sometimes I don't see him until halfway through the next day. Scandalous, I call it.'

'Yes, I suppose it is. Coming home from the pub the next day and—'

'Not my Pete coming home the next day,' the roller woman said scornfully. 'The fact that we ain't go no pubs in our own villages no more.'

'Oh, right, yes, of course.' Ella sighed. Maybe she should try a different tack? 'Um, so what's happening in the shop here, then?'

'Fat Stacey—her with the black and white hair what used to work at Londis—she's gone into labour by the dog biscuits.'

'Oh, dear, poor thing. Is that why the ambulance—'

The rollers agreed vigorously. 'Mrs Webb panicked if you ask me. No need for an amberlance. Fat Stacey has got at least five kiddies already. She'd probably have had time to finish her shopping, get home and have a nice bath and a bacon sandwich, then catch the bus into Winterbrook hospital before anyone needed to start boiling water and fetching towels.'

'Is that what they're doing in there at the moment, then?'

'As far as we can tell. Well, Mrs Webb is. She came out all puffed up to tell us when she barred us all from going in. Not that she'd know what's what, being childless, but she watches a lot of soaps, see, so she's always getting the wrong end of the stick so to speak. Doubt if the paramedics want boiled water unless it's for a cuppa. Pointless.'

'Yes, I suppose it is. But I'm trying to get to—'

The rollers quivered. 'If Fat Stacey's that far gone they might as well just let her get on with it and let the rest of us get on with our shopping.'

Ella nodded. 'But if she's in labour—'

'Yes, but like I said, it's only by the dog biscuits. In the far corner. We wouldn't bother her at all. We mostly only wants bread and milk. We could all skirt round her.'

A piercing scream tore through the gloriously bucolic morning. Ella winced and hoped George hadn't heard it. The Manchester United children looked excited.

'Won't be long now, thank the Lord,' roller woman said. 'My kiddies need their sliced white. It's one of their five-a-day.'

Ella felt too shell-shocked to query this remark. She tried not to listen to the horrendous noises echoing from the Miracle Mart. 'Er, look, while you're waiting, could you tell me how to get to Fiddlesticks from here, please?'

The rollers danced under their chiffon. 'Is that all you wanted? No shopping? Then why didn't you say so—Ah! Here they come!'

Ella, perspiration prickling her scalp and trickling down her back, stood aside as the paramedics emerged from Miracle Mart ministering to a large girl with badly striped black and blonde hair slumped in a wheelchair.

'Gas and air, lucky cow,' roller woman sighed

enviously. 'I could do with some of that. Good luck, Stace!'

The cry was taken up by the rest of the crowd which parted like the Red Sea to allow the procession through. Stacey, still sucking greedily, waved a regal hand like the Queen on the Mall as her wheelchair was expertly manoeuvred into the ambulance.

Everyone cheered as it roared away.

'Right!' A box-shaped woman in a floral wrap-over and ankle boots who, Ella knew, simply had to be the redoubtable Mrs Webb, stood in Miracle Mart's doorway. 'Excitement over. Let's have you in an orderly queue. There's people here desperate for their cigs and *Sun*s. And you—' she gestured at the Manchester United children '—Jay-Zee and Dizzy Crumpshall, you can go to the back of the line. You only wants to look at the mucky mags and I keep telling you we don't stock 'em.'

Ella giggled. 'Jay-Zee and Dizzy? Who on earth would give their kids names like that?'

The roller woman went ominously still. 'People like me and my Pete, actually.'

'Ah, right.'

'And we've got P Diddy and Li'l Kim at home too. Lovely names, they are. Modern.'

'Er, um, oh, yes, they are,' Ella said quickly. 'Lovely. And so unusual. Well, thanks for your help, um, I must dash.'

Hysterically, she hurled herself back into the car. George was making ambulance-siren noises, aided and abetted by Ash.

'What the hell was all that about?' Ash stopped nee-nawing and looked at her.

161

Ella started the car. 'Don't ask.'

'And did you get directions?'

She shook her head.

'Are you crying?'

'Laughing—I think.' The car bucketed away from the Miracle Mart. 'Hold tight—and for God's sake don't look back.'

## *Chapter Nineteen*

'We're just like a proper family now, aren't we?' Poll said happily to the dogs as she pegged out the following week's washing in the early morning's blazing sun. 'Sharing everything, getting together over dinner to talk about our day, but still respecting one another's privacy. It's working out just wonderfully, isn't it?'

The dogs wagged lethargic tails, too sleepy with the never-ending heat to argue.

'And I do hope Ella will want to stay until the three months are up,' Poll said, finally anchoring the last pillowcase to the line. It had bothered her because the pillowcase was navy blue and she only had green pegs left which wouldn't go with it at all, so she'd had to undo the cream towel, remove its pale-blue pegs, swap them over and start again. 'I know she must miss her Mark dreadfully, and of course I hope they sort things out, but not yet . . .'

The dogs thumped their tails again.

'And I must ring the solicitor and see where the contract has got to. She hasn't signed anything yet, but I love her so much, and she's just so wonderful with George, and it would break my heart if she decided to leave early.'

She hung the peg bag on the line and picked up the washing basket. The dogs rolled over in the welcome shade of the washing hanging listlessly on the line and blissfully closed their eyes.

Drifting back to the kitchen, Poll paused in the doorway. George and Ella were busily mixing something in a large bowl at the table. They both had expressions of fierce concentration on their faces and were totally immersed in their task.

What an absolute tragedy it would be, Poll thought, that Ella—if she and Mark got back together—might be denied children of her own.

'Hi,' she said. 'And what are you two making?'

'Fairy cakes,' Ella said, wiping a floury hand across her face. 'In Trixie's honour. We're going to put red and blue and yellow icing on them and call them scarlet pimpernel, speedwell and cowslip.'

Poll pushed the washing basket away and laughed. 'Ah, yes, I've been given the wildflower fairies routine, too. That's a nice idea, but you haven't forgotten that George is due to go to Doll Blessing's this morning, have you?'

'No.' Ella shook her head. 'We're going to put the mixture in the fridge now and finish them off later. George can't wait to play with Doll's brood.'

'No, it's nice of her to ask him. I know he's happy here, but he does need to mix with other children before he starts playgroup—and Doll, love her, has plenty of those. Blimey, though, it's so hot, isn't it?'

'Baking,' Ella sighed. 'It's practically impossible to sleep at night now as well, even with the fan going.'

Poll shuddered. 'I know. And the minute you

163

have a shower you need another one. Everyone is getting so scratchy. Right—I'm going to take some iced juice down to the barn for Billy . . . Oh, Ella, there's a shopping list on the pinboard—if you've got time when you go into Hassocks . . . ?'

'No problem. I'll drop George off first, then I'll be delighted to plunge into Big Sava—it's ice-cold in there with the air-con going full blast. I'll probably be in there for hours. Although I know I've promised to make a start on sorting out your paperwork.'

'You take as long as you like in Big Sava.' Poll smiled. 'And don't make me feel guilty about tackling the paperwork—it's total chaos.'

'I'm looking forward to it.' Ella grinned. 'It'll be nice to be doing some clerical work again, knowing that it's only temporary.'

'Don't speak too soon.' Poll shook her head. 'You haven't seen the paper mountain I've accumulated. I'm so very grateful to you for even offering to give it a go—oh, look, if you'll brave the correspondence muddle, please don't worry about collecting George again at lunchtime. I'll do that. I always like a chat with Doll to catch up with what Mitzi and Lulu are up to.'

'OK, thanks.' Ella ripped off cling film with her teeth and fastened it over the cake mixture bowl. 'Right, George, we'll pop this in the fridge and finish them later. Let's go and get you ready for the delights of Doll Blessing's paddling pool.'

With a whoop of excitement, George slid from his chair and scampered out of the kitchen with Ella in—literally—hot pursuit.

\*     \*     \*

164

'My word!' Poll said, twenty minutes later, as she walked into the largest barn's deliciously dark and cool interior. 'It looks like a proper building now. You've worked miracles!'

'Hardly, love,' Billy said, looking up from his improvised workbench, 'but I'm getting there. I'm really enjoying myself in here. And it's great to feel useful again.'

Poll set the jug of juice and glasses down, sat on a handy ancient hay bale sending clouds of dust into the solid air, and inhaled. 'I can't believe how much work you've done in such a short time—oh, and I love the smell of the fresh sawdust.'

'Me too. Budge up a bit.' Billy, joining her on the hay bale, drank a glass of juice straight down. 'Thanks, Poll, that certainly hit the spot. You're a great lass.'

Poll blushed.

Billy looked up into the barn's towering rafters. 'So, when we've got this all shipshape, and the electrics in, what are your plans for it?'

'No idea, really. I think, once upon a time, I thought it could be a sort of accommodation extension—you know—if I ever managed to have too many people in the house and could afford to expand, but I haven't got anything definite in mind. It's just lovely to see it all cleaned out and repaired and looking—well—like it might actually be something. I'm so grateful to you.'

'I'm the one that's grateful.' Billy smiled, the smile crinkling the corners of his gentle brown eyes. 'And always will be. And where's young George this morning? He usually likes to trot down here with you to see what's going on.'

165

'Oh, he's far too busy to be Bob the Builder this morning.' Poll laughed. 'He's been making fairy cakes with Ella and she's just taking him off to wallow in Doll Blessing's paddling pool with her brood, then Ella's doing the shopping and coming back here to sort out my paperwork.' She sighed. 'Do you know, I've just been worrying a bit about Ella. What if she wants to leave? It would be too awful to even think about, but the solicitor hasn't sent her contract yet and—'

'Then I'd suggest you chase it up. Ella seems very happy here to me but it's as well to get these things sorted out. Just make the phone call in case the contract has got lost in the post—that's all you have to do. Simple, love.'

Poll sighed. 'You make it sound so easy.'

'That's because it is. Don't do yourself down, Poll. Just because your Dennis found fault all the time it's knocked the confidence out of you. You're doing a great job here, love. A great job. And as long as you're not out of pocket by any of this . . .'

'Oh, no. Definitely not. It's all working out wonderfully.' Poll gazed at him. 'Do you really think I'm doing a great job?'

'The best. I can honestly say I've never been happier in my life.'

'Neither have I. And—' Poll, delighted that Billy thought she was making a success of something for the first time in her life, smiled happily '—Ash has got a job and has settled in nicely, and I think Trixie's OK too. She sings a lot.'

Billy chuckled. 'Ah, pity she can't hold a tune though . . . Still, we haven't heard too much more about her fairies recently, have we? And she's

166

managed to cook herself some decent meals without setting the place on fire, so let's be thankful for small mercies.' He straightened his back. 'Do you know, I fancy a break from all this. It's getting too darn hot . . . so, why don't you and me take a little spin out in the country?'

'Oh, that'd be lovely but I don't think I should. It doesn't seem fair to leave Ella with the shopping and then all that correspondence to deal with. I should be here to help her.'

Billy laughed. 'I think young Ella will cope much better without you, to be honest. You'll just start oohing and aahing over old junk mail and not let her throw anything away.'

'You know me too well.'

'Maybe I'm getting there.'

Poll tried not to blush or jibber. It really wouldn't do to let Billy know that just the sound of his burring Berkshire voice sent little shivers down her spine, or that the twinkle in his dark, gentle eyes turned her knees to jelly. That sort of stuff was for teenagers, not for silly old middle-agers like her.

They looked at one another. Then Billy reached out and squeezed her hand. 'Anyway, how about it, Poll? We can take a spin out, then collect young Georgie from his friends' place and be back here in time for a late lunch.'

Poll looked down at Billy's hand on hers and then up into his gentle brown eyes. 'Well, I told Ella I'd pick George up from Doll's, and he'd love it if you were there too.'

Billy smiled. 'He's a proper smasher is young George. Just the sort of lad I'd have wanted myself if things had been different. He's a great help when I'm down here doing my bits of DIY,

167

chatting away about this and that, not that I understand much of it yet—not like you and Ella—and always finding me the right tools. I love him to bits.'

And George loved Billy too, Poll knew. After having no father figure in his life she'd worried in case he'd be wary of having men in the house but he'd accepted both Ash and Billy with apparent delight. Especially Billy. Mainly, she supposed, because Billy was around all day and had all the time in the world to spend talking to George, explaining things to him, treating him as any proud father would treat his much-loved son. It was wonderful to see them together . . .

Poll dragged herself back from her rosy-tinted picture of the perfect family. 'We could have a little skive, couldn't we? Ash is at work, and Trixie said she was going to "top and bottom" her room so they won't need me on tap. Oh, yes, let's!'

Feeling like a truanting schoolgirl—not that she'd ever been one, of course, because she'd been far too biddable in her youth—Poll giggled as Billy took her other hand and pulled her to her feet. She was several inches taller than he was, but he was so strong, so comforting, so wonderfully kind.

'We make a good team, you and me,' Billy said gently, still holding her hands. 'I thought we would right from the minute we met at that first interview. And now we're proper friends—you've given me so much, Poll.'

'Me? I've given you a roof over your head—that's all. You've given me—oh, you've no idea what you've given me. Things that I thought I'd never have in a million years.'

'I'm not sure about that, but—' Billy reached up

168

and kissed her cheek '—all I want is to make you happy, love. You really deserve to be happy.'

Poll, wanting to touch her cheek with her fingers but not wanting to take her hands from Billy's, blinked back her tears. 'Oh, I am, believe me, I am.'

'Good.' Billy smiled at her and gently released her hands. 'Now I'll clear up here while you go and get yourself ready, and we'll go and have a little drive out.'

Poll, singing, rushed happily back to the farmhouse and galloped upstairs to change into her second-best going-out swirly skirt, embroidered gypsy top and sequinned flip-flops.

She knew now, thanks to Ella, that a spray of conditioner followed by a quick blast from the diffuser on the hairdryer would make her hair bouncy and full, and that a quick slick of mascara and lip gloss was all she needed to take a good decade off her face.

Although, she thought, studying herself in the dressing table's mirror, she already had very sparkly eyes and a very silly glow in her cheeks at the memory of Billy's chaste kiss and the thought of going for a spin in his disreputable car.

Dear me, all those years of never having a boyfriend, then the foolish marriage to Dennis, and then, when she least expected it, she'd fallen head over heels for a gentle, unassuming man who barely reached her shoulder and was certainly no George Clooney. And he seemed to feel the same way about her. What a wonderfully strange thing love was . . .

She'd liked Billy as soon as they'd met, and now, having shared the house with him and got to know

169

him, the liking had turned into something far, far more important.

Poll took a final look at herself. Yes, she'd do. Grabbing her beaded bag, she almost skipped along to Trixie's room.

'Just letting you know Billy and I are popping out and collecting George from his friends, and we'll be back in time for lunch,' she called through the open door. 'I'm not expecting anyone, and the postman's already been so you shouldn't be disturbed. Is there anything you want while I'm out?'

Trixie, dressed in her house-working clothes, appeared flapping a multicoloured feather duster exactly, Poll thought, like a fairy wand. 'No thanks, dear. Oh, you look very pretty. No, I'm well stocked up with everything and having a lovely time cleaning and tidying. I'm very grateful to you, Poll, dear, for giving me this lovely home—you do know that, don't you?'

Poll, suddenly in love with the entire world, gave the diminutive Trixie a swift hug. The feather duster stuck to her lip gloss.

Poll unpeeled it. 'It's, er, lovely to have you here. I'm just glad you're happy.'

'Ever so happy.' Trixie extricated herself from the hug. 'And would you like me to get lunch ready while you're out?'

Pushing away all thoughts of an impending incendiary accident, Poll nodded bravely. 'That'd be great, thanks, if you don't mind. But perhaps, as it's so hot, something cold would be best? Ella should be back soon, too, so that'll be five of us for lunch. Maybe we could have it in the garden. I'll leave it to you. I won't be long, anyway.'

170

And still smiling, swinging her handbag, Poll skittered happily down the staircases.

'You look really pretty,' Billy said approvingly as he opened the door of the cowpat Allegro for her. 'But, I hope you don't mind me asking, love, have you just eaten a budgie? You've got blue and yellow feathers all round your mouth.'

## Chapter Twenty

Ella, having delivered George to Doll Blessing and now driving away from Hazy Hassocks with the week's stock-up shopping, stopped at a zebra crossing. Hand-in-hand couples zigzagged in front of the car. Briefly she wondered if Mark was back from Prague. She supposed he must be—unless it had turned into the longest stag weekend on record. With a jolt she realised she hadn't spoken to him for ages. She still missed him, still missed being part of a couple, but the initial hurt of their parting was fading.

It was almost, she thought, as she turned on to the Fiddlesticks road, as if her previous life only existed in some parallel universe. And she knew she'd be happy to stay at Hideaway and be part of the family for the entire three months now. No question. What would happen when the three months were up, she had no idea. She certainly hadn't changed her mind, knowing now that working with children, and having her own eventually, was all that mattered to her. Maybe Mark would have changed his mind though. Maybe he'd take her back on any terms—simply because he'd found it impossible to live without her.

If only . . .

And then there was Ash—and Onyx. Ella had slid easily into the role of Ash's best mate, buddy, fellow-Roy-admirer, and all round good chum. And of course Onyx was as lovely as she'd first seemed, and had, since she made occasional visits to Hideaway, been very friendly.

And the solace of the countryside had quickly become familiar, and after one visit, the traffic and noise and bustle of Winterbrook, which wasn't a very big town really, had made Ella wince and long for the peace and tranquillity of Hideaway Farm.

It was all very strange. Mark and London belonged to some other time, on some other planet. It was like she'd been sucked into some delightful Berkshire Brigadoon . . .

Singing along to some ancient song on the car radio, Ella hoped George would have a great time with Doll's kids. It seemed very quiet without him and his plastic lorries and non-stop chattering in the car. And, despite the lure of the air con, the shopping in Big Sava had taken half the time— especially as there'd been no detour to Patsy's Pantry. However, it would be reassuring to get back to the farm and tell Poll that George had rushed off with merely a backward glance and causal wave to be surrounded by his noisy new gang of best friends.

So, this morning, now the shopping was done, all she had to do was sort out the post piled in the hall and the disaster zone of the three-legged table in the catastrophically untidy study that Poll called her desk.

172

With no computer and no mobile phone, Poll's life still revolved around Proper Correspondence. Consequently, both the hall table and the three-legged 'desk' were piled haphazardly high with envelopes, opened and unopened, of every shape and hue. Ella laughed to herself. Poll was the most disorganised person she'd ever met.

Pretty sure she now knew a short cut back to Hideaway Farm, Ella indicated towards Lovers Knot and drove confidently along the narrow road. Oh, yes, disorganised Poll might be, but she was definitely the kindest person in the world. She'd made not only her, but also Trixie and Ash and Billy feel effortlessly at home, and the odd collection of such different personalities had melded well together. It really was like a proper family now.

Oooh, no . . . not again . . .

Ella frowned. She really had to stop frowning so much. Especially as Onyx had the smoothest skin she'd ever seen. Botox, she'd reckoned, but Onyx had laughed and said no, her complexion was one of the few good things she'd inherited from her apparently extremely bad-tempered and therefore non-stereotypical Caribbean grandmother.

However, Ella felt on this occasion, a frown was warranted.

Having been daydreaming and not concentrating on the road signs, she must have taken a wrong turning after the one for Lovers Knot . . . Where was she? Wasn't this single-track lane dangerously close to the frightening Mrs Webb's Miracle Mart in Angel Meadows? She was pretty sure it was, and now she was waiting in a queue of traffic, OK then, behind two other cars, but it passed for a queue in the countryside.

Peering crossly through the windscreen and swearing that next time she'd stick to the tried and tested route, Ella frowned again.

There was a familiar flash of colour up ahead.

Neapolitan stripes: green, cream and pink.

Surely not?

Ella peered through the windscreen again. Yep, it certainly looked like it. And, yes, she thought as she moved forwards another couple of inches, it was.

Ash's Maxi's ice-cream van, complete with its huge phallic cornet on the roof. Parked in a lay-by at the side of the road.

And he wasn't alone.

Ella nudged the car slowly forwards to the junction. There was a second ice-cream van parked facing Ash's. This one was blue and white and also sported an impossibly large cornet rampant on its roof. They looked like stags at bay.

And Ash, looking disgustingly gorgeous despite the silly hat and a rather ill-fitting white jacket, was standing on the lay-by, having what looked like a fairly animated discussion with the other vendor who, while being several inches shorter than Ash, was much, much wider.

Had Ash, unfamiliar with the business, inadvertently encroached on the territory of a rival?

Oooh, Ella, thought. Ice-cream wars! Here, in the deepest of the deep Berkshire countryside.

She immediately pulled the car to the side of the road, clearly much to the annoyance of the perma-tanned, hair-extensioned would-be WAG in the sports car behind her, and leaped out.

Ouf! The heat was intense. The scorching sun spiralled from the road, bounced from the high hedgerows, and dazzled from the dusty verges. This was surely going to be the barbecue summer to beat all barbecue summers. For once Ella thanked Poll's hippy-chick influence on her wardrobe. The long floaty skirt and brief cotton top were perfect for a June heatwave.

If my friends could see me now, she thought cheerfully, as, tucking her long, unstraightened hair behind her ears, she flip-flopped her way towards the ice-cream vans. Not a designer label in sight. Nothing more than lip gloss and mascara on her face. Her city friends would probably have a fit.

As she approached the ice cream vans, she was aware of a crowd gathering on the far side. How weird the countryside was. People appeared from nowhere. There were no parked cars and very few houses along the route, but there were still people everywhere.

'Hi!' She approached Ash and the other ice-cream seller. 'Is this a private fight or can anyone join in?'

They turned and stared at her.

Ash grinned. 'Oh, hi, Ella, where the heck did you spring from?'

'Got lost coming back from Hazy Hassocks, saw you and the van—and him—' Ella nodded towards the other vendor '—and thought you might need some help.' She turned her attention to the second ice-cream man. 'Leave him alone. Look, I know you must be guarding your territory, but give him a break, can't you? He's new to the job, and the area, and I'm sure he didn't mean to stray on to

175

your patch. I'm sure there's plenty of room for both of you—there's no need to resort to violence.'

'Er, no,' the second vendor said, 'I'm sure there isn't.'

'Good,' Ella said. 'So, if Ash apologises to you, and you explain to him that this is your pitch and he leaves, that'll be an end to it, won't it?'

'Well, yes, but—'

'Good,' Ella repeated, amazed that the negotiations had gone so easily. She really should have a job with ACAS if not with the United Nations. She held out her hand. 'Thank you. That's very magnanimous of you. I'm Ella Maloney.'

'Mike Sparrow.'

They shook hands. It was at this point that she realised Ash was laughing.

'What's so funny?'

'You. I never realised you could be so fierce. And much as I appreciate your support, there's no need.'

'There's every need,' Ella said crossly. 'I hate bullies.'

'Hold up,' Mike Sparrow interrupted. 'I ain't a bully.'

Ella snorted. 'Well, you would say that, wouldn't you? It looked like you were being very bullying to me.'

'Ella,' Ash said gently. 'We weren't fighting. Mike's a friend.'

'Oh.'

Mike Sparrow chuckled. 'Ah, we just met up. I'm off to Bagley-cum-Russet—wouldn't touch this pitch with a double cone plus two flakes. Angel Meadows—blimey, they've got some odd 'uns here

176

and no mistake.'

Ella knew she was blushing. It probably clashed wonderfully with her rapidly turning gingery hair. Sod it. 'Oh, right, but it looked as if—'

'And it was very kind of you to stop and fight my corner,' Ash said, still grinning, 'but Mike and I aren't ice-cream rivals. We weren't going to challenge each other to a duel. There was going to be no Mivvis at a hundred paces at dawn. We're old friends. We belong to the same club.'

Oh, I bet you do, Ella thought crossly. The one where Onyx undulates in a state of undress and sad blokes like you leer.

She shrugged. 'Really? Which club's that, then? The Peppermint Rhino?'

'Spearmint,' Ash corrected, 'and no. Mike and I are actually fellow reptile owners.'

'Oh.'

'We were comparing notes on Roy and his Burmese python, Linda.'

'*Linda*?'

'After me ex-wife,' Mike explained. 'Mind, the ex-wife was a lot more vicious than the python.'

Despite her deep embarrassment, Ella chuckled.

'So, you can see there was no turf war breaking out. Still, now you're here,' Ash said, 'you could make yourself useful—if you wanted to. Unless you've got to dash back to Hideaway for any reason?'

Oooh, let me think. Time spent in the sun with Ash or alone in Hideaway Farm with a mountain of someone else's letters?

Ella tried not to look too keen. 'No, just the glories of sorting out Poll's desk. As it's probably all been there for months, I'm sure it can wait for another hour or so.'

'Brilliant—then if you could help me out for a while I'd be eternally grateful.' Ash indicated the growing knot of people sweltering in the sun. 'I've got quite a queue here and I'm still not quite up to speed on the new soft ice-cream machine. Mike's had a look but it's even got him flummoxed.'

'Good luck with it then, mate.' Mike Sparrow grinned. 'And like I say, Angel Meadows is one weird place. And—' he smiled at Ella '—it was lovely to meet you at last. Ash is always talking about you.'

'Is he?' Ella tried not to do a little happy dance inside. 'All good I hope?'

'Oh, yes. Down at the Snakes, Lizards and Dragons club we're getting pretty jealous of him being on such, um, close . . . terms with an exotic dancer.'

Bugger.

As Mike trundled away in his blue and white van, tantalisingly playing a tinny version of 'O Sole Mio' to the perspiring crowd, Ash smiled at her. 'If you just climb up into the back here and put that jacket on—oh, and wash your hands—got to be careful about Elfin Safety these days.'

'Now you sound like Trixie,' Ella giggled, squeezing into the ice-cream van, and trying to do up the jacket and rinse her hands at the same time. 'Oooh, sorry, it's a bit snug in here.'

'Don't mind me,' Ash said cheerfully as she brushed against him, 'I'm more than happy.'

Ella exhaled. Goodness, it was hot in here . . .

'Right.' Ash leaned over her shoulder, tantalisingly close to her. So close that she could smell the warm, lemony scent of him, and see the freckles dusted beneath his skin. 'There's a list of what's what up there with all the prices—some of the ice creams have odd names so you'll probably need to look them up. The till is manual and bad-tempered so mind your fingers. The lollies and ready-made ices are in this freezer here . . . and the wafers, cones and flakes are all in here . . . and if anyone wants a Maxi's Swirler—which is the soft ice cream—you have to use the new machine, which tends to have a mind of its own and takes ages to get right and therefore leads to a bit of a snarl-up with customers and then they all turn nasty. Which, in turn, is why I need you.'

Delighted to be needed by Ash—even if it was only to operate a recalcitrant ice-cream machine—Ella smiled happily.

Ash pushed the silly hat to the back of his head. He still managed to look heart-stoppingly sexy. 'So, you're OK for an hour?'

Very, very OK, Ella thought. 'Um, yes, fine. I'm really glad I can help out, but is it allowed? Won't you get into trouble having me serving? Aren't we breaking all the EU employment laws?'

'Probably, but who's to know? I'm not telling if you're not. And I really could do with some help—just until I get to grips with that machine. I need this job—and my sales targets are massively high and I'll never reach them if I don't get my full quota of Swirlers.'

'Oh, sales targets,' Ella groaned. 'Don't talk to me about sales targets. Doesn't matter if it's advertising space or ice cream there's always going to be some Suit scanning your figures and saying, "Must do better." Been there, failed dismally, ran away from it.'

179

Ash laughed. 'Can't imagine you running away from anything, somehow.'

Ooh. Ella hugged herself. Was that a compliment?

'OK, walked very, very quickly.' Ella looked out at the Angel Meadows crowd which, now restless, had somehow organised itself into a ragged queue. 'Er, I suppose we ought to start dishing up ice cream before your sales targets melt completely. OK, here goes . . .'

Leaning from the little window, with Ash only inches away, Ella beamed at the first person peering into the van.

'Don't I know you?' The woman with the extravagantly bouffant hair squinted upwards. 'You from Fiddlesticks?'

Ella shook her head at Roller Woman—now without the rollers or her embryo rappers—and continued beaming. 'No, we met outside the Miracle Mart. When, um, there was the hoo-ha with the lady in labour . . . You told me how to get to Fiddlesticks.'

'Ah, yes! Found it, did you? Good. Mind, you never said you was selling ice creams that day. My kiddies would have loved an ice cream. And oooh—' she eyed Ash lasciviously '—he's pretty damn sexy, isn't he? I wouldn't kick him out of bed anytime soon. In fact, I'd leave my Pete tomorrow to work in a little van with him. Blimey, love, you're not so daft, are you?'

Ella giggled. 'Um, what can I get you?'

'Well, if it's not him naked on a plate covered with chocolate and cream,' Roller Woman continued to stare at Ash, 'I'll have three Bazoomas, two Splashy Scoffs and a Swirler cone with double flakes and strawberry sauce—no nuts. The kids are all allergic.'

Squeezing past Ash who was chuckling and serving the next person in the queue—a very old woman wearing a sun hat tied with mismatched ribbons under her whiskery chin—Ella added up in her head as she went, diving into the freezers, consulting the list—blimey, it was harder than she'd thought it would be.

'There.' She handed the ices to Roller Woman and turned to operate the soft ice cream's levers and buttons. 'Just the cornet to do now . . . Have you heard what happened to, er, sorry, forgotten her name—the girl having the baby?'

'Fat Stacey?' Roller Woman skilfully manhandled her ice creams. 'Had a boy. In the amberlance. On a lay-by on the A34. Mind, it wouldn't be the first time Stace's been legs apart in a lay-by on the A34.'

Ella sniggered and grabbed the soft ice lever.

Roller Woman nodded her elaborate hairdo. 'She's called him Clint. She says it's after one of the parrermedickals. We all reckons it's after that cowboy builder what came to do her gutters back last autumn. Mother and baby doing well—Oops, love. Mind what you're doing.'

Soft ice cream squirted merrily up Ella's arms, down her tunic and on to the floor. With a little scream, she leaned on the lever.

Ice cream cascaded across the van in a projectile spurt.

'Down for on! Up for off!' Ash yelled, trying not to laugh.

'What? Oooh—sorry—mind out!'

Too late.

181

A whoosh of sticky gunge spat non-stop across the tiny interior and glooped down every bit of Ash that was available, hovered teasingly for a moment, then slithered on to the floor.

'Eeek! Sorry.' Ella bit her lip. 'Oh, look, it's all over you.'

'Not quite *all* over.'

Still giggling, they mopped up what they could with paper towels and slid and slipped round the tiny space.

Trying very hard not to touch him too much, Ella shook her head. 'I really am sorry. I was laughing so much I just got a bit muddled about which button was on and which was off.'

'The story of my life,' Ash said, licking his fingers in a way that made Ella go quite unnecessarily warm. 'Anyway, it's fine. It's vanilla. I like vanilla. Can't stand the pistachio.'

Abandoning Roller Woman's cone, Ella tried again. As Ash was still slowly licking ice cream from his fingers it was very hard to concentrate.

This time, having got to grips with the controls, the ice cream swirled out in a satisfying peak. With a squelch of strawberry sauce and two flakes rammed into the resulting mess, Ella triumphantly handed it over.

Roller Woman paid—all in small change—and, with a final red-hot look at Ash, elbowed her way out of the queue.

Wiping soft ice cream from her face and between her fingers, Ella grinned at Ash. 'Sorry, er, you've still got some in your hair.'

'So have you. Maybe we should do mutual grooming?'

They stared at one another.

182

'Three Ninety-nine Swirlers please, duck, when you've a-finished your courting—some of us are wilting out here.'

Ella dragged her gaze away from Ash, selected three cornets with trembling hands, and after two false starts, managed to produce three reasonable cones.

'Great.' Ash, still picking bits of congealing ice cream from his fabulous eyelashes, smiled. 'Looks like you've got the hang of it. Only another nine thousand customers to serve and we might be able to belt back to Hideaway and get this lot showered off.'

Pushing very, very vivid images of showers and smeared ice cream to the deep, dark recesses of her mind, Ella concentrated. Almost.

'Are you really OK doing this?' she asked, her voice muffled by the freezer as she reached for a clutch of Bazoomas. 'Selling ice creams? I mean, you're a chef.'

'Qualify that with unemployed and broke.' Ash sprinkled crushed nuts on to an oyster ice. 'And, yes, now I'm getting used to it a bit more. As a stopgap it'll do me fine. Ask me again in the depths of winter if I haven't got a restaurant job by then and I might say differently.'

Ella hauled herself from the freezer and leaned out of the window. 'Will you still be at Hideaway in the winter, do you reckon?'

'Probably. I can't see anything else on the horizon—and I love it there.'

'Me too. But I'll be leaving in August.'

'Will you? Why? Poll loves you, and so does George.'

'George will start playgroup in September.'

183

'Yes, but surely that won't be all day? And you're hard-working, funny, easy-going.'

Stunning, sexy and desirable might have been better, Ella thought, but as accolades went, those weren't too bad at all.

'Because I'm only on a three-month contract, which I haven't actually signed yet, and—'

'And there's the boyfriend and another life back in London.' Ash picked up a box of cones and ripped it open. 'Of course, I'd forgotten that you weren't a permanent fixture like the rest of us. I've . . . well, I've got used to having you around.'

'Thanks.' Confused, she played it for laughs and gave a mock curtsey, which was pretty difficult in the confined space. 'You're too, too kind.'

He grinned at her. 'No I'm not, I've got a nasty streak like everyone else, but I'm always honest.'

As the sun spiralled on to the van, the temperature inside soared. Sweating and sticky, with Ash pressed up beside her, Ella had never been happier in her life.

Eventually the Angel Meadows crowd dwindled away.

'Thanks.' Ash wiped his face on his sleeve. 'You were great. I couldn't have managed that lot alone without there being a riot.'

'Even though I've made you look like you only need a flake in each ear to make you into a walking, talking cornet?'

'Yeah, well, there are always drawbacks to any job.'

Ella concentrated on unpeeling now rigid strands of hair away from her cheeks. 'I had no idea selling ice creams was such hard work.'

'It isn't, usually. Most places are fairly

184

uneventful. But they're pretty cut off round here and on a day like this every man and his dog wants a Bazooma or a Splashy Scoff, or, sadly, a Swirler. Right, back to Hideaway, I think, to get cleaned up and maybe grab a bite to eat before my next stint. God, I'm really, really sticky, are you?'

Knowing there was no decent answer she could make to that remark, Ella simply nodded, tugged off the ice-cream-spattered jacket, and scrambled from the Maxi's van.

Ugh, she thought, as she started her car, her fingers were all stiff and encrusted. Disgusting. Then, following Ash and the cornet rampant in the direction of Hideaway Farm, and feeling very, very hot and very, very uncomfortable, she gave a huge whoop of delight.

It had been the best fun ever . . .

They were just turning into Cattle Drovers Passage when Ella noticed Billy's cowpat Allegro ahead of them.

She smiled to herself. George was waving from the back seat.

She waved back. Poll stuck a languid arm from the passenger side too. How lovely, Ella thought. Poll, Billy and George together. Like a real little family. Of course Billy was a bit older than Poll, but that didn't matter a jot. She really, really hoped that they'd realise soon that they were simply made for each other.

She sighed as she turned into the farmyard. If only her own love life was as simple to resolve.

Oh . . .

There was a strange car parked outside the farmhouse. A sleek silver car. And Trixie, accompanied by the dogs, cats and two chickens,

185

was standing in the doorway at the top of the stone steps looking agitated.

Dear God, Ella thought, parking between Billy's Allegro and the Maxi's van, don't let her have done something awful like burned the kitchen down or fricasséed Roy . . .

'Visitors?' Poll queried, blinking at the car then squinting at Ella in the full glare of the sun. 'Were we expecting anyone? Was there anything in the diary? And what happened to you—oh, and Ash? You're both all sticky and crusty.'

'Don't ask and, no, we weren't expecting anyone.'

Billy and Ash, emerging from their respective drivers' seats, also looked puzzled. George, having no such worries about unexpected visitors, simply hurled himself at the dogs, cats and hens, then finally at Trixie, clamouring about his paddling pool adventures and begging for his lunch.

'Thank heavens you're back.' Trixie flapped her hands at them all. 'You said you weren't expecting anyone but they seemed to think you were so I've put them in the family sitting room. I hope that's all right, dear? I said you wouldn't be long. I wasn't sure what else to do with them.'

Ella looked at Poll. Poll looked at Billy.

Ash looked at Trixie. 'Who, Trixie? Who have you put in the sitting room?'

Trixie shrugged. 'Don't rightly know their names, dear, although they did tell me. Something strange like Alphonse and Dee-Dee I think. They said they'd written and made a date for today.'

Ella and Ash exchanged bewildered glances.

'More waifs and strays?' Billy queried, looking at Poll. 'You didn't mention you'd invited more.'

186

'I haven't. And I don't know anyone called Alphonse and Dee-Dee,' Poll said. 'And if they'd written a letter I'd have answered it.'

No you wouldn't, Ella thought. It was probably still sitting, unopened, in the teetering pile on the three-legged table waiting to be sorted. By her.

'Where are they from, Trixie? Did they tell you?'

Trixie brightened. 'Oh, yes. Didn't I say, dear? It's really exciting, dear. They're from *Dewberrys' Dinners*.'

## Chapter Twenty-one

There was a stunned silence in the farmyard. Everyone looked at everyone else.

Ella, although totally wrong-footed, found her voice first. 'Poll . . . ?'

'I didn't know it was today they were coming. The letter said the ninth.'

'Today is the ninth. You've still left the calendar on Derwentwater, haven't you?'

Poll nodded.

'After everything you said, you *wrote* to them?' Ella asked, shocked. 'You've applied to be on *Dewberrys' Dinners*?'

Poll nodded again.

'And they wrote back and you *opened* the letter?'

'Well, yes—' Poll looked embarrassed '—I did, actually. You see, I was waiting for the reply, and I recognised the logo—I didn't want anyone to see it. Especially if it was a no thank you. I, um, didn't want anyone to know I'd written.'

'Er.' Billy cleared his throat. 'Actually, I rang 'em

187

up.'

'I emailed,' Ash said softly.

Ella grinned. 'OK—and I sent a text.'

They looked at one another and laughed. The laughter bordered on hysterical.

Trixie stared at them all. 'What's going on, dears? Would someone please explain to me what's going on?'

'Later,' Poll said, suddenly looking very excited. 'Later, I promise I'll tell you everything, Trixie. Right now, I suppose we ought to go and meet, um, Alphonse and Dee-Dee.'

'Maybe Ella and I should get cleaned up first,' Ash said.

'No time,' Poll said airily. 'We've got to see them together. All for one and one for all. Come along.'

Ella and Ash exchanged amused glances. Poll, for once, seemed fully in command of the situation.

They trooped into the peaches and cream sitting room, with Trixie, George and assorted animals bringing up the rear. Alphonse and Dee-Dee were sitting on one of the big squashy sofas.

One male, one female. One black, one white. Both thin. Both beautiful. One with a laptop. One with a clipboard and iPhone.

'I'm so sorry to have kept you waiting.' Poll stepped forward, holding out a hand. 'I'm Poll Andrews. I, um, was expecting you a little later.'

Ella tried not to laugh.

The man stood up and shook hands. 'We did say twelve thirty in the letter. And it took us ages to find you. We got lost—even with the sat nav. Hideaway is the right name for this place. Anyway, we're here now. I'm Anthony and this is Denise,

188

we're *Dewberrys' Dinners* researchers, and it's a pleasure to meet you at last.'

'And you.' Poll smiled. 'Now, can I get anyone a drink? Something to eat? It's so hot, isn't it? Would you like some iced lemonade? It's home-made.'

Please, Ella thought, surreptitiously scratching at the congealed ice cream in her crevices. Gallons of the stuff.

'No thank you,' Denise said briskly. 'We have our own supplies in the car. We're not here to be bribed by applicants.'

'It wasn't a bribe.' Billy rushed gallantly to Poll's defence. 'It was plain old-fashioned hospitality.'

Poll beamed at him.

Anthony frowned. 'We're running very late. We don't have time for hospitality, I'm afraid. Now, as you've applied to be on the programme, I'm assuming you know the basics. So—' he looked at the small crowd in the doorway then turned to Poll and nodded towards Billy '—you and your husband are a couple of the wannabe chefs, are you?'

'Oh, no,' Poll trilled happily, 'Billy's not my husband. My husband left me ages ago. And we all are. Chefs, that is, not husbands of course.'

Denise rose languidly to her feet, her eyes resting lustfully on Ash, who still looked drop-dead gorgeous despite his random coating of ice cream, in a predatory manner and for far longer than Ella liked. 'You mean the whole family cook? Including your children? And the grandson? And your mother?'

'I'm not her mother, dear,' Trixie said quickly. 'I'm Trixie Pepper—a.k.a. Gossamer Snapdragon, friend of the fairies.'

Anthony tittered.

Trixie fixed him with a gimlet glare and continued. 'And young George here is Poll's lad, not her grandson. And these two—' she indicated Ash and Ella '– aren't related at all.'

Denise and Anthony looked at one another and pulled anguished 'oh-mi-god' faces.

'We're all just friends who live together,' Poll explained. 'There's nothing in the rules that says we have to be related, is there?'

'No, nothing at all,' Anthony said quickly. 'So then, let's get this sorted out. As far as I can make out, we had four applications for this address.'

'Five, actually,' Denise interrupted. 'We had that last minute one from . . .' She scanned her clipboard. 'Onyx Smith.' She looked at Ella. 'That's you, is it?'

'Sadly not.'

'Oh, Onyx applied as well!' Poll trilled delightedly. 'Fancy! Mind you, she knows better than most how much Ash wants his own restaurant. No, no, Onyx doesn't cook. She doesn't live here.'

Yet, Ella thought.

Anthony waved his hands around. 'Am I to assume—'

'Best not to assume anything here,' Billy put in kindly. 'Always leads to confusion.'

Denise tapped her clipboard again. 'So, which of you—apart from the child and the absent, er, Onyx—wants to be the cooking team? If you're chosen, that is?'

'Just the four of us.' Poll nodded. 'There's always a team of four in *Dewberrys' Dinners*, isn't there?'

190

'Yes.' Anthony nodded, looking exasperated. 'But which four?'

'Not me, dear.' Trixie shook her head. 'I don't do much cooking unless I'm carefully supervised. Not since a bad elf burned my house down while I was making a cooker-top tagine.'

They all glared at her.

Anthony and Denise did the 'oh-mi-god' thing again but this time with the addition of raised eyebrows.

'We'll all be cooking except George and Trixie and Onyx,' Poll said. 'That's four of us. And you said not being related wasn't a problem?'

'No, the only problem—' Denise bared perfect teeth '—is making sure there's enough room for you all to work together, that's the trouble with this team cooking thing. Most kitchens are so small these days. So, first things first. Can we see your kitchen? The kitchen is a make or break. If the kitchen's too small we can't shoot, you see.'

Anthony nodded. 'We'll need to see the layout and measure up for lighting and sound, as well as the cameras, and Gabby and Tom *hate* being cramped and they do insist on maximum on-screen exposure at all times.'

'Oh, yes,' Poll said airily, as if discussing taking part in a top-rated television show was something she did every day. 'I quite understand. I'm sure we'll be able to accommodate them. Come along then, let me show you the kitchen. Oh, mind the step . . . and the dogs . . . ah, sorry.'

Ella felt as though she was dreaming. It was all too, too surreal.

'Pinch me,' Ash whispered as they all marched through the flagged hall. 'Ouch! Not literally.'

'Oh, yes!' Anthony enthused as Poll ushered him into the kitchen. 'Oh, yes, yes, y-e-s!'

'Lovely,' Denise breathed, all cool momentarily forgotten, flicking out an electronic tape measure and scribbling dimensions on her clipboard. 'Absolutely lovely—and so huge. Gabby's going to adore it. All that natural light. All these original features. All those wonderful old-fashioned utensils. And plenty of room for the crew. Super.'

Poll beamed at Ella. Ella, feeling slightly sick now, smiled weakly back.

'Right.' Anthony tapped things into his laptop. 'Kitchen—perfect. Now, we'll just need the names of the cooks.'

'Poll Andrews, Billy Booker, Ash Lawrence and Ella Maloney,' Poll said quickly, clearly in case Trixie, feeling excluded, revealed their fairy names as well and damned their chances from the off. 'We all do different things, you see. Specialise in separate courses.'

Denise held up French-manicured hands. 'We don't need your menu details yet. We'll ask for that later—if you're chosen. We've already seen several other applicants in the area and have two more to see today. If you're one of the five successful southern candidates we'll let you know by the end of the week.'

'What we do need,' Anthony said, 'is some idea of your theme.'

'Theme?' Poll's confidence started to falter.

'Theme.' Anthony nodded. 'Gabby and Tom always like to know what theme you're going to use for your food.'

Poll looked wildly at Ella.

'Er, rustic?' Ella ventured, still not able to

192

believe this was really happening. 'Traditional?'

'Oh, lovely—yes.' Poll nodded. 'And vegetarian, of course.'

'Fresh seasonal stuff,' Billy added. 'Locally grown and, er, locally picked, and, um—'

'Locally sourced produce,' Anthony interrupted, tapping into the laptop.

'Yes, so it'll be farmhouse cooking, then,' Ash said. 'We'll be doing real vegetarian farmhouse cooking in a real farmhouse kitchen. Er, with a twist.'

Anthony and Denise did the exchanged-glance thing again and both wrote things down.

'OK.' Denise looked reasonably happy. 'That sounds fine. Now, I'm guessing that you all know the format of the show, but we do need to run through it again here. If there's anything you're uncomfortable with then say so. There's no point in getting you through to the acceptance stage and then having you pull out because you can't cope.'

'Can't cope?' Billy chortled. 'This lot can cope with anything, let me tell you. No, sorry—you carry on.'

'Thank you.' Denise was slightly tart. 'OK, briefly. Unlike other prime-time cookery programmes, *Dewberrys' Dinners* is shown live. You have no second chances. And Gabby and Tom always go in blind. There's no pre-programme cooking. We don't do any test runs. If you can't cook and your food is inedible, then it'll be on air and your problem.'

'Oh, yes,' Poll chuckled. 'We especially love the shows where they can't cook for toffee. So funny.'

Ella winced.

Denise looked irritated. 'Yes, quite. Where was

193

I? Oh, yes. The show takes an hour—start to finish. Opening and closing credits take up three minutes. Gabby and Tom's ad-libbed intro another two. Their tasting and summing up takes five minimum. Of course, they'll be chatting, watching and advising you throughout. You'll have forty-five minutes max to prep, cook, plate up and serve. With me?'

They all nodded.

Anthony chipped in. 'You can do one, two or three courses, that's down to you, as long as they fit the time frame. So, it's no good planning to cook something that takes three hours in the oven, see?'

'As if,' Ella muttered.

'The ingredients are your choice and responsibility. There's no budget from us at this stage. If you can make cheap cuts taste like something that deserves a galaxy of Michelin stars then so much the better.'

They all nodded dutifully again.

'And please don't forget Gabby's Secret Ingredient.' Denise looked quite severe. 'We've had shows where Gabby has gone to the fridge or larder to retrieve Something Special that she can add, to find nothing but fish fingers or mouldy cheese.'

Poll and Ella nodded. Gabby's Secret Ingredient—where she added a last-minute surprise item from the contestant's own store cupboard—was one of the ongoing highlights of the show.

'Have something ready and conspicuous,' Anthony advised. 'And something that ties in nicely with the rest of your menu. But don't tell

194

Gabby what it is—it really is a secret, because she does like that unscripted element of excitement.'

Poll and Ella nodded again.

'Right, good. Well, as you clearly already know, each show has a team of four cooks, either friends, neighbours, family, workmates, what have you, and each series runs for five weeks. The regional north, east, south and west cook-off shows go out on five consecutive nights for four weeks. Prime time. The initial judging is solely down to Gabby and Tom. They'll choose their Weekly Winner, one team from each area.' Denise rattled off the words, clearly bored with the repetition. 'After that, the final is in the fifth week, Monday to Thursday. Live again. From your own homes. Again. With Gabby and Tom. Again. The viewers will then vote for the two semi-finalists.'

Ella swallowed. What on earth had they done? This was *massive*. The prospect was frankly terrifying.

Denise smiled. It stretched her enhanced lips but didn't reach her scarily catlike eyes. 'If you reach that stage then you'll be invited to the television studios on the Friday evening to cook again live, but in front of an audience this time. Just two lots of you. You'll go head to head. Then it's down to the viewers to phone in and choose the winner.'

'Like *The X Factor* or *Britain's Got Talent* or *Strictly*,' Poll said. 'Yes, we understand how it works.'

'The phone votes will be counted during an hour-long break for some other inconsequential programme.' Denise frowned at the interruption. 'Then we'll be back on air for half an hour when the winner will be announced live. We usually get up to ten million viewers.'

Ten million? Ella gulped. Ten *million*. She couldn't cook in a studio knowing there were ten million people watching her . . .

'And,' Anthony said, 'Gabby and Tom will present the lucky winner with a cheque and the *Dewberrys' Dinners* Winners Trophy. And of course afterwards there'll be the meetings to arrange the opening of a restaurant, run by the winners but initially funded and supported by Tom and Gabby's company. So, are we clear?'

They nodded silently. It had been fine in theory, but now the reality was all far too frightening to take in.

'And you still want to be considered?'

'Of course we do,' Poll said robustly.

'A couple of pointers here,' Anthony said, eyeing George who was eating rapidly melting chocolate while busily reversing his convoy of plastic lorries round Denise's stilt-high pink designer sandals. 'If you're chosen we can't have the, um, little boy or any animals on camera. Gabby doesn't do kids or animals. So if you could arrange to have them out of the way.'

Poll nodded doubtfully. Ella smiled to herself. Hiding George and the menagerie was probably going to be more difficult than cooking live in front of an audience of millions.

'Are there any further questions?' Denise, stepping over George's convoy and sticky fingers with obvious distaste, looked as though she hoped there weren't.

'Dozens,' Poll said happily. 'Like if we're selected, then when will we be on? I mean, how much time will we have to prepare?'

196

'Um . . .' Anthony tapped into his laptop. 'Right—well, in this next series, the southern heats will be first up . . . which means we'll be starting on . . . Monday the twenty-second of June. And this area's selected contestants will be cooking on Wednesday twenty-fourth.'

Billy coughed and Ella looked at Ash in horror. Just over two weeks . . . *Two weeks* . . .

Poll alone seemed unfazed. 'How lovely . . . not too long to wait then. Oh, and if we're lucky enough to be chosen, what time will Gabby and Tom and the cameras and what-have-you be arriving? I know the show goes out at eight—so will they be here say about half seven? I'd like to be ready.'

'*Half seven?*' Denise choked derisively. '*Half seven?*'

Anthony stepped in. 'It's an all-day affair. The crew will be here early in the morning. You'll get a running order in advance of course. They'll need all day to set up, check and recheck. Then there'll be the make-up girl and the hairdresser. They should be here in the afternoon. Gabby and Tom like to arrive a couple of hours beforehand to get a feel for the place and the contestants.'

All day . . . Ella gulped. All day . . . They'd be dead from exhaustion before they'd even started . . .

'How fabulous.' Poll beamed. 'Hair and make-up! What an exciting day it's going to be—oh, if we're chosen that is. And do we have a wardrobe mistress as well?'

'No, you wear your own clothes.' Denise bent down to remove a small dump truck from its parking place under her teetering heel and

197

inspected the shoe for chocolate marks. 'All this will be covered in the paperwork—if you're chosen—but a word of warning—don't wear black tops, it goes dead on camera, or white because it looks like a dirty yellow. And no diagonal stripes or tizzy ditzy patterns. Too dazzling.'

Ella stared at the floor. That was Poll's entire wardrobe wiped out at a stroke, then.

'Anything else?' Anthony asked, snapping his laptop shut. 'No? Good. Well, thanks very much and we'll be in touch as soon as we've seen all the applicants and had our meetings with Gabby and Tom.'

Ella wasn't sure she liked the look of dread that passed between Anthony and Denise.

Everyone rushed to wave them goodbye.

'Goodness me.' Poll was flushed with excitement as the silver car disappeared out of sight along Hideaway Lane. 'I think that went rather well, don't you?'

'Apart from us being caught completely off-guard, and George smearing chocolate over Denise's million-dollar Lanvins, and Trixie announcing that she was a fairy queen, and none of us having a clue what we were going to cook, and about a trillion other people applying?' Ella said. 'Then, yes.'

Billy laughed. 'Well, they'll certainly remember us, and that's a fact.'

'Please will someone tell me what's happening?' Trixie asked plaintively. 'I'm still not quite clear what that was all about.'

They all talked at once.

Trixie beamed. 'Thank you. That's made it all crystal, dears. Of course I'd guessed it was something along those lines. And if I'm not cooking then I'll look after young George and the animals during filming.'

'Always supposing we're chosen.' Ash said, looking, Ella thought, very pale.

'About a million to one chance.' Ella shrugged. 'It'll be a thanks but no thanks. But it was fun while it lasted.'

'Just suppose it isn't?' Poll, suddenly losing all her previous confidence, looked suddenly nervous. 'I can't believe it, can you? And aren't we all naughty? All applying without telling each other? Oh, though—suppose they pick us?'

They stared at one another.

Billy squeezed Poll's hand. 'If they do then we'll cope. No, we'll do more than cope. We'll be the best they've ever had, Poll, love.'

'Don't get your hopes up too much.' Ella, finally managing to convince herself that this wasn't some bizarre dream, nodded. 'But if—and it's a huge if—we're picked then we will be brilliant. And if it all goes, er, wrong then, well, it'll be a seven-day wonder, won't it?'

'It won't go wrong,' Billy said stoutly. 'We won't let it.'

Ash exhaled. 'And if we're chosen—and if we actually win . . .'

'You'll get your restaurant,' Ella said softly.

Ash smiled at her. She smiled back. It was his dream—not hers—but right at that moment she wanted it more than anything in the world.

'And Ash wanting a restaurant is why most of us applied, I reckon,' Poll said happily. 'Not just Onyx. And we'll also get a cheque which means we'll be able to open up more rooms at Hideaway

199

for more people without homes of their own. But if we're useless . . .'

Trixie looked up from collecting George's lorries. 'Oh, you won't be useless, dears. No fear of that. Not if your session is on the twenty-fourth of June.'

'Oh?' Poll frowned. 'Why's that?'

'It's Midsummer's Day,' Trixie said, her curls bouncing. 'It's the most magical day of the year. Couldn't be better, dear. It means me and the fairies will be on hand to make sure nothing goes wrong.'

## Chapter Twenty-two

'You're mad, you are.' Patsy looked scornfully at Ella over the counter of Patsy's Pantry on yet another scorching June morning, three days after Anthony and Denise's visit. 'What did we say to you? What did we warn you about? Letting Poll get into any more dopey scrapes, that's what. And what have you gorn and done? Ignored all our good advice and gorn and got yerself on the telly, that's what.'

'Well, not yet,' Ella said, amazed again at how the bush telegraph had spread the news throughout Hazy Hassocks within forty-eight hours. 'Maybe not at all. We don't even know if we'll be chosen. We haven't heard anything.'

'Best hope you don't.' Patsy frowned as she dished up two cream slices and two banana milkshakes and shook her head towards George building a sugar lump garage for his favourite lorry at the window table. 'Why you had to apply in the first place beats me. It's the child I feel most sorry for. Kiddies don't need their heads turned by all this celebrity nonsense. That poor little lad won't know whether it's Tuesday or Christmas at this rate.'

Ella laughed. 'George is fine. George knows what's going on, and if—great big if—we're chosen, then George will be kept out of the limelight. He won't be in any danger. Anyway, Poll always makes sure he understands everything.'

'That'd be a miracle,' Patsy snorted, 'given as Poll hasn't got a clue what's going on herself half the time. And another thing—' she pointed at the counter '—what's this, I ask you?'

Ella followed the trajectory of the jabbing finger. 'Er, two cream slices and two milkshakes?'

'Exactly! And what sort of breakfast is that for a kiddie? Oh, I'm not saying it's not tasty, well, I wouldn't, would I? But it's no substitute for a proper breakfast.'

Ella sighed. Sometimes Patsy's straight-talking became a touch too wearing. 'He's had a proper breakfast. We've all had a proper breakfast. Hours and hours ago. We were up before five. I was out in the dewy dawn—with George—collecting eggs from wherever the hens had decided to lay them. We then went indoors and boiled them. And we had them with soldiers made from Billy's bread. And he had freshly squeezed orange juice and milk. This is a treat because George is just off to play with his friends and he's already helped me with the Big Sava shop and he's starving again. OK?'

Patsy shrugged her pink-overalled bosom right

up into her shoulders. 'Hmmm, well, yes, all right then. Ah, and I've heard, from Constance and Perpetua Motion, that Poll was right worried you wouldn't want to stay on out there at Hideaway Farm seeing as how you hadn't signed a contract.'

Ella drummed her fingers on the counter. Was there no part of her private life considered untouchable by the Hassocks jungle drums? How on earth had that become Hassocks gossip?

Poll had only mentioned to her, on the evening of the day Anthony and Denise had visited, that she hadn't yet signed her contract. And Ella had said she'd sign it as soon as it arrived, and they'd all drunk quite a lot of wine in the dusky garden to celebrate the *Dewberrys' Dinners* thing, and Poll had said she'd chase the contract up with her solicitor the very next morning.

Patsy flicked imaginary flies away from her Perspex-covered display of what the older Hassocks residents referred to as bag-you-etties. 'That Amy Reynolds from Lovers Knot what works in Big Sava told Connie and Perpetua. Her sister, Amy's sister, that is—plain woman, face like a scone—Amy's sister, that is, not Amy—Amy got the looks but no brains to speak of—works in the solicitor's office in Winterbrook. Nothing gets past her.'

Not even client confidentiality, Ella thought, mentally untangling the torrent of information.

Oh, well, it was hardly a state secret.

'Actually, I'll be staying on for the full three months, with or without a contract.'

Patsy exhaled noisily. 'Well, I hope you know what you're doing. You're a grown-up and I suppose even working for Poll Andrews has to be

202

better than being on the dole. But I still worry about that poor child living in a houseful of oddballs. I worry about all of you out at Hideaway.'

'Please don't.' Ella smiled, turning away quickly before she said something she'd regret for ever. 'There's absolutely nothing to worry about.'

Not exactly true, she thought, joining George at their favourite table and sharing out the cakes and shakes. Since Anthony and Denise's visit, Hideaway Farm had been like—as Patsy would no doubt say with irritating smugness—a mad house.

They'd thought, dreamed and talked endlessly about nothing else but *Dewberrys' Dinners*, always carefully prefacing every sentence with '*if we're chosen, of course*'.

They'd discussed menus, and clothes, and nerves—they'd talked an awful lot about nerves—and menus again and cooking times and what it would be like to meet Gabby and Tom Dewberry in the flesh . . . And then they'd gone back to nerves again.

They hadn't—at any time—talked about winning.

'Excuse me.' Lobelia Banding leaned across from her neighbouring table. 'Lavender and I think we should give you some advice.'

Oh Lordy, not again. Ella smiled kindly at the Banding sisters. Today the cycle helmets were covered with a pastel mist of frou-frou netting, a mass of plastic flowers and several clip-on butterflies. Presumably their summer look. Sadly, Lav and Lob were also wearing hi-viz tabards. Over their lacy off-white vests. And very little else.

'Really? How lovely. I always welcome advice,'

203

Ella lied bravely. 'And—um—I do like the jackets.'

Lob preened. 'Well, we weren't too sure about them at first being as they're very bright colours and we tend to favour a nice neutral, but the cycle helmets have kept us safe for years, and now we're getting on a bit—I'll be eighty-nine next birthday you know, and Lavender is already eighty-six—and because we both want to live long enough to get our one hundredth birthday cards from our dear Queen—or that nice young Prince Charles if we should outlive Her Majesty—we didn't want to take any chances.'

'So,' Lavender joined in, 'we watched all the programmes on the television about road safety and safety at work and everyone was wearing one of these.' She stroked her Day-Glo yellow tabard lovingly. 'So, we asked young Lulu Blessing's Shay—because he gave us the advice about the cycle helmets—to find us some nice jackets to keep us doubly safe.'

'And,' Lob finished triumphantly, her net and flowers and butterflies wobbling furiously over the cup of tea she was sharing with her sister, 'he did. Not matching, of course. We've never copied each other. So I got orange and Lav got yellow. Both with the silver stripe though. Lovely and cosy they are in the winter but we do get a bit sweaty on these hot days.'

'Er, yes, I expect you do.' Ella bit her lip and concentrated on scooping up cream from her plate and wished it didn't remind her quite so much of that lovely time in the ice-cream van with Ash. 'Um, and you said you had some advice . . .'

'Oh, yes.' Lavender nodded. 'Lobelia and I think you shouldn't do it. You and young Poll and all

204

those bank robbers and axe murderers at Hideaway. Go on the telly, that is. You'll only end up in a prefab. They all do. We read it in the magazines in the dentist's surgery.'

George blew bubbles into his milkshake.

Ella shook her head. No, they'd lost her this time. She'd become pretty adept at translating Hazy Hassocks speak over the weeks, but this made no sense at all.

'A prefab? Sorry, but why, if we, er, go on the telly, would we end up in a prefab?'

'Because they all do,' Lob repeated. 'It goes to their heads. They go on the telly then they get hooked on pharmaceuticals and end up in a prefab.'

'She means rehab,' Topsy Turvey shouted helpfully from her corner table.

Ah, right . . .

Ella just managed to keep a straight face. 'Well, of course I'm really grateful for your concern, but honestly, we don't even know if we'll be chosen yet—there are loads of applicants—and if we are, then it's only a cookery show. It's not like sex 'n' drugs 'n' rock 'n' roll, is it?'

'*Only a cookery show*?' Mona Jupp interrupted. 'You don't want to tell Tarnia Snepps that. She thinks she's going to be chosen and it's her passport to becoming one of Simon Cowell's new best friends.'

'Ah.' Essie Rivers, who was, Ella noticed, holding hands across the table with Slo Motion, nodded. 'And that Geordie bloke that calls himself Giovanni over at Willows Lacey, he reckons he'll be picked and turn into the next Jamie Oliver.'

'Oh!' Lavender clasped her hands together. 'I

205

love him!'

'Me too.' Lob nodded. 'Specially when he was with that Merle Oberon in *Wuthering Heights*.'

Deciding that there was only just so much of Hazy Hassocks' elderly residents a girl could take without reaching for a machete, Ella made hurry-up motions with her hands at George, gathered her Big Sava bags together and stood up.

'I'm sure we'll be fine. And we're very unlikely to be picked for the show anyway—but I'll let Poll know you're worried about her. She'll be very touched.'

'She already is.' Patsy flicked a damp J-cloth across the table recently vacated by Gwyneth Wilkins and Big Ida Tomms. 'Not to mention being away with the fairies.'

'Ah!' Mona Jupp pounced on the word with all the relish of a terrier with a fresh marrowbone. 'That's another thing! Poll's got one of them daft old bats what believes in fairies living out at Hideaway now, hasn't she? She was at the Evergreens Club last week telling everyone they had a *fairy name*. Said I was known as Bladderwort Bramblemouth or something. Tosh and tomfoolery!'

'Ah, she's been in here with that nonsense, too,' Patsy said darkly, deftly flicking crumbs into the J-cloth. 'Daft as a damn brush, she is. She'll go down a treat with that bitchy Gabby Dewberry—if you gets picked for the programme. Specially if she starts telling her that her name is HoarFrost SpikyKnickers or summat equally apt. You'll be off before you've even started—you'll have to watch that one.'

As this was pretty close to Ella's own thoughts

about Trixie, she said nothing, smiled again at the Pantry's regulars, mopped at George's mouth and hands, grabbed him and her shopping, and dived out into the High Street.

Whoa—but it was even hotter today. As they made their way back to the Big Sava car park, Ella wiped the perspiration from her upper lip and tried not to stare enviously at a coterie of teenage mums with scraped-up hair and stomachs protruding over sportswear that had never seen the inside of a gym, and their obligatory accessories: cute plump baby in buggy in one hand and a mobile phone in the other.

She could do without the hair and the stomach and the sportswear—and even the mobile phone— but, oh, those babies . . .

She hurried quickly past. This morning, the sun shimmered in mirage pools on the road and even the colonnade of towering sycamore trees seemed to give very little relief from the soaring temperatures.

Hazy Hassockers were already drooping as they plodded to work or shop and the air was heavy with the mixed fragrances of Lynx and Ambre Solaire. It was exactly like being in Benidorm— only with less tasteful clothes.

'Right, I'll drop you off at Doll's.' Ella dumped the bags in the boot before strapping George into his booster seat. 'And Mummy or Billy will collect you. OK, sweetheart?'

George clutched his lorry, waved a fistful of sugar cubes, beamed broadly and said that would be lovely, thank you, in his own inimitable style.

At least, Ella thought as she negotiated the car park, one of the Hideaway residents was clearly unfazed by the never-ending wait for news from Anthony and Denise—or even Gabby and Tom themselves. The rest of them jumped every time a phone rang, and rushed to collect the post from the hall in the morning.

And tonight they were going to have a rehearsal of their first menu—just in case they were chosen. They'd all agreed, over and over again, that half the time they wanted nothing more than to be chosen for *Dewberrys' Dinners*, the other half they simply couldn't imagine anything more hellish.

Oooh though, Ella thought, squinting through the windscreen as she inched into the High Street, if only they *knew* . . .

## Chapter Twenty-three

'Shit!' Ash jumped around Hideaway's kitchen sucking his fingers.

'Oh, dear, you need dock leaves,' Poll advised from the other end of the table as she peeled artichokes. 'But as you haven't got any and we've got no time allowed to pick them, maybe running it under cold water would help? I knew there'd be a problem with nettle soup.'

'I didn't get stung once when I was picking them.' Ash, eyes watering, continued to shake his hand as he ran it under the cold tap.

'Probably,' Ella said as she vigorously beat butter in a basin with a wooden spoon and fought the urge to offer to kiss the injured fingers better, 'because you were wearing gloves then.'

'Yeah, OK,' Ash said wincing, 'but I can't cook in

gloves, can I?'

Billy, who was sifting cream of tartar and flour at the far end of the table, motioned towards the wall clock. 'If we're doing this to time, then stung or not, Ash, you're just going to have to get on with it. We've already had five minutes.'

The rehearsal was in full swing. Just in case . . .

The kitchen was stiflingly hot despite several fans whirring monotonously, and all the doors and windows being open. The evening sun streamed in, maliciously dancing across the cooking chaos.

Ella started to beat two large eggs together with a wire whisk. She looked across at Ash. 'OK now?'

'Oh, yeah. Just got three fingers blowing up like balloons and another ton of nettles to prepare.'

She giggled. 'No gain without pain.'

'Cliché alert,' Poll snuffled, peering into a small bowl of vinegar. 'Does anyone think I've over-soaked these artichokes?'

'And that sounds like the start of a bad poem,' Ella giggled, tucking her hair behind her ears again before resuming her whisking.

Maybe, she thought, one eye on the clock and the other on her adding beaten eggs slowly to beaten butter, this extremely retro menu hadn't been the best one to choose. However, that was the whole point of the rehearsal. The dishes they'd picked were ones they were happy to make and should be cooked to perfection after three-quarters of an hour. And they'd rehearsed the choreography of all working together, moving from table to cooker and back without getting in each other's way, many times—without the actual cooking.

Now it just remained to be seen if it all *worked.*

Just in case . . .

As there was clearly going to be no time for Billy to bake bread in *Dewberrys' Dinners'* allotted forty-five minutes of airtime, he was making 1930s Ballater scones to complement Ash's wartime recipe of nettle soup; Poll was cooking a main of Jerusalem artichoke pudding—a popular dish from the 1950s—with baby vegetables from the garden; and her own dessert was an ancient Athole pudding—one of her gran's favourites—with a wine sauce.

'Ten minutes!' Billy shouted, dissolving baking soda into a saucepan of milk. 'We've had ten minutes!'

Everyone looked panicky and worked even quicker.

Ella, still stirring, watched Ash, urticaria forgotten, as he chopped onions and garlic with rapid movements. The smell was gorgeous and it was, she thought, extremely sensual, watching someone so skilled, so at ease, so talented.

His movements were silky smooth. Unlike her and Poll, good amateur cooks, Ash was clearly the consummate professional. He was lost in his art, unaware now of anyone or anything else, his long fingers working their magic on the ingredients as he sprinkled and tasted and sprinkled some more.

Ella shivered.

Ash made cooking sexy. Very sexy indeed . . .

Billy, having thrown all his ingredients together and kneaded them quickly into a tacky dough, was industriously scattering flour everywhere. His face and hair were white. 'Fifteen minutes! Are we all on time?'

Ash and Ella nodded.

210

'I'm not sure.' Poll stared at her artichoke mixture. 'Am I supposed to have peeled my veg first? Are the potatoes supposed to be on now?'

'Twenty minutes for potatoes,' Ash said softly. 'You know that, Poll. You can do that in your sleep. No need to panic.'

'Oh, yes—right . . . Thank you.'

Ella smiled at him.

He grinned. 'See? I'm no shouty chef. I can be quite nice sometimes.'

'Most times.' Onyx, wearing tight cut-off jeans, very high heels and a tiny lilac top, drifted through the kitchen doorway. 'I passed Trixie and George outside, they said to come straight in.'

Everyone beamed welcomes. Ella sighed.

'It all smells fab.' Onyx curled herself sinuously into the rocking chair out of the way. 'But how's it really going?'

'OK, I think.' Ash gingerly scooped his nettles into the bubbling stock. 'No major incidents.'

'Apart from a few stung fingers,' Ella said tartly as she viciously grated lemon rind. 'The nettle soup has claimed its first victim.'

Onyx laughed. 'I told him he should just open a tin of tomato like normal people . . . Much safer.'

They worked on, getting hotter and hotter, more and more flustered, and more and more in each other's way.

'You know,' Billy puffed as he checked his scones in the oven to be met by a further blast of hot air, 'we're making far too much mess. And we're all wanting to use the same space at the same time. It's completely different now we're actually cooking. We're going to have to do this over and over again to get it right.'

211

Poll whimpered.

'Move over,' Ella muttered, carrying her Athole pudding carefully across the kitchen. 'This is going to have to go in now.'

'So's mine,' Poll said, spreading the last of her creamed potatoes over the artichoke mixture. 'Oh, this is awful. I've got lumps.'

Onyx made sympathetic noises from the rocking chair.

'All going well, dears, is it?' Trixie appeared in the doorway. 'Young George is just adding a new bridge to his motorway so I thought I'd just pop my head in and see what's what. Good Lord, what a bloomin' mess in here. It never looks like this on the telly.'

Hot, tired and frazzled, they all glared at her.

But, Ella thought, she was right. Four cooks, working together on four different dishes, collided all the time and made one heck of a mess. Even if the food was OK they were going to have to work really hard on the choreography and the clean-and-tidy aspect. Just in case . . .

'Um, and I don't like to mention it, dears,' Trixie said, 'but should that oven be smoking like that?'

'Bloody hell!' Billy rushed back across the kitchen. 'My scones have caught alight!'

Ella and Poll ran straight into one another.

'My artichokes!' Poll shrieked.

'My pudding!' Ella yelled.

Ash swore as his nettle soup bubbled teasingly to the top of the saucepan, hovered for a moment, then cascaded, lava-like, down the sides with a malevolent hiss and a torrent of flames.

'Stand back!' Billy commanded, flapping at the clouds of smoke billowing from the depths of the cooker. 'Everyone stand back! And where's the fire extinguisher?'

'You don't need a fire extinguisher,' Trixie said happily. 'After my own little incendiary incident, I know exactly what you need.' She patted her curls, adjusted her beads, threw back her head and started to sing: 'Dandelions so full of gold/Douse these flames to ashes cold/With your glittering water never ire/Use your magic on this fire.'

Ella, completely horrified, had a fleeting glimpse of everyone else just staring open-mouthed at Trixie before the sweltering kitchen became as cold as ice, and vivid zigzags of gold flickered everywhere like a million darting fireflies.

'What the . . . ?' Billy muttered.

Poll gave a little gasp.

Ash and Onyx said nothing at all.

Ella stared at the cooker. Everything seemed to go into reverse. The acrid smoke curled in on itself and disappeared. The darting golden movements were no longer there—if they ever had been—and the kitchen had returned to its normal sweltering temperature.

'There you go, dears,' Trixie said happily. 'All sorted.'

'What the hell was that?' Billy shook his head.

Onyx laughed shakily. 'Did someone just do something there?'

Ella and Ash stared at one another.

Poll clapped her hands. 'Trixie, was that *fairy magic*? Oh my word.'

Trixie preened. 'See, I told you. The fairies are always there to help. Now maybe you'll believe me.'

'Believe you nothing.' Billy tottered across to the

213

cooker. 'Good God, though—look!'

They looked.

Ash's soup had returned to its pre-eruption simmer and the hob was pristine. Inside the oven, everything was cooking as it should have been—with no taint of smoke, no sign of burning . . .

'There you are, dears.' Trixie patted her curls. 'That's the fairies for you. They've done good, as they always do. And that's certainly a bit of fairy magic I wish I'd known about when I had my little, um, conflagration. If only I'd known then I could have saved my house. I made sure I checked up on it afterwards, I can tell you, dears. You never know when it might happen again and there's always so much to learn about the fairy worlds. So that's when I discovered that the dandelion flower fairies are nature's firefighters.'

They all stared at her.

Billy shook his head. 'Sorry, but I just don't buy it.'

'But,' Poll insisted, 'you saw it. We all saw it. And it worked.'

Ella rubbed her eyes. She didn't believe in fairies. She simply didn't . . . But then, what in God's name had happened there?

'Actually,' Onyx spoke slowly from the rocking chair, 'I think that dandelions *are* connected with water . . . on a more, er, personal and basic level. Aren't they used in herbal diuretics?'

'Pis-en-lit!' Poll suddenly clapped her hands. 'That's what dandelions are known as—yes, Onyx, you're right. We always called them that as children!'

'Wet the bed?' Ella frowned, translating roughly. 'Nice.'

214

'Do you mean—' Ash looked at Trixie '—that these dandelion fairies—if that's what that was all about—*peed* on the cooker to put out the flames? Jesus, that'd go down well with the health and safety brigade—not to mention Gabby Dewberry.'

Ella giggled.

Trixie looked affronted. 'You can all think what you like. I know the truth. And believe or not, you've just seen fairy magic in action. No, please don't thank me—I'll just pop upstairs and have a little herbal tincture. Magicking always takes it out of me. Excuse me, dears.'

'She's not the only one who needs a drink.' Onyx exhaled loudly as Trixie headed out of the kitchen. 'I'm not sure I know what's what any more.'

'Neither do I.' Ella, shaken, clutched at the table. 'Come on then—tell me—did that actually happen?'

Ash and Billy shook their heads.

'Of course it did.' Poll clasped her hands, beaming. 'Oh, and wasn't it absolutely wonderful?'


## Chapter Twenty-four

'I think,' Poll said as she sat on a hay bale and watched Billy hammering nails into the barn's rapidly improving walls, 'that I do believe in fairies now. After last night . . .'

Billy looked down from his ladder and wobbled precariously. 'Don't, Poll, I'm still trying to forget it.'

'Why?' She looked up at him. 'It was amazing.'

'It was bloody damn scary.' Billy smiled at her. 'I

don't know about you, love, but I'm always a bit worried about things that have no rational explanation.'

'Oh, I'm more than happy to accept things with no explanation whatsoever. And it was so exciting, wasn't it?'

'Like I said—' Billy turned back to his repairs '—it was pretty scary. And, fairies aside, we're going to have to rehearse and rehearse just to stop getting in each other's way and making such a mess.'

'But the food tasted lovely.'

'OK, I'll give you that. It did. Young Onyx polished off loads of it, didn't she? And said it was delicious. We can certainly cook.'

'And Trixie can certainly conjure up fairies.'

Billy looked over his shoulder and smiled gently at her. 'You believe what you want to believe—me, I'll keep an open mind.'

She smiled back at him. The fairy magic had been exciting and astounding—but to her, nowhere near as exciting and astounding as these lovely times spent alone in the barn with Billy. It had become their special place, somewhere they could talk alone together, as it was being miraculously transformed from a tumbledown ruin into an extremely serviceable building.

Billy, Poll thought happily, was truly amazing . . .

'Anyway,' she said softly, 'and leaving Trixie's fairy intervention out because we're clearly not going to agree on it, I think that, forewarned being forearmed, we really should have our menu completely ready. I mean written down and everything? Don't you? Just in case?'

Billy, rocking slowly on the ladder as he

negotiated a particularly tricky repair, nodded. 'Good idea. Why don't you ask Ella to do that on her computer—always assuming she's got one. But Poll, love, please don't get disappointed if we're not chosen. I'd hate to see you disappointed.'

'I won't be,' Poll said quickly. 'Well, maybe just a little bit . . . So, have you and Ash finally decided on the first course? Is he sticking with the nettles?'

'Yes, I think so. Last night's run-through was a good idea because—fire and fairies apart—it showed us if we're going to cook three courses then we're going to need to be at the oven at the same time, and we really haven't got that much time to cook, have we?'

Poll sighed. They'd been over and over this already—both since last night and before. Sometimes she secretly wondered if this *Dewberrys' Dinners* thing was going to turn into another of her huge mistakes—like painting the house or the cannabis factory or the illegal farm shop . . . Still, at least this time Dennis wasn't around to pour scorn on her dreams, was he? And Billy—she glanced upwards and smiled as she always did when she looked at him—would never mock her.

'Well, we've done the timings over and over again, and, as long as there are no further disasters, it should work out OK. You and I will be using the oven, Ash is just using the hob and Ella will need both.'

'And, to avoid all that mess and confusion, we can divide the kitchen table into three sections like in a proper restaurant so we don't trip over each other all the time.' Billy fanned himself. 'Mind, if this heatwave don't let up we might as well just invite them out into the garden for a barbecue, if—'

'We're chosen,' they finished together and laughed.

Poll stretched her legs out in front of her. How lovely it was here in the barn, with clear blue sky outside stretching to the shimmering horizon, the sun dappling through the gaping doorway and the wild flowers sprinkled across the meadows like jewels. And there was no sound except the lazy bumbling of the bees and the constant singing of the birds and . . .

And—a car? On Hideaway Lane?

'Visitors?' Billy queried.

'Probably the postman.' Poll's mouth was dry as she scrambled to her feet.

'Poll.' Billy's eyes were gentle. 'Don't go getting your hopes up. I don't want you to have your heart broken. You're too precious to me for that.'

Poll swallowed. 'My heart will never be broken— at least, not by *Dewberrys' Dinners.*'

'And not by me, either.'

'I know. But if it is the postman, I'm going to have to dash. I want to get there before Trixie does—just in case . . .'

'OK, love,' Billy laughed. 'And don't forget I've got a nice handy shoulder to cry on should it be needed.'

'Thank you. Just keep your fingers crossed. I'll be back in a minute . . .'

And with her hair swirling round her face, Poll hoiked up her long skirt, ran out of the barn and across Hideaway's desiccated fields.

The postman, in the all-year-round uniform of shorts and polo shirt, was just clambering from his

218

van outside the front of the farmhouse.

'Morning, Poll. Another scorcher, eh? Lots for you all today—and one to sign for.'

'Really?' Poll tried not to look overexcited. Tried to stop the butterflies leaping from her stomach to her throat. Tried to stop her heart from crashing through her ribs.

It was probably Ella's contract from the solicitor. At last.

She reached out and took the fat brown Jiffy bag.

Oh, Lordy Lord! The *Dewberrys' Dinners* logo was plastered all over it . . .

Poll's hands shook as she scribbled an indecipherable signature in the little orange box. Stop it, she told herself, it's bound to be a thanks but no thanks. They'd have to write and tell you that, wouldn't they?

But, what if . . . ?

'Loads of them today,' the postman said cheerfully, tapping the logo. 'Didn't know so many people round here had applied to be on it. Loads of disappointed people this morning. Thought Tarnia Snepps was going to have me throat out when she ripped hers open. Envelope, that is, not her throat—sadly. Scream? I've never heard nothing like it.'

Poll worked some saliva into her dry mouth. 'Oh, so Tarnia wasn't lucky?'

'No, thank God. Me and the missus have been to one or two of her shindigs—you know the ones she put on for the hoi polloi when her old man was angling for a gong?—and she uses caterers, couldn't boil an egg herself, so she don't deserve to be picked. Pity in a way though, because she's a queen bitch, and her and that Gabby Dewberry would have made a fine pair. I'd have liked to see them go head to head on the telly.'

'And Tarnia had one of these packets?'

'Yep, and so has that Geordie geezer from Willows Lacey who pretends to be Italian—he hasn't made it either and his language was pure Tyneside, I can tell you.'

'Oh, dear . . . poor thing.'

'Ah. He didn't get selected—and nor has a good fifty more on my route alone.'

'Really? So these are the refusal letters, are they?'

'Looks that way. Sorry, Poll, if you was expecting different. It's been a right vale of tears this morning, I can tell you.'

'Yes, I can imagine.'

'Still, at least you're not too upset. No point really. Right, then, got to do Angel Meadows now—and I'm not looking forward to that either.'

Poll watched him drive away along the dusty lane. The sun beat down relentlessly on her bare head. She tucked the other letters under her arm and cradled the Jiffy bag against her Indian print frock, feeling icy cold.

They hadn't made it. These were the no thank yous. Everyone had got one today. Of course, the lucky applicants would have already been contacted by phone, wouldn't they? The also-rans would get a letter—this letter—to be signed for so that it was all legal and above board, and probably a Gabby and Tom cook book or something as a consolation prize.

It had been just another foolish dream.

Wearily she climbed the steps and plodded through the farm's open front door. It was dark and cool and she shivered. She dropped the letters on the hallstand as usual for everyone to take their own as they passed.

The Jiffy bag was too big to sit on the top so she slid it to the bottom of the pile. There was no point in opening it yet. She'd leave that for later, when they were all together, and by then she'd have shed all her disconsolate tears in private.

Poll exhaled slowly and realised, despite all she'd said to the contrary, just how very much she'd really, really wanted them to be chosen.

## *Chapter Twenty-five*

'. . . and then,' Onyx said, swinging her long legs from the kitchen table—legs, Ella thought, that looked even more amazingly never-ending in a pair of skimpy white shorts—'I got this weird phone call asking me to do a private show. Well, I was shocked. I mean, I'm not that sort of girl and I told him so in no uncertain terms.'

'Yes, well, of course, you would.' Ella looked up from folding George's clothes into the ironing basket. 'And what did he say?'

Onyx laughed and swirled the melting ice round in the water jug on the table. 'He said he wasn't that sort of bloke either and I'd got the wrong end of the stick and what he meant was would I dance for a private charity function he was putting on.'

'Oh, right . . . how funny. Um, do charity things have, um, exotic dancers, then? Sorry, it's not an area I know anything about.'

Onyx had arrived about half an hour earlier to

see Ash and, as he was still at work, had plonked herself on the table to wait and chatted non-stop. Mainly about the previous evening's fairy thing.

They'd agreed that *something* had happened, but neither of them was actually going to be brave enough to admit to it being—well—magical.

'And do you know what else Trixie told me last night?' Onyx fiddled with a huge hooped earring.

'No idea,' Ella laughed. 'But right now I'd believe it could be anything.'

'She told me I had a *fairy name*.'

'Oh yes, she's told us ours, too. I'm Sunshine Strangeflower.'

'Wow! That's really cool. How pretty. Mine's Serpentine Charmer. I might use it in my stage act one day. But Trixie said it went really well with Ash's—can't remember what his is now—but that it meant we made a really perfect couple because they were both linked to snakes.'

'Really? How fascinating.'

Onyx giggled. 'I thought it was really sweet.'

'Mmm, yes, it is.'

Ella folded another T-shirt. She'd had a brief and fairly miserable phone conversation with Mark earlier, and now really didn't want to listen to Onyx's cheerful chatter. Mark, it seemed, was getting more and more used to being a singleton and didn't seem to have had much time to give any thought to what their three-month break was supposed to be achieving. Even when Ella had tried to tell him—again—about how truly fabulous George was, he cut her short with the 'other people's children—boring' put-down.

So, despite feeling generally miserable, she was also well aware there was something not quite

222

right at Hideaway. And it had nothing to do with Mark—or fairies.

Trixie had opted for having sandwiches in her room while catching up on her beloved soaps, so she, Poll, Billy and George had had an early salad dinner because it was too hot to cook.

All through the meal, Poll had seemed distracted and unhappy and had hardly spoken. Even Billy had failed to get more than yes and no answers from her. Now Poll was putting George to bed, and Billy, having given up trying to get her to talk, was outside in the garden with the dogs and cats and hens, having his traditional after-dinner cigarette on the swing seat—and Ella was seriously worried.

Poll's uncharacteristic dark mood was strangely unsettling, and Hideaway Farm seemed to have an air of emptiness and broody foreboding. Surely Poll and Billy hadn't had a row, had they? Despite them thinking their burgeoning love affair was a secret, it was plain to everyone that they were deliriously happy in each other's company. Or they had been . . .

Of course it could be something to do with the weather, Ella thought, pushing her hair away from her sticky face. There seemed to be no let-up in the relentless heat, and even now, as the sun was sinking lower in the west, the temperature was still tropical and the evening was sultry and threatening.

'You should come along some time,' Onyx continued, still oblivious to Ella's distraction. 'I'd love you to see one of my shows—and it always helps to have as much support as possible.'

'What? Sorry?' Ella blinked. 'Me? Surely not.'

223

Onyx chuckled. 'Why not? We often get women in the audience. They love it—see it as an ace way of getting fit. They're always asking me for tips afterwards. This charity bash would be perfect—who knows, I might even convert you to the cause. It'd make you a nice bit of extra money.'

'Er, yes . . . well, thanks, but I really don't think it's quite my thing.'

'Nah? Ah, well, we can't all be the same, can we? This cooking on the telly is definitely your thing, and I'd run a million miles from that. Can't think of anything worse.'

'It's the main topic of conversation here, too—or at least, it has been.' Ella stopped. Funny, tonight, Poll hadn't mentioned one word about *Dewberrys' Dinners*. Even Billy's attempts to discuss the fairy magic had failed to raise any response.

'Blimey, if I hear much more about the precise chopping, cooking, dishing up times of your menu, with or without the addition of fairies and always qualified with the "if we're chosen, of course", I think I'll scream.' Onyx laughed. 'And I still can't get over how we all applied. I do hope you hear something soon. Anyway—' she slid from the table '—I think I'll go upstairs and give Roy a little cuddle while I'm waiting for Ash. Oh, and if you change your mind about coming along to this charity do just give me a shout, OK?'

Ella watched Onyx undulate out of the kitchen. Yeah, right! Liberated and fair-minded she'd always been, and if that was what Onyx wanted to do and it didn't make her feel exploited, then OK, but there were limits. If Onyx was happy baring all to strangers that was fine, but her? Never in a million years! And as for going to watch . . .

224

blimey, that was just plain weird.

'Hi.' Ash appeared in the doorway. 'Where's everyone disappeared to?'

Ella's heart gave a little leap of pleasure, then she thought about Mark and quickly concentrated on the washing basket. 'Poll's putting George to bed, Billy's having a fag in the garden and Trixie's watching soaps or reading or communing with the fairies or something.'

'Don't!' Ash laughed. 'And Onyx? Her car's outside.'

'She's gone up to see Roy,' Ella continued folding the laundry. 'Do you want supper? We just had salad.'

'Sensible in this heat.' Ash tugged off the silly hat and undid the ice-cream vendor's jacket to display a pale blue T-shirt, then collapsed on to one of the kitchen chairs and poured himself a glass of water from the jug. 'And no thanks. I ate at Maxi's after work. One of the perks. Er, so I'm assuming that as there were no frantic phone calls we still haven't heard anything?'

Ella shook her head. 'No. Poll must have got the post this morning, so my guess is that we haven't been chosen or the whole country would know by now.'

'Mmm, I reckon so too—which is a shame.'

He looked so bereft that Ella longed to comfort him. Concentrating fiercely on one of George's beloved Thomas the Tank Engine tops, she managed to fight the urge.

Ash sighed. 'Still, it was only a one in a million chance anyway, wasn't it? I suppose my restaurant will have to rely on a lottery win now.'

'But you won't give up? At least looking for a

225

decent chef's post to start with, will you?'

'No, I'm still looking. But without references it's practically impossible, and with Roy it has to be reasonably local so that I can carry on living here. And at the moment it seems like looking for the holy grail.' Ash shrugged. 'You know, I'd really hoped they might choose us.'

Ella nodded. 'Me too. It's really disappointing. Still, don't give up hope yet. No news is good news, as my gran always says.'

'Maybe, but I honestly think if it was good news then we would have heard by now. Ella, can I ask you something?'

'Yep—well, unless it's about fairies—we've done that one to death. Or geography. That was my worst subject at school. Although I do remember everything about oxbow lakes.'

Ash laughed. 'So do I. And no, it wasn't about geography. I was wondering if you'd like to come out for a drink sometime.'

Ella's heart did the treacherous climbing under her ribs thing again. She stared at him. 'Why?'

Ash poured another glass of water. 'Because I'd like you to. Sorry—if you don't want to that's fine. I just thought . . .'

Ella tried not to beam and turn cartwheels.

She arranged her face into what hopefully passed for a casually interested expression and tried not to think of Onyx or Mark. 'No, no—I'd love to. Thanks.'

'Great. I'd like to show you the hot spots of Winterbrook. You haven't lived until you've been to a karaoke night in the Masonic Hall or bingo in the Bricklayers Arms.'

Possibly not the venues he shared with Onyx,

then.

'You certainly know how to make a girl an offer she can't refuse.'

'I've been told I do have my moments of old-fashioned chivalry.' Ash shrugged cheerfully. 'Mainly by my great-aunts, it must be said. But, honestly, you've been here for a month and hardly been out at all. Certainly not in the evenings. You've got no social life and—'

'No, well, not a social life like I knew it before, with lots of friends and regular clubs and bars and things, because there aren't any on the doorstep like there were in London and I left my friends behind, but then this was supposed to be a complete change. And it is. And so far I honestly haven't missed the nightlife because I'm so busy during the day, and so—well—relaxed in the evenings.'

'And now you sound like you're Poll's age. Surely you miss the evenings out—your life must have been pretty hectic in London. You must miss London.'

'Honestly? No, not really. And it's a common misconception that London is one big whirl of fun. We're not all A-listers posing at premieres and piling in and out of private members' clubs at daybreak sozzled on the best champagne and being chased by the paparazzi.'

'Now you've shattered my illusions. As a poor country boy I imagined the big city to be non-stop sin and debauchery.'

'Sadly not. Living in London is much like living anywhere else. You go to work and you go home and you do housework stuff and watch the telly, and sometimes you meet up with your friends and

227

go out to clubs and bars and stuff like that, because there are plenty of them to choose from and they're all reasonably close, but . . .'

'Yes, but it's the going out with friends of your own age bit that you're not doing at all now. And I'd like to change that.'

Oooh!

'As friends?'

'Well, yes, as friends. No strings. I do know you've already got a boyfriend—and you must be missing him, too.'

And you've got Onyx, she thought. Much as she would love to go out with Ash—just as friends— there was no way she was going to hurt Onyx. But maybe he and Onyx had had a row or something? Like Poll and Billy? Maybe that was why Onyx was here? To tell him it was all over?

'Yes, I miss Mark, but I do still have my friends,' Ella said, shoving the laundry basket into the utility room. 'OK, they're just not on the doorstep any more, but they're still there. And Poll threatened me with an introduction or two to suitable girls of my own age when I first arrived. Fortunately, it hasn't happened. Honestly, I keep in touch with my mates all the time, but because my life here is so, well, different, I really don't miss them that much. Everyone here has become a friend. And, oddly enough, Onyx asked me out tonight as well.'

There. She'd said it. The Onyx word. Without mentioning two-timing or cheating or anything like that at all. Now it was up to him to explain that he and Onyx were no longer an item and she'd have one less complication to worry about.

Ash grinned. 'Damn. She beat me to it. We'd

228

been talking about you and we agreed that you needed to get out a bit because you were in danger of turning into Hideaway's answer to Cinderella and—'

Jesus! Ella blinked. Onyx knew about it! Did that mean they had one of those weird open relationships? They went out with other people and compared notes later?

'Sorry.' She shook her head. 'I'm not into that sort of thing.'

'What sort of thing?'

'Sharing. Ménage à trois. Call it what you like— I'm not into it.'

Ash laughed. 'No, clearly not. Me neither. Strictly a one-woman man, that's me. And I think you've misunderstood. Onyx and I just thought you needed to get out a bit, which is why we both agreed to suggest—'

Ella glared at him. 'You and Onyx thought this up? This isn't you asking me out then? This is you and Onyx treating me like some sad charity case? Thanks a bunch.'

'No. No, it isn't like that at all.'

But it is, Ella thought sadly. Just for a moment she'd let her silly dreams whisk her off into a pink and fluffy romantic world where Onyx and Mark no longer figured and she and Ash would fall madly in love and live happily ever after—with Roy, of course—in some rustic idyll.

'So—' Ash stood up '—I'll take that as a no, then, shall I?'

'Yes, please. Oh, and you can tell Onyx that I'm not interested in watching her twirl her tassels and gyrate her thong or whatever it is she wanted me to do, either.'

'Sorry, now I'm totally lost.' Ash frowned. 'But OK, whatever you say—it's far too hot to argue—but if you change your mind . . .'

'I won't.' Ella watched irritably as Ash slammed the door shut behind him. Men! Huh!

The door flew open again.

Ash waved a pile of letters at her. 'I thought you said Poll had checked the post?'

'I just assumed she had. She usually does. I haven't looked today. Why? Is there something for me?'

Ash waved a chunky pale-green envelope. 'Another letter from your gran.'

Despite her earlier irritation, Ella smiled. She loved getting her gran's letters. The rest of her family rang or texted, but her gran, who would never be a silver surfer, wrote weekly lovely long chatty letters on thick notepaper. And Ella dutifully wrote back. 'Ah, great. And? Is there anything else?'

'Only a great big Jiffy bag from *Dewberrys' Dinners*.'

'*What*?'

'Exactly. And it's been signed for so Poll knows it's here. What the hell is she playing at?'

Ella's hands were shaking. 'God knows. Open it—go on . . .'

'I can't. It's addressed to Poll.'

Ella groaned. 'Go and find her then!'

'Go and find who?' Poll, still looking woebegone, asked listlessly as she appeared in the doorway and looked over Ash's shoulder. 'Onyx is upstairs with Roy and Trixie is—'

'You!' Ella almost shouted, jabbing a finger at the Jiffy bag. 'We want to know why you didn't tell us about that, er, this!'

'Oh, that.' Poll stared at the package in Ash's hand. 'I was waiting for the right moment. When we were all together. So I could break the news to everyone at the same time. It's a no, I'm afraid. Everyone got one today.'

Ella felt suddenly sick. They hadn't made it. It was like a punch in the stomach. She really hadn't expected to feel like this.

'But you haven't even opened it,' Ash said, frowning. 'So, how do you know?'

'The postman told me about all the others, they were all the same, so there was no point in opening it. I expect there's a Gabby and Tom cook book in there.' Poll swallowed. 'It upset me a lot, and I didn't want to cry in front of George, so I thought I'd leave it until he was in bed.'

So that's why Poll had been so miserable this evening, Ella thought. And with good reason. Damn . . .

'Open it anyway.' Ash pushed it towards Poll. 'They might tell us who has been chosen.'

Ella snorted. 'How masochistic is that? I don't want to know, and I certainly don't want a stupid Gabby and Tom cook book.'

Poll fumbled with the envelope, eventually giving up on the 'tear along the dotted line' instruction and ripping it open.

A Gabby and Tom cook book tumbled to the floor.

'Told you,' Poll said miserably, staring down at it. 'And loads of bumph, no doubt telling us how great the show is.' She scanned the first of the many typewritten pages. 'Yes . . . yes . . . as I thought— and a lot of stuff about congratulations and how

231

they'll be in touch next week, how we should be prepared for the twenty-fourth and . . .'

Ella and Ash stared at one another, then back at Poll.

'What did you just say?'

Poll, who was now very pale, swallowed. Her voice shook. 'Um, I think I might have got it wrong—again. Er, it isn't a no . . .' She let the pages flutter to the floor and burst into tears. 'It isn't a no . . .'

Oh my God.

Ash gave a huge whoop of joy and swept Ella off her feet and swung her round and round.

Dizzily, she clung to him, laughing.

'What the heck's going on in here?' Billy stood in the kitchen doorway. 'Poll? Why are you crying, and what the heck are those two doing?'

'Er . . .' Poll sniffed. 'I'm crying because I'm happy—and they—' she looked at Ella and Ash, still clutched together and jigging up and down '—are, um, celebrating. And we—' she beamed at Billy '—are all going to be on the telly!'

# Chapter Twenty-six

As the June days grew ever hotter, life at Hideaway Farm became even more manic.

Within hours of the Jiffy bag being opened, everyone in every village for miles around knew they'd been picked for *Dewberrys' Dinners*. The phone never stopped ringing. Tarnia Snepps was apparently incandescent with rage and eye-bulging jealousy and demanding a recount.

232

None of them could set foot in Hazy Hassocks or Fiddlesticks or Bagley-cum-Russet or Lovers Knot without being pounced on and warmly congratulated or deeply commiserated with, depending on the viewpoint.

Patsy's Pantry had become a temporary no-go area because, owing to the verbal ferocity of the rival factions, there was a real fear that the heightened emotions, coupled with the soaring temperatures, might lead to one or more of the elderly regulars having a seizure.

And at home, the farmhouse kitchen was in constant use. Sweating, they rehearsed and rehearsed, and prepared over and over again, pared down timings, and planned where they would stand and work and move and still not get in each other's way, with military precision.

Tension was high, excitement was tangible, nerves were at breaking point. When they laughed it was verging on hysteria, and the frequent tears were blamed on the heatwave—never, never on *Dewberrys' Dinners*.

And there were umpteen calls, texts and emails from the programme makers. They could have recited the rules and regulations in their sleep. Poll's solicitor had guided them through filling in the myriad forms covering risk assessment and public liability and health insurance and various other disclaimers. And somewhere in there, Ella had also quietly signed her long-overdue contract, making her an official member of staff at Hideaway.

She and Poll had hugged each other and held a muted celebration—and promised themselves that *when it was all over*, they'd do it again, in style.

The internet communications—insisted upon in the copious instructions from *Dewberrys' Dinners*—had been a temporary stumbling block as Poll didn't own a computer and Ella had left hers in London.

'Use my laptop,' Ash had said, grinning at Ella. 'I'll delete anything incriminating.'

Poll, totally innocent of all things web-based, had been amazed that Ash's computer would allow Ella to use her log-in and email address.

'How clever!' Poll had exclaimed when she'd read the first email message from *Dewberrys' Dinners*. 'How on earth does that work? Can one of you explain?'

Ash and Ella had exchanged glances and neither had been brave enough to try.

'It's just like magic,' Trixie had said. 'Exactly like my fairy friends.'

Everyone else had managed to say nothing at all, but Poll had enthusiastically—and rather worryingly—agreed.

'I still can't believe that Gabby and Tom haven't been in touch, though,' Poll said now, in a break from their afternoon's rehearsals, when they were all sitting in the garden eating yet another version of their first planned menu. 'And I'm getting heartily sick of this food.'

'Me too,' Ella agreed. 'Although it does still all taste amazing. It improves each time we cook it. And my guess is that Gabby and Tom are way too important to do very much more than turn up on the day. That's why they have minions.'

'I suppose so,' Poll agreed. 'But I would love to talk to Gabby before she gets here next Wednesday. Woman to woman.'

Doubting that the imperious Gabby had ever talked, woman to woman or any other way, to any of her victims—er, contestants—Ella just smiled non-committally and tried to quell the mounting butterflies.

Next Wednesday . . . Dear God . . . Today was Friday—only four more days to go . . .

Was she the only one rapidly becoming paralysed with terror? She looked round the shimmering, baking garden. It seemed she was.

Poll looked serene; George, slathered in suncream and practically invisible under a huge baseball cap, quarried happily beneath the table in the increasingly rock-hard ground with his convoy of lorries; Billy and Ash were in deep discussions about improving their joint starter; and Trixie, under the shade of the willow trees with several prone dogs and cats, studied another of her collection of books and scribbled never-ending notes.

No one dared to ask her about them. Ella was pretty sure they involved fairy spells and witchcraft.

Trixie, presumably because she knew she wouldn't be on screen, had been the least frazzled of the Hideaway residents by the news. Ella secretly hoped it wasn't because she was planning her very own contribution by asking the fairies to conjure up Midsummer spells.

Onyx, wearing the smallest bikini Ella had ever seen, lay luxuriating in the full glare of the sun. 'Don't laugh.' She raised her huge Ray-Bans. 'I know you think I'm tanned enough already, but, believe me, I change colour in the sun like everyone else. Pass me the oil, Ella, there's a love.'

Life, previously odd at Hideaway, had turned upside down.

And through it all, Ella remembered how it had felt to be held in Ash's arms.

Stupid, she told herself now as she pondered on whether adding additional spices to her Athole pudding would be a mistake. He asked you out and you said no. There won't be a second offer. And he's made it very clear how he feels about you. He and Onyx are one of those together-forever couples and you'll never be more than a friend. A friend, more to the point, that he feels sorry for because you're separated from your boyfriend and leading such a sad existence . . .

And Mark, when she'd phoned him to tell him about being chosen to be on *Dewberrys' Dinners*, had been less than impressed. He'd laughed and told her she was mad, and that he wouldn't watch it because Jez from the sales office had tickets for a really hot concert and he thought it was probably on the same night.

'Clothes,' Ash said suddenly. 'We've done everything else a million times but we haven't done clothes. And—' he grinned at Onyx '—you're excluded from this conversation seeing as you wear so few.'

Onyx giggled. Ella didn't.

'I was thinking,' Ash continued, 'that we should all look the same—oh, I don't mean a uniform exactly, but similar outfits. That way we'll look like a team and hopefully stick in the viewers' minds.'

Ella stared at him. Due to her sunglasses, this was easy. She'd been doing it a lot all afternoon. The viewers, she thought, would never forget him, whatever he was wearing. Oh, God, but he was

236

gorgeous.

Ash nodded. 'I was thinking, if we all wear pale-blue tops and black bottoms.'

George clearly found this smuttily funny and chuckled loudly, sending up dust clouds from under the table.

'Careful, sweetheart.' Waving her hands, Poll blew the dust away. 'Oh, yes . . . clever you, Ash. A great idea. You boys can wear black trousers and pale-blue shirts, and I've got a lovely long floaty black skirt and a super blue peasant top. What about you, Ella?'

'Er, yes, I've got some black linen trousers and a pale blue T-shirt.'

'Great.' Ash stood up. 'Is that OK with everyone?'

They all nodded.

He held out his hand to Onyx. 'Come on then, Miss Sunworshipper. Grab what few clothes you've got and I'll give you a lift back to Winterbrook. There's no way on earth you're travelling in my ice-cream van looking like that. You'll cause a pile-up.'

Ella pulled a face then berated herself for being childish.

'Such a shame you've got to go back to work,' Poll said. 'Mind you, if you're on commission, this weather must be great for you.'

'Certainly can't complain,' Ash agreed. 'But I'll have to dash now. I'm due outside Winterbrook Ladies College at end of school. One of my best spots—and not just for ogling the sixth-form girls before any of you say anything.'

'Wouldn't dream of it.' Onyx, holding Ash's hand, stood up effortlessly in one easy motion.

'Although I'm sure they don't just queue up at your van for a Bazooma.'

'Probably exactly what they're queuing up for,' Billy chuckled throatily.

Poll and Ella shot him joint disapproving looks—although, Ella thought, for entirely different reasons.

Onyx, her glorious body glistening with oil, slithered against Ash as she hopped on one leg to pull on her shorts. Ella dragged her eyes away. It was too erotic for words.

Oh, stop torturing yourself, she told herself crossly. Just bloody stop it.

She scrambled quickly to her feet. 'It's too hot out here. I'm going to go indoors and type up our recipes and the final menu layout and email them to the programme. They want it before close of business today—so, is everyone OK with what we've got?'

They all nodded.

'And we're all agreed on Gabby's Secret Ingredient?'

They all nodded again.

Poll looked up. 'I thought we could leave both things we've agreed on. A prominent punnet of fresh herbs in the fridge, and a small plastic box of frozen crystallised fruits in the freezer. I know it's a bit belt and braces, but that way Gabby can pick either of those, and they'll garnish any of the courses nicely without spoiling either the taste or the presentation.'

'Good thinking,' Ella said. 'And no one wants to make any last-minute changes, do they? Because this is our absolutely last chance to alter things. Once this is sent, we're committed to it.'

Poll flapped her hands. 'Don't say that, Ella. It all sounds so final.'

'That's because it is. Once the weekend is over, we'll be watching the first two southern heats, one on Monday, the next on Tuesday—and then on Wednesday, it'll be us . . . *Us*. On live telly. Cooking. Our menu. The menu the Dewberrys need this afternoon. So, anything you want to alter will have to be now—or not at all.'

They all stared at her. She hated being so abrupt, but really, one of them had to try and keep a grip on reality.

'And the weekend will fly by,' Poll said faintly, 'because we're going to have to clean every nook and cranny of the kitchen before, er, before *they* arrive. And then it'll be *next week* before we know it.'

'Exactly,' Ella said, a shiver of excitement running unbidden down her spine. 'We honestly don't have much time left.'

'Oh, heavens above,' Billy sighed. 'It all seems a bit scary now.'

Trixie stirred under the tree and carefully placed her books and notes in a tidy pile. 'None of you have anything to worry about—so you run along and do what you have to do, Ella dear. I can promise you all it won't be scary in the least. I've just taken care of that.'

# Chapter Twenty-seven

Midsummer's Day dawned hot and mistily fragranced by scorched grass and overblown roses. Hideaway Farm shimmered drowsily beneath a wall-to-wall bluebell sky.

Ella, lying in the claw-footed bath, queasy with nerves and gritty-eyed through lack of sleep, stared up through the skylight at the diffused golden glow of the sun.

It was today.

Oh God—it was *today*.

In fact, she thought wildly, as the *Dewberrys' Dinners* crew had said they'd be arriving by eight, it was probably at any minute . . .

On Monday and Tuesday, the Hideaway residents had all piled into the peaches and cream sitting room and watched the first two southern programmes: one from Kent, with a team of four new-age hippies who did fusion food, but sadly one of them fused her love beads to her teriyaki chicken due to an overheated grill pan in the wrong place; and one team from Dorset, two middle-aged couples who bred and slaughtered their own livestock, something which totally horrified Poll into very bad language, angered Ella to tears, and shocked the rest of them into silence, and whose pigs trotters—'Mabel was one of our dearest and most-loved piggies, she was exactly like a member of the family'—with lavender mayonnaise had earned scathing remarks from Tom, and exaggerated oh-yuck face-pulling from Gabby.

240

And now it was their turn.

Now. Today . . .

Hauling herself reluctantly from the luxuriously scented water, Ella wrapped herself in a huge fluffy towel and padded to the bedroom.

What to wear . . . Not the black trousers and blue T-shirt, they'd come later when—Ella swallowed—Gabby and Tom had arrived and they were going to be filmed.

No, it would have to be something cool and comfortable . . . The tabloid forecasters had already said Midsummer's Day was going to be A Proppa Scorcha, so possibly one of the two floaty frocks she'd bought last week on a visit to Winterbrook with Poll would be suitable, and flip-flops, and her hair now freshly washed—scrunchied up so that she could wear it down tonight, and . . .

Ella swallowed again and wished she didn't feel quite so sick.

Get a grip, she told herself as she dressed. This is what you wanted. It's not for you, it's for Ash. Remember it's for Ash—and Poll. You've just got to pretend there's no one watching you and cook as you've been cooking for the last umpteen years.

Fat chance!

When she got downstairs, Poll, similarly dressed, was the only person in the kitchen.

'I know it's boiling hot but I'm shivering with nerves and my tummy's in knots—and I couldn't sleep,' Poll said, fiddling with the cutlery drawer. 'I'll be a zombie by this evening.'

'Me too.' Ella poured orange juice. 'No, I don't want anything to eat, thanks. I'll probably never eat again. Where's everyone else?'

241

'Trixie's taken George to feed the hens, collect the eggs and try to keep them inside their run, and Billy's down in the little paddock trying to get the dogs and cats to accept that they're going to have to spend today out of sight. He's built a nice little shelter for them to sleep in the shade and they've got loads of water and tons of dry food.'

'And they'll all have escaped and be back up here before he is.'

Poll nodded. 'That's what I think, too.'

'And Ash?'

Poll shuddered. 'Giving Roy his breakfast.'

'Oh, right.'

'Dear God, Ella . . .' Poll looked suddenly stricken. 'What on earth have we done?'

'We'll be fine,' Ella said with no conviction whatsoever. 'Once the film crew arrive it'll be so busy we won't have time to be nervous. Er, is Onyx here?'

'You mean did she stay over last night? Not as far as I know, although of course she's got Ash's spare key so I probably wouldn't know if she had.' Poll stopped fiddling with the knives and forks. 'I did have a little chat to Ash about her, you know. When I was telling him about you and Mark—oh, not the details, Ella, you know I wouldn't do that—but we were just talking about relationships in a general way. They've been together for such a long time and she's a lovely girl, and even Trixie says they're the perfect couple in fairy names, but it's very clear to me how you feel about Ash and—'

Ella held up her hands. 'Don't, Poll. Please. Ash is definitely off limits, I've got Mark, and enough other stuff to worry about today. And once this is over, Mark or no Mark, I'm going to get myself out

242

on the village social circuit and join in all the barn dances and find myself a nice young farmer or something.'

Poll laughed. 'Maybe you could find me one at the same time.'

'No way. You don't need one, do you?'

Poll, Ella noticed, simply blushed and didn't deny it. Oh, well, at least one of them might be lucky in love . . .

'Poll, forgetting the other problems for a moment, what about Trixie?'

'She's going to be wonderfully useful at keeping George and the animals out of sight today. She isn't miffed at all about not being on camera. She really doesn't want to be. She says—'

'I meant about her fairy stuff. You don't think she seriously thinks that today is magical in some way and she's going to, well, conjure up something?'

Poll shook her head. 'I shouldn't think so for a minute. Oh, I know you're still sceptical about what happened before, but I actually believe it *was* the dandelion fairies. Even so, I really don't think there'll be anything like that today, do you?'

'I hope not. But you know she said she'd take care of things tonight . . . like she was going to cast spells or something. You don't think she intends to hijack the programme in some sort of, well, fairy-ish way?'

'Good Lord, no! Trixie will keep right out of it tonight, with George and the animals—if they escape from their confines, which of course, they will—the animals, that is, not George. She's told me so. And, bless her, she can't help being a little bit . . . fey.'

A bit barking more like, Ella thought, still not completely convinced that Trixie wasn't preparing for Midsummer's Day by seeing herself as some sort of mumsy Titania in floral polyester.

The doorbell stopped them both in their tracks.

'It's not eight o'clock yet,' Poll croaked. 'It can't be the film crew, can it?'

'Well, it isn't the postman this early and as you've just said Onyx has a key, so I'd guess yes, it probably is. I'll go, shall I?'

Poll clutched the cutlery drawer for support. 'Please. Oh, do we look all right? Is the kitchen all right?'

'Perfect. Everything's as all right as it's ever going to be,' Ella said gently. 'And you'll be wonderful—you're a brilliant cook and you're kind and lovely and you make everyone welcome. So stop panicking and enjoy it.'

Yep, she thought as she slip-slapped her way along the tiled hallway to open the front door, now if only she could convince herself . . .

The film crew beamed at her from the steps. There seemed to be hundreds of them. And dozens of vehicles of every conceivable make skewed outside the farmhouse. Ella, fixing her best smile and praying that her teeth weren't chattering, ushered them inside.

The producer, director, two cameramen, lighting man, sound man, runner, various assistants and two very pretty girls with clipboards all introduced themselves. The names simply floated in and out of her consciousness.

The introductions were repeated in the kitchen and Poll, wearing a very bright glittery smile but with terrified eyes, welcomed everyone warmly. So

244

far so good, Ella thought, although she was pretty sure Poll hadn't taken in one word of what was being said either.

The crew, seemingly more than happy with the dimensions of the kitchen, explained they'd need to measure everything before setting up and then there'd be umpteen checks and run-throughs to make sure the light and acoustics were spot on. Then they'd have their own sound checks and position markers would be put in place and loads of other technical stuff that meant nothing to Ella at all.

'Food!' Poll exclaimed. 'You'll need food! And how can I feed you when you're going to be needing the kitchen and—'

'Chuck wagon,' one of the pretty girls interrupted. 'It'll arrive shortly, park outside and feed us—and you—all day.'

'My word!' Poll sighed, looking animated for the first time. 'It's just like being in Hollywood! And do we all get a Winnebago?'

Several heads were shaken. Ella felt this probably wasn't the first time they'd been asked.

After that, the crew took over. Poll and Ella, feeling very in the way, escaped to the garden and watched the comings and goings through the open back door.

It was quite amazing the amount of equipment needed as the crew bundled in and out with reels and reels of cables and loads of silver boxes and a strange big white umbrella thing, and more electrical stuff and chairs and little folding tables and even bigger silver boxes.

Slowly the kitchen was transformed.

'They've got railway tracks!' Poll hissed. 'Are we

having trains? George will love trains!'

'For the first camera,' the lighting man said cheerfully. 'So that it can run up and down in front of the table while you're cooking. Then we've got the swivel one in the corner to swoop over when you move across to the oven, and for Gabby and Tom's close-ups, of course.'

The boy they called the runner started stage dressing the kitchen.

'Oh, how pretty!' Poll peeked round the door. 'I'd never have thought of putting flowers there! And look at all those herbs in pots! And the fruit basket! Won't we look posh?'

Just as the big umbrella thing—'for making sure we have optimum and level illumination and bouncing light off the faces'—was being moved for the umpteenth time, Ash opened the kitchen door.

'Oops, sorry—didn't realise you were here yet,' he said cheerfully. 'Hi then, I'm Ash, and if I could just get to the freezer. Oh, sorry—right, that's great, thanks.'

Oh, erk, Ella thought as Ash opened the freezer. The remains of Roy's breakfast . . .

'Ash! Over here!' Poll waved from the doorstep. 'We're keeping out of the way.'

Ella grinned as Ash squeezed his way through the paraphernalia. One, because he wasn't accompanied by Onyx, and two, because the two pretty clipboard girls were gazing at him with wide-eyed and open-mouthed lust.

Within minutes they were joined in the doorway by Trixie and George, and a puffing and glistening Billy.

'Cats and dogs seem to be settled down there,' Billy reported. 'And unless they're going to start

246

tunnelling and do an animal version of *The Great Escape* they should be fine. Trixie's going to pop down and top up the food and water later. But blimey, Poll, love, this is a transformation, isn't it?'

They stared silently at the manic comings and goings in the farmhouse kitchen which was now, with the addition of spotlights and banks of blinding overhead bulbs, rapidly turning into a film set.

'And the hens are all rounded up,' Trixie said happily. 'And me and George have found some lovely fresh eggs for our breakfast.'

Quickly, Poll told them the eggs wouldn't be used until tomorrow because of the imminent arrival of the chuck wagon.

George clapped his hands and capered up and down.

Trixie, looking as if she was about to caper too but without clapping her hands as they were full of eggs, peered into the kitchen. 'Oooh—this is very exciting, dears, isn't it? And what's all that stuff for?'

With eye-watering inaccuracy and a huge lack of any technical knowledge whatsoever, Poll explained everything.

Ash looked down at Ella and laughed. 'Did you sleep at all?'

'Nope. You?'

'No. I honestly hadn't expected to feel this nervous . . . And I'm knackered already.'

'Onyx not with you?'

'No.'

'Oh.'

'She was working last night but she'll be coming along later. There's no way she'd miss this.'

'No, of course not.'

'What about your boyfriend? Mark? I bet he'll be watching and so proud of you.'

Ella nodded, knowing full well that he wouldn't be, but damned if she was going to say so.

Ash stared at the crew as they moved round the kitchen. 'God, aren't they all brilliant, though? I know they must do this all the time, but even so—all those different cameras, so much electrical stuff, so many lights and things, so many sockets and cables and plugs—and everyone is so cheerful and they all know exactly what to do and where to put everything.'

'As long as we do.'

'Don't.' Ash shook his head. 'But honestly, as long as we don't fall apart we've got to be better than the first two teams, haven't we?'

'The Hippy Fusions and the Pig Killers? Definitely.'

'Food!'

The cry went up from the runner who was nearest the hallway, his arms full of potted ferns which had been in the sitting room. The ferns were abandoned—so was everything else—as the crew galloped towards the front door.

'Come on!' one of the cameramen shouted cheerfully. 'Polly and Emma and the rest of you! Grub's up!'

'I can't eat a thing,' Poll muttered as they picked their way round the equipment and over the cables snaking all across the kitchen floor.

'Me neither,' Ella said.

'I think I'll just have a cup of tea.' Billy shook his head. 'I'm much too nervous to touch a bite.'

'Wow!' Ash blinked in the blinding sunlight as

248

they all trooped outside from the darkness of the house, and lined up behind the crew at the side of the food wagon. 'It certainly smells good.'

Within what seemed like a nanosecond, everyone had piled-high plates and was in the garden again, sitting round the wooden table or on the swing seat.

'Breakfast in the fresh air,' Ella said, forking up scrambled eggs with gusto. 'Fantastic.'

'Just what I needed,' Trixie muttered through a Hideaway-forbidden bacon bap, ketchup dripping glutinously on to her plate.

'Mmm,' Poll agreed over her poached eggs and hash browns. 'And to think I said I wasn't hungry.'

The pretty girls were nibbling toast and drinking black coffee and watching Ash. Ash, beside Ella on the swing seat, still appeared not to have noticed.

'They do a smashing lunch, too,' the sound man told them. 'One good thing about location work on this job—you never go hungry.'

'So.' Ella leaned forward. 'What are Gabby and Tom really like? I mean, of course we've watched them for ages, but surely, the way they snipe and snap at each other—and everyone else—is all an act for the television, isn't it?'

The crew looked at one another.

'I think,' the producer said eventually, scraping his plate clean, 'that it would spoil the surprise if we told you anything about them. You'll just have to wait and see for yourselves.'

'But surely you can give us some clues?' Ash said. 'I mean, how they expect us to behave, what we're supposed to say and when—and what we do in front of the cameras?'

One of the cameramen grinned. 'Oh, no. We

249

can't do that. Gabby and Tom will do all that. They like that part of the show best—the prepping of the contestants. It's like virgins to the slaughter.'

Oh, dear God . . . Ella gulped in terror.

The director chuckled. 'Just one word of warning, though. They'll be preceded by a bevy of outriders. They have separate cars—and chauffeurs—and Gabby refuses to go anywhere without her dresser, make-up girl, hairdresser, PA . . .'

'Doctor, dentist, lawyer, chef, minders . . .' The runner boy grinned. 'Not to mention florist, jeweller, butcher, baker, candlestick maker.'

'Oooh, yes,' Poll said, nodding, 'we know about most of those. We're having our hair and make-up done too, aren't we?'

'Not by Gabby's girls, you're not.' The director looked askance. 'You'll get staffers. Gabby employs her own.'

'Really?' Ella looked shocked. 'What, even for outside broadcasts?'

'Especially for OBs,' the producer sighed. 'It's like being on bloody tour with Mariah Carey.'

'Your make-up girl and hairdresser should be here in about half an hour,' one of the pretty clipboard girls said, smiling directly at Ash. 'They like to have everything done before the Dewberrys arrive.'

'Which will be when, then?' Poll started to collect up the empty plates. 'I'd love to have time for a little chat with Gabby and be able to show her round the house and the garden and—'

The crew stared at her in stunned silence. Then one of the clipboard girls giggled.

The producer shook his head. 'Possibly best not

250

to. That's my advice. Anyway, they'll be here in—
oh, about four hours.'

## Chapter Twenty-eight

And they were. But not before the programme's
hairdresser and make-up artist had arrived and
ushered Ella, Poll, Ash and Billy into Poll's vast
lilac and silver bedroom to be—as Ella put it
later—Gok'd.

It took simply ages.

First, they all had to dress in their black
bottoms—George had chuckled dirtily again over
the phrase and been shushed by Trixie—and pale-
blue tops and be covered with little plastic capes
which made them even hotter than they already
were, and allow the girls to do their best—or
worst.

Billy had laughed about having to wear powder
to lessen the shine. 'If our Mary could see me now,
she'd be all disapproving and say I was doing a
Danny La Rue.'

Ash, Ella had noted with some annoyance,
seemed perfectly happy to allow two very
attractive women to mess around with his hair and
get very up close and personal while they flicked
shader and highlighter over his face and cooed
together over the astonishing length and darkness
of his eyelashes and the spectacular angle of his
cheekbones.

'Gabby's going to lurve you,' the hairdresser said
huskily. 'She'll probably have you stripped and
washed and taken to her tent.'

Poll, taking this literally, had looked horrified.

But not quite as horrified as when she'd looked in the mirror and seen herself with very blue eyeshadow and very red lips and her fly-about hair smoothed into a sort of page-boy effect.

'That's not me!' she'd cried at her reflection. 'I look like my mother! Oh, look, I hate to complain and I know you're doing a great job, but, please, let my hair look more messy, and, please, please, can I wipe off my mouth and eyes?'

'No way,' the make-up girl had said cheerfully. 'At least, not the lippy or the eyeshadow. You have lovely eyes. The blue shadow will make them sparkle on the screen. And the red lipstick makes your mouth more prominent. It all has to be exaggerated, see?'

The hairdresser nodded. 'The eyes and lips stay, but if you'd like your hair to be a little more tousled . . . ?'

'Tousled!' Poll had nodded eagerly. 'Yes, I like the sound of tousled.'

So the page boy had been mussed up and sprayed into a more dishevelled style and eventually Poll and the hairdresser were happy.

Ella had found it very strange after weeks of the bare-faced country wench look to be made-up again. How odd she looked with heavily kohled smoky eyes and sleek, glossy hair. It was like having City Ella back again—and she didn't like it much.

'There!' The girls had eventually finished and stood back to admire their handiwork. 'Wonderful. We'll be on hand to touch up as necessary before the programme and, off screen out of shot, throughout the proceedings, but you're the most attractive bunch we've had for . . . oooh, ages. You'll all look absolutely great on the screen.'

'On the screen,' Poll had echoed, as the reality hit home. 'Oh, dear . . . Excuse me, I need the bathroom. I think I'm going to be sick.'

*       *       *

And then, as the crew continued to work tirelessly in the kitchen, checking and rechecking, and as the sun climbed ever higher and ever hotter in the midsummer sky, the Dewberrys arrived.

In a convoy of cars purring down Hideaway Lane.

And they weren't alone.

'Jesus!' Ella peered out of her bedroom window. 'Everybody from damn everywhere is outside!'

She laughed to herself. Of course there was no way that the residents of Hazy Hassocks and surrounding villages were going to miss something like this. They'd turned up in their hundreds, camping along Hideaway Lane with picnics and chairs and sunshades and cameras, eager to be part of the biggest day the area had ever seen.

'Ella!' Poll's voice wavered nervously up the stairs. 'Ella, I think they're here and I can't face them on my own.'

'Just coming.' Ella checked her make-up and hair in the mirror again, took several deep breaths, and ran downstairs.

Ash and Billy, looking pale, were in the hall. Poll, her hands fluttering, looked anguished. 'I know they're here because I saw the cars from the window . . . Should I go out and welcome them or wait until they knock?'

253

'I'd wait,' Ella said, not actually having a clue on the social niceties of greeting mega-star celebrities. 'They clearly have their own way of doing things.'

The doorbell rang.

Poll teetered forwards and after a couple of failed attempts managed to pull the door open.

Gabby and Tom Dewberry, with a crowd of minions hovering behind them, stood on the doorstep.

Ella felt quite odd. It was too surreal.

Gabby, all perfect and pouty, with her trademark golden curls and an exquisitely cut cream linen suit, and looking ice cool despite the searing heat, was far, far smaller than she appeared on television. And, Ella thought with surprise, underneath the make-up, far, far older.

And Tom was all tall and dark and brooding— like a culinary Heathcliff—but with gentle brown eyes.

'Hi.' Gabby just slightly extended a tiny pale hand that she clearly didn't want shaken, to Poll. 'I'm Gabby Dewberry. This is Tom—and we're delighted to be here at your home for this element of *Dewberrys' Dinners*.'

'Scripted,' Ash hissed.

Tom smiled and said nothing.

'Er, I'm Poll Andrews, and we're delighted to have you,' Poll, clearly awestruck, whispered. 'Please come in and let me introduce you to . . .'

Gabby, with Tom walking a consort-regulation two paces behind, swept regally into the hall with her entourage, stared for a moment then smiled coquettishly at Ash, and ignored everyone else.

Ella sniggered.

'Kitchen?' Gabby enquired imperiously over one

254

small shoulder.

'Er, um . . .' Poll fumbled. 'Oh, yes, across the hall, then go right to the end of the corridor and it's the last door on your right.'

Ella and Ash looked at one another.

'Cow?' Ash asked as they followed the herd.

'Definitely,' Ella hissed. 'Grade One Dairy Show Champ. And she clearly wants to be your Sugar Mummy. Oh, goodness, this is going to be fun. Not.'

The crew stopped chatting and laughing and stood back in deferential silence as Gabby and Tom walked into the kitchen.

'Hi, everyone.' Tom spoke for the first time.

The crew all said hi back to him. It sounded genuinely friendly, Ella thought, and everyone smiled. Maybe Tom wasn't so bad after all.

'What a perfectly lovely farmhouse kitchen.' Tom beamed at Poll. 'I grew up on a farm and this is exactly like—'

Gabby shot him a Look and he lapsed into silence.

The on-screen sniping and carping was definitely no act, Ella thought.

'It'll do.' Gabby gave the kitchen a cursory glance. 'Plenty of room. Plenty of light. We need more fans though. There's obviously no air con and I refuse to wilt. Fetch fans, someone!'

Three people skittered away.

Gabby preened. 'Now, first things first. I'll need a room for resting, changing, hair and make-up.'

Poll looked blank. 'What? Oh, yes, of course . . . um . . . well, there's my bedroom.'

'En suite, I trust.'

'Well, there's a Jack-and-Jill bathroom.'

255

'Really? Oh well, I suppose it'll have to do. Clean bedlinen?'

'What?' Poll looked helplessly at Ella. 'Oh, I'm not sure. I wasn't expecting . . .'

'Fresh on this morning,' Ella lied cheerfully.

Gabby nodded. 'Good. And floor-length mirrors?'

Poll coped with this one. 'Er, yes.'

Gabby flicked flinty eyes towards the crowd of followers. 'Find the bedroom. Check for dust. Set up the extractor and the diffuser. I'll have the lilies, the Evian, the rice cakes and the sushi. Get the rest of the usual stuff laid out. Bedroom and bathroom. Clean both rooms if necessary. Then I'll have the two Alexander McQueens—the blue and the red—oh, and the gold Stella McCartney. I'll decide later. And the Louboutins. All of them.'

Several more of the followers peeled off and, after whispered directions from Poll, disappeared.

'Next,' Gabby said, 'let's make this clear—Tom and I are consummate professionals. We never, ever use an autocue. You're simply amateurs of course, but you won't have an autocue either. I know you'll have been told how we want you to behave but I need to reiterate. Act just as if we're not here and the camera isn't there, and there are no viewers. Naturally. Talk to us only when spoken to. Do not look at the camera. Never, ever look at the camera. Do not look at the monitor screens. Listen to directions, and obey if necessary. And do *not* swear. Ever. If things go wrong then grin and bear it and put it right as damn quickly as possible.'

'We had a team in one heat,' Tom said, smiling happily, 'who lost the plot completely and used the

256

most amazingly bad language. Enough to make a docker blush, it was. We zapped away from them quickly, but not quickly enough and—'

Again, he was quelled with a Look.

Gabby then turned to Ash and flicked her tongue over her glossy lips.

Dear God, Ella thought, she's going to eat him alive . . . Mind you, he did look particularly delectable in his black jeans and a pale-blue Ben Sherman shirt with the sleeves pushed up to the elbow.

'Now you—' Gabby did the lip-licking again and purred '—are *exactly* what we need. The camera will l-o-v-e you. Not to mention the viewers. We'll have to feature you a lot. The majority of our viewers are women, which means, if you get through to the next round, when it comes to the public vote you should do v-e-r-y well.'

'Thanks, but isn't that a bit sexist?' Ash said. 'Surely—'

'Sexist, yes. Top viewing figures, definitely. I only care about the latter. Now, your menu . . .'

Poll stepped forward. 'Ah, yes, now, we're doing a proper farmhouse meal and—'

'Please, no interruptions.' Gabby frowned. Or tried to. 'I've read your menu. I don't need to go through it again. I just need to know that you haven't deviated.'

Ella and Ash giggled together.

'No deviations? Good. And your equipment is ready? Your food is all here? Nothing missing? And you've got your Gabby's Secret Ingredient ready for me to find reasonably easily?'

'Oh, yes!' Poll said with enthusiasm. 'We've got—'

'Don't tell me!' Gabby shrieked. 'I have to use my expertise, you know. And the viewers always love watching me rooting through your fridge and freezer and cupboards and discovering your murkiest cookery secrets. Everyone is a voyeur at heart, don't you agree?'

Ella bit her lip.

'OK.' Gabby tapped a tiny foot. 'So, you can assure me that nothing last minute can possibly go wrong, can it?'

'Yes, love,' Billy said comfortingly. 'And no, love. Yes, we can assure you and no, nothing at all will go wrong. Everything's ready. We're all shipshape and Bristol fashion. And we're all primed and raring to go.'

Billy was treated to a Look. Then Gabby screamed and pointed. 'A child! There's a child!'

Ella turned just as Trixie and George sauntered in through the back door.

'Lose the child!' Gabby instructed a minion. 'And the old lady!'

'I'm no old lady,' Trixie huffed indignantly. 'I'm probably around your age, and I do have a name.'

Ella held her breath.

'My name is Gossamer Snapdragon.'

Ella whimpered and didn't dare look at Poll or Ash.

'And,' Trixie continued, 'young George lives here and I'll thank you not to yell at him in his own home. I know tonight when you're doing the filluming to keep him well out of the way, but he's naturally curious and he isn't doing anyone any harm at the moment, is he? So you, madam, you keep a civil tongue in your head in front of the youngster, please.'

258

Tom sniggered and turned it rapidly into a cough. The crew all paled.

Gabby had two bright spots of colour on her cheeks. She looked like Aunt Sally. 'Excuse me, Mrs Snapdragon, but this is my show. I do not like children or animals or—' she narrowed her feline eyes at Trixie '—old ladies who aren't cooking on my set. It should have been made clear from the outset.'

'And it was.' Billy stepped bravely into the fray as George ran to be cuddled by Poll. 'Only they only mentioned the filming, see? They didn't say young Georgie or, um, Trixie couldn't be around beforehand. And, no harm done—so leave the lad alone, OK?'

'That's us out of the competition,' Ash hissed to Ella. 'Buggered before we even get to first base.'

Surprisingly, Gabby suddenly laughed. It was very shrill, and a bit tinny and discordant, but it was definitely a laugh.

'Oh, I do love you rustic characters who call a spade a digging thing with a handle. Give me an outspoken *character* any day over the sycophantic PC brigade. OK, I'm sorry, I may have overreacted a little, but the kiddie ban still holds good. And you—' Gabby fixed an indulgent smile on Trixie '—Mrs Snapdragon or whatever your name is, you can keep out of my way, too.'

'Pleasure.' Trixie sniffed, gathering her floral polyester frock more closely to her plump thighs and stomping out of the kitchen.

'Phew,' Ash hissed. 'That was a close one.'

'Mmm.' Ella watched Trixie's swaying rear end as she continued to stomp out of sight. 'But I'm still worried about her. I think she's got something

259

up her sleeve.'

'Probably just a hankie,' Ash said reassuringly. 'My nan always has hankies up her sleeve.'

'So does mine, but you know very well that wasn't what I meant.'

Gabby interrupted this conversation by clapping her hands. 'Right, I'm happy that everything here is as good as it's going to be. I'm now going to have my rest and then get bathed and changed. I do *not* want to be disturbed. Not for fire, flood or any other disaster. I rest—you deal with it. Understood?'

Everyone nodded.

'Good. Tom—' she cast a withering glance at her husband. '—will hopefully cope with any other questions. I shall return, ready to go live on air dead on eight o'clock, at seven-thirty. By that time, you—' she turned the withering glance on the rest of them '—will have everything—and I do mean everything—you need laid out ready to go. Your oven will be on—never mind the heat—your utensils will be to hand, your ingredients will be there, laid out on your work station, for the viewers to see. There must be no fumbling or bumbling or searching for things. If you haven't got it you do without it. Understood?'

They all nodded again.

The producer and director waited until, followed by the remains of the entourage, Gabby had swept out of the kitchen. Then they let out a collective sigh of relief and looked at Tom.

'Fancy a cold beer from the chuck wagon, Tom? And a sarnie or two? There's a very nice garden out the back. I think we all need a bit of R & R.'

'Er, does that include us?' Poll, still cuddling a

260

wide-eyed George, asked shakily. 'I'm feeling a bit strange. I couldn't eat a thing but I'm absolutely parched.'

'No beer.' Tom smiled warmly at them. 'Sorry. Can't risk any of you being pie-eyed. That's a cookery joke, by the way . . . But iced drinks, yes. And an hour of relaxing before we hit the ground running. We'll all need to come inside and have our hair and make-up retouched before the final countdown, but in the meantime, let's just chill out and enjoy ourselves.'

Was he completely mad? Ella thought. Relax? Chill out? Enjoy? When she was already gibbering with stomach-churning nerves? When Billy had sunk into a sort of terrified torpor? When Ash had suddenly stopped smiling and looked like he was about to have anaesthetic-free root canal work? And Poll . . .

She frowned. Poll was nowhere to be seen.

She nudged Ash. 'Where's Poll?'

'She's gone to be sick,' Ash muttered. 'And I think I might just be going to join her.'

## Chapter Twenty-nine

At 7.30 precisely, Gabby swept into the kitchen again. All dressed in gold, her curls teased and burnished, teetering on her Louboutins, and with more make-up than a drag queen, she gazed around.

Hideaway's kitchen was completely transformed.

The lights blazed from every angle. The cameras were poised. The monitors were rolling. The crew were in position. Everything the Hideaway contingent could possibly need to produce their best ever three-course meal had been placed artistically by the runner boy on the vast scrubbed kitchen table. Fans whirred everywhere, attempting to reduce the rapidly rising temperature.

Gabby, ignoring Tom, flicked at things here and moved things infinitesimally there. Then she nodded. 'Good. Very good. Right, let's get a move on here.'

Oooh, Lordy . . . Ella, who, with Billy, had earlier joined Tom and the crew in the garden, felt hot, sweaty, dizzy and very, very frightened. Tom, smiling benignly over his iced beer, had regaled them all with horror stories of what could—and probably would—go wrong during a live television show.

But, Ella thought now, he'd seemed like a genuinely nice man. Warm, gentle and funny—not at all starry. And not once had he mentioned Gabby or their seemingly caustic relationship. And he'd only had the minimum amount of powdering and fussing from the slap and hair girls. And, even more to his credit, he'd chatted with them as equals and friends. She wondered where the heck Ash and Poll were.

Gabby clapped her tiny hands. Diamonds glittered, showering rainbow prisms across the kitchen. 'Come on! Let's get mic'd up then and have the sound checks.'

Getting mic'd up apparently involved the sound man clipping microphones to their necklines and threading wires down inside their tops, and attaching more wires and a little black pack to the

262

back of their waistbands. And all the time, apologising and laughing, he'd told them that come eight o'clock, every single word would be broadcast to the nation and therefore to remember at all times not to say anything they didn't want the viewing public to hear.

'Sorry.' Ash appeared in the doorway. 'Am I late?'

'Not at all, sweetie,' Gabby gushed, fluttering her gull's wing eyelashes. 'Just in time for sound—oh, would you like me to fix your mic for you?'

'Say no,' Ella advised softly. 'Unless you *want* to be pawed to death by her, of course.'

Ash chuckled as the sound engineer wriggled the wires down his Ben Sherman. 'No thanks, Mrs Dewberry. I do appreciate the offer, of course.'

'Gabby to you, sweetie.' The eyelashes batted again. 'And if you change your mind at anytime, sweetie, just say the word . . . Now, are we all here and all mic'd-up? Oh, where's Polly?'

'It's Poll—and I'm here.' Poll drifted into the kitchen, looking far more serene than she had all day. 'I'm sorry, too. I was explaining things to my son and making sure that Trixie keeps him out of the way. Are we all ready to go?'

'Has she been drinking?' Ash whispered to Ella as Poll happily submitted to be wired up. 'Or is she on Diazepam?'

'Probably both,' Ella whispered back, indicating the microphones, 'and I don't think we should say that in case we can be heard.'

'Ooops, forgot.' Ash grinned. 'God, it's hot in here.'

'Boiling. Where did you go?'

'Just to check on Poll, but she was with Trixie

263

and said she was fine, then to make sure Roy was OK, then I phoned Onyx.'

'And?'

'Roy's fine, too.'

'I meant Onyx.'

'On her way. She'll be here before we go on air. She's going to stay in the garden until it's all over.'

Oh, goody . . .

Ella looked at Poll and mouthed, 'OK?'

'Fine, thanks.' Poll smiled dreamily. 'I was feeling pretty awful, but Trixie gave me one of her little herbal tinctures and I feel absolutely wonderful now.'

Holy shit, Ella thought, that's all we need.

Then, before she had time to panic about anything else, the director was ushering them into position behind the table, the producer was marshalling his troops, Tom and Gabby were standing in front of the railway camera, loads of little multicoloured flashes jumped and flickered on the banks of electronic equipment, and the lights were notched up to midday in the Sahara levels.

Someone shouted, 'Rolling,' and the familiar *Dewberrys' Dinners* theme tune—the jaunty 'Pickin' a Chicken' by Eve Boswell—boomed out around Hideaway Farm's kitchen.

Billy tapped his feet.

Jesus Christ, Ella thought in total panic, this is bloody *it*!

'Hello, everyone!' Gabby beamed at the camera. 'I'm Gabby Dewberry, and welcome to day three of the first heat in the new series of *Dewberrys' Dinners*.'

'Hi, and I'm Tom Dewberry, and on a scorching

264

and glorious Midsummer's Day—' Tom beamed a matching beam—'we're in rural Berkshire for our third southern area heat. And heat—' he grinned wolfishly '—is just the word for today. We're all baking in here. Or should I say, cooking?'

Gabby glared at him. 'Another one of Tom's pathetic jokes . . . Well, yes, today as you can see, we're in a gorgeous old farmhouse kitchen for a—hopefully—scrumptious three-course dinner, prepared and cooked for us, in front of you, by a lovely team of rustic wannabe chefs.'

The camera swung round and ran along in front of the table.

'From the left,' Tom said cheerfully, 'we have Ash and Billy who will be doing the starter; Poll who is cooking the main course; and Ella who is making the pudding.'

Ella knew her smile was a rictus. Her lips had gummed themselves to her teeth. Her tongue was anchored to the roof of her mouth.

'I shall be chatting to them as they cook.' Gabby moved effortlessly up and down in front of the camera, completely at ease. 'So, as we go along you and I will discover what it is they're going to tempt us with tonight. And you and I will also discover if they're good enough—' a pause and a stage wink to camera '—to become our Weekly Winner.'

Tom turned and smiled encouragingly at them all. 'So, off you go, chums. You have forty-five minutes to wow us with your culinary expertise, starting from—now!'

They froze.

Ella, at the far right-hand end of the table, glanced across at Billy and Ash. Neither of them moved. Beside her, Poll, was standing, grinning inanely at the camera, her hands by her sides.

'Right—' Gabby was clearly used to this sort of imminent disaster '—*now as we get started*, Tom and I will get you all to introduce yourselves, tell us a little bit about yourselves, and explain to us all what you're doing.'

Tom leaned over the table towards Poll and gave her a 'you can do it' smile. 'Let's start with you, shall we? You're Poll Andrews? And this lovely Berkshire farmhouse is your home—so what's your menu called?'

Poll, her eyes still fixed on the camera, swallowed. 'A Feasthouse Farm.'

'A Farmhouse Feast!' Tom corrected kindly. 'How smashing! And what's so special about it?'

Poll clearly couldn't remember.

'It's retro,' Ash ventured, huskily. 'All the recipes are at least fifty years old.'

'Like Tom!' Gabby shrilled.

'Er, and vegetarian,' Ella put in, her lips still gummed to her teeth, and not sure if anyone could hear her. Then she remembered the really important thing about their menu and took a deep breath. Her words came out in a rushed monotone, but at least they came out. 'And we're not only using the old-time ingredients but also the original farmhouse kitchen implements to prepare and, um, cook with.'

'So I see!' Tom enthused, nodding encouragingly. 'It's all graters and hand-whisks and sieves! Not a blender or a food processor in sight! Just like the good old days, eh?'

'Which—' Gabby gave a stage wink to the camera '—Tom remembers only too well.'

266

Tom flushed and nodded at Ella. 'And now tell us a bit about yourself—no, you don't need to stop.'

Ella, who suddenly couldn't even remember her own name, gulped. 'Oh, er, yes. I'm Ella and I live at Hideaway and I'm a sort of mother's help.'

'Lovely!'

'And,' Billy said gruffly, clearly forgetting the 'speak when you're spoken to' rule, 'if you're interested, the ingredients for today's meal arc all locally, er, sourced, and grown, most of them here on the farm, and seasonal.'

Annoyed at being pre-empted, Gabby's eyes glittered in competition with her diamonds. 'Really? Well, it all sounds very retro and very exciting and *very* different, which is what we *love* on *Dewberrys' Dinners*—so let's get cracking!'

Slowly, very slowly, they started to move. Started to prepare their food. Slid, albeit shakily, into the routine they'd practised over and over again.

'So—' Gabby shimmied behind the long table and pushed herself very close to Ash '—you and Billy are doing the starter? What is it?'

'Nettle soup.' Ash stopped slicing onions and garlic and had to stare down into Gabby's cleavage. 'From an original wartime recipe, but with my own additional herbs to give it a twist.'

'Nettle soup! Well, that's a first for *Dewberrys' Dinners*! And did you pick the nettles yourself?'

'Yes. Just fresh young nettles or the tops of the older plants. From the fields and hedgerows in and around the farm. Very, very carefully.'

Gabby trilled with laughter. 'I can imagine. And the rest of your starter?'

'Ballater scones,' Billy chipped in from the other

267

side. 'A recipe from the nineteen thirties and something I used to make with my old mum. Ash'll do the soup and I'll make the scones to go with it.'

'Mmm!' Gabby murmured falsely, again clearly annoyed at being diverted from Ash. 'Delish! And you are?'

'Billy Booker and retired baker, love.' Billy sifted flour and cream of tartar into a basin and started to rub in huge chunks of butter with consummate dexterity. 'Not much interesting about me. Ah, if you'd just mind yourself, I need to get to the baking soda.'

Gabby gave Ash a kittenish smile, trotting behind him to the cooker as he melted butter and fried the onion and garlic. 'Oooh, that smells good! So, Ash, let's know a little about you. Have you always cooked, and what do you do at the moment?'

'I've always enjoyed cooking. I was a professional chef, and now I'm an ice-cream man.'

'Nooo!' Gabby shrilled, turning to the camera. 'Oh, ladies, wouldn't you stop him and buy one any time at all?'

Ash, Ella noted, blushed furiously.

Tom sidled in between her and Poll.

'So, Poll, you're doing the main course. Which is?'

Poll shook her head. 'Er . . .'

'Jerusalem artichoke pudding,' Ella prompted, looking anxiously at Poll.

'Ah, yes. That's right. I grow my own artichokes in the little greenhouse in the garden.' Poll suddenly beamed, removing the halved artichokes from their vinegary bowl and putting them in a saucepan with half a pint of milk. 'A much

268

maligned vegetable these days. But this recipe comes from an old Berkshire farmhouse favourite and—'

Gabby was making 'cut' motions with her hands behind Poll's back.

Tom turned to Ella. 'And you're Ella and you do desserts? So what are you going to show us today?'

Ella ignored Tom and stared at the camera. She attempted to unpeel her lips, but was horribly aware of doing a bit of an Elvis thing with the side of her mouth. 'Um, Athole pudding . . . with a white wine sauce.'

'That's a new one on me!' Tom laughed loudly. 'Athole pudding!'

'Again,' Ella said, even more loudly, 'it's a popular country recipe from the nineteen thirties. It's unusual because it's cooked in a mould and is turned out while it's still hot. And it's something my gran taught me when I was a kid, um, child.'

Gabby and Tom moved together in front of the table and started exchanging snippy comments.

Ella, wiping the sweat from her upper lip and beginning to relax, somehow forgot that there might just be gazillions of people watching her, and beat butter and eggs together and grated lemon as she had done for more years than she could remember.

Beside her, Poll was also getting into her stride, and Billy was rolling out the dough for his scones. The non-stop practising had paid off: they were working as well and smoothly together as they had all through their trial runs, and were moving from the table to the cooker and back again with all the grace of synchronised swimmers.

It was going to be OK.

'Right, now we're really cooking! And believe me it all smells absolutely gorgeous in here,' Gabby simpered, shimmying back to the cooker and casting hungry eyes on Ash. 'Now, don't you all wish you had one of these in your kitchen, ladies? And how I wish my Tom could look as good as this when he's in the kitchen—or anywhere else for that matter!'

Ash, testing his cubed potatoes as they glooped with the nettles in his home-made vegetable stock, gripped the knife handle very, very tightly.

'Oooh, yes,' Gabby gushed again. 'Simply superb. That looks and smells good enough to eat! Which I'm sure it will be very, very soon. You certainly have a lovely touch, Ash.'

Tom watched Poll layering sieved artichokes, creamy potatoes and herbs. 'And if Gabby could cook as well as you, my dear, then it would make me a very happy man. You've also got a lovely touch, especially with that mash.'

'And Tom,' Gabby purred, 'should know. Seeing as sausage and mash is about his culinary limit these days.'

'Fanny!' Billy shouted.

Ella dropped the brush she was using to butter her pudding mould.

'Rude word alert!' Gabby shrieked.

'Not at all, love.' Billy expertly flipped his scones on to a baking tray and crossed to the oven. 'I meant you're just like Fanny Cradock. She was always giving her old man gyp, too, while they was cooking on the telly. I knew you reminded me of someone, and it's just come to me.' He slid the baking tray into the oven and stood up. 'And you must be about my age, love, so don't tell me you don't remember.'

Gabby, her eyes blazing, her pouty lips turning rapidly inwards, shook her head. 'I have no idea at all what you're talking about. I don't remember any television cookery shows prior to Keith Floyd. Oh, dear me—men,' she teased at the camera, 'useless creatures, aren't they, ladies? Well—' she fluttered at Ash '—with some very notable exceptions, of course.'

Ella chuckled, poured her pudding mixture into the mould, and managed to get it into the oven without disaster. Now, just the wine sauce to make . . .

'Right.' Gabby clapped her tiny hands. 'It's all going very well. I'm very impressed with the way you've worked. And all on time . . . So, Tom,' she bridled, 'shall we find out a little more about our contestants as they clear their work stations and prepare to serve? Tom? Tom . . . ? TOM!'

Ella stopped and stared in the middle of stirring white wine into her beaten egg yolks and sugar.

Poll stopped and stared in the preparation of her baby carrots and asparagus.

Ash stopped and stared as he tasted and seasoned his soup with black pepper.

Billy stopped and stared as he prepared pats of butter for his Ballater scones.

Tom just stared. Open-mouthed.

Onyx, wearing a silver bikini top and the little white shorts, had just undulated—out of camera shot—into the kitchen garden doorway.

# Chapter Thirty

Gabby, clearly mistress of the unforeseen circumstance, didn't miss a beat.

'Oh, dear, Tom's gone into one of his catatonic trances again. It looks as if it'll be down to me to carry on here in the kitchen.'

Onyx, behind the cameras, waved to everyone. Poll waved back. Tom still stared.

Ella chuckled to herself as she carefully stirred her wine sauce over a basin of hot water, one eye on the consistency, the other on Tom and Gabby.

With some sort of sixth sense, one of the clipboard girls padded across, out of shot, to Onyx and had a quiet word. Onyx simply smiled and pointed downwards. She wasn't alone. Two of the larger dogs, covered in dirt and dust, and having clearly done their *Great Escape* tunnelling were sitting beside her, tongues lolling, tails wagging.

Gabby's face, furious before, was now glitteringly angry. Her breath hissed like a stationary steam train. 'Oh dear we need to close the door very quickly. N-O-W.'

With a look of sheer terror, the runner boy dashed between the cameras and cables and crew, shoved the clipboard girl to one side, and kicked the door shut.

Tom blinked sadly as the glorious sight of a minimally dressed Onyx disappeared from view.

'Insects,' Gabby improvised cheerfully to the camera. 'Always a problem when we're cooking in summer, aren't they, ladies and gentlemen? Now it might make it even hotter in your kitchen, but I do

272

think closing all doors and windows is a must, don't you? Especially—' she glared at Tom '—if you want to keep pests out.'

Clever, Ella thought. No one watching the show would ever know that the 'insects' were in fact a fabulously sexy and underdressed exotic dancer and two large and shaggy and very dirty dogs.

But of course, we must have blown it now, Ella thought sadly, and just when it was going so well, too . . . Bugger.

Still, you had to hand it to Gabby. Ultimately professional, she managed to keep her clearly volatile temper under control—except, obviously, with poor Tom. As Ash lifted his soup from the hob, and Billy retrieved his scones from the oven, she remained icily cool and looked at her watch.

'Five minutes, everyone! We have five minutes before you need to start plating up! And Tom—' she gritted her teeth '—are you with us again, now, dear?'

Tom dragged his eyes from the closed door. 'Er, yes . . . yes.'

'So what's next on the agenda, Tom?'

Tom, still reeling from the sight of Onyx, clearly didn't know.

Poll, having checked that her carrots and asparagus were perfectly cooked, suddenly waved her hand in the air like an overenthusiastic schoolgirl. 'I know, Gabby! I know!'

Gabby shuddered. 'Really? Well, thank heavens one of us does. No, no—the rest of you carry on scuttling between the stove and the table and concentrate on plating up. Polly is going to tell us what Tom seems to have forgotten.'

'Poll, actually.' Poll blew damp strands of hair

273

away from her forehead. 'And it's Gabby's Secret Ingredient, isn't it?'

'Ah—' Tom muttered.

Gabby cut him short. 'Yes, clever, girl! That's right. It's time for Gabby's Secret Ingredient!'

The camera zoomed in for a sparkling Gabby close-up.

Ella, hotter than she had ever been in her life, glanced at Ash. He smiled at her. The smile crinkled his eyes and wrinkled his nose and made her heart turn backflips.

Ella stopped dead in decanting her wine sauce into a tiny jug. Sod it! She loved him. She really, really loved him.

She'd never felt like this about Mark—never had and never would.

But there was Onyx . . .

Afterwards, Ella could never quite remember what happened next. Or how. Still reeling from the realisation that liking and lusting and friendship had turned, on her part, to something far more intense and personal and romantic and altogether wonderful—if heartbreakingly pointless under the circumstances—she wasn't totally concentrating.

But at the point where they'd all managed to get their food back on the table without burning it or dropping anything, and started dishing up without spilling anything, and it was looking pretty wonderful in Poll's gorgeous old-fashioned dinner service—the one that matched the fat teapot with rosebuds and forget-me-nots—and were all mentally congratulating themselves that nothing had gone wrong at all during the cooking process, things started to change.

Tom was looming over the table, enthusiastically

274

wafting scents towards him with a big brown hand, while Gabby, followed by the second camera, had teetered across the kitchen and was rather dramatically opening the doors to all the cupboards and the fridge and freezer searching for the Secret Ingredient.

Everything seemed to be hunky-dory. Well, apart from realising that she'd just fallen hopelessly into pointless and unrequited love, of course.

Ella, keeping her mind off Ash, Onyx and Mark, and on the food, had just managed to turn the steaming Athole pudding out of the mould without any of it flopping, when she suddenly noticed a sort of silver flash out of the corner of her eye. It was nothing more than a glimmer, glimpsed and then gone, through the kitchen door in the darkness of the hallway.

How odd. It was almost like . . .

'Ah!' Gabby cried ecstatically from the depths of the freezer. 'Got it! I've got Gabby's Secret Ingredient!' Glittering at the camera, she held a small package aloft for the camera.

'What the hell's that?' Ash hissed to Ella.

Ella, mindful of the microphones and the fact that she loved him and mustn't let him know by going all stupidly gooey-eyed, simply shook her head.

'Oh, but that's not . . .' Poll started as Gabby sashayed her way over to the table.

Gabby silenced her with a Look.

'And what have we got for Gabby's Secret Ingredient today?' Tom cried with extremely false bonhomie.

Before Gabby could answer, Ella was aware of another shimmer of silver at the back of the kitchen.

Even more weird . . .

Was she seeing things? Was it lightning? Was the humid day going to dissolve into a thunderstorm at the last minute? Or were the lights about to fuse? God, she hoped not—it would be truly awful for *Dewberrys' Dinners* to go off air just at this vital moment.

'We've got,' Gabby purred, 'some lovely little dumplings.'

Oh God, oh God, oh dear God, Ella thought.

'Sweet or savoury, Gabby?' Tom was becoming more desperately obsequious by the minute.

'Well, we don't know that until we taste them, do we?' Gabby upped the purring. 'If they're savoury I shall pop them into Ash's nettle soup, and if they're sweet they'll complement, er, Ella's lovely Athole pudding. I'm just going to taste them to find out.'

Ash pulled a horrified face at Ella. 'Jesus, isn't that . . . ?'

'Roy's next dinner,' Ella muttered. 'Yes. For God's sake stop her.'

But they didn't need to.

The silver shimmer erupted and billowed from the hall and into the kitchen.

'Puck!'

'Oh, I say,' Tom stuttered.

'Rude word!' Gabby spat, the rolled-up deep-frozen mouse suspended to her lips.

'Puck!' Trixie repeated, storming into the kitchen in a flowing silver robe over her sturdy crossover sandals, and brandishing a twisted silver and gold wand wildly over her bubble perm. 'Puck! Cobweb! Peaseblossom! Mustardseed! Come my

276

fairy friends on this magical mystical Midsummer Night! Come and help your sisters Sunshine and Thistledown! Come and save your brothers Kalen and Pumpkin!'

Holy shit, Ella thought.

Ash laughed. Poll and Billy didn't.

Gabby and Tom were transfixed, standing like statues.

Trixie's warbling voice trilled tinnily, 'On this lovely Midsummer Day/Little folk come out to play/And all the fairies sweet and meek/Help to find the food they seek.'

Then oddly, the kitchen previously bathed in light, grew dark. The air tingled and tinkled and was filled with cascades of multicoloured stars. In the half-light the only sound was of gently beating wings, soft as a butterfly, as a refreshing, rushing breeze played around them.

The sensation could have lasted hours or the blink of an eye. Ella had no idea.

But suddenly it was gone. And so was Trixie. And the darkness. And Gabby was standing in front of them, holding the little basket of crystallised fruits.

There was no sign of Roy's leftovers.

'What the heck happened there?' Ash asked, blinking. 'Oh, surely not?'

Ella, pretty sure she knew exactly what had happened, just shook her head.

The crew were all frantically fiddling with dials and switches and checking and rechecking their electrical equipment.

'A tiny technical hitch,' Gabby spoke straight to the camera, without faltering. 'Probably because of the hot weather. I never mind those, do you, viewers? It proves that *Dewberrys' Dinners* is very, very live indeed and I hope it didn't spoil your enjoyment . . . Now, where were we? Ah yes, Gabby's Secret Ingredient! So what do we have?'

'Er, didn't you say dumplings?' Tom muttered, still looking perplexed.

'Dumplings?' Gabby screeched. *'Dumplings?* Are you mad? Do these look like dumplings, Tom? No, we have some darling little crystallised fruits. Aren't they pretty?'

Everyone nodded.

Ella, feeling as though she'd suddenly woken from a vivid dream and couldn't quite remember where she was, rubbed her eyes. The smoky shadow came off on her fingers. Damn, now she probably looked like a bloody panda . . .

And was she the only one who'd seen—or thought she'd seen—Trixie? Dressed as a panto fairy godmother? Gabby and Tom didn't seem to have been fazed by it at all. Had she imagined it? Dreamed it?

'What happened?' Ash leaned towards her. 'What the hell happened? Was it Trixie? Again?'

Ella shook her head. 'Not sure . . . but I think so.'

'Do not talk.' Gabby smiled a fixed smile. 'Just plate. You have two minutes!'

Ella plated. So did everyone else. It was as if the weird silver moment simply hadn't happened. Yet she was sure Gabby *had* heard Trixie's initial shout, and *had* been about to sample a dead mouse, and then suddenly, inexplicably, the dead mouse had turned into crystallised fruits— crystallised fruits that Gabby was now placing artistically on top of the perfect shape of the Athole pudding.

And Trixie *had* rushed into the kitchen wearing a silver cloak, Ella knew she had. She'd seen her. Hadn't she?

'Right! Time's up!' Gabby shimmied to the far end of the table. 'Step away from your food. Right away.'

They stepped.

Gabby eyed the table. 'Very nice. Beautifully served. Gorgeous old china. Well done.'

Ella looked at Poll and gave a little inner jig of pure happiness.

Tom, casting a longing glance at the firmly closed back door, shook himself. 'Ah, yes. It all looks absolutely wonderful. A proper Farmhouse Feast.'

The camera panned the length of the table.

It did look fantastic, Ella thought. From Ash's mouth-watering nettle soup in the ancient tureen, flanked by Billy's scones, piled high on the matching dish and dripping with butter, on to Poll's delicious Jerusalem artichoke pudding, layers of creamy vegetables, topped with thin curls of cheese and accompanied by the vivid arrangement of baby carrots and asparagus spears, and then her own Athole pudding, a perfect glistening shape, with the crystallised fruits dotted like jewels and the hot wine sauce steaming in its pretty little jug.

They stood back, exhausted, sweltering, pushing damp hair from even damper faces, and took huge life-saving swigs from the bottles of water provided by the crew.

Gabby and Tom took centre stage and took up their positions behind the food. Ella held her breath as they stirred the soup and cut into Billy's scones.

'Oooh, excellent, absolutely excellent,' Gabby groaned orgasmically, managing to shove what Ella considered a massive amount of nettle soup into her mouth without apparently dislodging her lipgloss. 'Oh this is absolutely sublime. This is can't get enough soup. Fabulous, fabulous flavours!'

'Oh, yes!' Tom agreed, soaking up the soup with a buttered scone. 'My word, and the scones, too—light as a feather. Yes, yes, yes indeedy!'

Then they moved on to Poll's main course. Again, the exclamations were of sheer gourmand delight. Both Tom and Gabby had second greedy mouthfuls.

Gabby was by now ecstatically tossing her golden curls and rivalling the Meg Ryan scene in *When Harry Met Sally*.

And then it was the turn of Ella's pudding. Drenching it with wine sauce, Gabby took a huge spoonful and went into further raptures. 'Sooo lemony, sooo creamy, sooo rich and sooo absolutely gorgeous.'

Tom followed suit.

Ella, aware that she was still holding her breath, uncrossed her fingers and exhaled.

It was OK. It was all OK.

'Well.' Gabby eventually dabbed her lips on a pristine napkin and spoke to the camera. 'I think you can tell that both Tom and I really, really enjoyed that. A fabulous old-time meal, thank you all. In fact—' she twinkled flirtatiously '—I think I'll have to ask Ash and, er, the others for their recipes so that Tom and I can try them out at home.'

'Oh, yes,' Tom put in, 'that would be fun, Gabby. A veritable Farmhouse Feast. Thank you. All of you. It's been an absolute pleasure.'

The camera switched briefly to Ella, Poll, Ash and Billy who all smiled stiffly.

'So,' Gabby summed up, 'we've had day three of our southern area heat. And I think you'll agree that our four cooks here in baking hot Berkshire have provided us with something very different, very old-fashioned, wonderfully cooked and beautifully presented. Tom and I are delighted and very impressed. Aren't we, Tom?'

Tom, who had just shoved another of Billy's scones into his mouth, nodded in agreement. Sadly, his reply was muffled and very crumby.

Gabby looked scathing, 'That made no sense at all—par for the course with Tom—but I think we more or less got the gist of it, didn't we? Well, today we've been treated to an exceptional three-course meal from four exceptional cooks. They've certainly raised the bar.'

Tom had swallowed his scone but still had crumbs round his mouth. 'Ah, yes, they certainly have—they'll be a hard act to follow. So, tomorrow, when we're in, um, Wiltshire, I wonder what delights there'll be in store for us there?'

'We'll all have to wait and see, won't we?' Gabby twinkled. 'So, we'll see you all the same time tomorrow when we'll be, as Tom says, in Wiltshire. Until then, it's goodbye from Ash and, er, the others here in Berkshire.'

# Chapter Thirty-one

Ella, simply thrilled that it was over and no longer caring that she had smudgy eyes and damp, lank hair, managed another rictus smile. She assumed the others did too. Poll waved at the camera.

'. . . and it's goodbye and good cooking from me and from Tom and from *Dewberrys' Dinners*—until tomorrow evening.'

'Pickin' A Chicken' plinketty-plonked from a hidden source and echoed round the kitchen.

'OK.' Gabby tore off her microphone. 'Let's go.'

Ella blinked. It was all over. It was really all over. And they'd survived.

'Fab food,' Tom said cheerfully. 'Really fab food. You should deffo become our Weekly Winners.'

'TOM!' Gabby screamed. 'We do not EVER say that.'

'Oh no, but they were sensational, weren't they?'

'Good, yes,' Gabby said, grudgingly. 'Very, very good. But who knows what Wilts and Beds will provide for us in the next two days.' She leered at Ash. 'Not two words very often linked together in your vocabulary, I'm guessing.'

Oooh tacky! Ella thought, trying not to giggle.

Ash didn't dignify the remark with a reply.

As Gabby, followed by the entourage of minions, disappeared upstairs to collect her unused frocks, shoes and probably enough make-up to stock a large cosmetic department, Tom leaned against the kitchen table.

'Well, that went really well. You're all excellent cooks. That was one of the best shows we've ever done—oh—but please don't tell Gabby I just said that. Will you? Please?'

'Of course not.' Poll, her eyes glittering with a massive happiness high, beamed at him.

'Um, and would anyone object if I went outside for a quick ciggie? Only please don't tell Gabby— she doesn't know. She doesn't like me smoking.'

Or much else, I'll bet, Ella thought.

Poll beamed a bit more. 'Oh, yes, of course, you go right ahead. And all your secrets are safe with us. There's an ashtray out on the table in the garden. Billy likes a smoke, too. I don't have any objections at all. Why don't you go with him, Billy? You must be gasping.'

'Ah, I am, Poll love.' He gave her a quick hug and a kiss on the cheek. 'Come along, Tom—let's go and get our nicotine fix together.'

'Oh, thank you.' Tom looked as though Poll and Billy had just jointly handed him the secret of eternal youth and King Midas's never-ending-gold recipe all wrapped up into one package. 'Thank you so much. You're both very kind.'

And, with the air of someone who probably hadn't known an awful lot of kindness, Tom picked his way across the kitchen—pausing for a quick word of thanks and a handshake with all the crew—and disappeared out of the back door with Billy.

Poll, still beaming from ear to ear, tottered to the rocking chair and sank into it. Ella, exhausted, but with adrenaline pumping non-stop through her body, wanted to skip round the kitchen and yell and grab everyone and kiss them—especially Ash, who was helping the film crew dismantle things. Oh, yes, especially Ash . . .

283

She didn't.

She smiled at Poll instead. 'Well, we did it. We actually did it.'

Poll nodded, pushing wisps of hair away from her face. 'We did. And nothing went wrong. Aren't we clever? I do hope someone has recorded it for us because I don't actually remember very much about it—except being very, very hot and very, very scared. Oh, and something funny with the lights going dim and then Trixie . . . or did I imagine that? Billy said Trixie came into the kitchen and did some more fairy stuff, but did she? I must ask her . . . She could have ruined it all.'

Ella, reckoning that discussing Trixie's intervention with an even more doolally than usual Poll right now, was possibly not the way to go. They'd talk about it later. When they'd calmed down a bit. If they ever did . . .

'There'll be plenty of time later to have a post-mortem on all of it,' she said carefully. 'We'll sit in the garden, when Tom and Gabby have gone, and chat. I think we just need to try to relax a bit now.'

Poll nodded. 'Yes, you're right. You're always right about things. But—' she gave a little giggle '—it was all such fun, wasn't it? And now it's over I really loved it! Oh, Ella what if we *win*?'

'God, Poll, don't. I can't think about that now. Because, if we win this heat it means we've got to do it all over again. But, yes, it would be amazing.'

Still buzzing, Ella leaned gratefully on the rocking chair and watched as the crew, helped by Ash, quickly and efficiently cleared up their equipment.

'Dunno what went wrong earlier,' the producer scratched his head as they rewound cables and

284

unplugged banks of sockets and repacked the silver boxes. 'Funny, that blip . . . Nothing showed up on the monitors though and it was all over in a second. Don't think it spoiled anything—I'll have to check the recordings back in the studio.'

'We've had no complaints from Up On High,' the director said, shaking his head, 'so I'm guessing it didn't interrupt the filming much—if at all. Very odd.'

'It'll be electrical atmospherics,' the runner boy said, rapidly removing the props, 'count on it. Thunderstorm somewhere. Right, is that the lot here? What's next?'

The crew, inch perfect and well organised, soon had the kitchen almost returned to normal.

'Shall we clear our stuff up now, too?' Ella, slowly coming down from her high, left Poll beaming benignly in a world of her own, and walked across the kitchen to Ash. 'Or are we having this lot warmed-up for supper?'

'No way,' Ash groaned. 'I never want to see it or smell it or eat it again. We'll ring out for pizzas, shall we? But—' he grinned at Ella '—we were bloody brilliant, weren't we?'

She nodded, still longing to hurl herself into his arms by way of celebration but managing not to. 'We were. It all worked really, really well . . . and even the things that could have gone horribly wrong, didn't.'

'Mmm.' Ash opened two more bottles of water and handed one to her. 'Onyx certainly made a stunning entrance. Almost.'

'Tom certainly thought so.'

They laughed. Then Ella stopped. 'Ash, the, well, fairy stuff that happened—when Gabby had picked

285

Roy's dinner out of the freezer. It did happen, didn't it? Trixie did rush in looking like a pensioner version of Titania? And she did sing another fairy song? And then it all went, well, odd, and Roy's food did turn into the crystallised fruits, didn't it?'

Ash shrugged. 'Not sure what happened, to be honest. I was just bricking it when I saw Gabby with Roy's food. But yes, I'm sure Trixie was there and I'm sure she sang some fairy stuff and then it went dark and, well, everything else was a bit of a blur.'

'But Gabby and Tom don't seem to have noticed anything really *weird* after the Puck-word, did they? Or the crew? They all knew *something* happened but none of them think it was—well—magical, do they? They'd have said something, and they didn't, did they?'

Ash laughed. 'What, like, "Oh, there's Gossamer Snapdragon and her band of fairies galloping in to rescue us from imminent disaster by changing deep-frozen mice into crystallised fruits with the whisk of a wand"? No, can't say they did.'

'But,' Ella insisted, 'that *was* what happened. Somehow. Crikey, last time I was prepared to think it was some sort of illusion, but now . . . You don't think Trixie can really work magic and conjure up fairies, do you?'

'I honestly don't know what to think. Either she's a very clever illusionist, or it was really fairies . . . Nah, it couldn't be, could it? More likely that she saw what was happening with Gabby, flicked the dimmer switch and did the changeover herself.'

'How?'

'I don't know. I really don't know, but I'm just

286

damn glad she did. I owe her one. Right now though, I just want to get some air. Come on . . . the crew are almost done and we'll have to say goodbye to Gabby and Tom. He's still in the garden, isn't he?'

'Bound to be, especially if a near-naked Onyx is still out there too. He doesn't look like he gets much fun.'

'No, poor bloke.'

They picked their way towards the door, and the producer and the crew said well done, and you never know we might see you again, and thanks for the hospitality and for making it so easy for us.

Like reluctant slimmers escaping from a sauna, Ella and Ash then rushed out into the garden and greedily inhaled the gorgeous evening freshness.

'Hi, superstars!' Onyx, surrounded by removed-from-confines dogs, cats and hens, waved languidly from the swing seat. 'Billy and Tom have been telling me all about it. It sounds really cool. Did you enjoy it?'

Together, grinning, their words tumbling over themselves and with a lot of repetition, Ella and Ash told her exactly how much they'd enjoyed it.

Billy and Tom, stubbing out their cigarettes, stood up.

'I'll go and see how Poll's feeling,' Billy said. 'And if young George is still awake I can tell him all about it, too.'

'And I,' Tom said sadly, with a last lingering look at Onyx, 'must go and join Gabby. She hates to be kept waiting.'

'He's a nice man.' Onyx smiled as he disappeared back into the kitchen. 'Very amusing and interesting. And much more handsome than he looks on the telly, don't you think? Bit henpecked though, I'm guessing. So how does it feel to be celebs? Oh, and sorry about almost barging in and messing it up.'

'It was really funny,' Ella giggled. 'I thought Tom was going to have a heart attack when he saw you.'

'I wasn't trying to scene steal, honest. I was trying to listen in and it all sounded really good, then the dogs came rushing up and jumped all over me and I sort of leaned against the door. I was mortified! Sooo—me nearly fouling up your culinary brilliance apart—do you think you've won?'

'Too early to say.' Ash patted the dogs, moved two cats to one side and sank down on the swing seat. 'I reckon we were definitely better than the first two, but there's still Thursday and Friday of the southern heats to go.'

'You'll walk it,' Onyx said confidently, stretching her endless legs out in front of her and snuggling up to Ash. 'I'm really, really proud of you.'

They smiled at one another.

Time to exit stage left, Ella thought miserably, suddenly feeling very weary. I know when I'm being a great big green gooseberry.

'We're having pizza later,' she said to Onyx. 'I'll go and see what Poll and Billy and Trixie want then I'll ring and arrange a delivery. Shall I count you in?'

'Oooh, yes please. I've got some money in my bag.'

'My treat,' Ella said. 'By way of an after-show celebration.'

'But I wasn't part of the show.'

'No, but you're part of the family,' Ella said

stoutly, thinking that torturing yourself was probably ever so good for the soul. 'And you're my friend—so what would you like?'

'Oooh, brilliant then—I'll have a veggie special with extra olives. Ta, Ella, you're a star.'

Yeah, right, Ella thought. And I'm also head over heels in love with your boyfriend . . .

\*      \*      \*

Two hours later, after answering umpteen congratulatory phone calls, none of them from Mark, as the balmy dusk spread gently over Hideaway Farm, and the midsummer sky was marbled pink and lilac and grey, they sat exhausted in the garden, round the wooden table, munching on pizza and sipping champagne.

They'd lived and relived every single minute of their appearance on *Dewberrys' Dinners*.

Gabby and Tom and the entourage, followed by the film crew, had swept off, cheered wildly by the waiting crowds, and the house had seemed suddenly empty and very quiet without them.

It almost seemed now, Ella thought, licking cheese from her fingers, as bats and moths skittered overhead, like it hadn't happened. Like it was all a dream.

Trixie, sitting beside her, in a floral shirtwaister, delicately nibbling at a slice of Seafood Special, had been very quiet all evening.

Making sure that the others were all busily engaged laughing over Poll's rather inebriated champagne-fuelled impersonation of Gabby, Ella leaned closer. 'Trixie . . .'

'Yes, dear?'

'That thing you did—in the kitchen—when Gabby was going to take a bite out of Roy's dinner, was it . . . ? Well, was it . . . magic?'

'I didn't do anything, dear.' Trixie wiped her lips delicately with a piece of kitchen roll. 'But my fairy friends helped avert a disaster, yes. However, as you don't believe in them . . .'

Ella sighed. 'I don't know what to believe. I do know that something odd happened—again—and if it hadn't then things would have gone very wrong indeed, and we certainly wouldn't have stood a chance of going through to the next round and—'

'And that's all you need to know, dear.' Trixie smiled kindly. 'I have no intention of trying to turn you into a card-carrying fairy believer. I'm just delighted that we were able to help out tonight.'

'But, can't you explain—?'

Trixie shook her tightly permed hair. 'No, sorry, dear. Explanations would kill the magic, and you don't need them. Just trust, dear, that's all you need.'

'But,' Ella insisted, 'I can't trust if I don't understand . . . and those names you called out . . . Puck—which was really funny because Gabby's a bit thick and thought you were swearing—and I've heard of him, of course. But Mustardweb and Cobblossom and Peaseed?'

Onyx looked up. 'Did you just say Puck? And Cobweb, Peaseblossom and Mustardseed?'

Ella frowned towards Poll, Ash and Billy. 'Yes, or at least I tried to. Clearly I didn't get the names quite right, but I don't really think we should be talking about them in public—oh, sorry, but I really, really don't want Poll to overhear this conversation because she's addled enough already.

290

But do they mean something to you? Do you recognise them?'

'Course I do. I'm Reading Uni's Eng Lit queen, remember? They're Shakespeare's *Midsummer Night's Dream* fairies—and a very suitable topic for tonight. But, honestly, Ella, isn't a literary discussion a bit heavy given what you've been through today? Why are you—?'

Ella looked across at a smiling Trixie then shook her head. 'It doesn't matter, but thanks, it explains a lot . . . I think.'

## Chapter Thirty-two

'Right.' Poll bustled into the peaches and cream sitting room. 'Are we all ready?'

Ella, Billy and Trixie nodded. George drummed his heels.

'Ash not here yet?'

Ella shook her head. 'He texted just now. He's on his way. He got stuck with a lot of customers out at Angel Meadows again.'

'Poor Ash.' Poll plumped herself down on the sofa beside Ella. 'It must be doubly difficult for him—selling ice creams in the middle of the hottest summer since nineteen seventy-six and being recognised everywhere he goes. No doubt he has to tell the tale over and over again.'

Ella chuckled. They'd all been treated like superstars ever since last week's programme. Everywhere they went they were asked the same questions. She felt like typing up a fact sheet and handing it out.

Yes, Gabby was exactly the same in real life.

No, Tom wasn't putting on a doormat act.

Yes, it had been scary.

Yes, they'd loved every minute of it.

No, they didn't think they were going to win.

But in a very short space of time, Ella thought now, butterflies racing up and down in her stomach, they'd know.

Now it was eight o'clock on Monday, *Dewberrys' Dinners* was about to start with week two: the eastern heats, and the southern area Weekly Winner would be announced.

'Don't get too disappointed—I still think they'd have rung us before now if we'd won, duck,' Billy said. 'Stands to reason, they wouldn't leave it to chance. And them ones from Bedfordshire on Friday night were right good, weren't they?'

Ella and Poll nodded. They had been.

On Thursday, the Wiltshire contestants, a quartet of very up-themselves self-made entrepreneurs, who'd already changed careers several times and thought it was 'a toss up between writing a novel next or becoming a celebrity chef— but honestly, Gabby, writing's easy, isn't it? Anyone can write a book. So, always wanting to challenge ourselves, we've taken the harder creative option . . .', had failed spectacularly with their culinary take on 'Foodie Food for the Twenty-first Century'.

Their samphire had gone gritty, their aubergine and venison stack with broad bean purée had looked like dog vomit, and their imaginatively arranged three minimalist puddings with spun sugar drapery—'just a little taste of heaven especially for you, Gabby'—had turned into a hellish, blackened, burned-on glob.

Hideaway Farm had whooped and clapped and cheered no end.

But the Bedfordshire team—two rather sweet, very young and very much in love couples—had produced a meal Cath Kidston would have killed for. Each tiny course was so artistically pretty—delicate and ethereal, sprinkled with little pastel flower petals and whimsy pea shoots—it had looked and clearly tasted—judging by Gabby and Tom's ecstatic reaction—wonderful.

They'd win, Ella thought sadly. She knew they'd win.

With trembling hands, Poll pressed the television's remote control and, after a couple of false starts, 'Pickin' a Chicken' bounced into the room.

Gabby, in silver tonight, and Tom, looking even more Heathcliff-dishevelled, prepared for their opening lines. Ella still found it funny that before last Wednesday she'd imagined, in her innocence, it was just Gabby, Tom and the contestants in the kitchen—now she knew just how many people were beavering away out of shot to make the programme appear that homely, relaxed and easy.

'Hello, everyone!' Gabby beamed at the camera. 'I'm Gabby Dewberry, and welcome to day one, of the second week, of the first heat, in the new series of *Dewberrys' Dinners*.'

'That sounds more like *Countdown*!' Tom guffawed.

Gabby gave him a Look.

Tom stopped guffawing. 'Er, yes—hi, and I'm Tom Dewberry, and on yet another scorching Monday evening, we're in Norfolk for our first eastern area heat.'

Gabby glittered. 'But before we introduce you to tonight's eager chefs, we have the results of last week's southern area cook-off. As you know, we select just one team of chefs from each area for our Finals Week.'

'Yes,' Tom agreed, 'and this time it was a very, very hard decision to make. Last week's cooks were all exceptional.'

'No they weren't!' Ella snorted. 'We were! OK, and maybe the Bedfordshire ones. Most of the rest of them were rubbish!'

'However—' Gabby twinkled '—after much deliberation, we've reached our decision, haven't we, Tom?'

'We have.'

'Oh, for Lord's sake!' Poll shrieked. 'Just get on with it!'

'It won't be us.' Billy reached over and clutched her hand. 'Like I said, they'd have told us before now.'

Gabby looked solemn. 'The southern area Weekly Winners are . . .'

There was a silence. Tom and Gabby stared at one another.

'God!' Ella exploded. 'I hate it when they do that to ratchet up the tension. They do it on all the reality shows, and it always irritated me before, now I think it's just unbelievably cruel.'

Poll buried her face in a cushion.

'And our first lucky Weekly Winners—who will be going on to cook for a second time in the *Dewberrys' Dinners* finals week commencing the twentieth of July—are . . .' Gabby paused. 'Ooh, shall we do this together, Tom?'

294

Tom looked a bit surprised but nodded.

More silence.

Ella wanted to punch the screen.

'The first Weekly Winners are . . .' Gabby and Tom moved together and glittered in unison. 'Berkshire's Hideaway Farm!'

'See,' Billy said, 'told you we wouldn't . . .'

'But we *have*!' Ella shrieked with excitement grabbing Poll up off the sofa and dancing round and round with her. 'We have! We have!'

'Have we?' Poll burst into tears. 'Have we really?'

'Yes, really!'

'Oh, blimey . . . Are you sure? And please could we stop jigging now?' Poll gulped. 'I feel a bit sick.'

George scampered round the room with his T-shirt over his head, punching the air—he'd picked up some very doubtful habits from Doll Blessing's children—while Billy sat and nodded happily. Only Trixie, smiling gently to herself, seemed relatively unmoved.

Ohmigod, though!

Totally stunned, Ella clapped her hands to her mouth. 'Bloody hell, we've done it! Oh, I can't believe it. Oh, I wish Ash was here—where is he? I can't wait to tell him! Oh, and there's the telephone going—it'll be half the county wanting to share in the glory . . . and . . . crikey, my mobile's going mad too.'

Poll, gently extricating herself from Ella's clutches, staggered out of the room to answer the phone, followed by a skipping and still air-punching George.

Ella, skimming through her barrage of congratulatory texts from practically everyone who knew her—except Mark, of course—still couldn't quite believe it. She'd hoped and dreamed that they would win—and now they had and they were one huge step closer to Ash having his own restaurant and . . .

Trixie folded her magazine as, on screen, the team from Norfolk started doing something pretty awful with the innards of a chicken. 'Well done, dears. I'm very, very happy for you.'

'Thanks, Trixie, love,' Billy said. 'But I was still sure it wasn't going to be us.'

'Oh, I knew it would be.' Trixie smiled sweetly.

Billy chuckled. 'The fairies told you so, did they?'

'As a matter of fact, they did, Mr Pumpkin Scoffer. They helped more than you'll ever know.'

'Whatever you say. I'm not going to get into any more arguments with you on that score. You almost spoiled our big moment last week, storming in and shouting "Puck" and all that malarkey, presumably because you didn't want to be left out of the telly shenanigans, but I've said nothing about it because Poll seems to have forgotten about it and I won't do anything to upset her.'

'But?' Trixie's bubble perm quivered.

'But—' Billy puffed himself up '—I'd ask you, now we're going to be on the telly again, to keep your fairy nonsense to yourself in future.'

'Oh, I don't have any control over the fairies,' Trixie continued to smile. 'They do whatever they like. I'm just a channel for them, but they do help me—and you . . . as young Ella knows only too well.'

Oooh no, Ella groaned, looking up from her phone, don't drag me into this.

'Do you?' Billy looked at her.

'Not really *know* as such, but I think I do understand a little more than I did before and . . .'

Oh, hallelujah! Saved by Poll drifting into the room, holding George's hand, looking stunned.

'That was Denise from *Dewberrys' Dinners*. She was ringing to confirm that we're the Weekly Winners . . . She said we couldn't be told that we'd won until Gabby and Tom had broadcast it because it had to stay a strict secret and we might have talked.' Poll looked shocked. 'As if we would!'

Ella thought they definitely would.

'Anyway—' Poll smiled vaguely round the sitting room '—we'll be filmed live again, from here, on Monday the twentieth of July . . . and if we win that one with the viewers' votes, we'll be in the television studio with the other lucky semi-finalist team, for the live audience final on Friday the twenty-fourth of July.'

At the mention of the dates, Ella noted with deep foreboding that Trixie suddenly looked animated.

'And,' Poll continued, 'Denise says we have to cook an entirely different menu on the twentieth, but if we get through to finals night we can use that again, or our original one, or another one again. Isn't it just wonderful?'

'Yes, it is, love.' Billy stood up and kissed her cheek. 'Now, have we got any more of that champagne left?'

'Mmm. I think so . . . It might be in the fridge, and if it isn't it should be.'

'Shouldn't we wait until Ash gets here?' Ella said. 'It doesn't seem fair to leave him out of the celebrations. And, we'll have to start thinking of a whole new menu, and he'll have to be here for that and—Oooh, just look what they're doing with those prawns.'

They all stared at the television screen.

'Looks like a satanic ritual.' Poll shuddered. 'Not that I've ever seen one, of course, but should there be all that blood? From prawns?'

'That's beetroot sauce,' Trixie said.

'Beetroot with prawns? Does that go?' Poll frowned. 'It's a very pretty colour, though.'

The phone started ringing out in the hall again.

'I'll answer the phone—bound to be someone from the villages having heard the news and wanting to have the latest low-down,' Billy said, 'then I'll go and see if the champagne is in the fridge. We'll have to have it nice and cold for when Ash gets here. Come on, young George, let's see if we can find some of that special cherry pop for you, too.'

'Ah, love them.' Trixie watched them leave the room. 'Lovely seeing them together, isn't it, Poll, dear? Like a proper father and son. Billy's a bit old to be George's dad, of course, but then, wasn't Charlie Chaplin still fathering children in his eighties?'

Poll blushed. 'I've no idea. And Billy is only in his early fifties.'

'And you haven't reached the change yet, have you?' Trixie enquired cheerfully. 'Plenty of time for you and Billy to give George a little brother or sister.'

Poll gave a little whimper and blushed even more. 'Er, um, oooh, yes. Who fancies some of my cheese straws with the champagne?'

'Me!' Ella said, laughing. 'And some goat's

298

cheese with your home-made pickled onions.'

'You've got a really disgusting palate for a winning cheffette,' Poll, still flushed with embarrassment, muttered as she headed for the door. 'I'll go and see what I can find.'

'OK—' Ella looked at Trixie as soon as they were alone '—forget all about Billy and Poll's breeding programme, what's so special about those dates that Poll mentioned?'

'You noticed, dear, did you? Well, between us— and the fairies, of course—they couldn't be better. July, in fairy speak, is known as Maed Monath— the flowering of the meadows. And the twentieth of July is very special for all the fairykins—it's Ruby Larkspur Day.'

Ella tried to keep a straight face. 'Who the heck is Ruby Larkspur Day? She sounds like a bit of a diva to me. You know—ahem—and here we have the latest chart-topping cloned offering from last year's cloned *X-Strictly On Ice Without Talent* winner—Ruby Larkspur-Day!'

'Don't mock, Ella. Ruby is the precious birthstone for July, and larkspur is July's special flower. They unite in magical power on the twentieth of July. Gemstones and flowers are very important to fairies.'

'And to divas. And to most other women really. The way to a woman's heart . . . Or maybe that's with food?' Ella pondered for a moment. Yes, definitely with food. Especially if it was created, cooked and served to her, just her, by Ash . . .

Although the gems and flowers would be quite nice, too . . .

Trixie shook her head. 'A woman's heart can't be bought with gems and flowers though, dear,

299

can it?'

'Can't it? Er, no, probably not. Too materialistic. No, I suppose hearts have to be given freely—if you love someone, then it's unconditional, isn't it? It doesn't matter what *things* they can give you or not, you simply love them for being them.'

Trixie smiled. 'Underneath all that cynicism and youthful bravado, you're quite a romantic, dear, aren't you?'

'Hopeless,' Ella admitted.

'I was, too,' Trixie said. 'But then I loved the wrong person. All my life I loved someone who belonged to someone else. Unhappily belonged to someone else. And he had no idea how I felt. No idea at all. Then he died . . . and it was all too late.'

Ella gulped. 'Oh, God, Trixie, I'm so sorry—I didn't know . . . That's so sad.'

'Don't make my mistake, Ella, that's all I'm saying.'

Ella stared at her. Did she *know*? How could she *know*?

'Look, dear, Poll's told me about your boyfriend in London. Well, not all the details, but enough to make me realise that there must be some problem for you to want to be away from him for three months. And I recognise a girl in love when I see one, dear. So, assuming it's not the boyfriend in London who's making you look all dreamy-eyed, I can only draw one other conclusion . . .'

'Please don't,' Ella said quickly. 'Jumping to conclusions, especially the wrong ones, can cause all manner of problems—and honestly, Trixie, I just don't want to discuss it, OK?'

Trixie sighed. 'Whatever you say, dear. But I'm here, dear, in case you ever change your mind and want to unburden yourself.'

'I won't.'

'All right, dear. So, where were we? Oh, yes—materialism, fairies and maybe food really being the food of love.'

'I thought that was music.'

'Only according to Shakespeare, and what did he know? But if you add music and flowers and gems and food together, what do you have?'

'The best date ever? A lovely romantic evening?' Ella sighed, suddenly transported to a daydream of Ash showering her with all of them in some secluded hideaway . . . 'Sorry.' She dragged herself back from the never-going-to-happen scenario. 'Go on then, tell me—what do we have?'

'You have the pure essence of Ruby Larkspur Day. And, before I carry on with the explanation, are you sure you're not going to mock again?'

'Sure. Promise. Absolutely.'

'Very well. Larkspur is a beautiful wild flower—so much rarer now what with building all them little houses over the green belt and the use of pesticides and the destruction of the hedgerows and very few fields left fallow, but then, you, being a city girl, don't know about that and you probably wouldn't even recognise larkspur, would you?'

Ella shook her head.

'Shame. I bet you never went on nature walks at school, did you, dear?'

'No. There actually wasn't a lot of nature round our way. Graffiti, yes. Nature, no.'

'Such a pity, dear. Oh, look at that!'

They both looked at the television screen. The team from Norfolk had just dropped their Victorian trifle.

'Anyway,' Trixie continued, 'the summer fairies love larkspur, they say it makes dreams come true, and in combination with rubies on the twentieth of July, it has some amazing magical properties. It makes it a fairy party day—hence the food and music.' She leaned forwards. 'And because of this I think you should suggest to the others that you all wear the Ruby Larkspur colours on the twentieth of July for luck.'

'Red for rubies?' Ella nodded, watching the screen with glee as Gabby glowered over the remains of the trifle as they were scooped up into a Tesco carrier bag. 'Er, OK . . . We've probably all got something red we can wear with our black bottoms. Yes, I'll mention it. I don't see what harm it can do. Is larkspur red, too?'

'Blue mostly, dear.'

'You think we should wear blue and red?' Ella chortled. '*Together*? We'll look like West Ham Second Eleven Reserves.'

'You said you weren't going to mock.'

'I'm not—Oh, look, Trixie, let's keep most of this between ourselves, shall we? I promise I'll mention about wearing the red and blue to celebrate some rural festival to the rest of them. But I'm not going to say a word about the Ruby Larkspur Day magical thingy if you don't mind . . . And, while we're on this fairy party day subject, what's so special about the twenty-fouth of July?'

'It's CandleKiss Day.'

'Don't you mean Candlemas?'

'No, that's from a completely different calendar. CandleKiss is a fairy festival of lights.'

'Like a miniature Diwali? My best friend Nalisha at home used to celebrate Diwali—we all used to

302

go to her house. It was amazing.'

'It's not Diwali or Candlemas. No. Do you remember I told you that I made my own candles? Added magical herbs to them? Well, CandleKiss is when those candles come into their own. All the fairy believers make and light their candles and make their wishes on CandleKiss and—'

'The wishes all come true and the frog turns into a handsome prince and marries the scullery maid who is really a beautiful princess and everyone lives happily ever after. The End.'

Trixie held up her hands. 'You're a lost cause, Ella. Too flippant for your own good. But don't say you haven't been given fair warning.'

## Chapter Thirty-three

The rest of *Dewberrys' Dinners'* eastern area heats more or less passed Hideaway Farm by in a frantic blur of on-screen recipes and recriminations. Ella, Poll, Ash and Billy had far more important things to think about.

Once the heady euphoria of further success had turned into blind panic, they just tried very hard to forget about the current competition, and concentrate on planning their next menu.

Having held several in-the-garden-where-it's-cooler committee meetings when, because of the temperatures and the overexcitement, tempers had become quite frayed, they finally agreed that they should stick with their retro theme for the next heat.

'No point in changing tack now,' Ash said. 'We

303

should keep to what we're best at and provide another pre-nineteen-fifties Farmhouse Feast. Really old-fashioned, farm-grown, veggie meals. That's obviously what we're good at, Gabby and Tom loved it, and that's what the viewers will remember us for. So far, no one has tried anything like it, have they?'

'No,' Ella said, 'they haven't. So, I'm happy to make an Eve's pudding, but with red, black and white currants instead of apples—because they're seasonal and we've got loads of them in the garden—and home-made custard. OK?'

'Fab!' Poll said, scribbling it down. 'But, it still looks like we're going to have a cheesy starter and a sort of cheesy main, do you think that's OK?'

Everyone nodded.

'It'll fit in nicely with the veggie theme, we didn't have cheese last time, and they're very different cheesy things, aren't they?' Billy said. 'Ash's baby leek and new potato soup is only flavoured with a sprinkle of cheese at the end, and my old-fashioned cheese biscuits are quite light in flavour and will just complement it nicely. Whereas your bread and cheese pudding will blow their socks off—bet they'll never have tasted anything like it before.'

'OK, we'll go with double cheese, and I'll have loads of fresh veg from the garden with mine anyway,' Poll continued, scribbling. 'Always assuming we have anything worth using in the garden in three weeks' time, that is. This hosepipe ban is a bit of a killer.'

'Me and young Georgie are on to it,' Billy said. 'We'll be out there first thing in the morning and last thing at night with all the leftover washing-up

304

water and what have you, making sure everything gets a good soaking. George is really excited to be playing a part this time.'

'And Ella has explained about the colours you should wear, hasn't she? And why?' Trixie leaned forwards in a nice, cosy, mumsy way. 'And you're all going to wear red and blue?'

'She has and we are.' Poll nodded. 'I think it's a lovely idea to celebrate Macd Monath—something else I remember from my Old English lessons at school. And we've all got red tops and we're going to wear blue bottoms this time.'

George chuckled smuttily again.

'Although,' Poll continued, 'I've never heard of that old country saying.'

'Which one is that, dear?'

'What was it, Ella?' Poll frowned across the dusky garden. 'I'm useless at remembering poetry.'

And Ella, avoiding Trixie's eyes, muttered, 'Er, July twenty, wear red for plenty; wear blue with red and keep the family fed.'

'So apt!' Poll beamed. 'And clever of you to know that one, Trixie. So, we're all agreed on everything? And Ella can go and type this menu up and email it to *Dewberrys' Dinners*?'

They all nodded.

'No one wants to change anything?'

They all shook their heads.

'Goody,' Poll said. 'Now all we have to do is practise and practise and rehearse and rehearse and work out timings—over and over again.'

And they all groaned.

\*　　　\*　　　\*

305

'Do you know what we need?' Ash said in the farmhouse kitchen, at the end of the week, after a particularly gruelling rehearsal when Ella knew that she'd never, ever make another Eve's pudding in her life once this was all over.

'A thunderstorm?' Ella pushed her damp hair away from her face and held up her hands in front of the constantly whirring fan, and wondered for the umpteenth time why, while the non-stop sultry weather made her look like a wilting wet rag, Ash still managed to look cool, relaxed, sexy and darkly devastating. 'A deluge of non-stop rain? Sub-zero temperatures? The new ice age?'

'A night out.'

Here we go again, Ella thought. It's the feeling sorry for me thing again. 'Thanks, but we've been through all this before and it didn't end well, did it? Anyway, I've been out,' she said. 'And at night. Two days ago, remember?'

Ash nodded. 'Oh, yes—the night the team from Cambridge made the all-pink Barbie menu.'

Their life, Ella thought with amusement, was now completely charted by *Dewberrys' Dinners*.

'Yep, that night. Anyway, because Poll was having a meal with her friends Mitzi and Zillah and Joss, she gave me a lift into Hazy Hassocks and I finally met up with those "nice girls" who work with Mitzi.'

'And were they? Nice girls?'

'Amber and Cleo? Yes, really nice. They're both married and both very loved-up, but despite not having an awful lot in common to start with, we had a drink or three at the Faery Glen in Hassocks and got on really well—and I'll definitely see them again.'

306

'Great.'

'Funnily enough, once we'd got through a couple of bottles of wine, they told me lots of things about the magic and stuff that goes on round here.'

'Yeah, a couple of bottles of wine can do that. It makes you talk about rubbish—but very seriously. You didn't mention Trixie, did you?'

Ella shook her head. 'No—well, yes, but nothing specific, not the dandelion firefighters or the *Midsummer Night's Dream* fairy thing. They'd both watched the programme and only noticed—like everyone else—just a slight technical hitch, a bit of a blip that lasted for an eye blink . . . but I was telling them about the set-up here and said that Trixie believed in fairies.'

'I bet that went down well.'

'It was OK, actually. Amber laughed. She said when she moved down here to Fiddlesticks from Manchester several years ago she thought everyone in the village was barking because they all believed in the moon and stars. They held—and still do—astral magic ceremonies. And in the end she's just accepted it because, although there was no rational explanation, things *did* and still *do* happen.'

'Belief without any understanding or explanation?' Ash frowned. 'Isn't that just the easy way out? You know, if you can't beat 'em, join 'em?'

'Maybe.' Ella shrugged. 'But Cleo lives in Lovers Knot and she said there was a similar thing there too. Only with magical wine. And then there's all sorts of rumours about herbal magic in Hazy Hassocks and love potions in Bagley-cum-Russet.'

'So I've heard since I've been doing the ice-

307

cream rounds.' Ash grinned. 'Completely bonkers, of course. But I guess it actually makes Trixie's fairy stuff quite mild by comparison.'

'Mmm . . . I've decided that it's just all old country folklore.' Ella nodded. 'But it was reassuring to talk about it. It doesn't make what happened here seem quite so weird somehow. Anyway—long story short—you see, you don't have to worry about me any more. I've met some friends and I'm getting myself a life in the country.'

'Great, again. And about time, but you can have another night out, can't you? Poll's OK about you having evenings out?'

'Of course. She always puts George to bed anyway, and does the bedtime stuff. She'd be glad if I got out more.'

'Fantastic. So—will you?'

'Not just because you feel sorry for me? Or think I'm pining for Mark in London or something and need cheering up?'

'I certainly don't feel sorry for you, as I've said before, and I'm not asking you out because I think you need cheering up, OK? Although, I know you must miss Mark.'

Ella just shrugged in a non-committal way. 'Yes, of course.'

'Mmm, Trixie has told me lots about him, and Poll has filled in the gaps.'

Oh, great.

'As they know less than nothing about him I shouldn't believe all you hear . . . Um, so, are we going out with Onyx, too?'

'No, just you and me. I've got tickets for a show, and, as we've done nothing but cook, and think

308

about cooking, and talk about cooking all week, I thought it would be nice to do something completely different.'

Just for a moment, Ella allowed the treacherous love thing to sneak in. Then she ignored it. She was getting good at that. But doing a show—a phrase she hadn't heard since leaving London—sounded pretty good, whatever Ash's reasons for inviting her. And she'd be out with him, wouldn't she? Just the two of them. For once. Oh, why not?

'OK.' She smiled. 'As long as Onyx doesn't mind.'

'Why should she? She likes you a lot. She knows we're friends.'

'OK again—that sounds great and I'd love to. When? Where? Are we eating out or do I eat first? And what do I wear? I mean, is it "dressing for the theatre" or what?'

'Hardly. It's only in Winterbrook. But yes, dressy rather than jeans, but, more importantly, whatever you're comfortable in. And there's a meal of sorts provided. And it's tomorrow.'

Pushing away the nagging 'tomorrow never comes' phrase, and trying not to skip round the kitchen, Ella took a deep breath and started making yet another Eve's pudding.

# Chapter Thirty-four

She was ready early. George, who had watched her dress in her pale-blue and silver strappy frock and her flat silver sandals, and add silver jewellery, and carefully do her hair and make-up, said she looked like the Little Mermaid.

Hoping this was a compliment, Ella swept down the staircases.

'Wow,' Ash grinned. 'You look lovely.'

'Thanks. You've scrubbed up nicely, too.'

'Right, princess, your carriage awaits.'

Ella stepped out of Hideaway's front door and shrieked with laughter. 'We're going in the ice-cream van?'

'Sorry, yes. I've let the MOT lapse on my car—got it booked in for next week—so, until then this is all I've got.'

'We could take my car,' Ella said. 'I don't mind driving.'

'But then you wouldn't be able to have a drink, and I really think you deserve a drink. I'm not fussed myself—a couple of shandys will be fine for me.' Ash looked quite worried. 'Or will you be embarrassed arriving in the van?'

'Embarrassed? Not at all.' Ella headed for the Neapolitan stripes with the cornet rampant. 'It'll add to the excitement.'

'No, Ella, look, I'll ask Poll or Billy to give us a lift and we can get a cab home.'

'No way. This is much more fun and I'm more than happy to travel in the van. But—' she stopped and looked over her shoulder '—only if you let me play the jingly-jangly music all the way into Winterbrook.'

'And have every child for miles around throwing themselves at us demanding a Bazooma?' Ash pulled a face as he hauled himself into the driving seat. 'I don't think so. But if you really must, give it a little blast now.'

Ella did. She wasn't sure if it was the 'Cancan' or 'Greensleeves' but it made them both laugh.

310

And they were still laughing when they arrived outside Winterbrook's Masonic Hall.

Slotting the ice-cream van in between a gleaming row of BMWs and Mercedes, they joined the well-dressed crowds heading for the entrance.

'Oh!' Ella blinked at the embossed poster outside as they queued to hand over their tickets. 'It's a charity do. Lovely—Winterbrook Homeless Shelter—that's great. Poll would definitely approve. Oh . . .'

Ash looked at her quizzically.

'Cleo, who I met the other night, mentioned this charity, I'm sure she did. I know she and her husband, er, Dylan, I think she said, do an awful lot of work for the homeless.'

'Maybe she'll be here tonight, then?' Ash said as they neared the imposing doors. 'And her husband. You'll have to introduce me to them.'

Ella shook her head. 'I don't think they'd be here. I gathered they work behind the scenes more. Hands on. They do soup runs and things like that. I sort of gathered that Dylan comes from a mega rich family and he's a patron—and donates oodles of dosh to these charities—but likes to stay anonymously in the background so that he doesn't lose his street cred with the rough sleepers and so that people don't think he's angling for a lot of back-patting.'

'Sounds like a nice guy. Oh, right, here we are—in we go.'

Inside the ancient gilded, chandeliered and curlicued Masonic Hall, colonial fans swirled and the myriad tables were covered in white linen, sparkling with crystal glasses and silver cutlery and tastefully decorated with white roses and tall,

311

flickering candles.

'How pretty!' Ella looked around in amazement. 'Blimey, Ash, thanks for this. What an amazing place. Is this our table? Oh, yes, there's your name—mine must be "guest"? Oh, and wow— thank you.' She smiled gratefully at him as he pulled out her chair for her. When had Mark ever done that for her? Never, ever . . .

There were four other couples round their table, strangers to both of them, and they all did the polite nodding and sketchy smile thing—with the addition of a discreet 'haven't I seen you somewhere before?' stare. Ella was getting used to it. Since *Dewberrys' Dinners*, she'd had loads of those looks.

Ella surreptitiously eyed the other men round the table: pleasant, middle-aged and comfy looking, none of them could hold a candle to Ash. In fact, she thought, gazing round the crowds in the loudly buzzing hall, Ash was the most gorgeous man in the place by a country mile.

The women at their table clearly thought so, and Ella felt a little frisson of pride. So what if she'd only borrowed him for tonight. No one else knew that, did they?

Ella, thoroughly enjoying herself, continued to people-watch as the crowds still poured in. At one end of the hall was a stage covered by long velvet curtains, but there was no dance floor area. So, not a dinner dance, then . . . presumably it was more of a cabaret, and maybe with some speeches. She settled back in her chair as the waiters bustled round, filling glasses.

'It's a set menu.' Ash leaned towards her. 'Not very inspiring—corporate catering—but presumably the idea is to make money for the charity, not splash out on ritzy food.'

'It looks OK to me. Very OK. Pumpkin soup.' She chuckled. 'Sorry, that reminds me of Billy. Oh, and roast chicken for the carnivores and mushroom risotto for the veggies, and crème brûlée for pud. Oh, and cheese and biscuits. Lovely—I'm starving.'

'You usually are,' Ash laughed. 'I had to tick boxes for the main course. I went for the veggie option for both of us—Poll's influence is really rubbing off—I hope that's OK.'

'Perfectly. I haven't eaten meat since I arrived at Hideaway. Don't think I ever will again, actually. Ash, thanks so much for this. It's great.'

'My pleasure.' He smiled.

Ella's heart did crazy somersaults and she suddenly felt quite giddy with lust. She took a huge gulp from her wine glass. There, in control again—well, sort of . . .

As soon as the last of the latecomers were seated, and she and Ash had properly introduced themselves round their table, and discussed their appearance on *Dewberrys' Dinners* with their very impressed companions, who all realised now that's why they'd seemed so familiar, the waiters circulated with the first course.

The footlights suddenly blazed into life, illuminating the front of the stage. A very made-up woman in a sequinned frock and big glasses strode up to a lectern and tapped the microphone.

'Please carry on eating.' Her elegantly modulated voice spiralled tinnily high up into the beautifully stuccoed ceiling. 'I just want to say, on behalf of the committee of Winterbrook Homeless

313

Shelter, that I'm delighted to see you all here and to thank you so much for your overwhelming generosity. Your money will make such a difference to refurbishing and extending our existing drop-in centre and in building our planned hostel. We've decided that entertainment while you eat is the best way to show *our* appreciation, so I do hope you'll enjoy our little supper show. And, of course, if you wish to leave another small—or not so small—token of *your* appreciation in the buckets by the doors when you leave, we'll be even more delighted.'

There was a lot of laughter and applause. Then, as the woman left the stage, the curtains drew back and a troupe of vividly dressed jugglers ran on.

Ella loved every minute of it. They had the jugglers with the soup, and a close-harmony choir with the main course, followed by a very clever magician during dessert.

And in between, she and Ash talked and laughed together. It was like being out on a real date. Ella couldn't remember when she had last been so happy.

The waiters circled silently, clearing plates, refilling glasses. Ella groaned greedily over the arrival of the cheese board.

From behind the closed velvet curtains, exotic music echoed. Ella tapped her feet under the table. It sounded very Arabic: sensuous and mysterious.

A gasp went round the Masonic Hall as the curtains drew back to reveal a belly dancer, moving sinuously in the spotlight. In a tantalising costume of flimsy, draped, brilliantly coloured fabrics, and dripping with jewels, she undulated

314

across the stage to the wonderfully evocative Eastern music.

The whole audience was transfixed.

'Wow,' Ella whispered to Ash. 'How beautiful. She's absolutely brilliant . . . God, I wish I could do that. Look at her—Oh . . . Jesus Christ! It's Onyx!'

Ash laughed. 'Well spotted. She always opens with "Arabian Rhapsody", but you wait until she gets into "Disco El Sharq"—that's amazing.'

Amazing . . . Oh, yes, Ella thought bleakly, leaving her blue cheese untouched. Onyx was definitely amazing . . .

And the dancing—not a pole or a lap in sight. It wasn't even slightly tacky. She'd got it all so wrong.

Onyx was a belly dancer . . .

A clever, talented, beautifully exotic belly dancer . . .

The tune changed to something even more Eastern and Kasbah-ish. Ella stared at Onyx, her sensuous body moving in perfect time with the mysterious music, in abject misery.

Onyx, in a filmy shimmer of hot pink and orange, every inch of her perfectly toned and lithe and glistening, the gold and silver bells and coins dancing, and the jewels glinting, seduced the audience with her brilliance.

Dear God, Ella thought sadly, how could I ever compete with *that*?

Even supposing that she got the chance to— which of course she wouldn't, because Ash and Onyx were rock solid.

Oh, why had he brought her here tonight? Was it to show her once and for all that she was his friend and Onyx was, well, Onyx, and Ella would never, ever be anything else but a good mate? Yes, Ella

315

decided, probably. In fact, obviously.

Well, she thought, watching Ash watching Onyx, it had succeeded.

Four more dances, each one more complex and daring than its predecessor, and Onyx took her bow.

The Masonic Hall's audience was on its feet, giving her a standing ovation. Ash and Ella stood too and clapped and cheered. Ash, no doubt, Ella thought bleakly, because he was secure in the knowledge that Onyx—with her beautiful body, her clever brain and her multitude of talents—was his. But Ella stood because, well, because Onyx was amazing and she truly deserved the accolade—even if she'd just finally broken her heart.

And it had all been so lovely up to then . . .

They sat down again as Onyx took her final bow and shimmied from the stage to be replaced by wall-to-wall music-to-talk-over.

'So?' Ash leaned towards her. 'What do you think?'

'Oh.' Ella crumbled her untouched blue cheese. 'She's incredible. Totally incredible. No wonder she doesn't want to hide herself away in some stuffy classroom teaching Shakespeare to kids who don't give a damn.'

Ash laughed. 'She'll do that one day, though. I always tell her she'll have to give it up once the varicose veins start to kick in . . . Would you like some more wine?'

'No thanks.' Ella stared down at her plate. 'Ash, I know why you brought me here tonight now, and it's OK, honestly. I do understand, and I'm not a child. I won't make a scene or anything.'

'Good.' Ash looked slightly puzzled. 'I hate

316

scenes—but I haven't got a clue what you're talking about. Oh, hi—' he stood up '—come and sit down. You were great. I'll get you a drink.'

Onyx, back to being Onyx now in her jeans and her vest and her heels, but still wearing the thick stage make-up, beamed at them. 'Thanks, I'm parched. Soda with ice would be great.'

The men on their table all became suddenly animated, Ella noticed as Onyx slid into Ash's vacated chair. Even the women smiled, albeit not quite so warmly.

'You were brilliant,' Ella said. 'Totally brilliant.'

'Ta—but it's like second nature now. Not clever or anything. Just something I'm able to do easily and reasonably well. Told you I was lazy, didn't I?' Onyx leaned towards Ella. 'But I'm so glad you're here. I told Ash you'd turned me down when I suggested you came along tonight; I knew he'd be able to persuade you. I so wanted you to see what I do.'

And now I've seen, Ella thought bleakly, and now I know why he loves you so much, and now I know why he wanted me here tonight, and it's left me feeling more inadequate and foolish than I've ever felt in my life.

Ash came back then, bearing iced soda for Onyx and a strawberry daiquiri for Ella.

'Oooh.' Onyx eyed the cocktail. 'That looks good.'

'Thank you,' Ella said, as Ash located another chair and squeezed in between her and Onyx. 'But there was no need.'

'I thought you'd like it.'

'I do.' Ella sighed. 'Look, please don't think I'm being a party pooper or anything, but would it be

317

OK if I got a cab home?'

'Why?' Ash frowned. 'Oh, God, you *are* embarrassed about the ice-cream van, aren't you?'

Onyx shrieked through her soda. 'Ash! You didn't bring poor Ella in the van?'

'She enjoyed it, didn't you?'

Ella nodded. She'd loved it. She'd loved every minute of the evening—until . . .

'Yes, it was fun. But right now I've got a headache and, um, I'd hate to spoil the rest of your evening. So you stay on here in Winterbrook with Onyx and I'll get a cab. OK?'

'Ella—wait!'

But grabbing her bag and leaving her strawberry daiquiri untouched, she blundered away from the table.

## *Chapter Thirty-five*

The Pink Barbie team from Cambridge was the eastern heat's Weekly Winner. Even before the western area heats had started, everyone at Hideaway was sure they'd win the whole thing.

'But,' Poll said to Ella on yet another July clear-blue-sky, spiralling-sun morning, 'I still don't really see the problem with you and Ash . . . I mean, I was so pleased when he asked you out—and then you came home alone—and now . . .'

'And now we're hardly speaking at all, mainly because I don't know what to say. It's changed everything. He keeps saying he thought it would be a lovely surprise for me.'

'Which,' Poll said, 'I suppose it was?'

318

'You're not kidding! Although I'd leave out the "lovely".' Ella sighed. 'Well, of course, the evening out bit was very lovely—it was just the surprise of Onyx being the mind-blowing incredible cabaret that threw me. And now Ash just thinks I'm being unreasonable.'

'Which you are, really, aren't you?' Poll said gently.

'Am I?' Ella looked at her as she collected up George's dirty washing from the kitchen floor and shoved it into the machine. 'Yes, OK, I probably am. But I felt such a fool . . . I thought . . . well, you know what I thought.'

'Yes, I do. But Ash doesn't. He must wonder what the heck he did wrong.'

'He does. He keeps asking me.'

'And?'

'And I just said it was a lovely evening, but I'd had enough and had a headache and wanted to come home—which even to me sounds pathetic.'

'And to me, too.' Poll frowned. 'Poor Ash.'

'Oh, I know I should have been more adult about it all and not let my feelings show, but I couldn't . . . I just couldn't.' Ella sighed. 'And of course, that was his point, wasn't it? To let me down gently. To make me realise that he and Onyx are a couple— and why—and there's no way I'm going to be anything other than a good friend. Still, at least I know exactly where I stand now.'

'But you always did. Oh, love, I'm so sorry you're upset. But you can't accuse him of cheating on you, or anything, can you? He's aware of your relationship with Mark, and you did know about him and Onyx—it couldn't have come as that much of a shock, surely?'

319

'But it did! I thought, stupidly, that for once the evening was an Onyx-free zone. I really thought this time he'd asked me out because he wanted to be with me, just me, and we were there, as a couple. No Mark, no Onyx. And it was wonderful. Really, really wonderful. We were chatting and laughing and, oh, I don't know, it all felt right and we were so close, and he really, really seemed to want to be with me—and then . . .'

'And then Onyx did her stuff?'

'And how. God, Poll, she was amazing. I mean truly amazing. Talented and exotic and erotic, but not sleazy at all. Just absolutely beautiful. Everyone went mad for her, and I can't blame them. Oh, how the hell could I ever have expected him to fall in love with me when he's got her?'

Poll, clutching a handful of George's grubby socks, hugged her. 'Ella, I'm really sorry—and I do think he should have mentioned that Onyx was part of the evening's cabaret—but they are a couple. As you and Mark are. And while I'm sure Ash asked you out with the best of intentions, he knows about Mark, and he has no idea that you, well, er, how you feel about him, has he?'

'No, but I think now he'd probably twigged that I fancy him and needed to tell me to back off. But he's a nice man, so he did it in a sort of non-verbal way.'

Poll shook her head. 'Are you sure?'

'Positive. I'm not stupid. I've been given the elbow before. I can read the signs.'

'And what about Mark?'

Ella bit her lip. 'I'm going to tell Mark there won't be a reconciliation after the three months is up.'

'Ella! Are you sure?'

'Yes, never more sure of anything in my life. Poll, I can't go back to Mark when I leave here. It's not fair on either of us. He won't change his mind about children, and neither will I. I realise that now. We're never going to resolve our differences. The gulf's wider now than it was when I left. It would be so wrong to try to rekindle something that clearly died ages ago. I love Ash; I don't love Mark any more.'

'But Ash is with Onyx.'

'I know. It doesn't matter. I'd far rather be on my own for ever than settle for second best. I'm going to ring Mark tonight.'

'Oh dear, oh dear.' Poll shook her head sadly.

Ella sniffed. 'I feel really awful, Poll, so please don't tell anyone. Not Billy or Trixie—and certainly not Ash. It's something I should have done ages ago.'

Poll hugged her. 'Ella, love, you know I won't say a word. But are you absolutely sure?'

'Yes, never more sure of anything in my life. Because of the way I felt when I *knew* how much Onyx meant to Ash. I was totally eaten up with jealousy. I've never felt like that when Mark's flirted with some pretty girl at a party.'

Poll was silent for a moment. 'And once Onyx had finished her act, she didn't mind you being there with him?'

'No.' Ella shook her head scornfully. 'She knew I would be there, apparently. She'd asked me to be there before and I'd said no. And why should she mind? Look at us, Poll. I'm no competition, am I?'

'You're a very pretty young woman. Beautiful. And easy-going and sweet and funny and kind.

321

And I'm sure Ash recognises that. While Onyx is . . .'

'Drop-dead gorgeously, stunningly, sexily, mind-blowing?' Ella smiled sadly. 'Intelligent? Well educated? Amusing? Friendly? Yep, all those—and more. Not that she seems aware of it.'

'No, she's a really lovely girl.'

'I know,' Ella sighed. 'And even if Ash *had* asked me there on a date, she wouldn't have cared two hoots. She knows no one else is important. They clearly have total trust.'

Poll sighed. 'It all sounds very complicated to me. Oh, why does love have to be so unfair sometimes?'

'Dunno. Mind you, if it wasn't, half the songwriters in the world would be broke. Oh, I'll just have to cope with it, and as far as I know, Onyx isn't aware of how I feel about him, either—thank goodness. She's just so bloody nice anyway. She came and joined us after the show, and was so pleased to see me and was just her normal lovely self—damn her.'

'But I still don't see why you're not talking to Ash.'

'Don't you? Oh, God—I behaved like some sort of spoiled child, and if Onyx hadn't appeared when she did I'd have blurted it all out to him. And now he just thinks I'm rude and ungrateful. Which is fair enough, but now I've no idea how to put things right.'

'Well—' Poll gave Ella another hug '—you'll have to try to patch things up with him before the twentieth of July. You'll have to be speaking to each other by then. We won't be able to work as a team if you're not.'

322

'No, I know, and I will, or at least I'll try. Promise.'

'Ready, Poll?' Billy poked his head into the kitchen. 'If we're going to grab a bite of lunch we ought to get a move on.'

'Yes, ready.' Poll smiled. She looked at Ella. 'You'll be OK having George for an hour or two, won't you? If you don't feel like it I can always drop him off at Doll Blessing's—he gets on so well with her brood.'

'I'm fine,' Ella said. 'George and I will quarry in the garden with his new lorry, or read under the trees, or go and look for fairies at the bottom of the garden, which is Trixie's influence and his latest craze.'

'Don't tell me.' Poll grabbed her beaded shoulder bag. 'I'm fiercely anti gender stereotyping, but since she bought him those books he's clamouring for a Flower Fairies duvet set for his birthday and it's beginning to bother me. Right, we won't be too long.'

'Go and have a lovely lunch and take as long as you like—you both deserve it.'

'And, Ella, remember, if all else fails, there's always Plan B.'

'What? Oh, yes.'

'What's Plan B?' Billy frowned.

'A barn-dancing young farmer,' Poll and Ella said together, but only Poll laughed.

*     *     *

Half an hour later, Poll and Billy found a table by the open window in Patsy's Pantry. The frilly curtains hung heavy and listless in the sultry air,

323

but at least, thanks to the air conditioning and a phalanx of fans, it was far cooler inside than out. And fortunately, at lunchtime, the place was almost empty, the majority of the more elderly Hazy Hassockers preferring to gather there for morning coffee and afternoon tea.

'. . . so my money's on the fish and chip team from Devon this week,' Billy said. 'Although we've still got another western heat to go tonight, haven't we?'

Poll nodded, enjoying every mouthful of her cheese omelette and salad. It was such bliss to be eating food cooked by someone else for a change. 'I don't think anyone will beat the fish and chippers though. So clever, making all three courses look like fish and chips, even though it was only the main that was, fish and chips, I mean.'

Patsy, clearing a nearby table, looked over. 'You're going to be on the telly again, I hear. Well, I must say, I said you was mad to go in for it in the first place, but you made a fine fist of it. None of that folderrol rubbish. Good wholesome food and plenty of it—some of them recipes you used took me back to my childhood and beyond, I can tell you.'

Poll beamed. High praise indeed, coming from Patsy, who, she knew from Ella and Trixie, was one of her harshest critics. 'Thank you. I appreciate that. I know you haven't always been quite so supportive. Either of us going on *Dewberrys' Dinners* or me personally.'

'No, can't say I have.' Patsy wiped vigorously. 'Thought you was doolally to want to go on the telly in the first place, what with all that head-turning nonsense that goes on, and you don't need that, Poll, do you? You're halfway there already. But fair's fair. You seem to have come out of it more or less unscathed. And, say what you will, that band of bad 'uns you've got living at Hideaway did you proud.'

'They are not bad 'uns,' Poll said hotly. 'They're all lovely people who are now my family. This is Billy and—'

'Ah.' Patsy nodded. 'We knows all about him. Heard from his cousin over in Tadpole Bridge that he murdered his first wife with a bread stick.'

'I did nothing of the sort,' Billy protested. 'Poor Mary choked accidentally on a bloomer.'

'Bread stick—bloomer—where's the difference? And accidentally? Well, that's between you and your maker, I say. But ' she looked at Poll again ' there's one thing that does ring true about the telly. It puts pounds on you. You looked like the side of a house.'

Poll flapped her hands and stifled her giggles in her napkin. She tried to stop the giggles erupting into a snort and failed. 'Oh, please excuse me. I'm so sorry . . . Er, um, yes, well, we're watching all the heats now to see what we're up against in the next round.'

'Ah well, there's the thing—' Patsy shook her J-cloth out of the open window '—you needn't get all het up because there's no point in thinking you'll win it. You won't get no further. That lot from Norfolk what made everything pink—they'll walk it. Still, you had a good try.'

Poll bit her lip as Patsy bustled cheerfully away to serve a clutch of customers who had wandered in from outside and were staring balefully at the Perspex-covered display of bag-you-etties.

'She's a bit outspoken,' Billy chuckled. 'Calls a spade a spade, doesn't she?'

Poll nodded. 'A good plain speaker is our Patsy. Oh, dear.'

'What's up?'

'Mona Jupp and Topsy Turvey have just come in. I hope they don't want to sit near us. Topsy's OK—old as the hills but still dances the cancan—but Mona can be a bit tart.'

'After Patsy I reckon we can cope with anything. Mind you, it looks like they're coming over this way. Must be because of the open window. Why can't they be happy with the fan and the air conditioning? Oh, drat and damn.'

Poll frowned at him. Billy, the most sanguine of men, was rarely irritated. 'Does the open window bother you? Do you want to sit somewhere else?'

'No, love. The fresh air is fine—I'd just hoped we'd have the place to ourselves for a little bit longer. That was one of the reasons I asked you out to lunch. So that I could talk to you privately without the phone ringing non-stop about *Dewberrys' Dinners.*'

Poll felt suddenly cold. All through her life, when someone had said they wanted to talk privately, it had been to impart Bad News. Whether it had been her parents or her teachers or even Dennis during the brief and disastrous marriage, those words had heralded something extremely unpleasant.

And always, she'd stood or sat, cowering and feeling sick and helpless, knowing the Sword of Damocles was just about to fall, and, well, just let it.

But that was then. Now she was a different Poll

326

Andrews. Now she'd made a success of things and her life was lovely and she had confidence. Well, OK, not loads of confidence, but some. Now she knew she'd never be a victim again. And that was in no small part down to Billy. But if he left . . .

She swallowed her last mouthful of omelette with some difficulty. Best face the horrors head-on. 'You don't want to leave Hideaway Farm, do you?'

'What? No way—of course not. Whatever gave you that idea? Far from it. I never want to leave. Ever. I've had the happiest couple of months of my life since . . . well, since . . .'

Mona Jupp and Topsy Turvey, in summer frocks dating back at least five decades, eased themselves into a neighbouring table and did the smiles-and-nods greeting.

Poll, mightily relieved on several counts, lowered her voice. 'Go on, I don't think they can hear us.'

Billy shook his head. 'Don't mind if they can. But no, let's not talk here—let's go back to the barn where we know we'll get some privacy for a while—if you've finished your lunch, that is?'

'Yes,' Poll screwed up her napkin. 'It was lovely, thanks. A rare treat.'

'OK then—' Billy wiped up the remains of his egg and chips with a huge doorstep of bread and butter '—let's go.'

*       *       *

Half an hour later they were sitting in the cool of the barn, side by side on a hay bale, watching the sun scorch its way across the parched meadows outside.

Billy sighed. 'I've been watching young Ella and Ash and thinking what a darn shame it is. Such smashing kids. They could be so happy, but this last few days they've been as miserable as sin. I know it's a bit of an infernal triangle there, but anyone with half an eye can see that they're just right for each other.'

Perceptive, Poll thought, knowing that she couldn't tell him what Ella had so recently confided in her. But had Billy really rushed back here to their almost completed bolt hole to talk about Ella?

'I know. But Ella, um, does have a boyfriend, and Ash and Onyx have been together for years. And I honestly can't see that changing. I don't think there's anything we can do. Even if Ash did like Ella as much as she obviously likes him, there's still Onyx. Oh, and Ella's Mark, of course. One or more of them's going to get terribly hurt. And it's probably going to be Ella.'

Billy shook his head. 'Poor little Ella . . . But, you see, Poll, that's what I wanted to talk to you about. Ella and Ash aren't happy. I had a darn miserable marriage and yours was—well—wasn't the best, was it, love?'

'Understatement of the year.'

'Exactly.' Billy reached for Poll's hand. 'I might be talking out of turn here, but what I've been thinking is why, when we've been so unhappy in the past, shouldn't we be happy now—and in the future? Life's so short. We clicked as soon as we met, didn't we? And since I've been here, we've got to know each other properly, and I know my first feelings were the right ones.'

Poll smiled. First feelings? Love at first sight?

328

Was that what Billy meant? Dare she even hope that was what he meant? She'd made so many mistakes in the past, and this was so important, she simply couldn't make another one now.

She nodded. 'I thought you were lovely at that first meeting. I thought you were the gentlest, kindest man I'd ever met. I didn't know how you felt about me.'

Billy shifted on the hay bale. 'I thought you were amazing, offering me the chance to start again— but more than that, I thought you were very beautiful.'

Beautiful? Poll relished the word. No one had ever called her beautiful. She knew she wasn't, but if Billy thought so then that was all that mattered. She sighed happily, not daring to speak in case her voice wobbled or she cried and spoiled the moment.

'But,' Billy continued, sliding his arm around her shoulders, 'it wasn't just that. Yes, I thought you were kind and generous and selfless and beautiful, but there was something else. Something I never felt with Mary or anyone before her. Oh, I know it sounds daft saying it like this, and at my age, but right there and then—at that first meeting—I loved you.'

Poll held her breath. Was this really, really happening? To her? Poll Andrews—slapdash, chaotic, confused, and, if her parents and Dennis were to be believed, stupid and totally unlovable?

'Poll?' Billy looked anxiously at her. 'Oh, Lord, Poll. I've upset you now, haven't I? Look, forget I said anything—I'm sorry, I shouldn't have . . .'

'Yes you should.' Poll finally gulped in the breath she'd been holding. 'Oh, yes, you should. Because

329

that's exactly how I felt, too.'

They stared at each other in delight, then Billy pulled her into his arms and kissed her gently.

He stroked her hair. 'Oh, Poll, I love you so much.'

'And I love you, too.'

They stared wordlessly at one another in total delight.

Billy spoke softly. 'And now we've both been given a second chance at making a decent fist of the years we've got left and—'

Poll, still floating, stared down at his hand covering hers, then up into his gentle dark-brown eyes. 'Are you suggesting that we should, um, put our, um, relationship on a more, er, serious footing? That we should go out together? Um, start courting or seeing each other, or whatever the current phrase is?'

'If that's what you'd like, then yes.'

Poll, completely overwhelmed with relief and love, beamed at him. 'Like? Oh, Billy, I'd love it!'

Billy kissed her again. 'Me, too . . . Oh, Poll, we're going to have so much fun and happiness, but now there's something else as well.' Billy gently pushed her away. 'I've got to say this bit now before I lose my nerve.'

Slightly awkwardly, he dropped on to one knee in front of the hay bale and took Poll's hands in his. 'Poll Andrews, I love you and I always will— so, will you marry me?'

The barn was silent.

'Marry?' Poll looked down at him. '*Married*? You and me?'

Billy nodded. 'You and me. I love you so much. Oh, Lord, Poll, sorry. You clearly don't feel the same way. The going out is fine, the marriage isn't. It's all too quick for you. I've got it all wrong here.'

'No, you haven't!' Poll said delightedly, throwing her arms round him, almost knocking him off balance. 'You've got it absolutely right! And I love you, too, and I'd love to be married to you. Oh, thank you.'

'Does that mean you'll say yes?'

'Yes!' Poll laughed as Billy struggled to his feet and snuggled even closer on the hay bale. 'Yes and yes and yes.'

'Now I'm the happiest man on the planet.' Billy kissed her gently. 'Mind you, we'll have to start dating right away, won't we?'

'Yes.' Poll giggled. 'But, Billy, seriously, the getting married bit—we won't mention anything about that until *Dewberrys' Dinners* is all over. We'll keep it to ourselves. It'll be our secret until the time is right. We've got enough going on, and with Ella being so miserable, well, it wouldn't be very fair, would it?'

Billy shook his head. 'No, it wouldn't. And anyway, I think you need to talk to young George before anyone else knows at all. Explain it to him properly. Make sure he's happy.'

'He will be. He loves you.'

'And I love him. And his mum.'

Billy pulled Poll to her feet and kissed her again. Properly. Poll, who had never been kissed properly before, thought dizzily that she hoped Billy would go on kissing her properly for ever and ever . . .

'So,' Billy whispered into her hair, 'we'll start courting for a few months, and then . . .'

'And then—' Poll sighed blissfully '—we'll have a small and very quiet winter wedding. I've always

331

loved the thought of a winter wedding.'

'Sounds perfect. Just us and George and the Hideaway family. But when we've announced it publicly,' Billy said, 'I want to buy you an engagement ring so that all the world knows.'

'Oh, that's lovely. But you don't have to. I don't need—'

'But I do.' Billy smiled as he kissed her again. 'I want this to be the right and proper start to the rest of our lives together.'

The rest of our lives together. Poll smiled dreamily. Oh, how wonderful that sounded.

## Chapter Thirty-six

In the fourth and final week of the *Dewberrys' Dinners* heats, the temperatures continued to soar, the country baked, the hosepipe ban had been extended, the tabloids forecast the end of the world as we know it, the fish and chips team from Devon won the western area heat, and the northern area heats were well under way.

Ella, curled on her bed, with the voile curtains hanging listlessly at the window, and with the sweat trickling down her back as the evening sun beat down across the farm, felt sick as she punched out the familiar numbers.

The wait for a connection seemed endless. The ringing went on for ever.

'Oh, um, hi, Mark, it's me . . . Are you? Which pub? Oh, yes—great. With? Ah, right . . . Yes, yes, we're going to be in the next round . . . You won't watch it? Oh, yes, of course . . . cooking was never your thing, was it? Well, have a nice time.' She swallowed. 'Mark, look, I just need to say something . . . What? When? Oh, with Nick and Andy—are you? And who? Oh, yes, the girls from Customer Services . . . A villa? Lovely. Look, Mark, I know I should do this face to face, but . . .' She took a deep breath. 'I think we should call it a day. Now. No point in dragging it out until August.'

She listened to the silence. Oh, God . . .

Then he spoke and she swallowed the lump in her throat.

'What? No, I don't know if I'll stay on here or come back to London when the three months is up, but whatever I do, I think it's unfair to you to keep you hanging on.'

Another silence. More words.

'Mark . . . ? Oh, has it? Well, that's good. Have you? Look, I know we've been together for ages but we weren't going anywhere, and now I know . . .'

She listened, her hands shaking.

'OK, that's fine, then . . . Yes, you too . . . As long as you're not—oh, you're not . . . Well, enjoy your holiday. No, there's no point in . . . OK, fine. Yes, of course.'

She snapped the phone shut, hurled it on to the bed and burst into tears.

'Ella?' Poll's voice floated up the stairs. '*Dewberrys' Dinners* is just about to start.'

'Er.' Ella dashed away the tears, hoping her voice sounded normal. 'OK, I'll be down in minute.'

She scrambled from the bed, feeling desperately sad, and stared at her face in the dressing table's

333

mirror. OK, so her eyes were red, but she could put that down to hay fever. She wasn't sure she'd be able to explain away the rest of the bleakness. Applying some blusher and lipgloss, a bit more mascara and fluffing at her hair, she stared at herself again.

Better—not great—but better . . .

So, she'd done it. Burned her boats. Now she had neither a relationship nor a life to return to in London. So after she left here, she'd be completely on her own.

A fresh start? Or a lonely future?

Whatever, it was up to her now, she thought, no one else, just her, as she headed downstairs to watch the opposition.

Knowing their next television appearance was rapidly approaching, the Hideaway contingent had practised their new recipes, and their cooking, and their timings, to perfection. It had become a rather out-of-sync routine, given that Ella and Ash were still awkward with one another, while Poll and Billy were constantly smiling and touching and wearing matching faraway dreamy expressions.

'Hi, just in time,' Poll said as Ella wandered into the peaches and cream sitting room and then met her eyes. 'Ah . . . OK, you come and sit over here.'

Not looking at Ash—or anyone else—Ella gratefully scuttled to the sofa.

Tonight's contestants were a quartet of very skinny students from Newcastle who looked like they'd never eaten a solid meal in their lives but who prepared an amazing traditional Geordie Slap-Up. With a combination of leek pudding, stottie cakes, pease pudding and singing hinnies, they sent an increasingly caustic Gabby and Tom

334

into the realms of culinary ecstasy.

'Blimey,' Billy groaned, as 'Pickin' a Chicken' bounced round the sitting room at the end of their show. 'They were brilliant.'

'Yes, they were,' Poll agreed. 'We've certainly got some very stiff competition. But we'll wow them again on Monday, you'll see. Our new menu's as good as any of them. Right, who's for a long cold drink?'

'Not me.' Ash hauled himself out of the armchair furthest away from Ella. 'I've got to clean out Roy's vivarium and then I'm off to the pub with Joe and the rest of the blokes.'

Ella watched him leave the room. 'Was that supposed to indicate that I'm Billy-no-Mates—no personal insult intended, Billy—? Well, tough.'

'I'm sure it wasn't anything of the sort,' Poll said soothingly. 'Dear me, the pair of you are behaving like George and his on-off best friend/worst enemy.'

'Thanks.' Ella stood up. 'I really needed to be told I'm being childish! Tonight of all nights!'

'Ella!'

'Sorry, Poll, but I've, er, I've just made the phone call.'

'Oh, love, have you? I'm so sorry.'

'What phone call?' Trixie enquired perkily.

'Nothing, nothing at all,' Poll said quickly. 'Just something work-related between me and Ella. Anyway, we're all feeling grumpy, aren't we? It's the never-ending heat and the build-up to next Monday, and, well, everything.'

Ella smiled gratefully. 'Yes—and sorry—I'm not usually a grouchy cow.'

'I know, love. I know. Shall I pour you a drink

and we'll sit in the garden and, er, chill out a bit or talk?'

Ella shook her head. 'No thanks. I'm really not very good company at the moment. I think I'll go and have a long, cool bath and find a good book to read and have an early night.'

'And that,' Onyx said, popping her head round the sitting room door, 'sounds about as boring a night in as I've heard in a long time.' She grinned. 'Ash said you were all in here, and also that I'm not needed in his plans for tonight because as soon as he's finished dunging-out Roy, he's going out with the boys—sooo—' she raised her eyebrows at Ella '—why don't you and I have some girlie time together?'

Ella knew Poll was staring at her with deep sympathy.

It was the last thing on earth she wanted to do.

'Oh, I don't know. It's quite late and I'm all hot and tired and bad-tempered. I really don't feel like going out.'

'Who said anything about going out?' Onyx chuckled. 'I thought we could have a girlie night in. Just the two of us.'

An hour later, in Ella's pale-blue bedroom, Onyx finished rooting through the jars and boxes on the dressing table. 'You're so lucky. This is such a fab room. So pretty and so much space—and that bathroom is to die for. And you've got some really super stuff here. Not that you need it, do you? Look at you. With your hair all in those gorgeous natural Pre-Raphaelite curls, and your skin all dappled and sun-kissed and lovely.'

'Me?' Ella, hugging her knees on the bed, letting the slight evening breeze now wafting through the voile curtains cool her, frowned. 'Since I've stopped going to the hairdresser and having facials, I'm sunburnt, ginger and frazzled.'

'You're so funny.' Onyx sniffed at one of the scent bottles. 'Ooh, Givenchy . . . lovely . . . Do you never look at yourself, Ella? You turn heads wherever you go.'

'Er, no. That's you.'

Onyx laughed. 'Because I'm black, six feet tall and wear minimal clothing—as Ash would say? Yeah, OK, but you do because you're truly beautiful. And I so wish you'd let me teach you to dance. You'd be like Isadora Duncan. All floaty hair and trailing veils and scarves.'

Ella smiled. It was difficult with a broken heart. 'And didn't one of those trailing scarves strangle her in the end?'

'Yeah, well, I wasn't suggesting you took it that far, but now you've seen how easy it is to dance.'

'Easy? You're joking. For you, maybe. You're brilliant at it. You're a natural. I couldn't do what you do in a million years.'

'You could, you know. I'm starting a class in Hazy Hassocks village hall. So many people have asked me, and it'll be something else to put off the dreaded "using my degree" thing for a bit longer. You must come along.'

Ella shook her head. 'No, honestly, I'm truly not the greatest dancer in the world. I can shuffle with the rest of them after a few cocktails, but I'd feel really silly trying something as difficult as that— especially in front of loads of other people.'

Onyx grinned. 'It's not difficult at all. And I'll teach you now, if you like. Just some of the basics. Then you'd be one step ahead of the rest of them

337

when you join my class.'

'I'm not joining your class.'

Onyx plonked herself down on the end of the bed. 'OK, look, I'll teach you the rudiments of what the non-purists call belly-dancing, and you can teach me how to boil an egg.'

Ella sighed. This was absolutely not what she wanted or needed tonight. 'You must *know* how to boil an egg.'

'Yeah, OK. But some basic cookery stuff. Ella, please. You're amazing at it, I'm rubbish, and I just need to know some basics.'

'Buy some books, or use the internet.'

'Not the same as hands-on, though, is it? I can't ask a book questions as I go along, can I? Cookery books and recipes will be OK later—when I know what I'm doing.'

Ella took a deep breath. 'So, why don't you ask Ash to teach you?'

Onyx shook her head. 'I can't.'

Ella cursed inwardly. Of course she couldn't. Because it was Ash that Onyx was wanting to impress with her new-found talents wasn't it? Or maybe even worse—Ash had suggested they live together—oh, God!—here? Yes, of course—and Onyx wanted to learn some sort of cookery skills so that they could share the chores in their newly found domestic bliss?

Oh, joy . . .

Ah, well, nothing like turning the screw a little bit tighter on your own pain and abject misery.

'OK, then. I'll wobble my tummy and while I'm doing it I'll talk you through some of the easy-peasy things about cooking.'

'Cheers.' Onyx looked animated again. 'Right,

338

you find something suitable to wear to get you in the mood, and I'll just nip down to my car for a CD.'

'Suitable? Like what?'

'Oh, anything loose—I'll suggest tracksuit bottoms and vest or T-shirt for my class to start with, and a long scarf or shawl to shimmy with, but you suit yourself tonight.'

Totally, totally mad, Ella thought, hauling herself off the bed after Onyx had gone downstairs to retrieve the appropriate belly-dancing music from her car.

The last thing—no, correction, the *two* last things—she needed right now, on this stiflingly hot evening when she was not only heartbroken but also tired and very, very angry both with Ash and herself—not to mention Mark who clearly didn't *care*—was to be shimmying about like a demented clumsy baby elephant *thing* in front of the sublimely talented Onyx, *and* teaching the sublimely talented and devastatingly gorgeous Onyx how to cook simply to impress Ash.

Of course, she thought, rooting through her pared-down wardrobe, she could teach Onyx all the wrong things. Give her a lot of false information, so that when she first tried to wow Ash with her new-found culinary prowess, she'd make a complete horlicks of it.

But, Ella sighed, chucking several unsuitable garments over her shoulder, she wouldn't and couldn't do that.

Because she really *liked* Onyx, damn it.

Eventually grabbing several of Poll's cast-off silk shawls from the bottom of the wardrobe, and deciding on a long layered skirt with jangly things

339

on it, Ella, with fairly bad grace, attempted to transform herself.

'Hey, you look really cool.' Onyx grinned as she opened the door. 'See, I told you you were a natural.'

'I've just dressed up; I haven't pranced yet.'

'*Prance*? We never prance! We shimmy and undulate and wriggle and writhe—and all in a sinuous, flowing, graceful, alluring motion. Read my lips—we do not prance!'

Ella, surprising herself, giggled. 'OK—is that the first lesson over then? Can I get changed back now?'

'Not a cat's chance.' Onyx slid the CD into Ella's stereo on top of the bookcase. 'Right—before we begin, get the basic rhythm by imagining you're hula-hooping, but don't just think you have to stand there and waggle your belly. This isn't just about your belly. This is about your whole body. You use your shoulders and your torso and your pelvis, all in turn, and then put them together. Oh, and especially your hands. Each dance is different and each dance tells a story—remember Scheherazade?'

As the evocative music flooded into the room, and Onyx put Ella through her paces, Ella breathlessly tried to instil some of the basics of cookery into Onyx.

It was the best therapy ever.

With much giggling and shrieking and joint exclamations of disgust and refusal, they passed a very quick and happy hour.

'I think,' Ella puffed, sitting exhausted on the floor in a heap of scarves, 'that maybe next time, we should do things separately. Dancing and cookery lessons definitely do not go together.'

'Next time?' Onyx looked up from the bed where she'd thrown herself. 'You mean you *do* want to learn to dance? You got the hang of it really quickly and you're very good. So does that mean you'll be coming to my classes?'

'Yes.' Ella nodded. 'If I'm still here, I think I will.'

'Yay!' Onyx stopped and frowned. 'And of course you'll be here.'

'Maybe—maybe not. Who knows.' Ella tried to regain her breath. 'But I'm clearly unfit—and I really enjoyed that—and I love the music, and you said ages ago that it was a great way to get in shape. Mind you, that was when I thought you were a pole dancer.'

'*What?*'

'Oh, yes, another one of my huge misconceptions.' Ella managed to haul herself off the floor, and padded across to the little fridge, her skirt jingling. 'I assumed, when Ash said you danced in clubs and you said it was exotic, that it meant poles or laps, or both. Sorry.'

'Don't be. I've got good friends who do both. All different skills. But not for me. Blimey, my mum and dad would have forty fits if they thought I was doing something even slightly sleazy. Oh, thanks.' Onyx sat up and took the ice-cold Diet Coke. 'And thanks for the cooking stuff. If you could write it all down for me some time I'd be dead grateful.'

'OK, no problem.' Ella swallowed a mouthful of Coke. 'But, it was mostly just cooking terms and things I gave you, not actual recipes. Is that what you wanted?'

'Mmm. To start with at least. I need to know

341

things like the difference between broil and boil and what reduction means and if a jus is gravy or not—it's like a foreign language to me at the moment.'

'If you turn up again on Monday night,' Ella said smiling, 'you could ask Gabby to explain it all to you. I'm sure she wouldn't mind—if she can spare the time from drooling all over Ash, of course.'

Onyx laughed. 'Ash laps it up. He's used to it. Anyway, he's a terrible flirt. He knows how to handle predatory women like Gabby. But he's dead decent—always lets people down gently. I've never known him deliberately hurt anyone.'

Ella was pretty sure they were about to walk on thin ice. She was also pretty sure that now would be a good time to change the subject.

Too late.

'Don't you ever get jealous, though?'

'Jealous? Of Ash? Never. Why should I?'

'Well, I know you've been together for ages and . . .'

Onyx tucked her long legs underneath her. 'When I first met Ash, at uni, I was desperately homesick and heartbroken. I'd never been away from home before in my life, not even for one night, and OK, Reading isn't on another planet, but my family were still miles away. Also, I'd just broken up with my one and only childhood sweetheart who gave me the "uni or me" ultimatum.'

Ella sipped her Coke, nodded, but said nothing.

'When I discovered Ash was my next-door roommate—' Onyx stared out of the open window '—I didn't even take in that he was drop-dead gorgeous. He could have been Quasimodo for all I

342

cared. I was still in love with Gaz. I missed my family so much it actually hurt and I thought I was going mad. I just needed someone who wouldn't laugh at me, who would listen when I needed to talk into the small hours of the morning, who wouldn't mind when I cried all over him, and who'd stop me from packing it all in and going back home.'

'And Ash did all that?'

Onyx nodded. 'He was a star. He was homesick, too. Of course, we all were, we were only kids, but I didn't realise that at the time. I thought it was just me. I just felt so alone. See, I'd been surrounded by this huge jolly family all my life, and been going out with Gaz since I was fifteen. I didn't know anything else. Ash was my rock, my shoulder to cry on, my best friend. And he still is. And, whatever he does, he always will be.'

'And, um, Gaz?'

'Still lives round the corner from my mum and dad in Winterbrook. Married my best mate from school. Two kids. Dead happy.'

Damn it, no chance of a quick Friends Reunited there, then . . .

Ella sighed sadly. 'Oh, I do love a happy ending.'

'So do I,' Onyx said softly, not looking at Ella, still staring out of the window as the deep purple night draped Hideaway Lane. 'I'm all for a Happy Ever After, but I'm not sure how there can possibly be one this time, are you?'

# Chapter Thirty-seven

The northern heats Weekly Winner was, as expected, the team of skinny students from Newcastle. The general consensus at Hideaway was that if they were up against them in the final then they wouldn't stand a chance.

Still, as Trixie said, at least they knew who their enemies were now: Pink Barbie, Fish and Chips and the Geordie Slap-Up.

It sounded like a cut-price street gang.

On Monday morning, Ella, still feeling pretty rotten, and haunted by Onyx's words of warning, and increasingly annoyed by Poll's complete inability to concentrate on anything at all and her sudden tendency to start every sentence with 'Billy and I think . . .', suddenly wished it was all over.

OK, so Ash wanted his own restaurant. If, just if, they won at the end of this week, Ash would have his own restaurant, and Poll would have a fat cheque and they'd have even more homeless people to live at Hideaway, which would be great. On both counts.

And, win or lose, Billy and Trixie would still have their new homes and new lives here, and Onyx would start her belly-dancing classes, and obviously move into Hideaway with Ash. Which wouldn't be quite so great at all.

But what was there for her? What exactly did the future hold for Ella Maloney?

She had a sudden urge to talk to her mum and dad, or her sister or her gran, but with typical Sod's Law timing they were all away on the family holiday in Majorca, and she really didn't want to interrupt and spoil their one longed-for break of the year with her troubles.

She'd just have to sort it out for herself. Like everything else in her life from now on.

'Ella! The film crew are here!' Poll shouted excitedly up the stairs, as the still and misty morning, already quivering with heat, showed no signs of cooling down. 'George has just spotted the trucks turning into Cattle Drovers Passage! Goodness me, I'm even more nervous than I was last time. I wonder if it will be the same people?'

'I expect so.' Ella walked slowly downstairs, feeling worn out already. How on earth was she going to cope with a full-on twelve hours of hustle and bustle and tension? Not to mention being made-up and having her hair done? Not to mention cooking in front of millions? With Ash.

George, who had Doll Blessing's brood, which included his best friend/worst enemy, to stay for the day in return for him being whisked away before the arrival of Gabby and Tom for a sleepover at Doll's in Hazy Hassocks, whooped past her in the hall, followed by a vociferous blur of little boys and girls in dungarees.

'Lovely day for it,' Billy said cheerfully, bustling out of the kitchen. 'Sleep well?'

'Not really.'

'I was out like a light.' Billy continued to smile from ear to ear. 'Once we'd finished all that kitchen cleaning and preparation last night, I was completely bushed. I was asleep the minute my head hit the pillow.'

Lucky, lucky you, Ella thought.

The film crew, followed by George and his gang,

poured through the house in a tidal wave of greetings and equipment, exactly as before. The hair and make-up girls said a cheery 'hiya' and set up their boxes and brushes and mirrors, exactly as before. Even the chuck wagon arrived and parked in the same place.

Ella, drifting out in the now burned brown garden and plonking herself down on the canopied swing seat, felt as though she was living in *Groundhog Day*.

'You look a bit surly, if you don't mind me saying so, dear,' Trixie said, as, carrying a bunch of wild flowers, she trotted into the garden from her job of corralling the dogs, cats and hens, once again, in their temporary out-of-Gabby's-way home in the lower field. 'Cheer up. It's glorious weather for Ruby Larkspur Day . . . and look what I've got.'

Ella stared at the armful of tall blue flowers.

'Larkspur!' Trixie beamed. 'Loads of them in that far field. Like a blue carpet it is down there, north facing, you see. I'm going to see if the film crew can use them in the—what do they call it?— oh, yes, the set dressing. It would be perfect.'

Ella frowned. She didn't care about the frowning any more. Wrinkles were the least of her problems. 'They're certainly very pretty, but you're not going to mention anything about it though, are you? The larkspur, I mean. About it being magical, or about today being a special fairy day? Or any of that stuff?'

'No,' Trixie sighed. 'I'm sure my fairy friends will have other things to occupy them today of all days. But if they're needed to avert a disaster for my earthling friends again, then I'm sure I can call on them.'

346

Ella groaned.

'Feeling really poorly, dear? Not surprising, this heat's enough to finish anyone off.'

'Yes, I suppose so. Oh, I'm sorry.' Ella smiled at Trixie. 'I just feel completely drained and I'm being a miserable so-and-so. I'll get over it.'

'You'll need to, dear, if you don't mind me saying so. After all, this is a very important day for . . .'

'If you say the fairies, Trixie, I'll probably scream.'

'Wasn't going to,' Trixie said huffily. 'I was going to say for Poll and Ash and everyone here. You've all done amazingly well getting this far. But you all need to be singing from the same playing field to pull it off today. One bad apple can curdle eggs and all that . . .'

Frowning at the mangled metaphors, Ella shook her head. 'Sorry again. Yes, of course, you're right. And I promise I won't let them down tonight. I just think, last time we were all so excited because it was all new, and now, this time, I know how *long* everything takes. I *know* about all the fuss. I'm just so tired . . . I can't imagine even being awake tonight when we actually go on the air.'

'The adrenaline will kick in and get you through it.' Trixie plonked herself and the larkspur down beside Ella on the swing seat. Ella found herself rocking wildly. 'But I can give you a little herbal tincture to help, if you like? It worked wonders for Poll last time.'

'No, thanks.' Ella said quickly. 'It's very kind of you, but I'll just grab some black coffee and give myself a severe talking-to.'

Trixie chuckled. 'But will you be listening?'

'Yes, no—oh, I don't know. I don't even know

what's wrong with me.'

'You're in love,' Trixie said softly. 'That's all, dear.'

'Hardly,' Ella snorted. 'And, anyway, isn't love supposed to make you all bright-eyed and bushy-tailed and smiling and happily on top of the world, and intensely irritating to other people?'

'Like Poll and Billy, you mean?'

'Exactly like Poll and Billy. I've no idea why they don't just come out and announce it—it's sooo obvious.'

'They'll have their reasons, dear. We must let them do whatever they think best. Anyway, Poll and Billy are going to be all right. I'm not so sure about you.'

'Thanks. No, sorry—again. I've really got to stop acting like a droopy schoolgirl and get over it.'

'And Ash?'

'What about Ash?'

'It's Ash you're in love with, dear, isn't it?'

'No! Well . . . maybe . . . anyway, I'm definitely over Ash.'

'No you're not, dear.'

'OK then, I'm not. Well, at least we're sort of speaking again. I've apologised for being rude when we went out, but he still clearly thinks I'm just a silly, moody girl—and anyway, Onyx said . . .'

'Yes, dear?'

'Oh, Onyx kind of warned me that there was no point in hoping that Ash would ever be interested in me in that way. She's lovely—and she's Ash's girlfriend—and I'm pretty sure she'll be moving in here with him really soon. She just told me not to expect a happy ending.'

'Oh dear. And what will you do then? When

348

Onyx and Ash are living together here?'

'Trixie, I have absolutely no idea. But I really love Hideaway and everyone and I really don't want to leave, even when my three months are up—so I suppose I'll just have to grin and bear it. But, please, promise me one thing—you'll never mention any of this to Ash. He has no idea, and I want it to stay that way.'

'I won't breathe a word, dear. To be honest, if I thought that by doing so he'd leave Onyx then I might. But—' she held up a chubby, wrinkled hand '—I know that under the circumstances that would do more harm than good, so my lips are sealed.'

'And you won't try to get the fairies involved?'

'Are you mocking again, Ella?'

'No, I mean it. *You* might not say anything, but then use the "it's not me it's the fairies" line.'

'I won't, dear. You have my word.'

'OK, thank you. You told me you'd spent your life loving someone who belonged to someone else, didn't you? I think, if I stay here, that's exactly what I'll be doing too.'

Trixie leaned over and patted Ella's hand. 'No you won't, dear. Forewarned is forearmed. I was silly. I wasted my life on a hopeless dream. I just waited and waited and hoped and hoped. But you *know*. You'll move on and meet someone else one day, and you'll forget all about Ash.'

Ella stared up at the cornflower-blue sky, mottled and dappled and dancing through the branches of the heavily scented lilac trees, and knew that she wouldn't.

*       *       *

349

Gabby and Tom arrived at six. Again, in separate cars with their retinue in tow. Again, the routine was exactly the same as before.

'It should be much easier for you all this time,' Gabby, cool and elegant in pale green, said, picking her way over the cables and round the cameras and flicking skinny fingers over the kitchen surfaces and inspecting them for non-existent grime. 'You know exactly what to do and what to expect, don't you?'

They all nodded with varying degrees of enthusiasm.

'And Tom and I love your new menu. It certainly sounds well up to the standard of your original one. And you're the luckiest of the Weekly Winners. You've had a decent gap between shows—and *if* you win the viewers' vote this week to appear in Friday's final, you'll at least have a few days to recover. If those emaciated *children* from Newcastle should be chosen, it'll mean they're cooking on Thursday *and* Friday. All in the luck of the draw. Eh, Tom?'

Tom, who was staring blankly out of the kitchen window, didn't answer.

'TOM!'

'Er, yes—what? Oh, yes, definitely.'

'Whatever.' Gabby gave him a withering look. 'Right, now you've all been to hair and make-up, and are all nicely gussied up, I see—red and blue, this time—very attractive, and I particularly like the red on you.' Her eyes lingered on Ash. 'That red T-shirt with those faded blue jeans . . . Oh, yes . . . the ladies are going to absolutely love you to bits—again.'

Ash looked, as he'd looked most of the day, only

mildly interested and said nothing.

'He got a lot of fan mail after the last show,' Tom spoke suddenly. 'Didn't he, Gabby?'

Gabby gave Tom a Look. 'Yes, he did. But we don't tell them about that until afterwards, do we, Tom?'

'Er, no.'

'Really? Fan mail? How thrilling!' Poll looked very perky. 'Mind you, I'm not surprised. Did you bring it with you?'

'No.' Gabby looked amazed that Poll should even ask such a stupid question. 'We don't bother ourselves with that sort of thing. We have a PR company that deals with it. They'll forward all mail on to all of you—once the series has ended.'

'Does that mean we all got letters?' Billy enquired.

'Yes, yes, most probably—there are all sorts of strange people out there who feel it's their God-given duty to write to anyone who appears on television as if they were their bosom chums and most of it is complete rubbish.' Gabby licked her lips. 'But Ash certainly has an extremely bulging postbag.'

Oh yuck, Ella thought.

Tom shook his head.

'OK, it all seems to be in order here—and I really like the wild flowers—very pretty. A nice rustic touch.' Gabby strode around, checking and rechecking. 'I shall be going upstairs now for my rest and subsequently my dressing, hair and make-up. Again, I want No Disturbances Whatsoever. Oh, and I trust—Oh, what's her name? Oh, yes, Mrs Snapdragon, and the child, the animals and anyone else who isn't taking part in the show, will

351

be kept well out of the way this time?'

Poll nodded happily. 'Oh, yes. There'll be no repetition of last time, Gabby. Trixie is upstairs, George is staying with friends in Hazy Hassocks, the animals are all securely locked in this time, and Onyx isn't going to be here because she's working. You'll have no problems tonight, I can assure you of that.'

'Good. Well, no doubt Tom will want to drink himself senseless—not difficult for him, he's got a head start—while I'm resting. I'll see you at seven thirty on the dot.'

As the crew continued their never-ending checking and run-throughs, and the lights were turned up to eyeball-burning level, and the sound man did the mic'ing up, and Ella, Ash, Poll and Billy made sure that everything they would need for their Farmhouse Feast Mark Two was arrayed on the kitchen table, Tom, clutching a bottle of beer, drifted out into the garden.

'Poor sod.' Billy watched him go. 'A miserable marriage is a dreadful thing.'

'Makes you wonder why so many people seem to go in for them, doesn't it?' Ash said morosely, rearranging the new potatoes and baby leeks he'd need for his soup starter. 'Can't see the point myself.'

'You will, lad,' Billy chirped happily. 'That's what we all say, but when you meet the right person, it all makes sense and—'

He caught Ella's eye and stopped abruptly.

Ella suddenly concentrated fiercely on the three piles of currants on her part of the table. Just think of cooking, she told herself. Don't think about Ash, or Onyx, or Mark frolicking in Portugal with the customer services girls, or anything else at all. Just think about cooking.

Strangely, Trixie had been right about one thing, though—the adrenaline rush had kicked in nicely, and she was no longer tired. Well, there's one blessing, she thought. I might want to bawl my eyes out all through the damn filming but at least I won't fall asleep, face down, in my home-made custard.


## *Chapter Thirty-eight*

Gabby reappeared in the kitchen dead on the dot of half past seven, just seconds after Tom had wandered in from the garden and hid a couple of empty beer bottles in the recycling box.

'Are you sober?'

'Of course. I'm not a lush. I just like to relax with a drink before going on air.'

'A drink or twenty,' Gabby snapped, smoothing down her skintight scarlet frock and stalking across to the oven on her stilt-high red patent Louboutins. 'Thank goodness one of us is capable of remaining professional, and upright. Oven on? Yes, good. Fans? Plenty. Good again. Tables prepped to perfection? Yes, fine. OK, now does everyone remember what they have to do?'

Everyone said they did.

'Right.' Gabby glanced at her watch and nodded at the producer. 'Let's get the count-down under way.'

The pre-programme checks flew by and it seemed to Ella that it was merely nanoseconds

353

before 'Pickin' a Chicken' echoed into Hideaway.

No one would have guessed Tom and Gabby had just been sniping at each other, she thought, as they stood side by side in front of the kitchen table, smiling warmly into the camera and seamlessly welcomed the viewing nation to *Dewberrys' Dinners*.

'This is the most exciting week of our series,' Gabby gushed to camera as soon as she'd done the 'you can start cooking—now!' bit. 'The first semi-final. It's been a real roller-coaster ride over the last four weeks, when Tom and I have been up and down the country, invited into so many lovely homes, and treated to so many fabulous feasts.'

'Yes,' Tom agreed. 'And it's always so hard to choose just four teams for our semi-final, isn't it Gabby? Or should I say, my Lady in Red?'

Ella cringed.

Gabby threw him a coy simper. 'We're all in red tonight, Tom.' Then to the camera. 'As you can see, our four hard-working chefs from Berkshire, our southern area heat winners, have chosen the same colour as me. Red for luck, or red for danger? We'll have to find out, won't we? So, Tom, if you'd like to introduce them once again, and find out what deliciousness they're cooking for us tonight.'

Ella faltered in beating her sugar and butter together, suddenly petrified. Her hands shook. Damn it, and her lips had stuck to her teeth again. Please don't let anyone speak to her just yet . . .

'Let's say hello again to Poll Andrews.' Tom was at his most kindly. 'Poll owns this lovely Berkshire farmhouse and she and her friends gave us a fabulous vegetarian Farmhouse Feast to win the southern heat. So, Poll, what's on your menu for this evening?'

Poll sighed happily, not a nerve in sight. 'Tonight, Tom, we're going to serve you and Gabby an Old-fashioned Farmhouse Cheeseboard.'

Ella marvelled at Poll's sangfroid. She was so self-possessed tonight. Love certainly was an amazing thing. Ah well, she'd just have to try to get through without it, wouldn't she? For cooking and being on telly and for the rest of her life . . .

'Oooh!' Tom exclaimed warmly, albeit a touch OTT, Ella felt. 'That sounds fascinating, Poll.'

Poll nodded confidently. 'We're using home-made cheese in the cooking of our first two courses, and rounding off the cheese in the time-honoured country manner—with fruit—for our third course.'

'Yummy!' Tom beamed. 'Right, so you all keep cooking, and Gabby and I will wander around and watch and chat. No pressure!'

Still completely tranquil, Poll started to gracefully gather the remainder of her ingredients together as Tom walked to the far end of the long refectory table.

'And here,' Tom announced, 'we have Ash and Billy, the Kings of the First Course. So, what's our starter this evening, boys?'

'A nineteen fifties leek, potato and blue cheese soup,' Ash said, chopping very tiny potatoes in half and seasoning them with coarse salt and black pepper. 'With baby leeks and these new potatoes, both dug fresh from the garden this morning, herbs gathered from the kitchen garden less than an hour ago, and the whole thing garnished with

355

Hideaway's own blue cheese.'

'Wow!' Tom said. 'Couldn't be fresher than that, could it, folks? And Billy? What are you making for us?'

'Cheese biscuits,' Billy said, also amazingly calm. 'From a family recipe that's umpteen years old. The trick with these little blighters, as well as using Hideaway's own cheese, is the addition of cayenne pepper to spice them up a bit. They go down a treat with that soup of young Ash's, I can tell you.'

'Mmm, I can imagine, and I can't wait to taste them. I must say I do love all these old recipes you use, and—' he looked knowingly at the camera '— if you remember, the cooks here at Hideaway Farm not only use old-fashioned recipes and home-grown ingredients, but also cook using old-fashioned kitchen implements. It's just like a trip back in time, isn't it, Gabby?'

'It is—' Gabby shimmied her tiny scarlet figure in between Poll and Ella '—although probably to an era that you remember far better than I do. Now, Poll, you said you were also going to produce something cheesy?'

'I am. I'm making a bread and cheese pudding.'

'R-e-a-l-l-y?' Gabby managed to give the word far more syllables than it deserved. 'Now that's something I've never heard of before.'

'It's a popular old country dish from the war years.' Poll seemed totally unfazed by either Gabby or the cameras this time as she cut her bread into neat triangles. 'But of course, I've made it my own by the addition of home-made goat's cheese and a selection of herbs from our own kitchen garden.'

Nigella, eat your heart out, Ella thought in admiration.

'So, it's a savoury version of bread and butter pudding, is it?'

Poll nodded as she moved on to skilfully chopping chives. 'Along those lines, yes, but maybe not quite so simple. And the bread I'm using is also home-made—' she did a Princess Diana-style coy downwards eye flicker along the table '—by Billy.'

'My, my,' Gabby said testily. 'We're really having a down home supper tonight, aren't we?'

'Of course my particular favourite thing to make is pastry,' Poll carried on cheerfully, clearly forgetting the 'speak when you're spoken to' rule. 'Any sort of pastry, but the cooking time we have on the programme would have meant *skimping*.' She looked coolly at Gabby. 'And I hate skimping or cutting corners. So when we devised our menu, it had to be dishes that were perfect for your allotted time slot.'

Ella gave her ten out of ten and a gold star.

'And,' Poll continued, 'I shall be serving it with scalloped potatoes—from another nineteen thirties recipe—and sweet grilled tomatoes.'

Gabby bared her teeth. 'Super. Absolutely super. And now, um, Ella . . . you're our pudding queen. That very strangely named Athole pud you made for us last time was a real triumph—so what are you going to top that with?'

'Er . . .' Ella worked some saliva into her mouth. 'Um, yes, tonight I'm making Eve's pudding, but again with a seasonal and local slant.'

Phew—she'd managed to speak without burbling.

'Lovely, and I'm sure you have a wonderfully light hand with sponge, but it's a bit early in the

357

year for apples, though, isn't it?' Gabby primmed her glossy lips into a little moue.

Ella nodded. 'Which is why I'm using currants instead . . . red, white and black—and again, like the rest of tonight's food, picked fresh from the garden this morning.'

'Oooh, yes! Aren't they gorgeous?' Gabby indicated that the camera should pan in on the currants. 'Like lots of tiny jewels, and we all love jewels, don't we, ladies?'

'And,' Ella said manfully, deciding that if Poll could suddenly become assertive then so could she—even without the love bit to spur her on—as she started to top and tail the currants, 'I shall be making an original nineteen fifties custard sauce to accompany it.'

Gabby again looked a bit put out that Ella had also volunteered un-asked-for information. 'R-e-a-l-l-y?'

'With, um, vanilla pods and grated nutmeg and lemon zest.'

'That sounds absolutely delightful! Well, don't let me hold you up. I think I'll just tiptoe along to the other end of the table and see what our favourite ice-cream man—the g-o-r-g-e-o-u-s Ash—is doing at the hob.'

Ella glanced at Ash and smiled to herself. He looked petrified.

Gabby squirmed herself very, very close to him. It seemed to make it pretty impossible for him to fry his garlic, onions, leeks and potatoes without burning one or other or both of them.

'Sooo, Ash, this all smells like heaven to me. How are you feeling?'

'Um, fine, thanks,' Ash muttered.

'Goody. You certainly look fine to me. And sooo fit.' Gabby shot a malicious look at Tom. 'Very fit indeed. It's wonderful to see a man who can still look like a Real Man in the kitchen instead of a limp rag, isn't it, ladies?'

Tom winced. Ella suddenly longed to comfort him. Poor man. How ever did he cope with this constant, and very public, humiliation?

Gabby squeezed even closer to Ash, leaning across him to peer into the saucepan. 'Oooh yes, Ash, you certainly know how to bring things to the boil, don't you?' She licked her lips lasciviously. 'The lady in your life is sooo v-e-r-y lucky. I'd say both you and your soup have simply oodles of va-va-voom.'

Oh, double yuck.

Still, Ella thought, as they chopped and grated and mixed and stirred in unison, and the kitchen filled with delicious scents, it would soon be over. Tom and Gabby would leave. Hideaway would return to normal. They might even win. They might not. But at least this time it had all gone really, really well.

Afterwards, Ella *knew* she should never have allowed her thoughts to stray in that direction. It was just asking for trouble . . .

The kitchen door flew open and Trixie, dressed in something long and flowing in blue and red, and with a lopsided garland of red and blue plastic flowers atop the bubble perm, frolicked in.

Oh my God—noooo!

Ella whimpered as Trixie waved an armful of larkspur round and round her head. Christmas cracker rubies glittered on her fingers.

Fortunately, Ella thought, pulling wild 'sod off'

359

faces at Trixie, so far she'd managed to frolic out of camera shot, so maybe she'd just frolic off again . . . Ah, no—sadly not.

Poll, Ash and Billy spotted Trixie merely seconds after Ella did but luckily before Gabby and Tom. However, the film crew, doubled up with silent laughter, were clearly way ahead of them.

Trixie stopped frolicking, pirouetted unsteadily on one foot and started to sing in a tiny, wavering voice, 'Hooray! Hooray!/It's Ruby Larkspur Day/When all the fairies come out to play!/Wearing blue for larkspur sweet/Together with red for ruby heat/Always means you can't be beat!'

Then she curtsied.

The kitchen was paralysed for a second. Then Gabby's face turned the same scarlet as her frock.

'Get her out of here!' Gabby hissed, ferociously angry. 'One of you! Get rid of her! Now!'

The crew were still soundlessly doubled-up and shook their heads helplessly.

Ella looked frantically at the rest of them. Ash and Billy were well into the last delicate stages of their starter, Poll was just about to check on her scalloped potatoes—none of them could leave their food. It was going to have to be her, wasn't it? Her Eve's pudding was in the oven and the custard sauce only needed heating. Yep, it was going to have to be her.

Backing away from the table as discreetly as possible, she grabbed Trixie by the arm and hustled her out of the kitchen and into the hall, just as the producer and director, shoulders still shaking with laughter, indicated that the cameras should zoom in on the table to cover her absence.

'What the hell did you think you were doing?' Ella ripped the microphone from her red vest and yelled, as, still clutching Trixie's arm, she bundled her up the twisting staircases. 'You've probably ruined it for us now! And you *promised*. You absolutely promised!'

'I promised not to tell Ash that you loved him,' Trixie chirped merrily, her garland now round her neck and gaily strewing a trail of larkspur petals behind them on the stairs. 'I didn't promise not to sing you a winning fairy song, dear, did I? I didn't promise not to celebrate Ruby Larkspur Day. I didn't promise not to . . .'

'OK, maybe not *promised*, but you said you wouldn't involve the fairies tonight. You said—' Ella peered at her as she bundled Trixie along the corridors towards her room ' loads of things— and why the hell are all the doors open up here?'

None of them ever locked their doors at Hideaway, but they were always closed.

'I was letting the fairykins have the run of the place. It's a special day for them, dear. They hate to be confined.'

'They're bloody fairies,' Ella roared. 'They fly everywhere! They don't need open doors!'

Oh God, she thought, listen to yourself.

Trixie tittered.

'Trixie, are you drunk?'

'I may have had a little herbal tincture or two by way of celebration, dear.' Trixie smiled, cross-eyed above the lopsided garland. 'It's a very special day for the fairykins, after all.'

Ella pushed Trixie into her room. 'I don't have time to argue with you. I've got custard to see to. Just stay there. Take those flowers off before they

361

strangle you. Drink gallons of black coffee, go to bed—and don't even think about bringing the damn fairykins downstairs again. OK?'

'OK, dear.' Trixie beamed. 'There's no need to shout. And anyway, I won't need to go downstairs again, dear. I'm quite happy up here now because I've left my fairy friends, Larkspur and Ruby, to help you and Thistledown and Pumpkin and Kalen in the kitchen.'

Dear, dear heavens, Ella thought, firmly closing Trixie's door, then tearing along the corridor, slamming every other door shut as she went—first Billy's and then Ash's . . .

Ash's . . .

Oooh, nooo. Holy, holy shit . . .

Tumbling over her long blue skirt, skidding down the stairs, sliding through the hall, Ella belted into the kitchen.

Gabby was just telling them they had five minutes before plating up. Tom was discussing the joys of scalloped potatoes with Poll. Billy was carefully removing his cheese biscuits from their baking tray.

Ella sidled back along the table and grabbed her custard. Stirring as she went, she moved towards Ash who was in the throes of crumbling his Hideaway Blue.

'Ash!'

He looked at her but didn't speak.

Oh, lordy, she thought, this was no time to continue the sulky cold shoulder stuff.

'Ash, when did you last feed Roy?'

He indicated the microphone, shook his head and turned away.

'Mine's off,' Ella hissed. 'Have you fed Roy

today?'

He frowned at her and nodded.

'And you locked the vivarium properly?'

He frowned again, thought, then nodded again, doing a silent mouthed, 'Of course. Well, at least, I think so—yes, I'm sure. Why?'

'Because,' Ella said faintly, 'Trixie's opened all the damn doors up there, and when I closed yours I could see the tank—and it was empty.'

## Chapter Thirty-nine

'Right!' Gabby clapped her tiny hands. There was a smile in her voice but murder in her eyes. 'Time's up. Stop cooking. Finish your plating up. Now!'

Ash and Ella exchanged frantic glances. The producer, giving her a thumbs-up, was also indicating that Ella should reattach her microphone—quickly.

Her fingers fumbled as she did so.

Now not only had Trixie managed to foul it up with her damn fairykins, but she had cold custard, and there was a python loose somewhere in the farmhouse.

Could things possibly get any better?

Poll and Billy, oblivious to anything but each other and clearly just relieved that Trixie had been dealt with, plated up on the fat roses and forget-me-not china with skill and pride. Ash, his hands shaking, slopped soup into a bowl and haphazardly added his blue cheese. Ella retrieved her—perfectly cooked, hallelujah!—Eve's pudding from the oven and decanted her lukewarm custard into a little jug.

'Well done!' Gabby spat angrily, glaring at Ella as if Trixie's interruption had been her fault. 'Exactly on time! Well, Tom, doesn't this all look quite, quite amazing?'

'It does,' Tom said. 'And just as well, because I'm starving. Right, shall we start with the first course?'

'Well—' Gabby raised sarcastic eyebrows '—what a novel idea! Of course, we'll start with the first course . . .'

She dipped her spoon into Ash's soup.

'Oooh, yes! Again, yes-yes-yes!' The fury left her eyes and she purred, almost rubbing herself against him. 'This is nectar. Food for the gods. My word, Ash, you are a man and a half, aren't you?'

Ash, agitated, simply stared.

Tom crumbled one of Billy's biscuits and dipped it into the soup. 'Oh, you must try this, Gabby, it's absolutely wonderful. These biscuits simply dissolve into deliciousness and you get a fusion of the cheeses and . . .'

Billy beamed along the table at Poll.

Gabby and Tom moved on to Poll's bread and cheese pudding. There were more fulsome exclamations of divine flavours, sumptuous blends of herbs, gorgeous textures . . .

'Now the pud,' Tom said greedily, licking his lips. 'Let's just pour some custard on, shall we.'

Ella held her breath. Not that cold-ish custard was her main concern. Neither, right at this moment, was her broken heart. Or even a very inebriated and fairy-mad Trixie. Her real worry was where on earth, in a house the size of Hideaway, were they ever going to find a stray python?

'Oh, fabulous!' Tom groaned. 'The sharpness of the currants, the melt-in-the-mouth sponge, the sweetness of the custard with just a little kick of lemon and the warmth of nutmeg . . . oh, yes, Ella, this is a triumph.'

Gabby followed suit.

Ella, relieved, swallowed and tried to smile.

Gabby suddenly clapped her hands to her mouth in a very theatrical manner. 'Oh, dear, what a silly woman I am! Aren't I, Tom?'

'You are, Gabby.'

'What have I forgotten, Tom?'

Tom clearly delighted at being allowed to insult Gabby on air, didn't have a clue. 'What have you forgotten? Is it old age creeping in?'

He got a Look. 'I've forgotten Gabby's Secret Ingredient!'

'Oh, yes, silly old you!'

Gabby shot him a Further Look. 'I think we can take that one as read, Tom, no need to over-egg the pudding, is there?'

Ella looked at Ash. He was very pale, his eyes were anxious. Oh, bless him. She knew all he wanted to do was belt out of the kitchen and find his beloved Roy before any harm came to him.

But obviously he also knew that this was his only chance of having his own restaurant.

Oh, bugger stupid Trixie and Ruby Larkspur Day and the rest of her damn silly fairykins rubbish, Ella thought fiercely.

'Never mind!' Gabby clapped her little hands together again and started tiptoeing exaggeratedly round the kitchen on her shiny red Louboutins. 'It's not too late. Let me see what I can find . . .'

Knowing that Poll had left a very obvious bunch of fresh herbs in the fridge, and that Ash had made sure every single one of Roy's frozen dinners was well out of reach, Ella didn't panic too much. Just let Gabby find the bloody herbs, go through her Secret Ingredient rigmarole, and get it over.

They let out a collective breath as, on cue, Gabby opened the fridge and brandished the herbs.

'Oooh, aren't these just d-a-r-l-i-n-g!' Gabby purred to camera. 'Sooo fresh! Sooo pretty! And won't they look just p-e-r-f-e-c-t on gorgeous Ash's gorgeous soup, ladies and gentlemen?'

Still wildly overacting, she plucked tiny leaves at random and, sashaying up to Ash and snuggling in closely, she scattered them like confetti over his soup.

'There! Perfect! Now I must taste the soup with Gabby's Secret Ingredient. Maybe Ash will feed me?'

Dear God, Ella thought, as Tom turned his head away in disgust.

Ash, obviously just wanting to get the pantomime over, dipped a spoon into the now herb-covered soup and held it up to Gabby's lips.

'Oooh, yes! Yes! Yes, and oooh, Ash, you are a *naughty* boy. Playing footsie with me! And I'm almost old enough to be your, um, older sister, but oooh, that's rather, oooh, yes, l-o-v-e-l-y . . .' Gabby's eyes closed with ecstasy.

Ella tutted in revulsion. Bloody men! Had he no shame at all?

Then she looked at Ash. He was staring, wide-eyed, down beneath the table. Weird or what? Did he actually *like* Gabby oozing all over him? Was he

366

*watching*? Was he going to add Gabby to his bedpost notches? Maybe he already had?

Ella leaned back and glanced downwards too. And nearly choked.

Roy was gently curling his huge coils round Gabby's slender ankle.

Ohmigod!

Now what did they do? Ignore it? Ash had said Roy had been fed today, so presumably he didn't want to eat Gabby—or did he? Ella swallowed. Having your Michelin-starred hostess eaten alive by a ball python on air would definitely put paid to any chance of them winning *Dewberrys' Dinners*, wouldn't it?

Billy and Poll hadn't noticed. They were doing a mutual self-congratulatory, billing-and-cooing, soppy, aren't-we-clever-and-madly-in-love thing.

OK, Ella thought. Stay calm. Presumably there were only a few more minutes of the programme to go. As long as Gabby stayed put and closed the show from that end of the table and didn't look down . . .

And as long as Roy didn't *squeeze* . . .

What had Ash said all those weeks ago? That if—big joke—Roy ever escaped he'd only be looking for warmth and company. Well, it looked like he'd found it.

The producer was making wrap-up motions.

Tom cleared his throat. 'Well, ladies and gentlemen, that was another spectacularly perfect old-fashioned three-course meal from the lovely and exceptionally talented cooks here at Hideaway Farm. And as we leave our first delicious feast in finals week in Berkshire to travel on to, um,—'

'Norfolk.' Gabby giggled. 'Oooh—I mean, yes,

367

tomorrow it's the turn of our eastern area heat winners, so don't forget to tune in, and, oooh, Ash, stop it, er . . . and now Tom has a really important message for you all.'

Tom looked blank.

'The voting details. Oooh, Ash, don't!'

'Ah, yes.' Tom nodded, his eyes bleak. 'This week, of course, it's down to you, the viewers, to choose the two finalists who will be cooking live in the television studio on Friday. You can ring or text your votes for your favourites on the numbers showing on your screen now.'

'The lines will be open every evening this week from nine until midnight.' Gabby sniggered, casting coy girlie glances at Ash. 'So to vote for tonight's contestants you need to add zero one and so on . . . and—' she giggled '—oooh, that's sooo lovely.'

Tom looked shell-shocked. 'Er, yes, and all the usual restrictions apply. You can find all the details on our pages in the listings magazines or on our website. And remember, this is down to you, the viewers—Gabby and I have no say in who you choose to be this year's *Dewberrys' Dinners* finalists—so vote for your favourites, and you'll see them cooking again on Friday.'

'But—ooh, yes, Ash!—the results will be announced early on Friday morning when we've seen all four semi-finalists and you've had a chance to vote—but do remember, oooh,' Gabby said breathily, 'just what's at stake for the lucky winner. A lovely cheque, a *Dewberrys' Dinners* trophy, and joining forces with Tom and me to open their very own—oooh-I-say-yesss!—restaurant—'

'So,' Tom butted in, white-lipped, looking like he

368

wanted to kill everyone, 'let's say goodbye to everyone here in Berkshire, and, please, start dialling now! Goodbye! Goodbye!'

Gabby waved. So did everyone else.

'Pickin' a Chicken' indicated that the ordeal was over.

The crew were clearing up even before the last notes had faded away.

'Wasn't that fab?' Poll breathed happily as she allowed herself to be de-mic'd. 'Didn't everything go well? Apart from Trixie, of course, but no one would have seen her, would they? The viewers, I mean?'

The director sniggered and said unfortunately not—she was off camera for the entire mind-blowing performance but probably no one would have minded because didn't everyone have a mad old bat relative tucked away somewhere?

'And no one noticed Ella had gone, did they, duck?' Billy grinned.

The runner boy said he doubted it. The cameramen were very good at covering up disasters of all sorts.

Gabby, Ella noticed, had her eyes closed and was rubbing up and down against Ash.

Oh Lordy—time to act . . . Ah, too late.

Gabby screamed.

And carried on screaming. And jumped up and down. And flapped her hands.

Everyone stopped what they were doing and stared at her.

'Gabby.' Tom frowned. 'Whatever's the matter? Do stop it, there's a good girl.'

Pretty damn ineffectual, Tom, Ella thought, walking slowly behind the table. Gabby's hysteria

369

really was becoming a little bit annoying.

'Shut up!' Ella hissed at her. 'You'll scare him!'

'Scare Ash?' Poll queried. 'Why would Gabby want to scare Ash? And why's Ash bending down? What's he doing down there under the table?'

'What's he done to you?' Billy frowned. 'Ah, he's a lad and a half is our Ash.'

'Shut up!' Ella hissed at all of them. 'Just keep quiet. Please. Roy's under the table. He's, um, hugging Gabby's leg.'

'Who's Roy?' Tom looked perplexed. 'Is he one of the crew?'

'Roy? Oooh nooo!' Poll howled. 'How on earth did he get down here? Oh, this is terrible! That's our chance of winning gone out of the window.'

'Sod our chances of winning,' Ash muttered from under the table. 'Right now, I'm just worried about Roy. Gabby, stand still and do *not* kick!'

Gabby, gibbering and whimpering, stood still at last.

Ella stooped down under the table. Ash was gently trying to coax Roy away from the slender ankle by stroking his head and making reassuring cooing noises.

'Shall I find him something to eat?' Ella whispered, kneeling beside Ash. 'And try to tempt him out?'

'No point. He's full up. I just don't understand how he got all the way down here without someone spotting him, and I'm sure I locked the vivarium. Mind you, I was thinking about other things when I fed him this morning. I was pretty distracted, so I suppose I could have just clicked the hinges into place and forgotten to do the locks. And he's very inquisitive, and I suppose with all the fuss today, no one would have noticed him.'

'Not with all these huge bundles of cables around, no,' Ella said, wondering if it was the imminent *Dewberrys' Dinners* or the imminent Onyx moving in that had distracted Ash and opting for the latter. 'He'd have been really well camouflaged.'

Ash sat back on his heels. 'I think we'll just have to play a waiting game.'

'Mmmm.' Ella pulled a face. 'He's anchored very firmly.'

'I do not want to hear that.' Gabby's voice wavered from above them.

Ella giggled. Ash suddenly grinned at her. Ella sighed. It meant nothing. Under different circumstances it would be really, really nice to be up close and personal with Ash under the kitchen table. But now . . .

'Seriously, we'll just have to wait until he's decided he's had enough cuddling,' Ash said. 'And that could take hours. There's no point in—Christ! What the hell is that?'

Ella blinked as a cascade of small red and blue stars swooshed under the table like a miniature whirlwind. The red and blue glistened and glimmered, danced together, and finally sparkled into a sort of shimmering purple mist. For a second she could see nothing at all, then the air cleared and the swoop of glittering coloured stars was gone as quickly as it had arrived.

And Roy and Gabby had parted company.

'What happened? Did I just dream that?' Ash frowned. 'Was that some sort of optical illusion?'

Bemused, Ella shook her head. 'Nooo, actually, call me completely mental if you like, but I think

371

that was Ruby and Larkspur doing their stuff.'

'OK.' Ash frowned a bit more. 'You're completely mental. Who the hell are Ruby and Larkspur?'

'Oh, you'll have to ask Trixie about them.'

'What? *Fairies*? You're telling me you honestly believe in Trixie's *fairies*? You think that . . . that . . . well, whatever that was just now was *fairies*?'

'I've got no idea what it was or what I believe in any more, but if it was Larkspur and Ruby—'

'*Who*?'

'Larkspur and Ruby—it's what Trixie was singing about—and they're the names of today's fairies and—'

Ash shook his head. 'Stop right there, Ella, please. Now you're scaring me.'

She shrugged. 'It's OK, I scare myself sometimes, too. But if it *was* Ruby and Larkspur, they seem to have done the trick, don't they?'

'Um, yes . . . I'll admit that. Whatever or whoever they are or that was, it's nothing short of miraculous.' Ash hauled most of Roy gently into his arms and stood up. 'I've known Roy do his cling-on act for days before now.'

Gabby, seeing Roy in all his massive glory for the first time, screamed again.

'Sshhh.' Ash shook his head. 'He's fine now. And so are you. You won't even be slightly bruised. He only did it because he loves you.'

Gabby, white-faced, was shaking from head to Louboutin'd toe. Ella, pulling herself to her feet, felt momentarily sorry for her. She'd probably have reacted in much the same way—only probably without quite so much screaming. A girl has her pride.

372

'Oh, blimey O'Reilly!' Tom's mouth dropped open at his first sight of Roy. 'No wonder old Gabby was upset. Where the heck did he come from?'

'Asia,' Ash said, still stroking Roy's head.

'Long journey,' Tom said, looking stunned. 'Nice snake, though. Are you OK now, Gabby?'

'No I'm bloody not. I think I'm going to faint.'

No one rushed to catch her so she didn't bother.

'Can you grab his tail end?' Ash said softly to Ella. 'Like you did before, when we first moved in? Then we'll get him back upstairs.'

'OK.' Ella grabbed.

'Oooh.' Gabby took a tottering step forwards and simpered shakily at Ash. 'My hero! You rescued me from that . . . that . . . awful creature.'

'His name's Roy,' Ella said, cross on Roy's behalf. 'And Ash didn't save you—ow!'

'Yes, I did.' Ash grinned cheerfully. 'Which means we're still in with a shout for the final, I hope?'

'Well, of course.' Gabby sat down in the rocking chair. 'Oh, sorry, I do feel rather wobbly.'

'That's because it's a rocking chair,' Ella said, shooting 'smug, slimy, conniving clever bastard' looks at Ash.

Gabby smiled weakly. 'We have nothing whatsoever to do with the voting on the semi-finals. That's solely down to the viewers' votes this week, but certainly, if I had my way, Ash, you'd not only get to the final but you'd get a bravery award as well.'

Ash was still beaming triumphantly as he and Ella manoeuvred Roy out of the kitchen.

# Chapter Forty

The rest of the week flew by. Again, the temperatures soared, and the east, west and north *Dewberrys' Dinners* finalists did their stuff.

The recriminations over Trixie's shenanigans, and Roy's escape, had been long and loud, with Trixie—who claimed a major part, with the aid of her fairykins, in the rescue of Gabby from Roy— being told in no uncertain terms that if she hadn't got squiffy on her herbal tinctures and thrown all the doors open for the sodding fairykins in the first place, then no rescue would have been required.

She'd stomped up to her room and sulked for ages.

Ella had almost returned to her former sunny mood. Almost. OK, so she was getting over being officially single again, and she and Ash were talking again, and friends again, and it was lovely, but it still wasn't what she wanted.

After Roy's escape, they'd returned him to his vivarium and stood and watched in relief as he'd hauled himself happily back round his sphagnum moss and watering holes before subsiding beneath one of his hot rocks. And Ash had thanked her a lot and then they'd left Roy and hurried downstairs, because Tom and Gabby were leaving and she knew Poll would want them there for the farewells.

So, Roy had thawed the ice, which was lovely, but there was still Onyx and the 'moving in' thing to deal with.

Ah, well, Ella thought, one step at a time . . .

Let's see if we get through to the final first, then I'll sort out the rest of my life. She'd always felt Scarlett O'Hara's method of thinking about nasty stuff tomorrow, not today, was a pretty good principle to follow.

Everyone who had watched the programme told them they'd been better than ever. Ella's parents phoned from Majorca and said they'd found a television showing the programme in 'Eduardo's English Eaterie' and, once they'd let it slip that they were related to Ella, they'd been treated to free sangria all night and her gran had had to be carried home.

And George, returning from his sleepover with Doll Blessing's brood, excitedly told Ella they'd been allowed to watch the show in their pyjamas while eating chips. This latter seemed to have impressed him far more than the fact that his mum had been on the telly.

On Tuesday, the Pink Barbie team had made everything they cooked lilac. It was very clever and exceptionally pretty, although they all decided that lilac ratatouille didn't look *quite* right. On Wednesday, the fish and chips team from Devon made a fundamental error by doing everything pasty-shaped. Sadly, their pasty-shaped pudding wasn't quite cooked and flopped into a gloopy pancake with lumps. And on Thursday, the skinny crew from Newcastle deviated from their original Geordie Slap-Up in quite spectacular style. They moved from Tyneside to Thailand and produced a totally stunning selection of beautiful dishes. There was no doubting their culinary ability, but as Gabby pointed out, with eye-watering acidity, curried rice pudding with a pickled lime sorbet was *not* one of her faves.

'Oh, dear me! I wouldn't know which one of them to pick, would you? It's anyone's guess,' Poll sighed, as the final notes of 'Pickin' a Chicken' died away in the peaches and cream sitting room. 'And we won't know if it's us until after midnight when the phone lines close for voting.'

'That's ages to wait.' Ella stretched her bare legs out along the sofa. 'But they said they'd ring whatever happened, didn't they? They'll tell us if we've won or lost. So it won't be just if the phone rings we'll know we've won, it could go one way or the other.'

They all groaned.

'I think,' Billy said, hauling himself from a deep armchair in search of yet more ice-cold drinks, 'that we ought to just forget it for the rest of the evening and get an early night and go to sleep and wait and see what happens in the morning, because they'll leave a message, won't they?'

'*Forget it*?' They all screamed. '*Sleep*? Are you joking? We're going to stay awake and be counting the seconds for the next three hours.'

And they were. Almost. George was put to bed at an almost unheard of ten, and Trixie gave up the ghost and said a sleepy goodnight at just after eleven.

So, when the phone rang at 1.15 am, the rest of them woke with a jump. Bleary-eyed, hot, uncomfortable and dry-mouthed, they blinked both at each other and round the stuffy sitting room.

'I'll go,' Poll said, yawning and stretching. 'If it's bad news I can cope with it.'

They all knew she couldn't, but said nothing.

376

Ella suddenly felt very sick. It was all so near now. And it mattered so much to Ash and Poll. And yes, damn it, to her too. To get this far—to have so much fun, to be actually cooking live on television, and to have proper professional chefs enthuse about your creations—had been absolutely brilliant. It couldn't end now, it just couldn't . . .

Oh, but Poll was *ages* . . .

The sitting room door opened. They held their breath.

'YES!!!'

They all leaped to their feet and hugged one another and danced round and round.

'It's us and the Pink Barbie team,' Poll said breathlessly. 'Now let me try to remember everything . . . Well, they're sending a car for us tomorrow afternoon. And putting us up in a hotel overnight afterwards, and it's just us—not Trixie or George or Onyx—oh, and they'll provide all the ingredients we need. So I said we were going to do a whole new menu this time and—'

'*What*?' they chorused in horror. 'A whole new menu? By tomorrow? Are you mad?'

Poll beamed. 'I didn't think it would be a problem.'

They all stared at her.

'What?' She frowned. 'Oh, come on, we've got loads of ideas. Things we rejected for the second round. And I thought we could just have a little run-through now and . . .'

'Poll, love,' Billy said softly. 'It's two in the morning.'

'Is it? Oh, well, maybe we could get up early and have a little run-through then instead?'

'No bloody way,' they groaned together. 'And no bloody time.'

'Well, it's probably best not to overdo it, anyway. We'll be perfectly able to go straight in when we're in the studio.' Poll beamed. 'Now, don't confuse me. What else did they say? Oh, we can wear what we like tomorrow as long as we stick to their guidelines, so I said I thought we might wear assorted pastels this time.'

'Pastels?' Ash and Billy looked horrified.

'Well, yes, because,' Poll smiled happily, 'I thought we could put together some of those recipes we tried out, before we settled on the cheesy ones for the second round, that we thought would go well for a country wedding theme, and that pastels would look really pretty, like confetti.'

They all frowned at her.

'But,' Ash said, 'I did the mains when we practised that menu, and you and Billy did the starter, will that be allowed?'

'Of course it will,' Poll said robustly. 'Anyway, you're the brilliant proper chef, Ash, you should have a chance to show off your talents. So, if Billy and I do the sweet-pea starter, you can make that incredibly intricate veggie tower with all those different blended layers, and Ella can make that lovely celebration strawberry fluff pud.'

'But we'll have to let them know, won't we?' Billy said. 'So that they can get all the ingredients in?'

'Ella can email them in the morning. Everything will have to be brought in fresh anyway.' Poll was still unfazed. 'And we have practised that one loads of times anyway. It'll all be absolutely fine.'

They sighed. And hoped it would be.

Ash suddenly flopped down on the sofa. 'God,

378

though, we've really, really bloody done it.'

'We have . . . It's going to be sooo incredible—oh, but no!' Ella groaned. 'We can't leave Trixie here alone. Not with George. Not tomorrow.'

'Why ever not?' Poll frowned. 'Not that I was intending to leave George here, anyway. I'd already arranged for Doll to have him again *if* we got through to the final. But surely Trixie will be OK here, won't she? It's only one night, after all. I don't think she's a nervous person, is she?'

'It's nothing to do with her nerves.' Ella shook her head. 'It's her fairy stuff. Tomorrow is CandleKiss Day—'

'What?' Ash pulled a face. 'Don't you mean Candlemass?'

'No, that's what I thought at first. But this is different. It's a fairy festival of lights. Trixie makes candles and adds herbs and sets them alight and the fairies magically make wishes come true.'

'Forget the wishes coming true,' Ash said. 'And the fact that you seem to know way too much about fairies. It's the lit candles and Trixie in the same sentence that scares me. There is no way on earth I'm leaving Roy with an arsonist.'

'Trixie is *not* an arsonist,' Poll said firmly. 'She's had one little accident in the past, that's all.'

'Yes, she has,' Billy said gently, 'but will you risk her having her next little accident here, at Hideaway, while you're miles away?'

'Oh Lord.' Poll sighed. 'No, of course not. Let me think. OK, so George will go to Doll Blessing—that's not a problem. And Mrs Tyler from the farm next door will see to the animals—Roy excepted, of course—but how do we tell Trixie we won't leave her home alone, and that

379

she's got to come with us?'

'Well, as yet, she doesn't know we've got through to the final or any of the restrictions, does she?' Ella said. 'She doesn't know she isn't invited? And I'm pretty sure that she'd assume that where we go she goes, so, we'll just take her with us and keep her out of the way.'

'But will Gabby and Tom allow her anywhere near the studio, after what she did?'

They looked at one another. They somehow doubted it, but they'd face that problem if and when it arose.

'Do you think it's too late to text my mum and dad and my sister and all my friends?' Ella asked no one in particular. 'I mean, I know my family are away, but some of my friends might be able to get to the studio to watch us as it's in London, mightn't they?'

'They might,' Ash said slowly. 'I bet you can't wait to see them again, can you? And I'm going to text Onyx now and tell her the news. Shame she can't come with us really, she'd have loved it.'

They looked at one another and looked away.

'Well, forgive me for sounding boringly grown up for once, but I really think any texting can wait. I think we should all go to bed and try to sleep now,' Poll said diplomatically. 'Because in case no one's noticed, we've got a *massive* day ahead of us tomorrow.'

# Chapter Forty-one

The television studio was amazing. Beyond their collective wildest dreams. Arriving there in the early evening, they'd been treated to a whistle-stop tour by one of the many young and trendy people with wires and phones and clipboards who seemed to populate every dark corner and every snaking corridor.

'It's like being a celebrity,' Ella whispered, sick with nerves now, as she watched the dozens and dozens of studio employees whizzing around, seemingly perfectly at home with all the lights and cameras. 'And we've got a proper dressing room with our names on. And I never realised that a green room wasn't green, and the place where we're going to get made-up is like a proper theatre dressing room with lights round the mirrors and all that.'

'And one of Pink Barbies is called Iris Freckles.' Poll gave a little skip of happiness. 'I saw it on her door next to ours. I didn't notice what they were called when they were on the programmes before, did you? Isn't it a lovely name? The Pink Barbies are all cleaners, too. They work in some huge office block. And everyone seems to know who we are, don't they? And my stomach is churning so much I think I'm going to burp.'

'Not on air, I hope,' Ash laughed. 'I don't expect Gabby allows burps.'

'Probably has too many of them at home from Tom,' Billy added. 'That lad certainly likes his ale.'

They all chuckled. They'd been chuckling

381

nervously at everything—funny or not—since the huge chauffeur-driven car had swept them away from Hideaway Farm and up to London, and deposited them at the swish and elegant hotel.

There had been a little problem getting Trixie into the hotel because they'd only got four single rooms reserved for them, but they'd managed to distract both Trixie and the receptionist during the booking-in process, and then sneaked her upstairs in the whispering glass lift without anyone counting heads, and she was sharing Ella's room.

'Trixie will have the bed,' Ella had said, as they left for the studio in yet another chauffeured limo. 'I'll sleep in the chair—it's huge. And she's really happy staying at the hotel for the evening. She loves all the gadgets and she's going to watch us on the flat screen TV and says she's made some sandwiches and doesn't want to come to the studio because she knows she'd be in the way.'

'And do you believe her?' Billy had asked.

Ella had nodded. 'Yes. Truly. I've had a really, really serious chat with her—about all sorts of things. And she's fine, honestly.'

'Ella's right. I've talked to her, too,' Ash had said. 'And as long as she doesn't want to celebrate CandleKiss in the hotel room, then I can't see any problems. I think she might just realise now how important all this is to us.'

'I think she does,' Ella had agreed. 'And it's OK. I've made her absolutely promise that she won't try lighting candles—any candles—or anything else, tonight. And while she was in the loo I searched her overnight bag and her pockets and, sorry to say, her handbag—'

Poll gasped in shocked disapproval.

'I know it's wrong, but I felt the end justified the means. Anyway, there's not a candle or matches or lighter or anything flammable in sight. She says she's left all her CandleKiss stuff at Hideaway so that the fairies can celebrate on their own.'

'Mad as a hatter,' Billy had sighed.

Ella had nodded. 'Anyway, I might even go home to my mum and dad's tonight—I've still got my key—so Trixie can have the room to herself.'

'Not if we win, you won't.' Poll had looked shocked. 'We'll be too busy celebrating.'

And they'd all looked at one another. *If they won* . . . It was almost too much to contemplate.

\*     \*     \*

Now they were in the studio proper with only an hour or so to go. Looking outwards, it was like a theatre, with rows of seats stretching as far as the eye could see into the gloom of the auditorium. But the studio floor was a state-of-the-art kitchen. Ella thought it looked like something from the Starship *Enterprise*.

'We shoot all our televised cookery shows from here,' Denise said, 'so we're well equipped with everything you'll need. Give yourself a few moments to look round, try out the cookers, acclimatise yourselves, plan your routine, get your bearings.'

'Your work station is here—' Anthony pointed to a long, stainless steel bench '—and all the ingredients you listed for your three new courses will be arranged exactly as you need them by our home economics editor just before we go live. And—' he'd grinned suddenly '—we've even gone

383

to the trouble of sourcing all the old-fashioned implements and utensils you favour.'

'Oh, wow—thank you.' Ella was overwhelmed.

Poll and Billy were simply speechless.

Ash swallowed. 'Thanks. It's amazing.'

Ella glanced at him. She'd never seen him so nervous. Of course this was just one step away from his lifelong dream, wasn't it?

She was still a million miles away from hers.

Then they were introduced to their rival chefs—Iris Freckles and her co-cleaners—who were also given the *Dewberrys' Dinners* introduction to the kitchen and their adjacent work station.

'They seem like nice girls,' Billy said. 'They're doing their original pink menu too—so at least we know what we're up against.'

They all sighed.

The next part seemed to Ella to pass in a blur. There was changing and make-up and hair and being mic'd up and having last-minute instructions barked at them from every direction.

'It's exactly the same as it was for your at-home shows,' the director said. 'All the same rules apply. Don't panic. Don't look at the camera or the audience, don't listen to the audience, just listen to Gabby and Tom. Forget the audience completely. Be yourselves and enjoy it.'

Enjoy it? Ella felt the forbidden panic rising. Enjoy it? With millions of people watching—again? He was madder than Trixie if he thought she could possibly enjoy any of this.

They stood to one side of the stage with Iris Freckles and her friends, who were all jolly, chatty and totally unperturbed, and watched as the studio audience filed in.

'We get loads of applications for the live show final,' Denise said, counting something down via a mouth-and-earpiece. 'There's always a massive waiting list. Nearly two years. Tom and Gabby's shows are always up there in the top ten.'

Ella nodded. None of her friends had been able to get tickets at the eleventh hour and had been told much the same thing when they'd phoned the show. In a way it was a relief to know she'd be cooking for an audience of total strangers. There was nothing worse than making a complete prat of yourself in front of your nearest and dearest.

Having obviously received the call she needed, Denise nodded. 'Right—on you go.'

'What?' Poll faltered. 'Now?'

'Now!' Denise said sharply. 'Iris, Jean, Dawn and Cathy first, then you, Ash, Billy and Ella. In single file. Take up your positions behind your work stations and smile!'

Trembling from head to foot and not smiling because she couldn't get her mouth to work properly, Ella followed the others out into the now brilliantly lit studio.

The audience erupted into foot-stamping and cheers and applause, and several loud wolf whistles when Ash appeared.

Ella, despite her terror, managed to smile to herself.

Blinking and sweltering under the serried ranks of lights, she looked down at the things arrayed in front of her and her mind went completely blank. What was she supposed to be cooking? Strawberry fluff? Raspberry sauce? How did she start? What did she do? Oh, heavens . . .

The audience cheered and whooped again as

'Pickin' a Chicken' played very loudly and Tom and Gabby walked on to the stage.

Oh dear God, Ella thought, this is it . . .

Gabby, glittering in and teetering on royal blue, did her usual smiling greeting. Tom, who looked a little distracted, joined in.

Then there were individual introductions and descriptions of their menus. There were more audience wolf whistles for Ash. And Gabby, Ella thought, spent a touch too long over Ash on both the introduction and the description. And did she really have to ogle him quite so much?

The audience were then treated to a few amusing stories about what had happened in previous finals. Then Gabby and Tom went into their familiar and much-loved sniping and putting-down insult routine. Tom's responses were even more lackadaisical than usual.

Ella thought there was something slightly odd about them tonight. They were still bitchy, but they weren't as brittle or cuttingly cruel as they'd been at Hideaway. Maybe it was the live audience that subdued them? Tom seemed especially quiet.

Mind you, she had to hand it to Gabby. Completely ad-libbing, she truly was the consummate professional in building the tension. The audience was now revved up and ready to go.

If only the same could be said about her.

'Right.' Tom smiled slowly. 'We know what you're making for us—Iris and her girls are going to produce their first all-pink menu again.'

Iris and her girls giggled coquettishly.

'And—' Tom beamed at them '—the Hideaway Farm team are going to produce a new meal for us this time—an old-fashioned Farmhouse Wedding

386

Breakfast.'

The audience screamed and whooped and whistled.

Tom continued to smile kindly. 'We know only too well what you can do, you're all wonderful cooks, so good luck to all of you, and off you go!'

'Start cooking—now!' Gabby said, baring her teeth in her most sparkly smile. 'And enjoy yourselves!'

After a pretty shaky start, when Ella had still completely forgotten what she was doing, and no one moved until Poll picked up a spoon and then dropped it noisily on to the stainless steel, making them all jump, everything suddenly seemed to click into place.

Ash reached for his pile of vegetables, looked along the pristine bench and smiled at her. Ungumming her lips from her teeth, Ella smiled back.

Damn it—she'd do it for him. She'd do her very best to make sure he had his restaurant, and if she couldn't bear to see him and Onyx living together in unadulterated bliss at Hideaway Farm, then she'd have to move on, wouldn't she? But tonight, she'd do everything in her power to help him win.

Strangely, Ella almost immediately forgot the audience. She was aware of them occasionally clapping or laughing or shouting, but she couldn't really see them, and it was no more distracting or intrusive than having a softly playing radio in the background.

Once she'd started cooking, the instinctive moves came back to her and she could have been in Hideaway or in her gran's ancient kitchen or anywhere. It didn't matter.

Glancing along the bench it seemed that everyone else had also fallen under the spell. Despite the heat and the blinding brightness of the lights, they were all working well. Even Tom and Gabby, moving between them, chatting, asking questions, didn't seem to distract them.

Iris and the girls were also working smoothly, their pink food colouring being liberally added to everything.

Time was concertina'd. Minutes were like nanoseconds. As far as she could tell, Ella reckoned it had all gone perfectly. They'd coped with the strange ovens and the unfamiliar surroundings and the relatively untried menu.

There had been no exclamations of horror from any of them, nothing had burned, they hadn't collided with each other or dropped anything.

'Five minutes!' Gabby trilled. 'You should start plating up—now!'

Ella's hands shook a little as she whisked her strawberry fluff. Please, please, please don't let it flop . . . no, it was fine. And the raspberry sauce was perfect. Oh, hallelujah! She'd done it.

Pushing her damp hair behind her ears, she glanced along the work station. Poll and Billy's sweet-pea starter—not the flowers, but fresh garden peas, cooked and mashed with herbs and shaped into little hearts—looked absolutely wonderful on their bed of baby salad leaves.

She looked at Ash, and heaved a huge sigh of relief and pride. His toweringly intricate and gorgeously colourful country vegetable stack, each layer sandwiched with a complementary creamy sauce, was an absolute triumph.

He'd shown the world tonight just what a

388

sensationally brilliant and versatile chef he really was.

Ella bit her lip and sniffed back happy tears.

'Time's up! Step away from your benches!' Tom said. 'Step right away.'

They stepped.

Ella allowed herself a surreptitious glance at Iris Freckles' girls' food. Oooh—it looked incredible. A whole vivid pink spectacular.

'Right.' Gabby clapped her tiny hands together. 'Tom and I can only congratulate you all on what looks like one of the best finals we've ever had on *Dewberrys' Dinners*. You've worked amazingly well. You've used some stunning ingredients and shown you have exceptional palates and presentation skills—the food looks gorgeous and smells delicious, doesn't it, Tom? TOM!'

'Er, yes.' Tom had been staring blankly offstage. 'Oh, yes. It does. We can't wait to taste it now, can we, Gabby?'

'No, we can't. But—' Gabby looked knowingly at the audience '—it isn't up to us, is it? Remember, it's you, the viewers, who will pick this year's *Dewberrys' Dinners* Winner! The numbers you need will be on the screen shortly and you have one hour—and one hour only—to vote for your favourite.'

'So,' Tom stepped in, 'if you want Ash, Ella, Billy and Poll to win, you add zero one, and if you want Iris, Jean, Dawn and Cathy to carry away this year's crown, you add zero two.'

'And we'll be back on air, live, in one short hour's time to crown this year's champion.' Gabby smiled invitingly. 'So get dialling and texting to make sure your favourite team wins. And in the meantime,

Tom and I will taste all this delish food. Aren't we lucky, Tom?'

'Er, oh, yes, we are.'

Ella relaxed. It didn't really matter now if Tom and Gabby liked their food or not. They would only win if the viewers voted for them. For the first time she wished it had been down to Tom and Gabby. Given the way Gabby was fawning all over Ash again, they'd have walked it . . .

'Oooh!' Gabby enthused, as she and Tom tasted the girls' gorgeous-looking frothy candyfloss pink food. 'Prawns and crayfish all in a pink Marie Rose sauce and with lollo rosso, too, to emphasise the colour motif. Oh, I absolutely love it! Clever, pretty, and very, very tasty.'

'Prawn cocktail,' Ash hissed. 'Easy-peasy.'

Ella giggled.

'Oh, yes—and followed by an all pink shepherd's pie, with pink veg.' Gabby didn't sound quite so enthusiastic. 'Now, I know this actually tasted wonderful in your first round, ladies, and it does again, but I think you may have used a touch too much cochineal this time. It's more candyfloss Day-Glo than Barbie, don't you think?'

'But the blancmange for pud is a triumph!' Tom muttered round a massive mouthful. 'There's nothing like a big, pink blancmange to take a chap back to his nursery days.'

'Sometimes I think you've never left them,' Gabby snapped. 'Well done though, ladies. A sumptuous meal well worthy of our final. Right, now let's see what we make of Hideaway's Farmhouse Wedding Breakfast. Especially as Ash has moved on from starters to the main course— and wonderful it looks, too.'

390

Tom and Gabby were ecstatic. They loved the way the food looked, loved the concept, loved the intricacy and the skill.

They ate lots of it, enthused hugely, and congratulated warmly.

'Fabulous flavours, very elaborate—and very, very clever.'

'Oh, Ash, you are soo talented. This tastes absolutely wonderful. I totally l-o-v-e it. Dear Raymond would surely be honoured to have this on offer at the Manoir.'

'And it perfectly complements the starter and the gorgeous frothy pudding.'

'A wedding breakfast fit for royalty. Well done, all of you.'

Ella, Poll, Ash and Billy beamed at one another. It was OK. It was all over now. There was nothing more they could do.

'Right folks, that's it from us for this segment of the show.' Tom wiped his mouth. 'You'll have an hour of soaps or something to numb your mind before we're back on the air. But don't forget—you only have this hour in which to vote. We'll be taking your phone calls and texts right here in the studio, then we'll be back with the results. So start voting—now! And do not go away!'

'Pickin' a Chicken' indicated that the ordeal—so far—was once again over.

While the studio audience were being treated to an hour of 'light entertainment', Gabby and Tom shook hands with everyone and the studio manager indicated that the contestants should all wait in the green room.

'I'm going outside for a smoke,' Billy said. 'I need some fresh air.'

391

'Contradiction in terms there, I think.' Gabby sniffed. 'No doubt you'll be joining him, Tom? Just another of your disgusting habits.'

Ash shook his head, then linked his arms through Ella's and Poll's and led them to the green room.

'God, I'm nervous now.' Poll sighed, collapsing on a sofa. 'No, no, I couldn't eat anything. I'll stick with this iced water. I think it went well, didn't it?'

They all nodded, suddenly both physically and emotionally exhausted.

Iris Freckles and her team, all of whom seemed completely untouched by any of it, piled their plates high with everything the green room had to offer and chatted happily about their vague plans for a seafront Multi-Coloured Snack Shack if they won.

'We don't care much one way or the other,' Iris mumbled happily round a cheese and pickle sandwich. 'We only went in for this to show our hubbies. They're all plain food, meat and two veg, sort of blokes. They hate our fancy cooking. Laughed at it. So, we thought we'd show them. Didn't expect to get this far, though, did we, girls?'

The girls all shook their heads.

'They're dead proud of us now, and we've proved our point, haven't we, girls?'

The girls all nodded.

'But surely the money would make such a difference to you?' Ella frowned. 'Even if you don't really want to open a proper restaurant?'

'Money's always nice, yes, but just between us, we four had a nice little lottery win last year on our syndicate at work—we're not short of a bob or two.'

Blimey, Ella thought. Lucky or what? They're *bound* to win.

Ash stood up. 'Excuse me a sec. Just got to make a quick phone call.'

As he left the room, Poll and Ella exchanged 'Onyx' glances and sighed.

Iris Freckles reached casually for a vol-au-vent. 'What about you? What's your plans?'

Poll smiled dreamily. '*If* we win we're going to open a Farmhouse Feast Restaurant in Hideaway Lane.'

Ella frowned. 'Are we?'

'We are.' Poll nodded. 'I've decided. I haven't even breathed a word of it—you know, tempting fate and all that. But that barn that Billy's been working on—well, I thought it would be perfect for Ash's' restaurant.'

'It would,' Ella agreed. 'It would be wonderful. But what about all the rules and regulations?'

'I've already spoken to my solicitor, who's done the necessary checks, and he says there's no problems. Also, access will be easy as there's a private road behind the farm, and there's also plenty of room for parking.'

'Blimey.' Ella blinked. 'You really have thought this through, haven't you?'

Poll nodded proudly. 'And Ash will run it, of course, and be the main chef, but we can all work there too on and off, and contribute ideas and recipes, and I thought we'd call it Hideaway Home and serve fresh, old-fashioned vegetarian food.'

'Wow. I'm impressed. It all sounds, well, perfect.'

'Oh, it will be.' Poll leaned over and squeezed her hand. 'If we win . . .'

Ella sighed. If they won—the phrase that had

393

haunted them for so long. And for so long it had all seemed a mad faraway dream. Now it was merely inches away—or not . . .

'Goodness me—it sounds really fantastic.' Iris started on the first of several cream cakes piled on her plate. 'I hope you win, then. You really want it. We don't, but we haven't told that Gabby-cow that. She's a bitch.'

Billy wandered back in then, closely followed by Ash, refused anything to eat and sat beside Poll and held her hand. 'That Tom's a nice chap, duck. But he's a bit, um, odd tonight. Distant. I reckon him and Gabby has had one heck of a row.'

'I expect they always do,' Poll said. 'He's probably used to it. Oh goodness, I wish they'd hurry up. I feel so sick.'

Ella looked over at Ash. He smiled at her.

Oh, I don't care about Onyx any more—just please let him win, Ella prayed to whichever gods were listening.

Please, please, please . . .

The green room door opened and the studio manager nodded at them. 'OK. We're ready for you again now.'


## Chapter Forty-two

Ella had never felt so terrified. Never wanted to win anything so much. Never been so scared of losing in her entire life.

'Come on.' Ash took her hand. 'Don't flake now. You've done brilliantly so far. And we've had such good fun, and Trixie and her so-called fairies didn't cause any complications tonight, did they? And there've been no news flashes about London hotels being razed to the ground, so we can safely assume Trixie's behaving herself as she promised—and all this will soon be all over.'

'But what if we don't win.'

'Then nothing much will have changed, will it? It'll be disappointing, but everyone gets over disappointments eventually. And we'll have enjoyed ourselves, learned a lot and had new experiences. It won't go to waste.'

She looked down at his hand holding hers and wanted it to stay there for ever. She stroked his fingers. 'Ash . . .'

'It's OK,' he said, gently removing his hand. 'We'll talk about it later.'

Then the floor manager ushered them all back onstage, and behind their now spotless work stations again, to rapturous applause.

Oh, sod it, Ella thought miserably, I've really, really made a complete idiot of myself now . . . Oh, come on, Ella, get over yourself and smile!

'Hello again!' Gabby, changed into shimmering silver, sashayed on to the stage waving to the audience. 'We've come to the most important and exciting part of all our shows! The culmination of weeks and weeks of travelling the country, being welcomed into your homes, cooking and experimenting! And I'm delighted to be able to tell you that the votes have all been counted, the lines have closed, and we have a definite *Dewberrys' Dinner* winner!'

The audience clapped and whooped and cheered.

'But—' Tom held his hands wide '—before we

announce that, Gabby and I have something to tell you. Haven't we, Gabby?'

'We have.' Gabby stopped smiling. 'Sadly, this is the last year of *Dewberrys' Dinners*. Tonight we'll be crowning our last ever *Dewberrys' Dinners* Winner.'

The audience gasped and groaned.

'Yes, but it's not all bad news,' Gabby continued. 'Next year, the live cook-in-your-own-home programme is going to be called *Gabby's Gourmets*. The format will be very similar to the current show with the same lovely cheque and restaurant deal for the lucky winner, but I shall be going solo.' She shot a killer look at her husband. 'Tom is keen to follow his own career off-screen.'

The audience was completely shell-shocked. No more Gabby and Tom? It was like Ant and Dec splitting up.

'We felt it was only right to tell you this tonight before it breaks in the media,' Tom said. 'And definitely before announcing tonight's winner. Because tonight belongs to them—and we didn't want to detract from their glory.'

'Sooo.' Gabby was twinkling professionally again. 'That's our news out of the way—now, let's get down to the really important business of this evening! Announcing this year's—the final year's—*Dewberrys' Dinners* Winner!'

The audience whooped some more.

'As you know,' Tom said, 'the winner will take away a nice cheque and our people—or rather, Gabby's people now—will be in touch with their people, to discuss the setting up, initial financing and running of their very own restaurant!'

The audience screamed with enthusiasm.

396

Ella looked at the others. They were very pale. Clearly the news of the demise of *Dewberrys' Dinners* came a very poor second to the result of tonight's show.

'Let's not keep you in suspense any longer,' Gabby said, dragging it out. 'I have the envelope with the number of votes cast right here.'

The studio grew dark. Roving spotlights criss-crossed over Gabby and the envelope, and Tom and the contestants.

'Tonight's winner,' Tom said in a gruff serious voice, 'is . . .'

There was a drum roll. Then silence.

Oooh, Ella groaned silently, not the damn stupid drawing-it-out-for-the-tension thing again.

The silence went on and on.

Gabby stepped forwards and tore the envelope open.

More silence.

Ella's stomach was in knots and she really, really wanted to scream.

Gabby glanced down at the envelope and smiled. 'Hideaway Farm! Congratulations, Poll, Billy, Ella and the sexiest ice-cream man in the universe, Ash!'

Gabby grabbed Ash and hugged him. Tom hugged everyone.

Suddenly the studio was filled with dancing golden lights and falling stars and rousing music. The audience were on their feet clapping and cheering.

Ella was then hugged by Ash, then Poll, then Billy.

Gabby and Tom were now shaking hands with everyone and talking but she couldn't hear a word they said.

Iris Freckles and her girls congratulated them warmly too. Then Tom presented Poll with the cheque and Gabby handed the trophy to Ash, then everyone kissed everyone else's cheeks.

Poll was openly weeping in Billy's arms.

And still the audience cheered.

They'd won. Ella tried the words out for size. They'd actually bloody won.

She really didn't know whether to laugh or cry so ended up doing a little of both as she and Ash grinned stupidly at each other over the huge crystal trophy.

'You've got a restaurant,' she said. 'You've actually got your own restaurant.'

He nodded. 'I know . . . No, that's not true. I still don't believe any of this.'

'Press call tomorrow.' Gabby barged between them, talking very loudly above all the noise, as seemingly hundreds of people crowded on to the stage, more glittery stuff exploded from the roof, and champagne corks popped along with the flashbulbs. 'At your place. Berkshire. They like you in situ. Already organised. Celebratory five-star meal on the programme makers tonight—Denise and Anthony have all the details—then back to the hotel for more champers for all of you.'

'Well done,' Tom, looking more like a wildly dishevelled Heathcliff than ever, said gruffly to Ella. 'I'm so glad you won.'

'Thank you.' Ella blinked back the tears. 'I actually can't take it in.' She stared out into the auditorium and at the vast audience, who were now noisily unpacking their after-the-show goodie bags of Gabby and Tom cook books and prettily wrapped treats, as if seeing them for the first time. 'I can't believe we've actually done it. And thank you so much for changing our lives.'

'And thank you for changing mine,' Tom said, solemnly shaking her hand, then drifting away through the ever-growing crowd.

Ella stared after him. Why on earth had he said that? Was he more drunk than he admitted? Was he just as shell-shocked as everyone else about the professional Dewberry split? Poor, poor Tom.

And now she couldn't see Ash at all. The noisy, laughing crowd had swallowed him up. In fact she couldn't see anyone she knew.

Then she blinked. Surely that wasn't . . . ?

Surely that wasn't Onyx standing in the wings?

She squinted, then pushed her way through the throng.

'Onyx? Onyx! But Ash said you wouldn't be here and—'

'Ella! Oh, I'm so happy for you!' Onyx, in skintight jeans and a very tiny vest and even taller in her killer heels, leaned down and hugged her. 'Isn't this just wonderful? And congratulations! You were all totally brilliant! Oh my God, I'm so pleased for you all! Now everything—absolutely everything—is going to be just perfect, isn't it?'

Well, no not quite everything, Ella thought, but she kept smiling.

'Yep. Ash'll have his restaurant, Poll's got the money she needs to enlarge her home from home for the homeless—although she says we all have to have a share of it too, which is lovely—and she and Billy can come out of the darn closet about being in love.'

She couldn't quite bring herself to say, 'And you

399

and Ash can live happily ever after.'

She just couldn't.

'Ash is over there somewhere, talking to Gabby and a million other people, shall I try and find him and tell him you're here?'

'No, he knows.'

Of course he does, Ella thought. Silly me. There'd been that phone call that he'd left the green room to make, hadn't there?

'I'm not here to see Ash anyway.'

'Well, no, hopefully you're friends with all of us, but surely it's Ash who you most want to see? Tonight of all nights?'

'Oh, yeah, I'll congratulate Ash later.' Onyx smiled gently. 'But actually, I'm here for him.'

Ella turned and looked over her shoulder. There was no man in sight. Well, only Tom, who was talking to Iris Freckles. And Onyx couldn't mean *him*, could she?

'Who?'

'Tom,' Onyx sighed dreamily.

'TOM?' Ella practically screamed the name. 'TOM! Er, sorry, have I missed something? You— and *Tom*?'

'Me and Tom.' Onyx's huge eyes were dreamy. 'Lust and love at first sight. Mutual lust and love at first sight.'

Onyx and Tom? Ella frowned. No way! Surely not . . .

It was like someone had torn the middle pages out of a book she was reading and the story now bore no resemblance to the one she'd started.

Ella shook her head. 'No, that can't be right. No, sorry, that's just wrong on so many levels. You mean, you and Tom have been having an affair?

And that even tonight when you *have* to be with Ash because it's the biggest night of his entire life, you're going to go swanning off with Tom? Sorry, Onyx, but—'

'I'm not having an affair with Tom. And why on earth should Ash knowing about it matter to him? And . . .'

'But, you and Ash? You've been a couple for years. And—'

'Whoa!' Onyx held up her hands. 'Where the heck did you get that from? Yes, Ash and I have been best friends since uni and shared everything. But not *that*. We have never, ever been a couple. Yes, he's completely gorgeous, but he's not my type any more than I am his. We don't even slightly fancy one another. We're *friends*. Truly, just good friends. Dear God, thinking about sleeping with Ash would be about as incestuous as contemplating sleeping with my brother Jet.'

Ella, her head swimming, exhaled. 'Really? No, I can see . . . Um . . . OK, right, I might have misunderstood . . . I might have got it all a bit wrong somewhere along the way.'

'A bit?' Onyx shrieked with laughter. 'Only about two hundred and ninety per cent of it!'

'But *Tom*?'

'Tom Dewberry is a lovely kind man. A lovely kind very unhappy man.' Onyx smiled gently. 'And absolutely my type. We met at Hideaway that first time and we talked, and afterwards we texted, and then we met up secretly a few times more and talked a lot more, and we fell in love. End of.'

'Beginning of,' Ella corrected, still stunned. 'You said you weren't having an affair.'

'We're not. You can call me old-fashioned, but

401

I've been brought up by my parents' strict moral code. Much as I'm madly in lust and love with Tom, I haven't slept with him. I'd never have a relationship with a married man. Nor could I give Tom an ultimatum. I mean, him and Gabby might be desperately unhappily married, but they're linked together by more than their wedding vows. The business is huge. I was never going to ask him to give either of them up for me.'

'But now he has?'

'Of his own volition, yes.' Onyx practically fizzed with happiness. 'What Gabby didn't say tonight— but the press will tomorrow—is that the Dewberry partnership split is professional *and* personal. They're getting a divorce. *He's* divorcing *her*. And he's told her about me.'

'Really?' Ella's jaw dropped. 'Ohmigod—and she's not going to kill you?'

'Couldn't care less, apparently. Gabby's not only a cruel-mouthed cow, she's also a serial cheater. She's got plenty of Tom-replacements lined up in reserve.'

Oh, God, Ella thought, Ash was definitely one of them . . .

Onyx sighed. 'She's been unfaithful to him for years and years. But Tom's a decent man—and he took her back time after time.'

'But now he hasn't, er, isn't? And he's divorcing the business as well?'

Onyx nodded. 'I didn't—couldn't and wouldn't— have asked him to do it. He had to do it because it was what he wanted, not because I was making demands. I had to know that he did it for his own future happiness, not just mine.'

Blimey. Ella shook her head again. It was all far

402

too intense for her to take in. Then she suddenly grinned. 'So, the cookery stuff you asked me about—that was to impress Tom?'

'Got it in one. We'd talked and talked about everything under the sun,' Onyx said, nodding. 'But I felt such an ignoramus not knowing anything about his business and I so wanted to be able to talk to him on all levels. I mean, I'd hung around Ash for years and loved what he cooked but knew nothing about the inner workings of how the food arrived on the plate. And I couldn't ask Ash to teach me, because at that time no one on earth knew about me and Tom, and I was sure, knowing me so well, Ash would guess.'

'Wow! So, what happens now? I suppose this is the end of the belly-dancing classes in Hazy Hassocks village hall? I suppose you and Tom will be shacked up in some ritzy London penthouse?'

'Wrong on both counts!' Onyx grinned. 'Tom's a country bloke at heart. Grew up on a farm. Loves the countryside. We're going to find a place locally—in one of the villages. I'll continue dancing until I feel I really have to get a teaching job, and he's going to take some time off to write some more cookery books and potter in our own little garden and grow stuff and just recover from being a celeb, which he absolutely hated, poor love. And maybe, one day, when all the dust has settled, he and Ash might join forces in the restaurant business—who knows . . .'

Who knew indeed? Ella took a deep breath. It was all too much to take in. Suddenly she felt very, very tired. There was no way on earth she could go out on the town and carry on celebrating into the small hours. She really just wanted to go home.

403

'But Ash knows now? About you and Tom?'

'Oh, yes. I texted him tonight. Once I knew Tom and Gabby were going public, then I knew it was OK for me to do it, too. He was dead happy for me.' Her smile increased and her smile softened as Tom joined them. 'Hi.'

Tom looked deep into her eyes. 'Hi, yourself. Have you been telling Ella?'

Onyx nodded.

'Um, congratulations,' Ella murmured. 'I think it's wonderful. I'm so pleased for you both, and I honestly hope you'll be very happy together.'

'Oh, we will be,' Tom said softly, discreetly holding Onyx's hand. 'We will be.'

He was a lovely man, Ella thought, and Onyx was clearly equally besotted. But who in their right mind would honestly fancy the large and shaggy middle-aged Tom more than the divine and delectable and oh-so-sexy Ash?

How very strange love was . . .

She bit her lip. 'Actually, I wondered if you could do something for me?'

Tom nodded. 'I'll certainly try.'

Ella nodded towards the middle of the studio where Poll, Billy and Ash were being plied with champagne and surrounded by a huge noisy crowd. 'I wondered if it would be possible for you to apologise to everyone, and explain to Poll and the others that I really can't cope with anything more tonight, or even staying at the hotel or anything, please.'

'Of course I can. I hate all the after-the-show luvvie stuff myself. But why do you want to go? Are you not feeling well?'

'I don't know how I feel, honestly. I think I just

need some peace and quiet to sort my head out. It's all been a bit overwhelming.'

'Understatement,' Onyx said. 'But I can't imagine you wanting to turn down the opportunity of an all-night celebration after being in the wilds of the country for so long.'

'Normally, no. I guess I must be getting old. You can just call me a party pooper—again.' Ella smiled. 'But I really do want to go home to the wilds of the country. Now.' She looked at Tom again. 'And I wondered if you could tell me how to find my way out of here so I could get a cab to Paddington?'

Tom smiled gently. 'There's no need to worry about getting a cab. I'll arrange for one of the show's drivers to take you home to Hideaway straight away if that's what you want.'

'It is,' Ella said gratefully. 'Thank you so much. Right now, it's what I want more than anything in the whole world. Well, almost.'

## Chapter Forty-three

Hideaway Farm loomed dark and silent in the still, humid July night. As the *Dewberrys' Dinners* car disappeared along Cattle Drovers Passage, Ella just lifted her face to the black sky and inhaled the sweet-scented air.

She was home—and it was sheer bliss.

The outside security lights clicked on, one after the other, as she walked slowly round the side of the farmhouse and into the garden. Moths danced in and out of the misty beams. Somewhere an owl hooted and small nocturnal creatures rustled unseen through the tinder-dry grass.

Ella smiled to herself as she sank down on the canopied swing seat and kicked off her sandals in the stifling heat. How much had she changed? Not so long ago, those night noises would have had her gibbering with fear. Now tonight London had exhausted her, and Berkshire was home. She'd become countrified.

She leaned her head back and rocked slowly in the oppressive darkness. Somewhere close by the dogs were sleeping soundly on the cool flagstoned floors, and the cats were probably curled up dreaming, and the hens were locked up snug and safe against any prowling predators. And Roy, being nocturnal, was probably sunning himself under his lamps.

But she was the only human being here at Hideaway. And it didn't bother her one little bit. Not any more. She absolutely loved the silence and the solitude.

All the way from London, in the back of the luxury limo while the driver sang along to a compilation of crooners, she'd had time to think.

Not about winning. The reality of that was slowly sinking in, and the full ramifications were delightfully obvious. Nor about missing out on a celebration of A-list proportions. Poll and Billy would lap it up, having a chance to be together in all that luxury, and Ash would no doubt be the star of the show.

All the way back to Hideaway she'd thought about Ash.

And Onyx. Because now, knowing that Ash and Onyx hadn't been romantically linked at any time, made her feel even worse.

There hadn't been any reason why she and Ash shouldn't have got together, had there? He and Onyx had never been a couple, but he'd never told her that, had he? He'd always let her assume that they were together, when all the time he was, and always had been, young, free and single. Which meant . . . she groaned . . . that he simply didn't want to be with her . . .

Oooh, how humiliating was that?

He liked her, was happy to be her friend, but that was it. And tonight, with the silly hand-squeezy-stroking thing, she'd left him in no doubt about how she felt.

And he'd pulled his hand away . . .

Feeling more miserable than she ever had in her life, Ella closed her eyes. It would have been far, far better to be rejected because Ash was in love with Onyx—anything on earth would have been better than just not being wanted. Oh God, how was she ever going to be able to face him again? How on earth was she ever—?

What was that?

Ella opened her eyes again. Had there been a noise? Not a night-creature noise . . . not one of the dogs . . . not even one of the cats . . .

A noise like a car driving slowly along Hideaway Lane and stopping, and a door closing, and then the car purring off again. Ella strained her ears.

And now there were footsteps . . .

Ella swallowed and it wasn't just the sultry, airless night that was making her heart race and her palms sweat. Sensibly she knew she should just sit there, silent and unseen, and hope whoever it was would simply go away. Sensibly, she knew she should quietly reach into her bag for her mobile phone and be ready to ring the police. Sensibly, she knew she should hold her breath and hide back in the black shadows.

But she'd never been particularly sensible.

Especially when the footsteps were coming closer and the security lights were once again popping on one by one . . .

'Who's there?'

'Jesus!' Ash's voice echoed from the darkness. 'You just scared me to death! Where are you?'

'On the swing. And why are you sneaking round the back of the house?'

'Because—' he loomed into view from the shadows '—it's so damn hot that the garden held certain attractions, and because the house was in darkness so I thought you weren't here yet.' He stared down at her.

'I've been here for ages. But why aren't you at the party?'

'Probably—' he lowered himself on to the swing seat beside her '—for the same reasons that you aren't. Too overwhelmed by it all. Too exhausted. Enough was enough. And when Onyx told me you'd left, it finally lost all its appeal.'

Ella frowned. That obviously didn't mean what she hoped it did. Why should it? How could it? And she'd got everything else wrong, hadn't she?

'Er, right, um, and it was really great to see Onyx, wasn't it? But her and Tom . . . weren't you gob-smacked when she told you?'

'A bit. OK, a lot. I certainly didn't see it coming. But it was about time she met her soulmate.' Ash leaned back, making the swing seat rock gently. 'And he's a great bloke—they'll be really happy

408

together—but I was still a bit surprised to see her there tonight.'

'Why? You rang her. When we were in the green room.'

'I didn't. I rang Joe.'

'Oh.' Joe the Art Garfunkel lookalike mate. 'Er, why?'

'Joe's just dropped me off. I rang him and asked him to come and pick us up.'

'Us?'

'You and me. I was being a bit presumptuous, but that's me all over. I hoped I'd be able to persuade you to leave the bright lights with me. I didn't want to spend another minute being pawed by bloody predatory Gabby, or shrieked at by people I didn't know who kept calling me Ashley and making really bad ice-cream jokes.'

Despite everything, Ella giggled.

'No, once it was all over I wanted to come back home, here to Hideaway, to talk to you.' He looked at her. 'Living here is wonderful, but we're so rarely alone, especially recently, and tonight seemed like a perfect opportunity to have some time to get things straight between us. Then Onyx said you'd beaten me to it and already left. So, I thought you might have gone out on the town with some of your friends.'

'I did think about it,' Ella admitted. 'Being back in London and everything, but then I knew I couldn't cope with it. Not tonight. I'll invite them all down here for a catch-up soon.'

'Then I thought—and it nearly drove me mad—that, of course, it wouldn't be your friends you'd want to be with. It would be Mark. Anyway, Tom and Onyx said you'd gone home—so I hoped you were on your own, made my apologies, and asked Poll and Billy to bring our stuff back from the hotel tomorrow, and Joe brought me home. Alone.'

'And now you want to talk?' Ella stared into the darkness. She had a nasty feeling that the talk was going to involve the hand-holding-stroky thing and have a just-good-friends-like-me-and-Onyx ending.

'Not just talk. I wanted to show you something. Before all hell breaks loose tomorrow with the press arriving and more filming and everyone here is talking about winning and nothing else.' He stood up. 'Do you fancy a walk?'

Managing not to admit that even if it was over hot coals or broken glass she'd say yes, Ella nodded non-committally. 'With you? Now?'

'Yes—and not far, I promise. Just round the back of the farm—we can cut across the fields because it's quicker than using the road, and it's still way too hot to contemplate a five-mile hike . . . but how high are your sandals?'

'High but not Onyx-level.' Ella slid them on and Ash hauled her to her feet. She was very careful to shake her hand free again this time. 'I'll cope. OK, lead on.'

The familiar tracks and fields round Hideaway were very different at night. And as there was only a faint misty moon and neither of them had a torch, there was a lot of stumbling over desiccated grassy tussocks and laughing as they stepped unwarily into huge concrete-dry ruts in the darkness.

'Where exactly are we going?' Ella puffed as they eventually negotiated the fields and reached a solid shingle path. 'Am I allowed to know? Oh . . .'

410

She peered at a large looming building. 'This is Billy and Poll's hidey-hole barn. The one Poll has earmarked for your restaurant *if we won*?'

'Yes, she told me tonight. So welcome to Hideaway Home.' Ash grinned. 'The best restaurant in Berkshire. Sadly it has no doors yet, no windows, no kitchen, no working gas or electricity and no chairs or tables—but it's rock solid and it's got a roof and refurbished walls and a solid floor.'

'Always a good start.' Ella stepped through the looming doorway and peered into the gloom. 'Blimey, it's absolutely huge in here. Billy's done a fantastically good job. It's amazing. Oh, Ash, it's going to be phenomenal when it's all up and running, isn't it?'

He nodded. 'A dream come true. And something I haven't quite managed to get my head round yet. Would you like to take a seat?'

Ella looked around. 'You said there weren't any chairs or tables.'

'Not as such, and Poll apparently favours hay bales, but Billy's work bench is over there and he's left a couple of folding chairs underneath it that he and George drag out for their lunch breaks, and if you use your imagination . . .'

'Oh, I've got plenty of that.'

'So I've heard.'

They sat on the tiny uncomfortable chairs and Ella blushed. Onyx had *told* him. Damn her . . .

'Yes, well it was an easy mistake to make. Poll and Trixie said you were together. And neither of you actually said you weren't a couple, did you?'

'It never occurred to us that we had to.' Ash leaned towards her, his face shadowy in the

411

darkness. 'And anyway I always knew about you and Mark.'

Ella said nothing.

Ash looked at her. 'Right from the start I knew you were with someone else, and I probably didn't stand a chance—so I asked Poll what the score was.'

'Did you?' Ella's heart sank. 'And?'

'And she said that you and Mark had been together for ages but were having problems and that you were really vulnerable, so there was no way I was going to go charging in and messing things up for you.'

'Oh,' Ella sighed.

Ash shrugged. 'So, it seemed easier to just let you think that Onyx and I were a couple—because everyone seemed to think we were anyway—and that way, you and Mark could work out your differences without any complications from me.'

'But—' Ella frowned '—you asked me out?'

'Because I had to,' Ash said fiercely. 'I'm only human. I wanted to be with you—but then when you went all distant and defensive every time I suggested we went out together, I was convinced that you and Mark were sorted and you'd be going back to London and him when you left here and—'

'I was never distant and defensive—OK, well, maybe I was a little bit.'

'Believe me, you were—a lot. And then, when we did actually manage a date, you went all sniffy at the Masonic Hall.'

'Sniffy isn't even in my repertoire.' Ella sighed. 'Well, OK, maybe there was just a *hint* of sniffiness, but I thought you were simply showing me that I didn't stand a chance with you because

412

of Onyx.'

Ash laughed. 'Cross purposes all round then.'

'Absolutely,' Ella continued, knowing now that all the stumbling blocks had to be removed if they were going to share Hideaway in any sort of harmony, 'and I apologise for being silly at the studios tonight and doing the hand-stroking thing. I just got a bit carried away with everything. It didn't mean anything.'

'Didn't it?' Ash sounded disappointed.

'You snatched your hand away pretty damn quickly, so, no it didn't.'

'Because,' Ash said in the darkness, 'it was just about the most erotic thing ever. And as we were just about to walk onstage in front of hundreds of people in the studio and had a television audience of millions, I felt that the timing was pretty lousy. *Dewberrys' Dinners* is a family show after all, and my feelings towards you at that point were definitely X-rated.'

'Oh.' Ella swallowed, suddenly giddy with lust.

'So, now you know Onyx and I are not a couple, can we go right back to the beginning and start again?'

'Probably best not to, actually.' Ella smiled. 'Remember, in the beginning I thought you were gay and that Roy was your live-in lover?'

'Seriously? I always thought that was a joke.'

'No joke.'

'Christ.' Ash shook his head. 'OK, let's skip the beginning. But, oh, God, what about Mark?'

'History.'

'Really?'

She nodded. 'I told him it was over a little while ago.'

413

'I'm really sorry.'

'Don't be. He wasn't.'

'Then he's got to be insane,' Ash said quickly. 'And I so wish you'd told me.'

'I couldn't. It would have sounded a bit desperate, wouldn't it? And I thought you and Onyx—'

Ash held up his hands. 'Enough about me and Onyx. Let's talk about you and me. OK, so now how do you feel about a first date?'

Ella didn't look at him. 'Yes, please. Tomorrow, when all the hoo-ha is over?'

'Right now . . .' Ash leaned under the table and pulled out a cool box. 'I've been planning and planning the best recipes ever to win you over— food being the way to a woman's heart and all that—but as we never seemed to be alone, and you didn't seem to be very interested in me, I thought that maybe tonight we'd be here alone, so very early this morning I came down here and . . .'

Ella watched in delight as he opened the cool box and produced two glasses, two plates and a small container.

'Not quite the complex and genius quail's eggs and truffles spectacular I'd had in mind. And not champagne either. Rosé wine—pink and sparkling, though—and these . . .'

'Chocolate-covered strawberries!' Ella squealed with delight. 'Ohmigod! I absolutely love chocolate-covered strawberries!'

'Thank the Lord for that . . . and—' Ash looked happily at her '—there's something else in here.'

'Oh? Oh, yes, er, what the heck are they?'

'Candles. Two candles.' Ash lit them carefully. 'One made from geraniums, juniper, roses and

414

crushed raspberries for everlasting love. The other made from sweet peas, lemon, meadowsweet and saffron for happiness and fulfilment of dreams.'

Ella blinked as the flames danced and flickered, and the glorious scents mingled together and the essences entwined, filling the barn with enchantment.

'Ash, are they . . . ?'

'CandleKiss candles, yes.' Ash nodded.

'You made them?' Ella stared at him. 'For me? Us? You've been talking to Trixie? And that's why she didn't have anything with her in the hotel tonight because it was all here?'

Ash nodded. 'Well, I thought you seemed quite taken with the fairy stuff, and Trixie was very helpful, and pointed out that her fairies have only done good things and were really helpful in getting lovers together, and I reckoned, even if I don't think the fairies exist, it had to be worth a try, and oh, Ella, come here.' He pulled her into his arms and kissed her.

Ella, her entire body dissolving, kissed him back. Again and again.

And ages later, when the kissing had been interspersed with a lot of spilled pink fizz and inebriated giggles, and they'd fed one another with chocolate strawberries and made quite a mess, Ella held his face between her hands in the sweet-scented candle glow.

'This is the best first date ever, ever, ever. I think you're totally, amazingly sexy and talented and adorable and—Oh, what the heck's that noise? Thunder?'

'Who cares,' Ash murmured, stroking her hair as the roaring got louder and louder, drumming on the slate and tile roof and echoing deafeningly through the cavernous barn. 'Carry on—you'd just got to the good bit.'

'Ash, look! It's raining!' Ella stared through the open doorway where the rain was falling in solid, vertical sheets, dragging the sweetest scents from the rock-hard earth. 'Rain! Oh, bliss! For the first time in months it's raining, and I'm so hot and sticky and—'

Ash smiled at her. 'What on earth are you doing?'

Ella paused in kicking off her sandals and pulling her T-shirt over her head. 'I'm going outside to dance naked in the rain—it was always one of my favourite songs.' She tugged off the remainder of her clothes. 'Come on . . . get your clothes off! All of them!'

'Shameless.' He grinned at her, pulling off his T-shirt, undoing his jeans and easing off his shoes. 'Ella Maloney, you are totally shameless. Are you trying to corrupt me?'

'Way, way too late.' Ella danced happily towards the non-stop torrent in the dark doorway. 'Come on! Race you!'

And, equally naked and still laughing, Ash beat her outside by a nanosecond.